RAGE

FROM THE WOMB

a journey into madness

a novel

DANIEL MARTINEZ

Rage from the Womb: A Journey into Madness
Copyright © 2013 by Daniel Martinez Publishing

For information about this title or to order other books and/or electronic media, contact the publisher:
Daniel Martinez Publishing (Costa Rica)
U.S. Mailing Address: 6703 NW 7th Street
Suite # SJO–12708
Miami, FL 33126
DMPublishing@zoho.com

ISBN: 978-0-9882677-0-1

Printed in the United States of America

Cover and Interior design by: 1106 Design

Dedication

To two important persons who lived the nightmare with us:

In Memory of my Aunt Carmen—The Brave

She had the courage to confront The Beast face-to-face.

She taught us about hope in our house of terror.

&

In Memory of Doña Mariquita

She made corn tortillas for us when our mother was away dying.

Even though weak, frail, and very old, she treated us with kindness

In our otherwise depraved world.

My Love to these two women who held our hands as best they could during our Darkest and most horrifying childhood years…

Chapter One
A Wrongful Birth!

If my mother were alive today I would have to kill her. Oftentimes I have imagined myself going for her throat and breaking her neck while at the same time beating her face with my fist, burning with an intense rage against her for the tragic and ghastly childhood which she provided to all of us. You see, I feel that in our childhood home there was a catastrophic failure to nurture, to protect, and to parent, a failure that for whatever reason left all of us spiritually and emotionally damaged forever. And we, the living dead, are the lucky ones, for my brother Benito, an innocent child who came to know nothing but hunger, neglect, abuse, and the bone-crushing sound of his baby skull repeatedly impacting against the unforgiving surface of the cement floor, lies in a box, having been unceremoniously put away in the ground as a final assault on his integrity as a human being. His frail body and budding spirit were no match for the unbelievable horrors that those whose job it was to be our parents created and unleashed against all of us.

Yet, this homicidal impulse which I feel against my mother, as evil as that may sound, is a positive step for me, a step in the right direction in my attempt to achieve mental and spiritual health after many years of sorrow and almost total abandonment of human decency. Prior to my feeling this sickening response to my years of tortured hell in the various homes where I lived as a child, I actually did not believe that my childhood years had been that bad. And herein lay the sinister delusion that provided the foundation for a chaotic, impulsive, and destructive life as an adult.

For many years I was spiritually lost, but it is only now, in retrospect, that I comprehend and feel the extent of my sickness, a sickness borne out of my having been surrounded by evil, perversity, neglect, violence, chronic hunger, abuse, lovelessness, addictions, human filth, and physical deprivation during my most vulnerable and formative years. I was deep in the spiritual depravity of hard-core pornography, sexual addictions, lying and cheating, financial irresponsibility, stealing, animal torture, vandalism, child abuse, and fraud. And this was as an adult, after I graduated from the sexually depraved experiences of my childhood years.

If my courage or my ego had been stronger, I envision with revulsion that I would have been a truly abominable serial killer, stopping at nothing until the end liberated my soul. I tremble when reading case histories of vicious killers and seeing childhood accounts of depravity and abuse that could easily have been written about me. "That's me!" is what my inner wretchedness says, identifying with the ugliness and vileness that is the scourge of our planet. Some unknown force in the universe must have intervened at the right moment when I was at the threshold beyond which there is no known redemption even from the most charitable of the Gods. Yet even though I never took any person's life, the cumulative effects of my immeasurable sins against humanity make me feel that the weight of my wretched history upon my soul is too great to be lifted by any force on this Earth, except, perhaps, by death. But then, I would be like my mother, who left this world almost in the middle of the night, denying me as a young adult the opportunity to protest with indignity her having placed all of us in an unimaginably abusive situation. No, I won't exit, for the evil of my history and my past behavior would stay behind just as the filth and spiritual wreckage remained after my mother bit the dust.

My name is Victor Alameda. Yeah, I do have a last name. Well, maybe I don't, or maybe it's the wrong one. It's the one my mother put on my birth certificate, but I have angry suspicions about it. As you can tell by now I have very mixed feelings about my mother, ranging from homicidal rage to empathy and sorrow about her own pain in the short time that she lived on this planet. It has not always been like this, for I recall when I only ideal-ized her, feeling that she was *my mother* and therefore practically sacred. Yes, I had clear memories of the uncountable times that we suffered; but those did not matter, because we were poor and therefore had to endure the hardships. She was beautiful, I recall. Long auburn hair, red lips most of the time, her skin whiter than ours, and gorgeous green eyes. In photos of her youth she was absolutely stunning, almost like those 1940s Hollywood goddesses with fancy hairdos. But one thing about my mother that stands out for me is her breasts. Big and nicely rounded, with pink nipples. Even when I was twelve years old and raging with the sexually explosive power of adolescent hormones, she would open her blouse in front of me and out would plop what appeared to be massive 44-D breasts. This memory is forever imprinted on my soul, along with the resultant sexual excitation and the fantasy of sucking her enormous breasts and of even dying with her nipples in my mouth. Yes, yes, yes, suck my mother's bountiful breasts all night long—that is heaven. My God, that is heaven! But, it took me years to realize how much damage this wonderful and ecstatic fantasy had done to my concept of sexuality, love, and human relations.

My sexual relationship with my mother began, I believe, when I was about age four or five. My recollection is still not clear on this, but I do recall our first house in El Paso, Texas, and a woman whom I believe was my mother took me to the only bedroom in the house and placed me on the bed. She proceeded to lie on her back, while totally naked from the waist down. She opened her legs and then placed my small face on her pubic area, asking me to lick her vagina with my tongue. I recall vividly her wiry bristles scratching my face and the musty aroma of her vagina making me feel like no child should feel. I can't remember if I liked it, but I know for sure it was not an unpleasant experience. Afterwards she let her naked legs hang from the edge of the unmade and urine-soaked bed (we all peed the bed in our sleep), and I lay with my back on the dirty and creaky wooden floor, sucking her toes with an incredible passion that I had never experienced in my five miserable years of life. With my little hands I desperately grasped my mother's foot to push her big toe deeper into my mouth, and I sucked and sucked until it hurt. I was desperate, I was hurting, I was in a near-orgasmic bliss, I was crying, I was sucking, I was trembling, I was sucking, I couldn't breathe, I was loving it, I was in a strange passion, I wanted my mother, I wanted my mother! Oh, God!

Yes, it was an ecstatic passion I had never felt and have never experienced ever since. For me it was an event that made me feel "sexual," the memory of which elicited sexual excitation in me for years as an adult. In fact, only recently was I made aware that it was not appropriate for my mother to have done that with me. I was so stupid and ignorant. Yet, I cannot deny that it was a positively memorable moment with my mother.

Her name was Esperanza, probably the most incompetent mother that Mother Nature could have designed if she wanted to destroy the children who should be sent into this world with all possible goodwill. My mother's grievous failure as a parent to all six of us kids encompassed just about all aspects of human existence, including being emotionally distant from all of us. Of all the abuses, tortures, hungers, diseases, neglect, humiliations, and depravities that I suffered, none damaged my soul so profoundly as my mother not having given me the chance to properly bond with her when I was an infant, something that every child needs from its mother. Of all the reasons that I have for feeling a murderous rage towards her, this is perhaps the most significant and over-riding. Over the years several events and symptoms tell the story about my early years when my mother didn't bother to love me as a child.

Quite simply I do not remember anything about my mother prior to my session in bed with her when I was four or five. I can recall literally hundreds of events prior to age five, with most of my relatives being part of the picture, but I can recall only one scene with my mother, and in it she was hysterical about her arm hurting. We lived in Mexico with my grandparents and aunts and uncles. I recall all of them, but my mother is missing from the picture. Where was she? Did she ever hold me as a baby? Why do I recall sleeping with all my aunts and my uncle in their beds, but I don't remember ever being in the same bed with my mother when I was a baby? Where was the bitch when I was an infant? Was she fucking or sucking dick?

The logical thing was to ask my Uncle Felipe about these early years. Major disappointment. He said that he too could not remember anything about "those years" in Mexico. What angered me most is that he told me that even if he couldn't remember, he knew for a fact that my mother loved me dearly. My rage came to the surface upon hearing those words, for I knew in my heart that they were fraudulent, not in that he was deliberately trying to deceive me, but in the sense that he too was so deep in the hole of desperate emotional confusion that he had no inkling about love, caring, and the proper responsibility of parents towards their children. His assertion about my mother's supposed love for me was an affront to my understanding of the proper relationships between decent human beings, so at this fateful meeting with my Uncle Felipe I reached what I felt was a monumental realization in my life: My mother had been so emotionally and spiritually sick that she had had only a delusional understanding of love, and worse yet, she had had almost no capacity to love her children in any real and concrete manner.

I didn't fare any better in asking other relatives about the years in Mexico. They too fumbled around for answers and had unexplainable gaps in their memories. But the pattern was consistent with a massive case of dysfunctionality and perhaps pervasive sexual abuse in my mother's family of origin. None escaped without significant character symptoms. What added an ominous tone to my suspicion of my having been abandoned as an infant was my realization that I had peculiar symptoms consistent with this interpretation. This had to do with a set of baby hamsters.

Normally people enjoy their pets and are excited when they give birth. But in this case I wasn't. Some years ago I had hamsters, a small bird, and a squirrel at home because my kids liked them. One day I discovered that the pair of hamsters had given birth to five pink-skinned critters whose eyes were still closed. I was shocked to realize that I was feeling extremely jealous when the babies would squirm and attach themselves to their mother's nipples to nurse. Imagine feeling jealous about this! That is real sick. But it's also true. It bothered me immensely to see the mother hamster lying down lovingly and accommodatingly so that her offspring could suckle as they pleased. My discomfort and jealousy continued to increase daily and I became obsessed with creating disturbances which would interrupt the family meal time of these innocent hamsters. Soon enough my jealousy gave rise to anger and a strong resentment against these creatures until I actually physically removed the babies from their mother's breast when they wanted to nurse. My continual disturbance of the family unit eventually led to the mother hamster becoming very anxious, and she ended it all by eating all of her babies alive. I watched with intense pleasure as the mother chewed off their tiny limbs while the babies struggled against death. She then crushed their heads between her bloody jaws and chewed and chewed until they were all gone. I was much relieved—I had lived through a life and death ordeal. But deep down I felt I was more sinister than the serial killers who roam the streets at night looking for innocents to dismember.

It was a pathetically sick episode in my life. Normally people are pleased when their pets give birth or at a minimum will respect the integrity and privacy of the animal. But my intense jealousy was all-consuming, as if somehow my soul felt, rightly or wrongly, that this adult female hamster was my own mother and that I wanted exclusive right to those nipples. How dare these babies latch on to those nipples—they belong to me, to me! I can't think of any other explanation for this bizarre emotion that makes me think that my soul is sick beyond redemption. Imagine depriving an infant hamster of its natural desire to bond with his mother's nipples. The parallel with my own life is terrifyingly close.

Other road signs point to my conclusion of emotional neglect. I do not recall ever having been kissed by my mother, or, for that matter, by any other person during my childhood. I now know what normal affection is between parents and children, and I have given my own children perhaps thousands of kisses in the few years since they were born. This, plus my knowledge of other families has given me an idea of how children develop in this area, so I know that kids as young as a few months will pucker their lips when they kiss their parents or other people. But I on the other hand was 17 years old when I finally realized that I did not know how to kiss. I was interested in this girl at my high school so I wanted to be well prepared for our romantic date. Maybe too naively I was anticipating that I might even try to kiss her lips, and this is what brought on the terror of my realization that I actually had not kissed anything in my entire life. Retrospectively, that was a very sorry situation for any human being. At 17 not only did I have a long history of hunger and of having had my body used by dozens of people, but I also had never been kissed. So here I stood, a scared teenager trying to have a normal date but not knowing how to plant a simple kiss. So I took action and decided to practice. The back of my hand seemed not too threatening to me, so I placed my lips against it in my first kiss ever. Only in retrospect can I analyze what happened, and it was very frustrating to place my lips to my hand, but feeling that the kiss was "dead." Nothing happened—no smack. Over the next several days I attempted to kiss my hand repeatedly whenever I could find a private moment so that no person would ever witness what I felt was shameful. I think that it was about a week later that I discovered quite by accident the "puckering" part of preparing my lips for a kiss, and the loud "smack." Wow, I had finally delivered my first real kiss ever, even if it was to the back of a hand that would never protest or reject me. Little did I know then that it would still be several years before I would have the chance to deliver my first kiss to another human being.

This shows why I feel that my mother failed me and all my brothers and sisters right from the beginning. I believe that she was essentially absent from the home, that she sent me away to live with my grandparents, and that she visited only occasionally. No one knows what the bitch did during my first four years of life. There are only little bits and pieces of history, in spite of three aunts and one uncle who were surviving witnesses to the ongoing chaos and tragedy. My own angry suspicion is that my mother was in another town enjoying a series of romantic liaisons, opening her legs for pleasure while her newborn son was left to face the forces of destruction much as the infant hamsters would many years later. The bitch didn't eat me to get it over with, but I have wondered many times if that cannibalistic solution wouldn't have been preferable to the torture that was to follow. But let us start somewhere closer to the spot where her whoring must have begun.

Chapter Two

Infant, Surrounded by Confused Adults

As angry as I have been for years at my mother, I still miss her. However cold and abusive she may have been, my mother is the only link I have to my creation and my sense of family history. For better or worse, probably more on the worse side, there is no way that I can deny the central place that my mother occupies in my spiritual and emotional life. Oftentimes she would sing to us in our darkened dungeon to help us sleep when our stomachs would protest about the several days' worth of hunger we frequently endured, and the melodies in the dark must have etched their sweetness against the barren landscape of our wilted hearts, for now my soul seeks out similar melodies in all opera. For years now I have had an enormous penchant for the soprano operatic arias of Puccini, Delibes, Mozart, Faust, and Dvorak, feeling an enormous uplifting force from the female voices. In Catalani's *La Wally* I cannot help but feel that my mother would have sung that way to me if she could speak from the grave for just a few moments to ask for forgiveness for the grievous wrongs which she inflicted upon us all. If the request came in that form I would gladly forgive her for everything that she ever did, and the rose which I have withheld for many years I would tearfully place upon her unvisited grave, marked only by a stone from the street. But I am not so sure that my baby brother Benito would forgive her, for I suspect that my mother, for whatever reason, neglected him the most, so much so that she contributed directly to his death when he was still a baby.

This tragedy actually began around 1951 when I was about six years old and we were living in the house on Salinas Avenue, our second home in El Paso, Texas, after I was brought from Mexico hidden under the spare tire in the trunk of a car by my mother and some strange men. So in that year there were four of us kids, and my mother was pregnant by the most brutal, vicious, caustic, and malignant man that I have ever known; unfortunately for all of us, this monster lived with us and faked the role of husband while pretending to be a stepfather to some of us and a father to the others. It was a normal nightmare for all of us kids—I was the oldest—to cower under the oily blankets while our parents had their nightly vicious arguments. We suffered these nightly traumas for years on end, imagining the worst was happening as we heard the awful venom spew from our parents' mouths. No wonder I wet my bed until I was ten years old; I never knew if I would find a cadaver next to me in bed at night.

On a particularly cold night the arguments started as usual, but there was something more sinister this time around. We kids knew that the intensity of the argument was beyond anything that we had ever seen or heard before, in spite of our desensitized hearts. The face of hatred and homicidal rage was what I saw on my stepfather, who was ugly to begin with anyway. I'll never forget the day I stared at Satan in the face. He was there. He was in our home, and I believed at that moment in time that he would kill my very pregnant mother.

It was a dimly lit room with only a cheap bed on one corner—no other furniture. As she was standing next to the bed holding her belly, the beast hit her and then pushed her against the wall. She bounced off the wall and fell to the floor with an ugly thud we will never forget. We kids cowered in the far corner of the room while the demon kicked and stomped on her. Even I, who by the age of six was already a full coward in the face of the Demon, felt horror in my heart about my mother's totally defenseless position, yet I was terrified that he would snuff me out just as easily if I went to my mother's side. My cowardly failure to assist my bleeding mother when she desperately needed me was to haunt me for the rest of my life.

When it was all over my mother just lay on the floor whimpering softly, holding her very big belly with one hand while supporting herself against the leg of the bed with the other. All of us kids had urinated from the terror, but we didn't dare crawl towards her for fear of being vaporized by the hate-stare of the monster, who just stood by admiring his macho victory. Eventually he left and we ran to her side, but neither she nor we could provide comfort to the other. We were all in the same sinking boat, unable to rescue ourselves from the sea of misery that had come to engulf all of us so completely. It was normal for us to not even think there were alternatives to our tragic and hopeless life.

As far as I can remember, the severe stomping that my mother suffered must have done something to the baby inside her because she later said he was going to be born much earlier than expected. More complications occurred and my brother Benito was born a few days after the beating, savagely forced into this world by his own father's hatred. But this was to be only the beginning of a brutal life that no human being should ever have to know.

We all sensed that something was not right with the new baby in the family. His face was strange, and even after a few months he didn't seem to progress. Years later, as an adult, I looked at the one existing photograph of my little brother and could see that he appeared floppy and unnatural. Quite soon after his birth he began having all sorts of medical problems, and as a consequence he was in and out of the public welfare hospital quite routinely. I do not recall any of us older kids ever playing with, enjoying, or kissing my baby brother. And I do not remember seeing my mother give him any affection either. But I do recall vividly the many times that his head slammed against the bare concrete floor.

I cannot understand how this could have happened, but it did. When Benito was a few months old we had to move out of the house on Salinas Avenue because, as usual, we did not pay the rent (the ironic thing here is that this house on Salinas Avenue was owned by our stepfather's parents, who none the less kicked their son out. What else could you expect from parents who created such a vile human being?). We moved into the welfare projects popularly called The Jacinto Projects, known for their commercial-grade concrete floors; none of us knew then that my brother Benito would not live to see the next house.

My mother had the habit of putting the baby on top of a rather high bed and then walking to the vanity mirror to adorn her face. The first time that the fall occurred I cringed from the inhuman sound of a baby's skull landing squarely and cleanly on the concrete floor, followed by the echo-like noise of my brother's brain jarring inside his skull. I can't describe it any other way. Benito didn't cry much—he just looked more strange. This same deadly scenario was played out several times over the next few weeks, my brother all the while going to the hospital for "routine" admissions. In retrospect I feel sickened by how all of us failed to protect this innocent baby, but most of all I have a disgusting feeling that my mother may have subconsciously wanted him dead. Why else would she show such a catastrophic and monumental failure to protect my baby brother? Didn't she know not to put a baby on such a high bed? Didn't she know there were bare concrete floors throughout the roach-infested apartment? Didn't she know that you never leave a crawling baby unattended on a bed? Didn't she know that even one fall from such a height can be fatal to a baby? And didn't she learn anything the first time Benito fell off the bed? This was just another sick episode in our miserable lives, and the answers to the above questions rot in the grave along with the mother who failed her baby—the mother who may have even killed her infant son.

The inevitable end was yet another ugly chapter in our lives. It was a very hot summer day in El Paso, and as usual we were all sweaty and sticky in part from the heat and humidity, but mostly because we took showers only about once a month. I don't know why. Our miserable welfare apartment sat directly next to a large baseball field which was usually busy with all the other unkempt welfare kids, most of whom had in one way or another beat me up, sexually abused me, or had broken windows in our home. Our brother Benito had been in the hospital for about two weeks, apparently getting worse from what I could gather from bits of overheard conversations here and there. Since we never had a phone in our house the hospital would communicate daily with my mother through a neighbor whose apartment was exactly on the opposite side of the baseball field and who was one of the richer poor folks in the neighborhood. We kids got the kick of our lives just *sitting* next to the phone when my mother was allowed to use it. That morning we were in our apartment pulling lice out of each other's hair when one of the neighbor's kids came running and said that our mother should come quickly to his house because there was an urgent message from the hospital. My mother jumped from her chair, revealed for the first time that I could remember a face of concern and distress, and started walking and almost running along the pathway that connected our end of the baseball field with the neighbor's. For some reason I decided to go out of our apartment through the other door which was on the opposite side. As I arrived in the open area I got a panoramic view of the entire baseball field, and I could see my poor mother running along the far pathway towards the neighbor's house. At that very instant the neighbor woman also appeared at her end of the pathway, walking very briskly towards my mother. I can only conjecture about what my mother must have felt as she ran and saw the woman with the message. When they were about 25 yards apart and still running towards each other, the woman yelled out the message from hell: "The doctor said Benito just died!" Those words froze this image of the baseball field, and the two running women, in my heart forever.

My mother stopped in her stride and sobbed hysterically; a few moments later the woman arrived at the spot where my mother was, not knowing what else to say or how to comfort her. She just stood there looking out of place. By that time the entire neighborhood had focused on the unfolding event, with other neighbors stepping just outside of their doors to observe us. Soon all my brothers and sisters had gathered around my mother, and we all walked back to our roach-infested apartment to cry. As I think about it now, I feel so sorry for my mother because not only did she lose a son, but there was no dignity to the manner in which she received the bad news: The baseball field became a public stage for our terrible misfortune and our hopeless lives.

At the funeral home we kids waited outside in a car belonging to a kind neighbor who agreed to transport us for the day. I don't know why but we played and romped around in the car as if nothing was happening. We laughed a lot. Nobody cried when the cheap box went into the ground; we just wanted to get back into the car to play. After this, nobody ever talked about Benito again. It's almost as if he had just been a bad nightmare. An innocent baby, hammered while in the womb, had his skull slammed against the cement more than once, and put away in a plain plywood box in the ground. It was normal for us. He quickly became a big zero in our desperate lives—totally forgotten.

Beginnings in Mexico, Late 1940s, with Dirt Floors

It was in Ciudad Juarez, Mexico, that this story began in the late 1940s. Ciudad Juarez is located just south of the Rio Grande, adjoining El Paso, Texas, as a sister city. The poverty in Ciudad Juarez was beyond desperate, and the focus of the day was survival, with common decency and moral values optional if the stomach permitted it. Most of the streets were unpaved, but if you were lucky you lived on one that was covered with *caliche,* a kind of soft, grainy stone that provided a slightly better surface for travel but which unwittingly also became a projectile used by the ever-present misfits who inhabited the streets. And it also meant that the streets became small rivers when it rained, carrying with them raw sewage from the thousands of outhouses that dotted the city.

The house I was born in was a one-room box with walls covered by salvaged wood slats that were already peppered with countless holes where thousands of nails had been. It was so poorly put together that even mild wind made it creak. That was alright during the day, but at night those sounds made everyone afraid. In this rickety, leaky, never-painted house lived my grandparents, my mother, my aunts Julieta, Marisa, and Sonia, and my Uncle Felipe. I was the first grandchild in this home although I don't know if that made any difference. I have a few memories of the two years that we lived in that house, only one of them about my mother. We had an outhouse just like most of the neighbors, and my mother would tell me to be careful when I used it, because the green lizards that habitually hung around the inside of the seating area would love to crawl inside my anus. Even at age two, I had already started to ponder about some of these bits of "wisdom" that were being handed down to me and was perplexed by the need of these green critters to identify and enter a dark, smelly anus. It just did not make sense to me at that age. Now, as an adult, I think about my mother's anal anxiety and wonder just how she acquired it.

About a block away from our house was a residential-construction project in progress, providing me with excitement. Sometimes I would actually enter the house that was being built, and I would talk to the workers who periodically would give me a round wafer of pure, grainy chocolate. One day, on the way back home, I ventured onto a concrete sidewalk that had been freshly poured, and, of course, I sank down to my knees. My cries brought the men running, and I was quickly rescued from my sinking predicament. They hosed my legs down with water and gave me another delicious chocolate wafer to take home (or to shut me up). Other than this, there were no other significant events at the house where I was born. Or at least events that I can recall.

However, there was one very perplexing fact that I have yet to understand the meaning of. When I was much older, my mother showed me several boxes that must have contained perhaps *hundreds* of photographs, mostly of her. In these, she seemed to radiate pure vanity, always looking intensely at the camera, raising a coquetish eyebrow yet almost never betraying a smile. Interestingly enough, most, if not all, of these photos were taken when she must have been between the ages of 15 and 25; she was 25 when I was born, and the photo mania came to an abrupt end. Unfortunately, her look of vanity remained, transferred from her amorous social relations to her role as a mother and thus poisoning the images we came to have of her. Little did I know that, many years after my mother's death, this same arrogant and detached look would come back to haunt me; it came in the form of a cat (more on the "psychotic" cat later).

Second House in Mexico and Some Strange Events

They said that my mother was married to my biological father, Arnulfo, when I was born in 1945, but I suspect some kind of a cover-up. I recall just one event with him in the picture at the first house; here, at the second house in Mexico, he is nowhere to be found. My sister Ana was born when I was about 15 months old, but she, too, is invisible to my mind's eye, for I have no recollection of her at all at this place.

Here, poverty was a culture; we were well acquainted with its norms and in the customs that reflected our sense of values. The kitchen had no floor, or rather had a floor that was the bare ground, making it dank even during the scorching Mexican summers. Having no toothpaste and no toothbrush, my Uncle Felipe improvised by applying salt to his wet index finger and using it as a bristleless toothbrush.

I slept usually with one of my aunts in a huge bed covered with a sheet for a canopy to keep away the persistent Mexican mosquitoes. As I said, I don't ever recall having my mother there, except once when she came to visit, I believe, and got hysterical about her arm hurting, as I mentioned before. Someone in the house applied alcohol to her arm, and she apparently felt better. Was it psychosomatic? Then afterwards one of my aunts guzzled the remaining amount of *rubbing* alcohol directly from the bottle. Was she an alcoholic at what must have been age 13? Where was my mother the rest of the time? As unbelievable as it may sound, *none* of my aunts or uncle currently recall where my mother was during those two years at the second house in Mexico.

Not too many bad things happened here that I can remember. But I believe that by this time the abandonment trauma had taken its toll, as I conjecture from the fact that during my formative years up to age four I recall perhaps one or two times that I interacted meaningfully with my mother. Quite simply she was not available to me, but neither was there anyone else in that maternal extended family that I could identify as my main caretaker. There was, however, one pleasant and memorable event that stands alone as the *only* flower from my childhood years in Mexico.

My grandfather used to take me with him to do things about town—things like collecting the fruit from neighbor's *Mesquite* trees and smelling the sweet aroma from a freshly peeled banana. I don't recall his demeanor too well, but I do remember that he was a big man who always smelled like old sweat and urine, something that I came to like about him. One day we walked together for a few blocks, eventually coming upon a huge open field circumscribed by tenacious Mesquite trees. We had a homemade kite that we soon had in the air high above any of the reaching tentacles of the trees. I wanted to sit on the ground to enjoy our kite a bit better, but I was hesitant due to the carpet-like covering of the prickly *cadillos* on the ground. My grandfather must have noticed my dilemma, for he promptly took out a sticky red handkerchief from his back pocket, and opened it on the ground for me to sit on. He then sat next to me on the prickly *cadillos,* neither face nor words betraying if he felt any discomfort from the ground. For the next few minutes we sat there together, wordlessly enjoying that wonderful homemade kite, the kite that was witness to what was to be my *only memorable moment* with an adult male figure during my entire childhood years.

My first four years of life in Mexico were essentially not emotionally charged or explosive, but there were some things going on that profoundly determined the course of history for us and perhaps set the stage for the misery that was to come when we moved to Texas. Of greatest concern to me as an adult searching for answers to the layers upon layers of mysteries in my family was my mother's sexual behavior.

There is a part of me that feebly believes that a son has no right to judge his mother's past sexual behavior, that out of respect for her he should stifle any impulse to judge her. I even have to contend with The Bible's teachings in Solomon's book of *Proverbs* (1:8): "Listen my son to your father's instruction and do not forsake your mother's teaching." Maybe on the theological level that may be so, but if I am to escape the damnation my mother brought down on all of us, I must judge her behavior so that I may see more clearly through the moral fog she conjured up for us. In any case, it makes me feel less guilty if I adopt this self-serving attitude of finding it necessary and ethical to judge her.

From what I have been able to gather from relatives and others who knew the family during 1945–50, my mother very much enjoyed men, so much so that when she was 15 (circa 1935) she eloped with and married a man in his 40s. I suppose that many a love-struck girl has done that in the history of the world, but it doesn't feel good that *my mother* did it. It didn't last more than a few days (I am glad!) and soon she was back at home in Mexico. Family history also has it that she was caught in bed with a married male relative the same year, precipitating a lifelong hateful relationship that she endured with the relative's wife. And then there was her fateful decision to leave Arnulfo, her second husband and my father, at about the time I was born.

Many sources have told me that Arnulfo appeared to be a good man, treating my mother with love, dignity, and respect. Sure, he was poor, they said, but he had already set up a home complete with furniture for my pregnant mother to move in to and set up house. She hedged, preferring to continue to live at her parents' home in Mexico during her pregnancy, even though towards the end of the pregnancy they were already legally married. At some point a relative also told me that my grandmother never wanted my mother to leave home. If that is so, I might be right in thinking that my grandmother felt emotionally distant from my grandfather, so much so that she depended on her own children, especially the oldest, my mother, to provide her with emotional and spiritual support in her loveless and empty marriage.

I was born in 1945, and my mother sought a divorce from my alleged biological father a few months later. About the most coherent reason for this I have been able to uncover is that she felt that Arnulfo was "too weak, and not man enough." While the divorce was in the courts my mother got pregnant again; I believe that it was finalized a few months before my sister Ana was born.

For many years now there has been a virulent suspicion in the family about the paternity concerning Ana and me: It has been alleged that Ana and I have different fathers, and I personally have heard from the lips of Arnulfo that he is not my father. My mother the bitch left us with this miserable uncertainty that was further compounded by events that were to take place many years later.

When I was between the ages of about 5 and 12 my mother would routinely take me on long walks about the city, strutting along the sidewalk in a seductive manner with her vain face and raised eyebrow, as usual. On one occasion she took me to the *Hotel Central* in El Paso, going to the rear kitchen entrance instead of through the front door. By the door she told me, "Wait here, don't move, and I'll be back soon." Patiently, I waited just outside the greasy kitchen door, listening to all the seemingly choreographed banging of pans inside and furiously playing with my testicles through a torn pocket in my pants. I was six years old and a co-conspirator in a seductive affair that my mother was carrying on behind the back of the miserable monster whom she had chosen to be my stepfather. I did not know it then, but I was probably learning a valuable lesson in clandestine techniques which would come in handy in the future when I found myself similarly unhappy with my own spouse.

Never once did I see the face of the mystery man in the hotel kitchen, the one banging my mother between his duties as dishwasher. For all I know his penis and his ardor could have been the ones responsible for my being on this planet in the first place. Years later one of my aunts related to me how my mother pointed to a man and said to her, "Do you see that man over there? Well, that is Victor's father." As per my aunt, this man worked in the kitchen of none other than the now infamous *Hotel Central*. My father, the dishwasher who fucked my mother every week in the kitchen broom closet, and sent her on her way full of sperms.

So there was certainly enough going on during the first four years of my life to set the stage for the lifelong problems that all of us were to encounter. Years prior to my birth my mother already had a sexual track record with men, apparently having a penchant for much older men when she was 15. At the time she was dating and would eventually marry my alleged biological father, Arnulfo, we all suspect she was having secret rendezvous with the prize short-order cook from the hotel with the greasy door, if not with a swarm of other low-lives as well. Then she got pregnant. Did the whore even *know* which of all these worms gave her the sperms at the right time, or was she just mostly interested in opening her legs and swallowing as many male organs as she could? As if all this whoring was not enough she then proceeded to bed one of her married male relatives in my grandparents' substandard house, *and got pregnant again!* This was in 1947. Since then, many members of our extended family, as well as this man's wife and children, have viewed the pregnancy—announced shortly after the romp in bed—as having been caused by this illicit affair between family members. The man's wife and children never let an opportunity pass to let my mother know, in the most caustic and acrimonious manner possible, that the resulting baby was the most damnable human to ever arrive on Earth. My poor sister Ana consequently suffered from the hate that this family spewed at her throughout the years. Thus, this act of my mother's resulted in inestimable damage to family relations, a legacy that survived well beyond her years. My mother was truly the whore from hell.

And what about her probable sexual improprieties before, during, and after she was pregnant with me? Her dubious history certainly leads me to believe that she may have been having sex with a variety of men when she was pregnant with me, the visualization of which makes me sick. In fact, many years later when I entered psychotherapy as an adult I went through hypnosis and free association. My therapist asked me to let my mind's image roam free as I visualized my humble beginnings in my mother's womb (I would prefer to call it the womb from hell). The very first thing that spontaneously came to my mind as I visualized myself as an unborn baby was an army of invading penises attacking the integrity of the womb by entering through the vagina and cervix. Indeed it sickens me to think that as I was in my mother's womb there may have been several penises virtually just millimeters away from me, all squirting sperm and all belonging to different men who then left and played no part in my life. My honest and spontaneous visualization of my mother welcoming an army of penises into her vagina, scant millimeters from me, is the *rage from the womb;* this is the sin from which there can be no redemption, for in my view the womb is sovereign territory when a child awaits within.

Some Early Psychological Problems

By the time I was four years old some very major developmental problems had been cast by the unseen hand of pathological family forces. Most corrosive in my view was my mother's apparent abandonment of me after birth. I believe that she may have had very mixed feelings about the pregnancy, and my birth may have triggered a panic reaction in her. All evidence seems to show that at the very least she was reluctant about being a mother, and I paid the full price by having been denied that special infant-to-mother bond that is the cornerstone of normal socio-emotional development. Thus the first four years of my life I spent in a whirlpool of dysfunction created by confused adults all desperately trying to deal with their own misery as well as they could, all groping with their own inner demons of abuse, hunger, lovelessness, anger, and destitution. Retrospectively I can see that there were no adults in that home in Mexico that I would consider "normal" by our current standards. From what I now know I can state that most tragically no one in that loosely-knitted household had any real concept of love, an intolerable situation further aggravated by the multitude of terrible symptoms that perhaps were just seen as normal "character" traits of the individuals.

I was already grievously wounded by the time that I was four years old, having lost the opportunity to "bond" properly with my mother because she was not physically and emotionally available to me. I played, set fires, urinated in my pants and my bed all the time, tortured and killed tarantulas, and developed a fierce attachment to an oversize safety pin that I hung to any shirt that I may have been wearing.

My Safety Pin, My Opium.

I suppose that this may have started when I was about one or two years old, but as far back as I can remember in my childhood I *always* carried with me a large safety pin, the kind used with diapers. Vividly I recall how I would panic if for some reason I misplaced this wonderful little tool, my constant companion, my safety net, my security, my non-threatening amulet to the world. Soon I devised a method of never losing my companion: I ran the pin through the fabric of my shirt, if I had a shirt on, or through the elastic waistband of my pants. Of course, pretty soon I also had a lot more holes in the rags I wore as clothes. No matter what was going on around me, I could make myself feel better by just thinking about my trusty pin that was attached to me. If it was dark in the house and the walls tried to grab me, I would feel for my pin. The vicious monsters under the bed would stay at bay if I felt for my pin, and the loneliness of our house full of confused and sick adults would be less scary if I ran my fingers through the center part of the pin. Yes indeed, I found a self-absorbing, autistic world into which I could retreat when the never-ending storm around me got too hard to bear. Only, sometimes, the intensity of the scary things around me seemed to require a greater degree of detachment, of autistic-like withdrawal, so I began to utilize my friendly pin as a tool for self-inflicted pain.

Of course, when it was happening I did not know what was going on or what to call it, but I recall vividly the progression of my more intense use of this sharp, metallic pin. Things at my grandparents' house went from bad to worse as my mother now found herself with two kids and no husband, and one never-mentioned uncle of mine drowned at age seven when he went swimming in the unforgiving waters of the *Rio Grande* with my Uncle Felipe, then about 13 years old. As I understand it, alcoholism severely affected several members of the household, and I have reason to believe that there also was rampant sexual abuse of all offspring in the house. Many years later my Uncle Felipe told me that at about this time my grandfather was inflicting severe beatings on him, especially when my grandfather would come home after roaming the streets aimlessly all day, as he had done for his entire life. Still, my mother was like a cat, coming to visit only sometimes, only when she needed something. And even then she had that vain, haughty look. Didn't she see that I was deteriorating and retreating, needing adults less and less? Didn't she see that I no longer ran towards her when she came to visit, a detachment symptomatic of inner withdrawal and despair? And didn't she see the severe tears and marks that I had on my hands? Probably not. She was never much for little details like that on her children.

Having used my pin almost around the clock, I became an expert at manipulating it between my fingers. I quickly learned that if I forced one of my fingers through the open center part of it that I would experience pain and pleasure. Since my finger was too large to go through the center part, I would have to force it. To most people, it would be painful, but to me it felt good. As I got to be about age four I learned to rotate my captive finger inside the loop for additional pressure and additional pain. The more pain I inflicted on myself, the more I wanted. This I did almost all day long, and at night I needed it to fall asleep, numb from the 24-hour self-inflicted pain that was obviously preferable to feeling the chaos and dealing with the confused adults who had no eyes and no ears. It sounded like an addiction to self-inflicted pain at age four.

My nails, too, suffered, for they were mostly stubby, not growing fast enough to keep up with the ravenous appetite of my very anxious teeth. Sometimes I mutilated myself by driving the open sharp point of my pin through the external layers of skin on my hands. I enjoyed it. What I didn't enjoy was this thing that I called the "hot vomit" feeling that began just about age three. Numerous times a day I would feel that whatever food I may have had, if any, would come up from my stomach and stay just below my throat. It felt like hot vomit that never made it all the way out. For years and years I suffered with this condition; it became part of me; it became so normal; I didn't know any better. Unfortunately for me, I believed it to be so normal that I never mentioned it to anyone until about 30 years later. Now I know that it was my nervous physical reaction to the intense anxiety that had enveloped me so completely during my childhood.

Another peculiar symptom that I had was a chronic desire to suck my tongue in a rhythmic fashion resembling that of sucking a nipple. In fact, I would suck my tongue perhaps as much as 16 hours per day, pausing only to talk whenever necessary, as when someone asked me a question. Somewhere along the line I learned to integrate my self-inflicted pain from the pin with my sucking habit, and soon the start of one would trigger the other.

As I look back at these terrible times of my early childhood I feel so sad that so many things went wrong, that so many adults around us *failed* in their ethical and moral duties to protect us all. The habits I had already fully developed by age four were nothing less than *real psychiatric symptoms indicative of serious emotional disturbance.* If the proper authorities at that time had seen my condition I probably would have immediately received psychiatric care or would have been placed in a children's psychiatric hospital. Here I was, exhibiting autistic, self-mutilating symptoms, and having phobias about walls becoming alive and about other, threatening objects around my environment. Here I was, exhibiting a chronic, nervous condition resembling somatic heartburn more typical of a financial executive in a high stress job. And why did I have to suck my tongue 16 hours per day *for years*? Was it because I experienced some disturbance or trauma in what we would call the Freudian *oral stage*? Was it because I experienced a significant deprivation in bonding with my mother's breast? Indeed, at age four I was already a walking basket full of psychiatric symptoms, the product of a severe failure in parental duty and responsibilities.

Unfortunately the evils of our wicked home viciously surrounded me when I was born, so I stood alone as a young child in defending myself against unseen demons who tormented me in every corner of my life. My mother who should have been the source of love and security for me was one of those demons who looked at me with disdain, vanity, and haughtiness, expressions which made me want her and fear her at the same time. I think that at one point my child's heart simply shut down, unable to survive the onslaught of abuse and the mixed messages coming from my mother's eyes—the eyes of a cat. Had I known at age four that this was to be only the beginning of a horrific childhood, I would have lain down across the railroad tracks and allowed the cold wheels of mercy to cut my body in half to save myself from further agony. But as bad as things were at this point, they were merely the backdrop of more evil to come.

Chapter Three
The Evil Stepfather and The Early Years in Texas

"Unconditional love corresponds to one of the deepest longings, not only of the child, but of every human being...."

The Art of Loving, 1956
Erich Fromm (1900–1980)

Ciudad Juarez, Mexico, in the late 1940s, was even more destitute than it is today. A miserable border town of about 25,000, it was home to many rural poor who had come to the big city to find their fortune, mostly in the form of backbreaking labor digging ditches for the city—ditches whose purpose I never figured out. Thousands upon thousands of children were born to passive mothers who wondered loudly why God kept sending them little angels to homes without beds, plumbing, food, heat, or fathers. These little accidents of nature had the enormous misfortune of having to work for their food starting at around age 3, for by the thousands they would pepper the city streets selling whatever cheap junk their parents could design from trash or leftover garbage from the city dump. Not that before age two they could just slack off, play peek-a-boo with mom, or simply enjoy a good tantrum. Babies hung on for dear life to empty, prune-like breasts, sucking hope into their wasted stomachs while mom was busy defending herself against invading armies of flies and simultaneously holding out a hand for a kind gesture from a passing Christian. And at night, after walking miles throughout the city in search of that elusive fortune but settling for a nice, warm, bean taco, mothers and children would typically sleep wherever they wouldn't get run over by the decrepit automobiles or by fortunate pedestrians with shoes.

But one thing that was very popular in this town that should have gone down with Atlantis was the town square called *Plaza de las Rosas,* a meeting place for all those grownup children who now wanted a mate they could call their own, so that they could make more little angels to pepper the city of joy. (It is amusing to me how nature has such a relentless drive to replicate individuals of a species, even if thousands of babies must die so that a few survive to carry forth the genes.). *Plaza de las Rosas* was beautifully landscaped with very tall palm trees, flowered shrubs, grass, and dozens of sturdy cement benches—quite an anomaly in a dirt-poor town like Ciudad Juarez. As a town square it was always bustling with hundreds of colorful merchants offering their cheap, home-made trinkets, and self-professed cooks selling giant beef tacos and lemonade. Lemons in the lemonade, yes, but beef in the tacos, I cannot say. This was the center of the universe for the townspeople.

But I suspect that sometime in 1948 or 1949 there was a sick and sinister man slowly walking among the dispossessed throngs, a *man looking for someone to be ugly with,* looking for someone to complement his spiritual sickness, looking for someone whose life he could suck dry like a vampire. A man so vile that no one would give him a second look, so vile that even rabid dogs quickly got out of his Satanic path. Yes, that infamous and wretched day my mother was there too, somewhere, looking for a real man in her life, and the crossing of their paths would doom both of them forever.

About a mile from this pitiful scene of human misery was my grandparents' house. At about that time I was three or four years old and deep in my own nightmare without a mother, not knowing that the bitch was at the *Plaza de las Rosas,* neglecting me but scouting the throngs, and about to cross paths with the sinister shadow of Satan, a man whose outward sickness must have captivated her from the beginning. He was rough, he was ugly, he was unshaven, he was dressed in soiled mechanic's clothes, he was uncouth, he had no manners. But he was a real, real man. Her subconscious must have surely come alive with her womanly vigor: Can he rough me up to show me his love, just like my father? Can he hit me hard? Can he drag me by my hair? Can he spit on me and abuse me with no compassion? Can he ram his obviously large tool mercilessly into me until it hurts? I gather it must have been love at first sight between these two pathologically compatible rejects from the human race.

All my relatives have said that they have never figured out what attracted my mother to this low-life scumbag, for he was "not good-looking," didn't have a steady job, and had a drinking problem. There was no logic, as, perhaps, there never is when the heart alone dictates our path in life. But my mother herself told me eye to eye years later that she met this beast at the famous *Plaza de las Rosas,* and that in her careful judgment he would make a "good father" for all of us. Fuck the bitch! How can anyone misjudge as badly as my mother did on such an important issue? This was one of my mother's most devastating and ruinous decisions, a judgment call that resulted in incalculable suffering for all of us, and for herself as well. This monster stalking the dispossessed at the plaza came home with my mother, to suck our spiritual blood and to steal our souls. But why did it have to go from worse to catastrophic?

They must have dated many times back in '49 while I was still in Mexico in my usual trance, compulsively applying pain with my pin. His ugly name was Merengueno Zalmar, son of a vicious El Paso, Texas, family, or rather, a collection of humorless adults who clawed at each other under the same roof. He was not just "not good-looking"; in my untrained-eye view as a child he was positively ugly, having scary black eyes that never looked at you unless he was about to deliver a blow to your body or an insult to your soul. He was short but stocky, as all hyenas are, with black hair and a grotesque rounded face with hideous dark eyebrows drooping towards the top of his nose that gave him a permanent look of being in a rage. The monster had half of one eyelid missing, much as rabid dogs have bite marks or torn ears after a territorial fight. For years I wondered what kind of vicious fight he'd been in that allowed another beast to have gotten its teeth so close to his eyeball. The fool gloated that he had blinded the guy who had eaten his eyelid. He sure looked like the winner, left with an eye that just wouldn't shut. Many years later when we kids wanted to sneak out of the house and he was passed out on the floor during the day, we found out that his perpetually open eyeball was terrifying when we were trying to see if the monster was still asleep. It was a positively ugly thing to look at, especially because even the white of the eye was evil, having jagged purple veins all over it.

There's more. His two upper front teeth were chipped diagonally in half, courtesy of a bad spill he'd taken when trying to kick a dog on the street. It didn't ruin his smile, for he didn't have one anyway, but it added an extra dimension of viciousness to his Satanic stare. His mostly round face had several scars and small ears, small, stubby nose, kinky black hair. He had powerful short arms, but for us kids they were massive, especially when he lunged at us to deliver random blows. He stood about 5'3" and always walked briskly as if he had something important to do. His occupation: bar patron, brawler, thief, child abuser, wife beater, and, when he had extra time, refrigeration mechanic. In time all of us kids came to call him *El Diablo* (The Devil).

So whatever it was that my mother saw in this half-man, half-dog, remains a secret. Maybe she was excited by his I'll-take-charge-or-I'll-break-your-face attitude. Or, maybe she just felt she didn't deserve a real person for a mate. At that Mexican plaza for the poor, in 1949, my fate and my sister Ana's, as well as our future brothers' and sisters', were sealed when my mother and *El Diablo* decided to set up house together in El Paso, Texas, and combine their mutual moral turpitude into one colossal blunder that resulted in abject misery for themselves and spiritual damnation for all of us kids. And so it was that The Devil became our live-in stepfather.

Cunnilingus on Lincoln Avenue

We were still in Mexico in 1949, I was four, and for several days I had been hearing of going to the other city—El Paso—to live there permanently. On the scheduled day two men arrived in a shiny black car—quite an unusual occurrence since never had a car stopped at our house. I was overjoyed to know that I would be riding in this beautiful car, but my exuberance did not last long when I was told that I had to get in the trunk under an old tire. Someone told me that it had to be this way because "The gringos will send you back if they see you." After the adults adjusted the tire's position so that it would not crush me (too much), I braved the situation and saw the trunk lid close. With my safety pin furiously exacting pain on my fingers, I just played dead under the tire as the car sped toward my new life. After a very long time the trunk lid opened and someone took the tire off my back and helped me out. I didn't want to tell him I had left behind a puddle of urine out of sheer terror.

Our very first house in El Paso, Texas, was located on Lincoln Avenue, a poor area but the best that we were ever to see in our childhood. The street itself looked decent, was paved, and connected other similar poor homes in the area. About half-a-block away were the tracks of the Missouri-Pacific Railroad—tracks that would bring us hours of delight in the year that we were to spend there. The house itself was made of unsanded wood with flaky white paint, a rickety porch, and short stilts that supported it above the ground. Behind the house was a rather small yard that contained, again, an outhouse and a bath. The kitchen was large enough for only a small table which I believe we stole from a Salvation Army charity store. Our furniture was chipped all over, but it didn't matter, for we *never* had any visitors in this or any other house we ever lived in. We were the only ones who looked at it. Besides, I didn't know what "normal" furniture looked like anyway, so I was quite happy with it and the ticks that lived in it.

So there we were, in America, and supposedly forming a "real" family, with the required mother and (step)father, and the two zombie kids. My safety pin was always with me too. Oddly enough, I do not recall feeling ecstatic about having my mother at home; maybe she had been away so much that it didn't really matter much anymore. The situation reminds me of that of institutional babies whose souls shut down and simply ignore mom when she comes to visit. In my case, though, it appears that I had developed some sort of institutional syndrome living right at home in Mexico. In contrast, my mother must have felt something, for it was here where she took me to the bedroom.

Yet strangely I cannot recall too many details of the bedrooms of the house, except for the one where I performed my first reluctant cunnilingus at age four or five, soon after we had just moved in. I was amazingly compliant when my mother put my face in her pussy, as if I really didn't have any say about it. Even though I was only a young child, I was already like an insatiable sex maniac.

But I wonder just what was going on. We all know that this was wrong, yet my *feelings* about that event do not involve this moral judgment. That probably was the *closest* that I ever felt towards my mother in all my life, even though it was her pussy and then her toe in my mouth instead of her breast. I felt comfortable, safe, secure, nourished, and almost symbiotically attached to her. Apparently the toe-sucking must have awakened some neglected infantile desire in me, something that I had repressed deeply during my four years of life, so consequently, as much as my conscience may now punish me for having engaged in such a repugnant act with my mother, my inner soul relishes what only infants are permitted to enjoy: sucking one's mother with vigor, delight, and excitement.

The cunnilingus too, must have had an impact on me, for I recall that on two separate occasions when I was four or five years old I asked two neighbor girls if I could suck on their vaginas. They lowered their panties, and I licked and sucked. Their young, hairless vaginas didn't taste like my mother's, so I never asked them again.

Everything we've learned from child sexual abuse cases tells us that this kind of abuse leaves destructive wounds that take years to heal, and that other effects may go unrecognized for the life of the victim. My sentence, of course, is that I have this conflict about *interpreting how I am supposed to feel about what my mother did to me.* Only through the grace of psychotherapy did I come to realize how wrong this sexual contact was, but this spiritual enlightenment cannot erase the positive emotion that my mother placed in me by having crossed this sexual boundary. At no time have I ever felt anger, resentment, or fear about this event. It may have been that I was so severely deprived of maternal physical contact that I wholeheartedly welcomed this moral intrusion into my innocence. I had been essentially motherless.

There were no other cunnilingus sessions that I can remember, although sexual and personal boundaries were practically unheard of in our home. My mother typically would dress and undress in front of all us kids, readily displaying her voluminous breasts. She would sometimes grab my crotch through my clothing and fondle my balls, and even up to age 11 she would make comments about what it was that I had hanging inside my pants. Our family boundaries were so unusual that I slept in the same bed with my mother until I was 12. My God, my hormones were raging at age 12, and I was totally snuggled up to my mother for the entire night in (Satan had his own bed because he smelled and our mother refused to sleep in the same bed with him). I would place my arm across her breasts, enjoying the soft sponginess throughout the night. It was this type of pathological family culture that conjured up psychic forces in my subconscious which later contributed to my own sickness as an adult.

In contrast to my mother's sexualization of almost everything, my stepfather, *El Diablo*, never really did anything that I would consider sexually deviant within our house. In spite of being basically subhuman in his treatment of my mother and all us kids, he never touched anyone sexually and he never said anything that was sexually suggestive. On the contrary, he spoke only to bark at someone or to tell that person how stupid he or she was. Sometimes the best strategy was to avoid both sick parents altogether.

But not everything that was happening at our first house in Texas was sexual or abusive. There were other strange events, the most peculiar of these being the "bamboo incident."

Sometime during that year when we moved to Texas I befriended a boy on the block who apparently liked fishing at a nearby creek. I knew that I needed a fishing pole just like his, but buying one was out of the question, since I never received anything from my parents. Even though I was stupid and emotionally disturbed at that age, I figured out that I would have to solve the problem on my own. And that is what I did. About a block from our house was this shallow creek surrounded by marshy ground, and, guess what? Fishing rods were growing out from the swamp bottom! At age four I decided to take executive action and fetch myself one of those nice poles growing there, only

I didn't count on the pole offering so much resistance. I didn't think of using any kind of sharp tool to cut the tenacious bamboo stalk from its base, so I just used my bare hands. After I had been twisting, pulling, and jerking for some time, a few of the fibers in the thick bamboo began to break, creating sharp and jagged edges where I was holding and tearing at the stick. I began to cry from the pain and my hands began to bleed. For some reason the pain made me work harder, although I also began cutting the palms of my hands more severely. The bizarre cycle of crying and pulling proceeded for about one hour until my hands were dripping with blood. I know that I was scared at seeing so much blood ooze out of what must have been hundreds of bamboo cuts on my two hands, yet I was somehow caught in a strange duel with this uncooperative fishing stick and I had to win. All the bending and twisting finally won the battle against the bamboo, and I was able to slush out of the swamp with my trophy in my blood-drenched hands.

When I got to the house a block away the blood had already dripped all over my legs so I was a sorry sight. What followed is something that I cannot recall exactly, only that my mother cleaned me up and threw the bamboo stick away. I had worked so hard for that fishing pole, but I never got to use it at all. That I did not complain to my mother about her having thrown out my hard-earned fishing rod probably attests to the generally passive attitude that I had in social relations. This was to be a key factor in the expanding circle of sexual abuse which was just around the corner.

As I think about this episode where I was so nonsensically persistent, I feel sad and sorry. My empathy for that little boy is strong (please excuse my dissociation—I am more charitable with myself if I break my psyche into parts), and had I been there when he was struggling with his fishing rod I would have stopped everything—everything!—that I was doing, and I would have assisted him. I would have made a clean cut at the base of the bamboo of his choice, sanded it smoothly, and attached the most handsome string and hook that I could find. We probably would have gone to find earthworms nearby, and then, along with his little friend, we would have gone fishing for the whole day. But better still, I would have asked him if he was happy at home and if he had everything that he needed. I would have protected him to the best of my ability against all threats physical and emotional, with all my strength, my resources, and my life. I am sad that I wasn't there to protect him, so the forces of evil overran his little soul.

The bamboo incident started and ended pretty much on the same day, with no more mention about the fishing rod or the bloody hands ever again. That was pretty standard fare at our house, where we never actually sat down with an adult to talk about anything. Besides the sexual, physical, and verbal abuse that was going on, not much other interaction with our parents was happening. But there were little pockets of joy, once in a blue moon, and one of these was the Missouri-Pacific Railroad track.

About half-a-block from our house was a slightly elevated long mound of dirt that supported the railroad tracks in their closest pass near our house. As anybody who lives near tracks knows, the earth rumbles as the mammoth machines barrel their way along to deliver never-ending supplies of coal, cars, trailers, boxes, and other unseen stuff. All of us kids would drop whatever it was that we were doing and run towards the tracks at the first sign of vibration on the floor or on the ground. If we ran to the backyard of the house next door, we would have an excellent view of the curve that brought the track within feet of our fence. We would wait, all eyes fixed on the curve to see who could spot the locomotive first. The intensifying rumble of the ground made it feel almost as if the subterranean gods would split open the entire backyard and show their faces to us, but at the right moment in the earth-moving crescendo the massive MoPac Locomotive would show its huge green face at the beginning of the curve. We would all quickly abandon the subterranean-god fantasy and marvel at how the slow-moving behemoth would gently sway ever so slightly from left to right as it approached us almost in a straight line with its twin vertical lights burning as brightly as the Texas sun. At this point nothing else that was going on in the area mattered, for this mighty steel giant commanded everyone's attention, if not by its herculean appearance then by its unmistakable concentration of weight, power, and steel. As the bright green engine roared directly in front of us we would all feel that we were on the threshold of being annihilated by the sheer thunder and acoustic power emanating from the friendly giant. As we were totally engulfed by the earthquake-like presence of the titanic machine, we would then marvel at the many fancy parts dancing in harmony as the gigantic wheels rolled over the seemingly indestructible track. Some hoses looked like they were thick enough to swallow an unsuspecting kid, while some steel nuts securing enormous bolts were as big as bicycle tires. And those massive steel wheels looked like they could roll over anything that was unfortunate enough to stand in their way; their unchallenged supremacy was one thing that was never in question, and I respected them with fear and admiration.

There never was a dull moment when we watched awe-struck as that huge green locomotive breathed powerfully and roared in front of us. In spite of its commanding and intimidating presence, we knew that this MoPac Locomotive was friendly to us, for its engineer would always wave at us, and, much to our added joy, would throw dozens of wrapped pieces of chewing gum in our direction. We always waved back, took the gum, and were glad that the green titan was on its way, for we probably could not take that high level of sensory stimulation for very long. Soon enough we would again start waiting for tomorrow's rumble.

Besides this joyful experience with the train, there really was not much else that I could look to for excitement. My Aunt Julieta and my Aunt Marisa would visit only infrequently from Mexico, where they still lived at the time. In fact, being Mexican presented a big problem for us in Texas, where the gringo racist made his dislike for us well known. On several occasions my Aunt Marisa was picked up by the Texas Border Patrol undercover car because she "looked suspicious." Her only crime was that she had darker skin than the gringos who drove the undercover cars. For years and years we had to be careful where we went about town, for the abundant bigots would sneer at us from every direction. "Meskin," "Wetback," "Pocho," "Greaser"—we had to endure bad service, name-calling, and bad faith. From my perspective at that age the world was a frighteningly hostile place.

Normally one can take refuge from the troubles of the world in one's home, one's safe haven. Not here! My own stepfather, the evil Devil, would frequently threaten my mother by saying that if she would not comply with his wishes and demands that he would call the Border Patrol himself so that they would come to arrest my mother and all of us kids for being illegal Mexicans. This was a source of terror for me since age four.

Imagine the tragedy of having a live-in informant for the Border Patrol, right in our own home. Imagine the daily horror and severe anxiety over worrying that at any moment the police would show up and take us all away, never to be seen again. Imagine feeling that none of us could speak our mind because the monster would unleash the Omnipotent Police and Border Patrol on us. When I think about this horrific breach of safety and parental duty, I feel homicidal fury against this animal who lived with us. Had I been old enough and strong enough, I would have gladly cut his head off and fed it to the rabid street dogs that came out to hunt at night.

It is frustrating for me to think that when all these crimes were committed against us, I was so young, stupid, and cowardly. Not once or twice, but perhaps thousands of times the bastardly Devil violated our human dignity and our safety, committing crimes enough and so heinous to be sentenced to public dismemberment. I personally would have loved to have put a 12-gauge shotgun into his mouth and forced *him* to ask for forgiveness for all his outrages against the family. I would have made him repent for all he did to us. I would

have made him recount each and every one of his abuses against the family.
I would have made him cower just as we all did under his total domination. I
would have made him promise he would never do such hideous things again.
I would have made him squirm and beg for his life. But for all he did, there
is no forgiveness. He would have to die. So I would have to ram the barrel of
the shotgun deeper into his evil throat so that blood would gush. And then
I would have to pull the trigger and completely blow his entire head off. His
bloody carcass I would throw into the river. Fuck him. No more terrorizing
the family!

Had I done him in when I was four years old I would have spared the
world untold misery from this piece of garbage. But, there I was on Lincoln
Avenue, terrified about the Border Patrol and about when my aunts would
visit again, for I had seen my Aunt Marisa in the back seat of the Immigration
vehicle, looking like a criminal. Luckily for me, one day my Aunt Julieta came
to visit and she brought me a brand new toy truck. A gift—I was ecstatic!

Aunt Julieta had always been the more quiet type—quite reserved. And
she was so pretty. Maybe I secretly admired her. She was about two years
younger than our mother. Well, that day she and my mother stayed inside the
house, talking I suppose, while I went outside through the front door onto
the rickety, squeaky porch with my beautiful red truck in tow. I walked off
the porch onto a sandy part of the lot to play with this new toy, and then it
happened. For some unexplainable reason I got a brick and I pummeled the
new, shiny, red truck until its cab was completely flat. Not knowing exactly
why, I had just destroyed the only toy that I had received in years, perhaps in
my entire life. From the moment that I first put my hands on it to the moment
when I snuffed it out, it must have been not more than 10 minutes. Hearing
the enormous crunching of metal just outside their window, my mother and
my Aunt Julieta came rushing outside the house, but they arrived only to see
the remains of what just minutes before had been the most handsome truck
that I had ever seen.

Years later it still hurts me to think of what I did to that little truck. I feel
sorry that in destroying the truck I also hurt my Aunt Julieta's feelings, since
I am sure that her poverty must have made it difficult to purchase such a nice
toy. And besides, I *know* that she was fond of me and was giving me something
from her heart. Along with the massacre of many tarantulas in Mexico not
long before, this was one more incident that showed I had a destructive streak
in me. Retrospectively, as an adult, I see the clear pattern that had begun by
around age two and was in full bloom by age four. It really does sicken me to
contemplate how many objects and *living animals* I would eventually destroy,

so much so that some part of me feels that the world would have been better off if the wheels of the MoPac Locomotive had done me in when I was four. My life for the next three decades would have been such a sin against humanity anyway. How can I legitimately and morally criticize the vile and vicious Devil when I sinned in other equally monstrous ways? How can I rant about his wicked and evil nature when in many respects I as an adult came to be just like this monster who ruined our lives? Herein lies a most sinister of truths about our inner life and soul: *For better or worse, our parents place their spiritual and moral essence in our hearts when we are children, and if we do not examine our nature as adults we are destined to follow their footsteps either to heaven or into the fires of hell. It was only recently that I finally realized how much I had been walking with Satan himself.*

Perhaps that is what Philip Larkin (1922-1986) had in mind when he said, "Above all, though, children are linked to adults by the simple fact that they are turning into them. For this they may be forgiven much." (In *Required Writing*, "The Savage Seventh," 1959.) I welcome the opinion of this British poet since it tends to provide me with a bit of dispensation concerning my spiritual dilemma. For it is revolting for me to see the mark of The Devil in my soul in the form of my past adult behaviors similar to his, and in the form of personality neuroses and sickness bearing his imprint. It feels like my soul is mortally contaminated with his vileness, filth, and wickedness, so that when I morally criticize this subhuman predator I simultaneously condemn my own soul. It's mental illness in its many forms.

So in destroying animals and my toy truck, was I already copying my stepfather's example at age four? Was I identifying even then with El Diablo?

What this means to me is that in my heart I have some very fundamental identifications with The Devil, since he certainly was the source of extreme anxiety and even terror for me. As an adult I came to abuse people like he did. I cursed like he did. I was destructive as he was. I stole like he did. I eventually physically abused my own children as he did us. When I married, I disrespected my wife much as he did my mother. I abused animals like he did. I insulted neighbors like he did. I identified with this monster, only I didn't even know it! And while I have been able to break away from some of these chains of psychic and emotional bondage in the last few years, I still have a way to go to free myself from my hellish childhood.

If at age four I was identifying with El Diablo's violent nature, then probably the little red truck fell victim to my budding destructive nature at that time. A more normal boy might have treated it with care and respect, but the poor little truck, like me, did not get to choose which home it would go into. It was something beautiful which I admired, and I could control it, for it didn't fight back.

If I could rationally apologize to that little red truck, I gladly would. It never caused me any harm, it never looked at me the wrong way. Maybe it was just trying to be my friend—I don't know. If there is a heaven for little trucks that never made it here on Earth, then my truck is there. Please forgive me. I promise that all the nice, bright trucks that I give my son Andrew will be respected and well cared for.

After that destructive incident, I never again got another truck from my Aunt Julieta. I don't blame her. I had no respect for anything.

As for family life on Lincoln Avenue, well, there simply wasn't any. I do not recall any tender moments with anyone. If we all ate together as a family I can't say. I do not remember anything at all about my sister Ana who is about one year younger than me. I think that my mother continued to work at the International Hat Company as a quality control checker, a job she had gotten while I was still living in Mexico. There weren't too many fights here that I can remember, but all that was about to change, for evil was about to overrun our family in our next house.

The Horrors on Salinas Avenue

We must not have been doing too well financially on Lincoln Avenue, since we stayed there only one year and then moved on to a house several miles away on Salinas Avenue—a house owned by the sinister parents of The Devil. They lived next door. This moving out of a house after a short period apparently established a pattern, for after that we moved almost every year.

The house on Salinas Avenue was a definite step down for us, since it was located on a very busy street, was squeezed between two other houses, and looked a lot worse that our previous one. It was yellow, had a drooping porch that seemed to be sinking due to severe rotting of the foundation, had two bedrooms, and, like our previous house, had a severe case of peeling paint. The wood boards that served as walls were so poorly placed that at night we could see the lights of passing cars through the slits between them. My guess is that this poor house had been abandoned by the last tenant, who probably got smart and fled in the middle of the night.

One question that comes to mind is why El Diablo would agree to rent a house from his parents who lived next door. We were the only two kids in the family at this point, and we had no telephone bill (no phone), no car payment (no car), no mortgage, no vacations, and no new clothes from the department store (all were from the second-hand store or stolen from neighborhood clothes lines). Either money was being mismanaged, or The Devil was spending it all on beer (his favorite past-time)—or he just wanted to be closer to his parents.

We moved the sorry furniture from the previous house, although I think that it would have been cheaper to have simply abandoned the junk and bought a new batch of sorry furniture at the local Salvation Army Thrift Store. They delivered. All our mattresses were unusually heavy from all the urine still inside them, and reeked badly. As far as I can tell, all of us kids, including new arrivals, wet our beds every night up to age 10. It was normal for us. We knew that it was so uncomfortable to sleep all night in a pool of urine—the mattress refused to soak up after a certain level of saturation—yet, it seemed that we could not stop. I, the oldest, suffered embarrassment at school when my teachers would comment on the strong urine odor that was so much a part of me on a daily basis. Some of my teachers and some students would deliberately avoid me because of my odor. Yet my mother never bothered to bathe me in the morning or at least wipe me with a wet cloth to remove the smell. Why not? She sent me to school smelling so bad, day after day, year after year. Urine was my constant companion.

All our dishware was mismatched, or, rather, we didn't own a set of anything but a collection of individual cups, plates, and utensils that were found in trashcans or stolen from cantinas (bars). Mind you, I didn't complain, for it was perfectly normal to me, not having any other frame of reference than this sick environment. We had no bed sheets but slept on bare mattresses with a bath towel covering the usual pool of urine. In the morning my mother would normally take the soaking bed towel outside to hang dry—without washing!—and it would be ready for the next night's gallonage of new urine.

How about blankets to protect us from the night chill? Nope, we never had any that were *meant* to be blankets. What we had were moving-company blankets for large appliances such as stoves, washers, and refrigerators. I believe that The Devil had stolen these from his place of employment, and by the time we got them they were very filthy with dirt and grease spots. Not only that, but they were bulky, lumpy, abrasive, smelly, and really did not protect against the cold. As bizarre as this may seem, it did not bother me, for I had nothing else to compare it with. As far as I was concerned, the hostility of the world was natural.

I was now six years old, settled into the new prison, stupid beyond description, and—who knows why?—ready for school. About five blocks away was Escuela Primaria, a massive brick building with abundant playgrounds all around, but surrounded by busy streets. My First Grade Teacher was Teacher Aracelis, a beautiful young woman whom I fell in love with right away. In my opinion I had never seen a face more beautiful than hers—not that I had seen too many faces anyway. But the best part was that she was very kind to me, always *looking* me in the eye when she spoke to me. That was new in my world, for The Devil *never* looked at anyone in the eye, and I can't remember if my mother ever looked into my eyes except for once when she told me she was sick—very sick.

Of course I had my own desk in Teacher Aracelis's class, and I had wonderful books with pictures and drawings and photos of kids having fun. Every day I marveled at the many objects in class, things such as pencil sharpeners, flags, erasers and chalk, crayons, maps, and all that. The classroom was always clean with shiny floors and well-painted walls—it was a whole other world for me.

But the best part was my teacher, especially when she just sat at her desk and spoke to us about some topic or other. I would just look at her angelic face and her sweet, friendly voice. Where did she come from, this angel? Sometimes she would walk from student to student, distributing papers or other material, oftentimes lightly putting her hand on the student's shoulder as a supportive and kind gesture. *It's my turn, it's my turn!* I would eagerly say to myself, for I wanted her to hold me, even for those short five seconds. It meant the whole world to me.

I totally enjoyed the year I spent with my first grade teacher and was heartbroken when I learned that I would have a new teacher for the next grade. I didn't know what to do, and I had no one I could talk to about my sadness.

But during that first year in school I encountered several difficult spots. This was America and I had to learn English. The city of El Paso, Texas, has always had a large concentration of Mexican-Americans—some estimates put that at about 80 percent—so consequently there were lots of businesses which were run entirely in Spanish. Thus, one could easily transact any kind of business and survive without knowing one single word of English. Up to the time that I began first grade I did not know any English, so I had to learn very quickly how to deal with a teacher who spoke to me in a "foreign" language. It was not easy starting from scratch with a new language, but the good part was that 100 percent of the students in my class were similarly confused Mexican-American kids who turned to me after the teacher spoke and would ask, "Oye, que esta diciendo la profesora?" ("Hey, what is the teacher saying?") The Spanish gossip behind the teacher's back made the new-language experience more palatable.

Another thing that stands out in my mind were the countless times during the winter when I shivered almost uncontrollably while I was just outside the school building waiting for the bell to ring. I shivered and froze. Why? I was wearing *shorts during the winter!* Yes, I was wearing summer shorts during freezing cold weather. What the hell was my stupid mother thinking when she sent me out in shorts in the wintertime? May I say it again: Fuck her! The image is forever imprinted in my mind how I would stand next to a dried-out Mesquite tree, shivering uncontrollably and looking at the reluctant goose-pimples all over my legs. Next to me would be the more fortunate kids with their nice jackets, hats, gloves, and warm long pants. I had none of these—I just did not deserve warm clothes, that's why.

At that time the only thing that hurt was the cold itself. I looked at the other kids with their warm clothing and wished silently that I too could have something warm, but yet I just knew in my heart that I did not deserve warm clothing, that it was meant for the other children only. I felt that my life was simply one of suffering and wanting and never getting. That philosophy made palatable extreme deprivations such as this.

As an adult, though, I feel renewed rage against my mother for this kind of extreme neglect. This is indicative either of a gross disregard for her six-year-old son, or of a pervasive ignorance of common parental duties towards the care of children. Either way, it shows that my mother was totally unfit and unsuitable to raise children, and eventually all six of us kids paid a dear price for this. This bitch should have scraped me off her womb with a fork when I was but a squirming larva sucking her blood.

Sperms from the Janitor

By age six, I had suffered enough abuse and neglect to require hospitalization, but the worst was yet to come. One day, in the first grade, I asked pretty Teacher Aracelis if I could go to the hallway to get a drink of water. I had just finished drinking from the kid-sized fountain when the school janitor firmly grabbed my hand and quickly led me into the boys' bathroom. For whatever reason I did not resist, probably because he did not do anything threatening in the hallway, but I was so stupid and ignorant that I wouldn't have known anyway if he had been a clear threat. He was a big guy in khaki shirt and pants and was carrying a cleaning rag in his back pocket. Without saying anything he led me into one of the stalls, lowered his pants, and sat on the toilet seat. I passively watched as he then lowered my own shorts, not finding the fortitude to resist. By that time I could see his enormous penis standing straight up as he proceeded to spit big globs of saliva onto his hands and then transfer them to the head of his penis. He then raised me up in the air and slowly lowered me onto his lap. I felt the head of his penis make contact with my anus, and bit by bit he forced his entire organ inside me until I came to sit flat on his lap while his hands pushed my buttocks apart for maximum penetration. I gasped for air as he completed the insertion, because my lungs felt as if they were being squeezed from below. The sharp pain was only momentary, I recall, perhaps because after the initial penetration I just felt a terrible fullness inside me. As he moved his pelvis he started playing with my limp penis and kept asking me several times if I liked it, but all I could do was struggle to keep on breathing. He then groaned and squeezed me hard. I felt his penis pulsate inside me, and then he released the tension of his arms around me. For a few moments I did not know if I should move or not, for he sat motionless but all sweaty. The fullness of his penis inside me made me feel that I wanted to poop, but this condition was somewhat alleviated as he came to life again and slowly moved me off his lap. As I was coming off his lap I sensed that his penis was sliding out of my anus for what seemed like a long time, creating an uncomfortable vacuum inside me. I gasped, and then it was all over. The whole episode lasted perhaps three minutes. At age six I had now been introduced to a new low in my wretched childhood.

I didn't cry, I wasn't afraid, I didn't hate him. He spoke nicely and gently to me. He said his name was "Teodoro" and that he wanted to see me during the lunch hour to share his lunch with me. I readily agreed when he mentioned sharing his food with me, for I was always hungry from the lack of food at home. As I walked out of the bathroom I felt some liquidy stuff begin to ooze out of my anus, but I didn't pay much attention since many times I had wet shorts anyway. Of course, I was walking back to my first grade class with a full load of the janitor's sperms inside me.

At noontime I met him just outside the school building where he told me he would be. Out of a brown paper bag he took out a sandwich made from a huge Mexican roll. It contained scrambled eggs, onions, and tomatoes. It was one of the best sandwiches I ever ate. But, without knowing it I was tacitly and innocently making a pact with the devil: The janitor said he wanted to see me again in the same bathroom, that he would be happy to continue sharing his lunch with me. I was more than happy to oblige since I saw nothing wrong with it.

So it was that many times during first grade I met the janitor in various bathrooms throughout the school for more of the same. And he continued to share his lunches with me. I had become accustomed to his semen oozing from my anus all the time, wetting my pants quite embarrassingly. And since my mother never got me underwear, it would even drip down my legs.

Throughout most of my adult life I had considered myself the "responsible" party because I "let" him do those things to me—I never reported it even to my mother. It was not normal for me to tell her about my life, my problems. As an adult in therapy I came to realize the awful nature of what this janitor did to me, even though I have never felt anger or rage against him. From the point of view of an ethical, moral adult, we can condemn sexual abuse because it is wrong and because we know that it causes long-term damage. However, from my neglected-child perspective *at that time*, I can see how the attention and the lunches he gave me would make me feel that he was indeed my friend. Therein lies the sickness of how my soul interprets this memory from long ago.

The dichotomy in my feelings is divisive for my spirit and my soul, for it positions my moral view against my inner child who remembers this event with feelings positive and negative. In many ways my whole life is a tug-of-war between the reality of what happened and what I did long ago, and my current moral views of such behaviors. I believe stealing is wrong, and I do not currently steal, yet I stole many things as a child and do not feel terribly bad about having done it under those conditions. The fact that I may not feel like condemning with my soul what the janitor did to me may attest to the unfortunate state of my spiritual and mental health right before it happened. I was so low on any measure of normal development that the janitor's attention, however horrid, was a welcome relief. My ambivalent feelings of responsibility may indeed have started with the sexual session with my mother, where love, attention, and premature sex became pathologically confused. In fact, therapist-author Patrick Carnes in *Contrary to Love* (1989) wrote that numerous compulsions, impulses, and love/sex addictions are the result of adults having given warmth and attention to a child in return for some form of sexual performance from that child. In my case, it was difficult for me to emotionally separate the sexual abuse from the warmth, the attention, and the Mexican sandwich.

But if that same janitor were to ever touch one of my children today, I would destroy him by ramming a screwdriver into his brain, and pounding his head with a sledgehammer. I would guarantee that he would never do it again. He would be left unrecognizable and without his offending organ.

Yet, one thing that is puzzling about this is how my mother never suspected anything. The janitor's semen was my constant companion. I knew it was coming from him, but I just did not know what it was. It was always oozing out of me, especially because my anus was so distended from his unusually large organ. Did my mother notice anything unusual when she did the occasional wash? What about the liquidy tracks down my legs? On this count maybe I cannot blame her entirely since we do know that for the most part children will generally not reveal abuse of this sort right away. But was this sexual abuse the basis of my suicidal gestures at home?

Not long after we moved into this Salinas Avenue house, and after the bathroom sessions with the janitor had begun, I developed a terrible temper which I directed at my mother. On numerous occasions I would get angry at my mother and proceed to run to the bed to throw a terrible tantrum which consisted of hyperventilation and odd contortions of my body. I would tense my entire body as if I was having a heart attack, and this was generally sufficient for my mother to give me what I wanted. And when this outburst didn't work, I would go for the razorblade.

Again huffing and puffing, I would place it against my wrist, poised to cut through all the tendons right down to the bare bone. I would give my mother terrible looks that would apparently convince her that I would definitely do it if she called my bluff. But, like me, she was a coward, and she relented. Funny thing, though, I don't remember if I was bluffing or if I really felt like doing it.

My anger, from the sexual abuse, I suppose, or from the pervasive malady of our lives, also revealed itself in an incident that involved a large number of beer bottles.

Two Thousand Beer Bottles

When I was six or seven years old, the evil Satan was drinking a lot more. His favorites were cheap Texas beers such as Falstaff, Jax, and Lone Star, bottles of which he would bring home in brown paper bags every night. Of course, by the time he did come home, typically after midnight, he was fully intoxicated, but would continue his binges in the house. Consequently he had accumulated a huge stack of empty beer bottles in boxes in our backyard. This cubic stack was about 10 to 12 feet on the side and rested securely against the back of the house. One day, at about the same time I was doing the razorblade thing with my mother, I decided, I don't know why, to take each bottle and slam it against the brick wall of the house next door. One by one I hurled each bottle into the wall, and it would explode into a million little slivers. Box after box I would empty as the mountain of broken glass by the wall grew higher and higher. I don't know why I did it, maybe I was full of rage, but when I finished I had broken about 2,000 beer bottles. I knew full well that The Devil would be coming after me.

And he did. Not surprisingly he beat me up as usual, by grabbing me by the upper arm with one hand and using the other brick-hard hand to hit me wherever he could. I always screamed in a very high pitched, nervous, terrified whine. His military-hardened body and his rabid-dog look made him terrifying and nightmarish when he came at you. Then it would take about 24 hours for all the bruises to show their magnificent colors. The situation was so desperate and hopeless that my sister Ana and I developed a contest to see who had the most colorful bruises.

"Look at this one on my knee. It is red and purple," Ana would say.

"That's nothing. Lookie here on my rib. Let's see. Red, green, black, and a little bit of blue. Ha, mine's better," I would proudly retort.

"Hold on, Victor, let me count. One, two,…twelve. I have twelve, maybe thirteen if you count this little one here."

"One, two, three,…fifteen. Ha, ha, I won!" I would say triumphantly. What a sorry game for children to play. But it was terrifyingly real.

So after the fiend from hell beat me, he ordered me to go clean up the mess that I had created. It took me several hours and several tubfulls, but I got it done. I got satisfaction from having broken them anyway, yet I could not tell the beast, for he would surely snuff me out. As was usually the case with all the beatings that I got from him, I felt *glad and thankful* that he didn't kill me. His ferocity was equaled perhaps only by that of rabid and hungry wild dogs fighting for a morsel in the desert; my life was always on the line when he beat me, so today I still wonder why it was that he never finished me off.

El Terrible (The Terrible One)

The bottle incident was soon forgotten as there was never any sense of history in our family. No lessons were extracted to be applied to the future, and the boxes of empty beer bottles in our backyard on Salinas Avenue continued to increase. Oftentimes in the middle of the night we were awakened from our urine-soaked beds by El Diablo arriving drunk and slamming doors, cursing, and threatening to kick all of us out of the house. Our stomachs would churn out plentiful acid under the refrigerator-cover blankets from the constant state of terror and readiness as the vicious predator prowled around the house, keen on who would attract his attention so that he could unload his wretchedness on this unfortunate victim. We would all cower, and I feel sorry to say that each child, including myself, would *feel glad and relieved* when some other sibling was chosen for the nightly abuse. Living at the miserable level of mere survival, each of us was willing to sacrifice someone else to spare ourselves the agony of dealing with Satan in the middle of the night.

No child should ever be placed in this position of having to save oneself at the expense of someone else. Yet it was a profound part of our lives. The emotional and psychic forces at work probably made each of us feel that *somehow the chosen victim for the night deserved to be chosen.* "If I just *think* that I am good, he will not select me." The tragic secondary result of these nightly terrors was that my brothers and sisters and I felt *no common sibling bond*. This was to be demonstrated in many different ways throughout the years, but never so forcefully as when we all split up when my mother died several years later. These nightly traumas also had another important player: the neighbor across the street.

The title of El Terrible (The Terrible One) might easily have been applied to The Devil, but in this case it was reserved for this huge beer-bellied Mexican man who lived with his wife across the street. Like El Diablo, El Terrible was a beast of a man who terrorized his wife every night when he would come home drunk and become a major neighborhood nuisance as he typically hit trashcans, fire hydrants, trees, and parked vehicles with his battered white truck. His chest and arms were so huge that his arms could not hang vertically from his shoulders, but rather had to extend outward at about 45 degrees. In the middle of the night his truck would arrive in front of his house, but we all knew from experience that it would be about 20 minutes before he actually could reach his front door. From the street, he would yell and curse at his wife for whatever it was he imagined she was doing to make parking so difficult. His pig-squeals, grunts, groans, and barking were legendary in the community, and even though we kids listened every night from the anonymous darkness underneath our oily covers, we secretly enjoyed the momentary distraction that this nightly drama provided us. His wife we never saw, for she never came out of the house. But we knew she existed because there was another voice in the house that did not belong to El Terrible. One can only imagine what kind of suffering this poor, invisible woman must have endured.

It was good that we had El Terrible to talk about since it brought us a degree of distraction and emotional respite from our own ongoing suffering. Night after night it was the same for us in our little hell; night after night it was the same for the poor woman across the street. There were beatings at night; there were beatings during the day. The two-thousand-beer-bottle incident was perhaps an angry cry against the daily beatings, the first one, I think, and others were starting to materialize. Soon enough, I turned against our next door neighbor, a young woman named Jill.

Defecating on Their Gifts, Setting Fire to Their Couch

There was a thin, short-haired woman and two of her brothers who had the misfortune to move next door to us on Salinas Avenue. She must have been in her twenties, her brothers slightly younger, and they seemed to us to be good folks. But right from the beginning I started doing things to them that might be construed as some form of terrorism. At the ripe age of seven I was already a "Peeping Tom," for I would watch through a hole in the wall when Jill would take showers. Since their house was made of wood and was rotting just like ours, I had easily managed to widen a hole that I had located near the base of a wall in the shower area. Sometimes Jill would detect my presence and shout some obscene remark that would make me stop for the night, but at other times I would relish seeing her pubic hairs, which looked very much like my mother's.

On numerous occasions when they were all at work, I would force open a favorite window in their kitchen and have a feast from their refrigerator. In the beginning I stayed pretty much in the kitchen area, but in time I began to explore the other rooms. That is when I discovered the living room with the Christmas tree and the presents under it.

There were so many of them; I had no idea that there could be that many under *one* tree. Maybe envy, maybe anger, maybe a total disrespect for everything, but something prompted me to lower my shorts and defecate directly under their Christmas tree and onto the presents. When I finished with this ugly task, I wiped myself with yet another present—a red one with a beautiful white bow which I needed to ruin. From there I went to the small hallway and located a pack of cigarettes, from which I took one and lit it, enjoying the total control which I had of the entire house and contents. At age seven I felt "sexy" doing this, if that's even possible. When I was climbing out the window in the kitchen I remembered that I had left the lit cigarette on the arm of the couch; yet, fully realizing that it might cause a fire, I decided that it might *be fun* if the house did catch on fire. I closed the window behind me and walked to our house next door.

Reflecting on this incident in therapy as an adult, I came to realize what a terrible thing I had done. Even though I was only seven, I had committed a gross violation of the privacy and rights of these innocent people next door. Especially unforgiveable was my defecating on their Christmas presents under the tree. The spirit of Christmas is of family, love, compassion, giving, get-togethers with friends, and of sharing, and I'm afraid that I certainly did spoil this particular holiday for our neighbors. Here in the second grade I began to create terrors of my own which rivaled those that I was experiencing with my family and under the manipulation by the school janitor.

Perhaps prior to this incident and the other one with the 2000 beer bottles, I could claim justifiably that I was an innocent seven-year-old victim of a horribly abusive household and a predatory janitor, but now in having planned and executed a house break-in and a subsequent despicable act of vandalism, I was transforming from innocent child into a juvenile criminal, so that the lines of responsibility suddenly became vague and ambiguous. In my therapy and recovery I felt that more than any other incident in this time frame, my repeated break-ins of our neighbor's home clearly marked for me the beginning of a stage in which I was no long an innocent victim of an abominable family. Did my mother pass through these same stages?

So would it be fair for me, her oldest son, to "blame" her for her horribly inadequate efforts at being a mother? If her feelings were grievously damaged because of abject poverty, neglect, and abuse, could we still accuse her of having "neglected" her children? Can we realistically and legitimately "blame" someone for neglecting duties and responsibilities which that person may not even have known were hers? And, if my mother was a victim herself, would I not be victimizing her all over again by trampling all over her memory and calling her a bitch and a whore?

These intellectual questions have made my own therapeutic recovery more difficult, for they tear me apart inside as I attempt to be true to "reality" and to my need to interpret my past in a manner which will provide peace and closure. Even if it is true that my mother suffered severe abuse herself, and that this in turn caused her to be a poor mother, the "infant" in me who rightly expected proper care during those years would *not accept any excuse for its mother not being able to provide proper physical closeness, oral satisfaction, and safety.* Thus, it is the infantile memories within me that despise my mother so much, and which do battle with my more adult conscience that attempts to understand my mother as a human being who suffered much and then eventually died a painful, dishonorable death without her children.

Nevertheless, the issue remains: if my mother herself was a victim, I do not feel totally justified in raging against her for what she did to all of us, for it does not feel morally right to do so. But that is my conscience which speaks, since my inner soul, my inner child so grievously wounded, still feels the rage of the abandonment and the confusion of the sexual abuse. Consequently, my conscience often battles with my inner soul and I feel like a divided person. As an adult I am a broken man.

In dealing with this issue of my mother's "responsibility" for her neglect and abuse, and perhaps for even contributing to the death of my baby brother Benito, I cannot help but feel confused about this ill-defined term. What I did to the Christmas presents in our neighbor's house was my own doing. I wanted to do it. I made the decision to do it. Even though I did not succeed,

I did want their house to burn down to the ground. Nobody forced me. I did it. I *feel* responsible. But why did I do it?

Several driving forces led up to it, in my view. Primarily, I did not have a sense of respect for others' property. I simply did not *care* at all about their feelings or property. Am I "responsible" for this? No. Parents are charged with the duty to inculcate proper values in their children, since it is not possible for children to simply teach themselves morals. Secondly, I believe that I was full of anger, hatred, or rage which I unjustly directed to these innocent neighbors. Was I "responsible" for this rage? No. My grandparents' family, my mother, El Diablo, and the school janitor put it there in the way that they treated me. While it may appear that the "blame" may fall on these tormentors, it would be counterproductive for me to go through life believing that all my bad behavior was or is due to these experiences. Feeling that would make me conclude inevitably that I am merely a puppet of external psychic forces—that I can do no wrong.

As I got to be an adult the issue of "inner or free will" came more prominently into the picture. Don't we all have a "free will" to do what is right in our lives? For most of my life I really believed that, until in therapy I realized how much of my "free will" was really a sickness of the soul, an illness driven by impulses, anxieties, fears, jealousies, insecurities, hostility, neuroses, obsessions, and compulsions. But more on that later.

So there I was, clumsily climbing out of the neighbor's window, and wishing that the lighted cigarette that I had left behind would ignite the house. Yeah, let's burn this shit down! Before age seven, I can recall two incidents with fire, although I would not say that at this time I was what therapists call a "fire-setter." Yet, I was at the threshold of graduating into the serious business of deliberately setting fire to valuable property like houses. As it turned out, the cigarette did ignite the couch, which then almost burned completely, causing extensive smoke damage to the entire inside of the house. I watched as the lady next door assisted her two brothers in frantically carrying pails of water to douse the flames in the couch. Of course, after they managed to bring this problem under control they then discovered all the poop covering their Christmas presents. They knew right away it had been me since they had caught me doing other dastardly deeds to their property in the past. It was only by divine intervention that they did not retaliate against me or my family. Meanwhile, I continued to peek at Jill through the shower hole whenever I got the chance, as if nothing had happened. My mother never really saw what I was doing because we kids spent lots of time alone in the house—alone and hungry.

Chronic Hunger and Bricks for Breakfast

One emotion that was born early in my life and continued for my entire childhood was hunger. Some children have to contend with arranging their clothes neatly for their parents. I only had rags and some shorts for clothes, and I had to deal with hunger. Other children have to clean up their rooms. I had no room, but I did have hunger. Hunger, hunger, hunger. I was chronically hungry. Sometimes we had some food in the house. Oftentimes we had *none*. Not even salt. And when we did have food it was basic rice and beans and corn tortillas. No complaints here. I ate whatever I could voraciously, since some part of me felt so unsure about how long our table would have food on it. The house on Salinas Avenue did have a kitchen, but it might as well not have had one since we practically never used it.

Besides the usual chronic anxiety and rage I also had these hunger pangs which as a child I had to learn to ignore, for there was no connection in our family between stating a need and having that need met. After a while *none of us kids even mentioned our hunger to our parents.* I thought that the body was indeed made to produce this terrible discomfort in the stomach, but even more tragic, I thought that our family was just not deserving of food. Sometimes we would have to go for about one, two, or three days without a single meal. By this time, when I was seven years old, there were already four of us kids in the family, and all of us had sunken eyes and broken souls. It was just a matter of time before we found an alternative to food.

Hunger had so overcome me that one day I decided to experiment with some old bricks that we had piled in our backyard. Yes, these were bricks for building homes, but for me they looked tasty, given that they were made from the red earth of Texas. I got a heavy rock from nearby, and I pounded one of these bricks until it broke into several manageable pieces. I began to eat the brick, and much to my surprise it did taste pretty good; I especially liked the crunchy feel of the brick between my teeth and the sandy-gritty sensation on my tongue. The next day I was still alive, so I concluded that bricks were OK to eat. Henceforth I always ate bricks to push back the ever-increasing hunger pangs. (Years later I realized that this consumption of non-nutritive material is a disorder known as *pica*.)

Another thing that comes to mind surrounding our chronic state of hunger is the nature of my relationship with the janitor at school. It is patently clear to me that in a sense I was prostituting my body for food, since the janitor would regularly share his lunch with me if I agreed to see him in the boys' bathroom for sex, something that at that time I was all too happy to do. My body for food. That one fact alone attests to the desperate state of neglect that we were in.

Also part of our culture of hunger was the song that my sister Ana and I composed in honor of our hunger. For hours we would stare quite delusionally out of a window, waiting for some person to suddenly appear with food for us, and we would chant the following hundreds of times on end:

> *Tengo hambre. Tengo hambre.*
> *Rabo prieto, culo negro.*
> *Tengo hambre. Tengo hambre.*

The literal translation of this is: "I am hungry. I am hungry. Dark anus, black butt. I am hungry. I am hungry." We would practically go into a trance repeating this song hundreds of times, and we would forget soon why we started singing it in the first place.

Hundreds, perhaps thousands of times, all of us went to bed crying from the hunger. During the day we obsessed about food, sharing fantasies about strangers just stepping from the street to bring us some happy surprise. Yet when darkness finally came, we had to deal with the reality that there really would be no food for the day. My mother had the pitiable job of having to sing to my younger brothers and sisters to help them fall asleep fighting the deep hunger which tenaciously tormented us all, while at the same time she had to deal with deep sobs of, "I'm hungry, mami, please, mami, get me some food, mami, please, mami, I'm hungry…" Innocently, my mother would sometimes try to comfort us by saying that maybe when El Diablo comes home (usually at midnight or thereafter) he might bring something for all of us to eat. What a wretched deal this was! All this did was to awaken in us the hope that The Devil's arrival would maybe relieve us of the terrible, all-consuming hunger, but what it actually did most of the time was to expose us to his drunken wrath when we were both hungry and half-asleep. He sometimes would bring maybe one or two small hamburgers for the five of us, but in a cruel manner he would have us wait around for as much as an hour until he felt that it was OK to open the bag. We had to deal with the monster out of natural necessity.

Oftentimes each of us would just collapse into sleep in odd places, wherever the hunger would overtake us: under tables, in the bathroom, under the kitchen sink, outside in the backyard. It was a common sight in our house for my mother to be carrying limp bodies from odd locations to urine-soaked beds. I even remember that on some occasions when I would come home from school for lunch, as was the custom, there would be no lunch, so I would just play in the yard and go back to school for the afternoon session. I just knew that we somehow did not deserve to have lunch.

Another time I was invited to the home of this boy from my class. He also was from our poor neighborhood, but at least he had food in his house. I guess that my interest in his kitchen was obvious for he asked me if I wanted a slice of bread. Of course! I would have settled for the potato peels in the garbage can. But he had an ulterior motive, for no sooner had I beamed a clear yes to his answer when he told me that I could have one but on one condition: he would have to put some red-hot pepper chili sauce on the bread. My stomach made the decision, as always, and my pride and dignity were thrust into the background. He placed a slice of Buttercrust White Bread on the table and started soaking it with Louisiana Red-Hot Chili Sauce from a slim bottle. When he finished there was no white to be seen on the bread, just a sea of red liquid waiting to challenge whatever tongue dared go near it. I had no choice but to bite into it, feeling the acidic burn of the red-pepper sauce all over my mouth, down to my stomach. The little sadist watched with joy as I chewed my bread in agony. Food or no food, somehow misery always seemed to find us.

Another curious chapter of our culture of destitution and hunger occurred about four years later when we were living in a different house. As usual, the cupboards were empty except for the cadavers of some cockroaches who died waiting for some food to be brought in. The sometimes-functioning fridge had a few bottles of beer and ice-cubes, which it was probably tired of keeping frozen for no apparent reason. One afternoon The Devil came home early, much to everyone's surprise. While in the kitchen he announced that he had gotten "supper," and he proceeded to take a raw, unwrapped piece of red meat from his pants' front pocket. Where did he find it? Why did it not have a wrapper? We didn't care. The meat had a few hairs and lint from his pocket, but it looked edible to us (we ate bricks, remember). As soon as he placed the meat on the table, our cat, who also was on the verge of starvation, jumped up, grabbed the meat between his teeth, and ran under the table. Bedlam broke loose. The Devil grabbed a broom and chased the cat all over the house as the cat dragged the three-inch-square piece of meat under the bed, around the garbage can, behind the refrigerator, under the stove, in and out of the bathroom, and over the beds. Many times he was able to hit the cat with the broom, but the cat defiantly refused to give up his supper and continued to run as fast and as evasively as his weak legs permitted. But it didn't count on the stamina of the rabid dog Satan, and the cat finally reached the end of the line in a corner of the living room, where it cowered and perhaps thought that it wasn't hungry after all. El Diablo got the cat by the neck and ripped out the piece of meat from its mouth. He hit the cat several times on the head and hurled him out the rear door into the hot and steamy Texas afternoon. Needless to say, the cat had had enough of our dysfunctional family and elected to be homeless thereafter. He must have felt that it was preferable to starve alone than in the company of such vicious losers.

After catching his breath The Devil took the battered piece of raw meat and rinsed it under the faucet, removing cat saliva and vomit, hairs, lint, dirt, mouse shit, a moribund ant, pieces of paint, and two unhatched cockroach eggs. I then fried it in our only frying pan, and we all happily ate it for supper, no questions asked.

As I can see now from an adult's perspective, hunger becomes such a commanding force when ignored and left unattended that soon it grows to take over one's life, outlook, and perhaps even one's personality. All of us kids fought for and secreted away morsels to eat at more opportune times when there was less of a chance of losing them to someone else. On one occasion we kids had gone exploring a Catholic church in the neighborhood (San Joaquin Church on Morelos Street) during mass and quite ignorantly stood in line for the communion. To our delight we noticed that people were kneeling and were being given cookies or crackers, and they were not even paying for them! More than that, the man in the black and white clothing was *putting* the cookies in people's mouths. This was just a blessing from God, we thought! Just like the other people at the altar, we knelt, but we kept a keen eye on the dish that the man was holding since we thought that he may have been running low on his cookie supply. At the same time I felt hostile or antagonistic towards the other people there at the altar, for it was they who were eating my meal away. The thing that surprised me was how all these people could be so *orderly* in waiting for their cookie. They looked down at the floor and seemed sad, when in fact I thought it should be a joyous occasion to be getting a free cookie in one's mouth! Well, I was not about to worry about their being sad when they should have been happy, or about their being so slow and orderly when grabbing would have made more sense to guarantee a meal. When the formal, stiff, and well-dressed man finally got to me I opened my mouth real wide and practically bit his fingers off as he placed the cookie in my mouth. He looked at me strangely as I chewed my cookie with delight and a happy face. But I was confused because I thought that since he was the one who was *giving* his cookies away, he would be happy that people would be eating them.

Several days later as I related my good fortune to my mother and to other people, I learned that the cookie was actually the Catholic communion wafer.

Call it whatever you want; it didn't matter to me, for I had already planned to have more meals at the church. On subsequent visits I had gotten smarter, going to the altar several times during the same service and getting my lunch piecemeal as I munched on the communion wafers. Sometimes I would quickly change shirts, other times I would pair off with different families so that the priest would have less chance of detecting my multiple visits. But no matter how many schemes I tried and executed, I still was left hungry after the Mass. That is when I saw that I had to go a step farther.

One Sunday after Mass, I stayed behind kneeling in my pew, as if praying (I was praying that they wouldn't catch me!). When everyone was gone I went past the altar to a door next to a huge statue of some Virgin, the most sacred symbol of motherly perfection and love throughout all of Mexico and among the vast majority of Mexican-Americans everywhere. I always wondered why *she* hadn't bothered to send our starving family some food. Once behind the altar I saw all the sacred stuff that they used when the church was filled with poor people seeking redemption: the long poles with a cross at the top; beautiful multicolored cloths that surely would be warmer than our refrigerator blankets; shiny brass dishes, cups, and utensils; soft, velvety chairs with luxurious cushions that were even softer than our own urine-stained mattresses; strong, wooden tables with no cracks, holes, or wobbly legs; beautiful paintings of natural scenes that warmed my heart; long, elegant robes made from enough fabric, I felt, to produce at least a dozen shirts, pants, and socks; enough books to educate 10 or 20 classes of poor children, had the church wanted to; also, the box that I had been after. I knew from observation that the priest and altar boys kept the communion wafers in a shiny brass box which they always took behind the altar after the service. This was the box. This was my meal.

I opened it and felt a wonderful, joyous feeling as I saw what must have been *hundreds* of wafers. Quickly, I stuffed my pockets with as many as I could while I also filled my mouth. As usual, they were brittle, and they seemed to dissolve and disappear in my mouth before I could enjoy swallowing them. But, no complaints.

In the weeks that followed I must have eaten thousands of wafers, equivalent perhaps to having gone to Catholic communion every Sunday for about 300 years. In this respect I was more devoted than even the Pope, but it didn't matter, for the church officials must have gotten smart, so they terminated access to that wonderful room behind the altar.

Without the communion wafers to stem the pains of hunger, the daily struggle shifted to another bizarre area: pigeons. Yes, those filthy, ugly birds that desecrate every statue that has ever been erected on this planet. As is the case in all cities, these pigeons would have no pride and would frequently approach people to beg for food. I could certainly empathize with *that*. That is when I got the idea that maybe these stupid birds might make a good meal, even though they must have been filthy from eating all sorts of rotting food and putrefying dogs which were an abundant source of protein throughout the city. But how to catch one? I soon found out they only looked stupid. After all, they had survived millions of years of predatory attack from the Texas chicken hawks, and in more recent history had managed to adapt to the competition from hundreds of poor people who scoured trashcans and would never even *think* of throwing a playful morsel to a hungry pigeon.

Several plans involving huge blankets, wire nets, arrows, and poisoned darts failed. I was only about eight years old, not too fast, and weak from the lack of food and communion wafers—I was no match for these sorry scavengers. Then it occurred to me: Get them while they sleep!

For days I followed a flock of them, although I feel that "flock" is not the word. They were typically downright nasty and hostile to each other, sometimes even stealing morsels right from each other's beaks. If not for some natural instinct, why would they want to stick to each other? In some way they reminded me of my own "family." One evening they must have thought I wasn't looking and went into a hole under the eaves of the second floor of an old house about two miles from ours. I had located their sleeping quarters!

Now, I asked myself, how do I get up on the porch roof of this house so that I can get to the second-story eaves? The funny thing here is that at no time did I ever stop to think, "Should I trespass on this property so that I can get a pigeon?" No, I did not even think of *not* doing what I had to do to get that pigeon. My moral guide was my stomach. There was no other light to follow. Since there was a tree next to the porch it was a cinch for me to climb on it and onto the porch. It was getting dark, so I had to move fast, or I would not be able to see into the hole.

As it happened, I couldn't see into the hole where the pigeons had gone, but I could hear their collective cooing. Even though I was scared to put my hand into a dark, unknown hole, I forced myself to reach in as far as my arm could go. There must have been an extended family of them in there, judging from the commotion they made. Finally, I grabbed on to a warm body that did not resist too much, and I pulled out a baby pigeon. Little did he know that his life would soon be sacrificed, and that he wouldn't have to push and shove to eat morsels of rotting dog flesh as his parents did for a living.

I didn't even think about the owners or renters of this house. Soon enough a big, burly man came out of the house and started yelling and cursing at me for being on his roof. My plan had been to get at least two baby pigeons for supper, but I would now have to be content with this one skinny specimen. Never before in my malnourished history had I gone down a tree so fast. As soon as I placed my first foot on the ground the angry man appeared again and said, "Hey you, come here. I said come here you cabron, pendejo, chinga tu madre!" He was almost a replica of The Devil, having a menacing look and piercing eyes, and coming at me at a threatening speed. I froze at the bottom of the tree, clutching the warm pigeon which itself was now in double jeopardy, and feeling that my life, again, had come to an end. It must have been an act of Providence that a man passing by on the street yelled out at me, "Run, boy, run, don't just stand there!" Those words gave me the strength and the courage to flee as fast as I could without looking back, all the while holding on to my supper for dear life.

Back at home my hunger pangs blended with the jitteriness which I felt after that close call with the pigeon master, bringing tremors and a sensation of weakness in my legs. Most important, I had worked too hard and now I had to have my supper, three days overdue. I grabbed the baby pigeon by the head and swung it around in a large circular motion in front of me, and as a result the body went flying while I was left with the head in my hand. It did not take long for the body to stop squirming, so I immediately started the task of de-feathering my supper. Under warm water in the kitchen sink my mother and I pulled out all the feathers, cut it open, saved the guts for a soup later, and then placed the pigeon in a boiling pot of water. It must have taken about thirty minutes, and the kitchen didn't smell too good, but finally we felt that supper was ready. All four of us kids and my mother shared this small pigeon, which didn't taste like anything that we had ever had before (in our limited menu). Subsequent to this, we ate pigeons whenever and wherever we were able to catch them, especially if they were lame or looking sick.

Though we had found a source of food that provided us maybe one or two meals per week, the rest of the week we had to keep on praying for the occasional groceries we sometimes managed to buy. One time we thought we had gotten lucky when I discovered quite by accident a chicken's nest in a wooded area next to a neighbor's home.

This neighbor was actually the landlord of a house we lived in when I was about nine years old. He had a grown daughter in her 30s who used to live at home with him and his wife, and sometimes I would try to peek through their bathroom window when she was taking a shower, much like I had with

Jill at the other house. One time he saw me outside and came at me with a stick, but luckily my legs could still outrun someone who was well-fed as he but older. We ended up going to court where the judge told me to promise never to do it again. I said OK and I kept my promise.

Well, this neighbor had many chickens, and I had been eyeing them to see if I could steal one for supper. After the incident with the judge, I was a bit more scared about dealing with this landlord, but the opportunity presented itself in a different form. One of his chickens had gone AWOL and had apparently decided that *she* was the one to decide where she would lay her eggs. Serendipity played its part and I discovered the nest as I was playing in a wooded area not far from this man's house. The thing that opened my eyes wider than the sewer ditches in the city was that the nest was full with the chicken's eggs. I could not even remember when it was that we had had any eggs! But now, at least, we could feast to our heart's content with the 50-or-so eggs that were in the nest. Running joyfully, I made my way back to our dilapidated house to tell my mother of our good fortune. She gave me a big bowl and told me to bring all the eggs back so that we could immediately have supper. One by one I carefully placed our precious booty into the bowl, and I slowly walked back home with our treasure.

We couldn't wait so we prepared to fry our first egg, but as my mother cracked the first shell our innocent enthusiasm turned to nausea as the putrid stench of extremely rotten eggs swiftly permeated our entire kitchen, leaving no doubt that these eggs had been in the sun for days, weeks, or even months. Just to tempt fate my mother cracked open several more eggs, confirming with each viscous, putrid, rotting, maggot-filled mass that the eggs had to go. This was the only time in my history of chronic hunger that the filth and stench of our food had effectively obliterated the hunger pangs for at least a day.

Meanwhile, what does one do with 45 rotten, unbroken eggs? Gagging and with profuse saliva—as happens when you're about to vomit—I took all the eggs back to the wooded area and hurled each one at the landlord's house. It was his wayward chicken, and thus he deserved to have these eggs back. I never went into those woods again. He never knew who had covered his house with that awful stench.

Indeed, hunger was a major driving force in our lives at the Salinas Avenue house and in all other houses that we lived in. Love, safety, and discipline should be the cornerstones in a child's life, but not for us, for we had to do daily battle with insecurity, hunger, terror, abuse, and lovelessness. Hunger alone accounted for a major portion of our recklessness and my general disrespect for others. As Woodrow Wilson (1856-1924) said in a New York

City speech in May of 1912: "In the Lord's prayer, the first petition is for daily bread. No one can worship God or love his neighbor on an empty stomach." While that admonition certainly applies to adults, it is doubly relevant for children whose personalities will be affected far into the future even after the hunger has subsided.

Though our life in our Salinas Avenue house was marked by this endemic hunger, I personally had a small respite from this daily toil when my mother sent me to San Antonio to spend some time with my Uncle Felipe.

Summer of 1952 in San Antonio

It was almost a shock to me when I finally arrived in San Antonio, since everything was so different: huge buildings, all the streets were paved, the city blocks that seemed five times the size of El Paso's, large covered pools where the waste from the toilets went (later I learned one calls them "septic tanks"), the water that tasted different, not too many Mexicans, but lots of "gringos" and lots of "negroes." In fact, I had never seen a person with black skin before; all this time I thought that the world was basically Mexican and Gringo, so now I had to revise my primitive views. One thing that also struck me immediately was the pervasive smell of freshly cut grass which permeated the entire neighborhood where my Uncle Felipe lived. Even today, every time I smell cut grass I think of the Summer of '52 in San Antonio.

It was in late '51 or early '52 that my grandfather died suddenly from a heart attack as he was walking the streets in Ciudad Juarez, Mexico. The newspaper published the shocking photo of his smashed and bloody face exactly as he looked when the photographer turned over his dead body on the street. With my grandfather's death, my mother's family of origin completed its years-running disintegration. My Uncle Felipe had moved to San Antonio at about that time after searching for his soul and fortune in other cities, most notably Chicago, and subsequent to that my Aunts Julieta and Sonia had joined him temporarily in his home on Wakefield Street in the mosquito-infested part of this gigantic metropolis. Immediately after my grandfather's death, my grandmother moved to spend her last days in my uncle's home in San Antonio. This was essentially the situation when I arrived there.

They were poor, but they had *food!* For the whole month that I was there I ate whenever I wanted, whatever I desired. It seemed unreal that food could be so readily available in a home, that there were human beings somewhere who lived with such a miracle! Needless to say, the ready availability of food in my Uncle Felipe's home was the highlight of my visit. Soon after I got there, my Aunt Julieta told me that I needed to go to a barber shop for a haircut, something that I had never done before but to which I readily agreed.

She took me to the downtown area, where the enormous buildings were located, and I was awed by how these glass and concrete giants could stand without tipping over. And who would want to live in these huge buildings with no front or back yards? Well, she knew where she wanted to take me, and we ended up at a barber shop run entirely by gringos. Because of my isolated experience in El Paso I had had no contact whatsoever with white people, so I was afraid of them. The ones I had seen in pictures in magazines had blue eyes and blond hair—they seemed just so different from Mexicans. Besides, there was the enormous language problem: I could barely communicate in Spanish, even at age seven, and definitely not in English. They, in turn, felt that Spanish was a "gutter" language, so it was to be shunned. Luckily for me, at this gringo barber shop in downtown San Antonio, my Aunt Julieta served as the connecting link between these two mutually suspicious worlds.

I can just conjecture about what those white barbers must have been thinking as I was sitting in the waiting area, along with other "regular" Americans (non-Mexicans). They kept giving me unfriendly and exploratory glances probably meant to determine if they really should cut my hair or not, for I did look raggedy. Sitting in the waiting area with my Aunt Julieta I did not feel as if I was waiting for a haircut, but rather that I was waiting to be evaluated for acceptance or rejection. That was how I approached human relations in my life, and the disapproving glances of the skeptical white barbers a few breaths away from me were making me feel that, yes, this place was too nice for a gutter person like me. I probably should be looking for salvageable scraps of food in the trashcans outside.

The big moment finally came, after there were no other gringo customers in the waiting area. They had to call on me, ignore me, or tell me to get out. The grumpy white barber with the permanent frown motioned me with his head to come to his chair, but I was confused about his signal and looked at him with worry and stupidity on my face. Aunt Julieta, who had experience in dealing with white people, quickly told me that the man wanted me to go sit on his chair, that it was my turn.

It was a very comfortable and cushiony barber's chair. The big cloth that he put around me smelled clean and aromatic. But not a word came from him; rather strange I thought, but perhaps for the best since I would not have been able to understand anything anyway. As he silently began to comb then cut with the humming electric razor, the little dark critters began to drop by the dozens from my bushy head onto the snow-white cloth around me.

Lice! My head was crawling with hundreds of well-fed lice. Oh, yes, I guess we hadn't warned him.

Actually, having lice in my hair and on my raggedy shirt was very normal for me, for I had never not had lice. "Doesn't everybody?" I thought. Scratching my head was just part of life, just like being hungry and not having long pants in the wintertime. Since the original nest of lice in my hair had never been treated, it had through the years multiplied maybe a thousand-fold and established a solid base on my scalp, with the shiny, oval, white eggs adorning clearly all of the hairs on my scalp, much like a row of white pearls adorn a string. Oftentimes I would play with the adult lice that constantly would be falling onto my shoulders, and finally I would have to crush each between the fingernails of my two thumbs. Some of them—the selfish fat ones—would pop due to the excess blood that they were engorged with. My sister Ana and I would take turns plucking lice from each other, something that could easily occupy several hours in lieu of playing with toys we didn't have. In fact, in the Mexican culture we call it "espulgando"—a past-time that serves to remove lice and also to promote a "bonding" between family members and or friends. This lice subculture extends even to the fingers of the hand as each finger is given a special name: the little finger is the "niño chiquito," or the little baby; the ring finger is the "señor del anillo," or the ring man; the middle finger is "tonto y loco," or the stupid and crazy one; the index finger is the "lambe-cazuelas," or the pot licker; and, finally, the thumb is the "mata-piojos," or the lice killer. I would only surmise that it is because this lice-killing practice is so wide-spread that this children's game developed within the culture.

Even at inopportune times these lice would fall off my hair and onto my shoulders, as when I was in school. On many unfortunate occasions my fellow students alarmingly pointed out the dark-colored crawling critters on my shoulders, which made me suspect that maybe not everybody had these little animals in their hair. And on one particular occasion, when I was about nine years old, my Aunt Sonia, The Brave, came to visit us at home, and when she found out that all of us were totally infested with lice, proceeded to cut *absolutely all our hair* off to remedy the problem. It was such a humiliating feeling for us all to then go to school totally bald and face the stares of the entire student population. I had felt better with my lice in place.

Not that the scalping did any good, for the contamination at home was total: the lice were on all the beds, sheets, blankets, pillows, sofa, chairs, combs, brushes, clothes, and if that was not enough we could always count on the neighborhood kids to bring in fresh supplies daily. For the first 12 years of my life I had to share the nutrients in my blood, and my scalp, with these silent pets of mine. But I finally got rid of them when I landed in the permanent foster home, at age 12. Meanwhile I had to deal with a potentially volatile situation while sitting on the barber's chair.

From the gigantic mirror in front of us, I could see the face of the distraught barber whose eyes were locked onto the white sheet that surrounded me, locked more specifically on the dozens of pepper-like moving specks that soiled the otherwise pure whiteness. Not exactly pepper, I knew, for these black dots were crawling desperately all over, looking for the safe haven of my filthy and unwashed hair. The barber's worst prejudices were indeed confirmed and strengthened, as he had before him another raggedy and smelly Mexican kid with a whole anthill-like swarm of wiggly lice all over. His distraught look changed to a kind of nauseous repugnance—much like you would get if you discovered part of a mouse in your half-eaten hamburger. He immediately untied the string around my neck, disgustedly rolled up the sheet, and placed it in a large paper bag. In it he included the comb and razor he had used on me. Then he instructed his assistant to take the bag through the back door to the outside trashcans, and hatefully motioned with his head for me to get off his chair and leave his shop. This time I found no trouble interpreting his wordless signals; I knew that my lice and I were not welcome here, so my Aunt Julieta and I left the gringo's barber shop in a hurry and forever. As the glass door closed behind us, I was able to see him furiously washing his hands to cleanse himself of the putrid filth he had just encountered from this poor and shaggy Mexican kid.

Looking back at these experiences with lice I cannot help wondering just how low and desperate our expectations were. *For us, having lice all the time was a way of life, not just a medical condition that needed attention.* Lice are the least of one's worries when the stomach is empty and when one has to watch out for daily terror from a tormentor. We rarely made any attempts at getting rid of the infestation; when we plucked them out of each other's hair we did it more as a bonding past-time than to clean ourselves. But, my Aunt Sonia's drastic steps in cleaning our heads were in my opinion demonstrative of poor judgment. It really caused us great distress, and we suffered significant malicious ridicule when seemingly all the kids in our school made comments about our total baldness. I cannot see under what conditions one would have to take such action, especially during the school year. But, as we shall see soon, my Aunt Sonia's poor judgment was predictable.

My Uncle Felipe's house was on a huge lot, with a lawn that required apparently constant cutting. The house was neat, well furnished, and well stocked with all the foods that a kid could ever want. At this house I didn't have to worry about daily beatings, for my Uncle and my Aunt Julieta treated me very well. But, something happened one hot, steamy afternoon when I was getting ready to take a nap on the floor, together with my Aunt Sonia.

As I was preparing my blankets on the floor, my Aunt Sonia told me that she had these little "chiggers" all over her legs, and asked me for help in removing them. These little pests looked to me like red dots that were imbedded in the pores of her skin, so my Aunt gave me a small needle to help dislodge them. I started the process near her knees, but she soon told me that I should move on to her inner thighs. At this point she was lying on her back on the floor, with her skirt raised to the waistline and her legs wide open. Soon enough she asked me to go higher and higher in extracting these little red dots from her inner thighs, even though I wasn't sure if these particular ones on the inside of her thighs were "chiggers" or just freckles or moles. Before long I was staring right at her crotch and working at the edge of her panties, right where some pubic hairs peeked out reluctantly. Through her almost transparent panties I could see the slit of her vagina, and I felt right at home as it reminded me of my mother. In a final move she used her hands to slide the panties' crotch out of the way so that I could get to "the other chiggers" which were in there somewhere. That is about as far as it got, although I do not quite remember just how it ended.

Of course, this encounter was totally inappropriate, yet I feel sorry for and not angry at my Aunt Sonia. She had always been very emotional, impulsive, explosive, socially awkward, "histrionic," inappropriate, daring, adventurous, risky, confrontational, brave, talkative, and fearless, and even though I knew she would never beat me up I also did not feel love from her. Throughout the years she was the only woman whom I knew who had the balls to stand up to and do battle eye to eye with The Devil. Incredibly, the monster actually *feared* her, something that we secretly relished. In high contrast to our stupid and weak mother, Aunt Sonia The Brave never allowed El Diablo to push her around whenever she came to visit. She would spew caustic venom and frothing saliva from her mouth, challenging him to hit her first so that she could then break his face; The Devil, we were happy to see, would try to avoid her and never dared even to threaten to raise a fist against her. If he had, she said, she would have cut off his shriveled testicles.

One day when she came to visit us about one year before my mother's death, she locked horns again with The Devil. As usual, she was doing most of the screaming, complaining about how El Diablo mistreated all of us. At one point she said to him, "Oye, pendejo, sabes tu como hago yo mi dinero?

Con mi panocha. Yo hago mi dinero con mi panocha. Asi es que no te temo a ti ni a nadie." The translation is: "Hey, you fool, do you know how I make my money? With my vagina. I make money with my vagina. So therefore I do not fear you or anyone else." Even if she meant that she prostituted herself for money, I cannot condemn my Aunt Sonia, for at about the same time I was selling my body for food. Even though we kids had a healthy respect and fear of her volatile temper, we knew that she would not harm us. We thoroughly enjoyed Tia Sonia when she came for her always-unannounced, explosive, Devil-bashing visits. She was the fiery one of the family, she was our hero.

She also must have had a very thin skin. During this summer visit to San Antonio, she had spent several days back-to-back knitting what I felt were some very beautiful table cloths in various designs and colors. It amazed me how human hands could do such intricate work which seemed to have end-less connections between the many loops in the cloth. When she finished with her work, she asked me to take it around the neighborhood to see if anyone would like to buy individual items. Not having any sales experience, and being socially inept, I felt reluctant to accept the assignment, agreeing to do it only after much persuasion by my Aunt. So I went to maybe two dozen homes in the neighborhood, meeting new people, but not being able to make a single sale even though the price of each item was a mere 75 cents. Having completed the big loop around the neighborhood, I came back to my Uncle Felipe's house and reluctantly told Aunt Sonia that I had not sold any items. She was tremendously upset, feeling that her work was worthless, and, I suspect, she too felt valueless as the creator of this beautiful knitting that nobody wanted. In a convulsive fit of angry despair, she took her mightily sharp seamstress scissors and violently shredded all her beautiful completed projects to pieces in front of me, sobbing in a hurt and angry manner that I had never witnessed in any human being before. When it all ended, her work lay scattered all over the floor, looking like a thousand colorful pieces of spaghetti, many of which were soaked with her painful tears. My poor Aunt Sonia, normally The Brave, just whimpered softly on the couch, her melting mascara creating black winding rivers down her cheeks. I just stood there, speechless and paralyzed, not knowing which foot to move first.

This scene, like many others in my early years, I shall never forget.

Aunt Sonia lived her chaotic life with its many ups and downs until she was killed in a terrible late-night car accident just outside the San Antonio city limits in 1973. I wish that I had known her better as an adult. In spite of her one violation of appropriate sexual boundaries with me as a child, I still feel fond of her and I treasure her memory in my heart.

Besides this sexual encounter with my Aunt Sonia, I also had two more in San Antonio that summer. One involved my Uncle Felipe.

One morning we were all in the kitchen standing around and waiting as Uncle Felipe's wife, Tina, prepared the usual delicious breakfast of scrambled eggs with flour tortillas, a staple in San Antonio. My uncle was seated on one of the kitchen chairs while I was standing by the doorway next to him. He was wearing only his underwear shorts, with the fly section fully open because of the position he was seated in. I could see his penis, which was of considerable length, I thought, even though it was down and not up. I guess I was trying to compare it with the janitor's massive organ, which I had seen only in its upright position. For several long minutes I just stood there catching as many glimpses as I could, until my uncle finally noticed and closed his fly promptly, but not before asking me if I really wanted to see the whole thing. I was so embarrassed by his comment that I left the kitchen and I never even glanced at his shorts again.

The other incident involved a family that I had met while on my sales route with Aunt Sonia's beautiful creations. There was one girl and one boy about my age in that family, so one day I went over to their house to play. As we played hide and seek inside the house I lowered my pants while I was hiding, hoping that the little girl would find me like this and would then start to play with my penis. Well, she did find me, but she just told me to put my pants up, that they had fallen down. I just gave up on my ploy and went home.

Along the way I stopped next door at the house of a family I had also met selling door-to-door. Something would happen here that signalled a new stage of my moral sickness.

This family had one mother hen which had about five baby chicks. For some unknown reason, I chased the mother hen with a garden rake and deliberately killed one of the chicks by smashing it into the ground with this tool. I held the lifeless body in my hand and didn't know what to do with it, although eventually I decided to just place it on the ground. That night I worried about what I had done, thinking that the mother hen would probably stick to the area where I had placed the dead chick's body. So in the morning I hurriedly went over to the spot and was amazed to see that there was a hole where the baby chick used to be, but there was no body. I innocently thought that the earth had swallowed it.

The family somehow found out about it and confronted me. I did not deny it, and I told them honestly that I did not know why I did it. The lady of the house, a white woman who salivated profusely from the sides of her mouth, excoriated me for the crime, pointing out that the mother hen did not mean to scare me since she was only protecting her babies. Now as an adult I can see that somewhere in the family dynamics which I observed in the chicks' relations to their mother lay some very profound personal triggers which prompted me to react aggressively towards these baby chicks. It was only the beginning of a long career as an animal mutilator. I was already a seven-year-old fiend.

Besides these events there was not much else that was significant in my 1952 summer vacation in San Antonio. My Aunt Julieta took me to the Greyhound bus station and dispatched me alone on the 550-mile trip back to El Paso. I was not too keen on going back to the same old hunger, but I guess that San Antonio had had enough of me to last a lifetime, for I never went there again as a child.

Back at home in El Paso I had a new challenge to face up to: long stretches of daily abandonment.

Babysitting in the Second Grade

As the oldest child at age seven, I had the responsibility to care for my two younger sisters and one younger brother, and to do all the housework on a daily basis—with no adults at home. At that age it never dawned on me that babysitting at age seven was highly dangerous and that prudent parents would never allow it. But, my mother did, nevertheless. As a matter of routine, I was left alone with my sister Ana, my sister Tencha, and my brother Elizeo—all younger than me—for the entire day, for a whole year. Apparently my mother was working at the International Hat Company during the day, and she needed a babysitter for my three younger siblings. So she kept me home from school during the second grade, which resulted in my having to repeat it.

She left early, at about the same time that The Devil left for his freelance jobs at fixing refrigerators in people's homes. There was no schedule, of course, so I got up whenever I got up and attempted to find something to eat, even if it was some old and brittle corn tortillas, with margarine.

There was no television, no radio, no crayons, no pencils, no paper, no telephone, no snacks, no milk, no games, no clock, no air conditioning, no heat, no shades, no curtains, no relatives, no hope. There was absolutely nothing to do in that hellish house when we were left alone for the entire day. I did the best I could in changing the cloth diapers for my younger brother, but because we had no clothes washer I would soon run out of diapers. Consequently it was not unusual to see him walking around naked from the waist down with poop smears on his butt. When his milk bottle would run dry I would keep on refilling it with water, but his eyes would just roll back, and he would collapse from hunger, neglect, and exhaustion. At least we were careful not to step on him wherever he collapsed.

One of my sisters presented a special problem when she would suddenly become very rigid when in a standing position, locking her legs to prevent a normal bowel movement. She would stand in that catatonic state for nearly an hour as the urge to expel would eventually subside. I would just leave her alone and hope that she could join us for the imaginary games we would play on the floor.

It was just about this time when Ana and I would stare out the window into space and chant monotonically our hunger song, sometimes for an hour or two on end. During this time I would have no idea of what my other two siblings were doing, although I would have a sense that they were not outside getting into trouble. However, it was during this period, too, when I did most of my break-ins into the house next door, and my brothers and sisters had an even worse level of supervision. Above all, there was the benefit of my bringing some stolen food over from the house next door.

It was nothing less than a miracle that nothing serious happened to us during that year of abandonment—not physical, anyway. A child rapist-killer could have come through the front door with no resistance whatsoever. We could have gotten electrocuted, since we played with frayed electrical cords quite frequently. We liked playing with matches, but miraculously none of our "little fires" on the living room floor ever got out of control. There were only minimal cleansers and poisons in the house, yet we never had any accidents with these. Our kitchen had about two little-used knives which we used to practice stabbing the wall but fortunately never each other.

Of utmost interest to me is how it was that my mother's judgment allowed her to leave us alone, especially when I, the oldest, was only seven years old. And for up to eight hours at a time. And for what? She "had" to work? We were starving anyway, with or without her additional measly salary. So where was the extra money going? We had no amenities to speak of, no appliances to pay off, no car or phone bill, no vacation to save for, no wardrobe, no new furniture, no shoes, no drug habit that I ever detected. The only thing that possibly could have been consuming their two measly wages was The Devil's alcohol habit—he drank like crazy every day no matter what. And the fool would then wake up vomiting in the morning, stinking up the whole place. Whatever the reasoning, whatever the logic, my mother and my evil stepfather exhibited monumental incompetence and an incomprehensible lack of awareness of basic parental responsibilities and duties in leaving us alone for such lengthy blocks of time—for the whole year, in fact. What is even more perplexing and frustrating is that on top of leaving us alone all day for the entire year my mother also knew of these problems we were having when we were alone, yet she ignored them or felt they really were not problems at all. As I have said, Maria-Esperanza was unfit to be a mother, even to a dog.

But, why? Why did she fail? I have asked myself that question hundreds of times as an adult. It's not that my mother did not understand the situation, it was that she simply did not love us, or, rather, that she had no capacity to love us or anyone else. But, even if one does not love another person, one should at the least exercise moral duty in caring for that person, especially if it is a defenseless child, right? Yes, that would be true under normal circumstances, but our hellhole was anything but normal. *I now believe that my mother was driven by an over-riding motive that catastrophically compromised her sense of moral duty as a parent. That motive created a tragic and insufferable childhood for us all, and later ruined our lives as adults, spouses, and parents. That motive even turned fatal some years later and led to my mother's grim and preventable death.* It would be many years of sorrow before I would finally see the light.

As for El Diablo, he was unqualified to even be a member of the human race, for it was here, at this house on Salinas Avenue, where he so savagely beat my mother in front of all of us kids, and left an indelible image of his fundamental bestial nature in our hearts forever. Merengueno Zalmar, ugly and vicious maggot from a cesspool, should have been run over while he was still in his mother's fetid womb to spare the innocent children of the world the pain he brought us all. Too bad he was born alive. Too bad he was born already breathing. Too bad he was born with a pulse. Too bad he was not born with the umbilical cord wound several times around his neck—and in a knot. Too bad he did not slip out of the obstetrician's bloody gloves when he was being delivered from his bitch-mother's womb. He should have splatted then and there on the bare concrete floor. His evil brain would have rattled inside his satanic skull. Surely they would have had to just throw him in the hospital incinerator after that. The world would have been a much better place.

Bad parents, bad janitor, bad house. The house on Salinas Avenue had brought experiences that molded our personalities and that we would never forget. The rent was about one day's work, yet apparently The Devil's parents, who owned this exalted dog house, were demanding that he move out, for reasons that we will never know. We know for sure that The Devil's father hated him, for some years earlier the father had broken a heavy chair on the back of El Diablo. A dog begat another dog. Since my mother's side of the family was nothing you could gloat about at a dinner party, it would appear that my mother searched out just the right complement for herself, and found it in this prize husband with only one eyelid, broken teeth, and nothing whatsoever that his future children could point to with pride. In any case, two years after we moved in, we were moving out. It was looking as if we were really nomadic Mexicans. But not by choice.

Chapter Four
Worsening Family Chaos at The Jacinto Projects

By the time El Diablo's parents kicked us out of the Salinas Avenue house, the nest of evil and suffering was almost full. The baby was Benito, then there was Elizeo, Tencha, Ana, and I. It occurred to me afterwards that The Devil must have kept the impending move secret from the bill collectors who came very frequently to our house, since I, at the age of seven, was given the responsibility of telling them lies about how nobody was home, even in the evening, when, in fact, sometimes my mother and my stepfather would hide in the back room. There are no memories of us kids worrying too much about the move or about leaving school friends behind (who needs Louisiana Red Hot Chili Sauce anyway?). It was only later that I thought about not ever again being able to see my wonderful teachers at Escuela Primaria, especially my very elderly music teacher, Dr. Haskell, who, with her joyful piano music and beaming smile, instilled in me a lifelong love for classical music.

When we left, we were able to put all our belongings *and* furniture in one load on a stepvan, a slightly larger version of a pickup truck. Of course, we did not have to worry about the extra weight of toothbrushes, *since throughout our entire childhood, we never owned a toothbrush, and we never brushed our teeth*. As incredible as that may sound, it is so tragically true. I saw my first dentist and my first toothbrush years later, when we all went permanently into foster homes. Shoes? One pair for each kid, and the soles were always falling off, so we had to double on socks or place home-made cardboard inserts inside our shoes to provide a cushion against the pain of walking on pebble streets. Age seven and no underwear, just my famous shorts. My sister Tencha had just recently fallen off a bed and hit her head (sound familiar?) on a pin that protruded about one inch from the floor. She consequently got a clean, cylindrical hole, about one-quarter inch wide and half-inch deep, on her forehead, but that was taken care of with a bandaid (we called them "curitas"). A doctor never looked at it, so it *just had to heal on its own,* as there was no other way. Maybe it just filled up with brain fluid that simply solidified later. The unattended wound on my baby sister's forehead had no other choice.

From the Salinas Avenue house in El Paso, Texas, we moved to a series of about four other houses, always having to leave because we didn't pay the rent, and changing schools, leaving semi-friends behind, painfully saying goodbye to kind teachers who ignored my chronic urine smell. The housing selection, I recall, was not that great, for we had to look for the rock-bottom cheapest, which usually meant paper-thin walls with no insulation, sometimes no hot water, peeling paint and Texas-sized spiders throughout, and, of course, a minimum of one million fearless and aggressive cockroaches, plus their pregnant concubines. Not that these repugnant scavengers did any better than we did, for we made sure we ate even the crumbs of our infrequent meals and any small pieces of tortilla that may have landed on the floor.

The Devil continued to drink heavily, beating us for any infraction, real or imagined. Standard fare continued to be all of us kids watching and trembling as he would terrorize and finally beat our mother also. These vivid memories of the vile beast savaging our mother on uncountable occasions left me with agonizing feelings best characterized as anger, hatefulness, rage, fear, terror, shame, gloom, panic, confusion,and a soul-crushing and debilitating cowardice at the realization that never once did I defend my poor mother as the sadistic fiend pummeled her while she asked for mercy on the bloody floor. My adult mind tells me that of course I was not responsible for El Diablo battering my mother, yet my child memories make me feel like a worthless coward for not defending her against this cockroach masquerading as a dog. Had I had at that time the knowledge and the physical capacity that I now possess, even with my small size I would have lunged at the attacking sewer-rat and with my bare hands gouged out his evil eyes. And if that hadn't stopped him, with pleasure I would have stomped on his face with a steel-spiked boot a thousand times until it looked like chopped liver. Our hungry cockroaches would then have feasted on the real vermin of the house, the low-life, the criminal dog, the rabid larva, the faceless maggot, the putrid hemorrhoid, the aborted tapeworm, the vulture's vomit, the cesspool sperm, the bag of cancerous pus—The Devil. Merengueno Zalmar, Satan's cruel misbegotten slime intended for the fetid womb of a syphilitic slug, would have been no more. He should have been electrocuted as he was coming out of his mother's maggot-infested pussy.

Well, one time I almost did overcome my terror to go to my mother's side as Satan was upon her, ready to snuff her out, I thought. I was seven, the others much younger. It was dusk and all of us kids were playing in the backyard, poking sticks at fresh turds we had laid on one corner of the lot, trying to annoy the dozens of squiggly white worms wrestling their way out of the disgusting mass. But our fun with our tapeworms ended abruptly when we heard The Devil arguing with our mother inside the house. She was complaining that we had no food in the house while he viciously accused her of giving our food away to the neighbors. When the tenor of their voices reached what we knew was the horrible crescendo, we all dropped our worm-sticks and ran inside out of fear that our mother might not survive this new violent episode. We wanted to see but we did not want to see. We wanted to hear but we wished we wouldn't hear. We wanted to hug our mother but we did not want to hug her for fear of being annihilated by the monster in our home. We wanted to be there but we wanted to be far away with God instead. Satan then crossed the line again as he breathed toxic alcohol fumes from his flared nostrils and spewed foamed saliva from his ugly mouth with the broken teeth. As always, almost like a werewolf he changed from being a worthless, antisocial lowlife to a heinous animal with murderous rage. His eerie black eyes seemed to grow to twice their size, especially the hideous one with no eyelid, making them look absolutely terrifying—a living nightmare we could not wake up from. My brothers and sisters and I were quickly overcome with terror which made our legs weak and our knees ready to buckle. We huddled in the nearest corner to us but farthest from the horrifying scene unfolding before us. Then it happened. Lucifer cranked his massive right arm all the way to his left and unleashed such a powerful back-handed blow to my mother's face that she spun around, her auburn hair flying behind her as she fell to the floor. The cracking noise of the blow sent chills down my spine, and I believe that all of us helplessly urinated in our sorry corner.

But he was not done, this detestable macho beast from hell. After my mother landed on her back on the floor he sat on top of her, straddling her at about the hip area, and continued to beat her face as she yelped, cried, sobbed, whimpered, and tried to cover her face, saying, "No, please, no, I won't complain again, you know I love you." It didn't matter what she said because the werewolf wasn't listening.

Even though we too were crying and whimpering I began to think I should take the opportunity to stab the monster with the screwdriver he had sticking out of his back pocket, but then again, I thought, what if I cannot take it out fast enough and what if he does not die after I stab him? If he does not die for sure he will kill me right here. My mother's life, my mother's suffering, my terror, my life, my indecision, my cowardice. I failed in protecting my mother, and the scumbag delivered several more blows before spitting on her bloody face. He got up victoriously, perhaps feeling he had taught my mother a lesson again. Ignoring our terrified cries the sombitch just went to the bathroom. As soon as he closed the door we all ran toward our mother, mixing blood, urine, saliva, and tears as we held each other tightly.

This became another horrible episode to add to the nightmares which tormented us every night. Perhaps none of us kids should have been born. Perhaps I should have suffocated under the tire in the trunk of that car.

The next day we went about our miserable lives, scavenging for food, playing with worms, and absorbing our traumas like unfortunate soldiers who have to endure, because that is what we did—that was our destiny, to suffer the malice that tormented our entire wretched childhood.

The Radio, the Bicycle, and the Promise Unfulfilled

Yes we were destitute and traumatized and miserable, but that did not prevent us from wishing for what we saw in the windows of the few department stores in El Paso. Our poor mother must have felt overwhelmed with the endless pleadings she got from all of us, for we expressed fierce hunger for items that other, normal children took for granted. We had passed a large department store, "Bressner's," in downtown El Paso many times on the way to the International Bridge on Relicario Avenue, at that time the only bridge which connected El Paso, Texas, with Ciudad Juarez, Mexico. In that window was a beautiful two-transistor radio (the rage when they first appeared) that I had fallen in love with, so I begged my penniless mother to get it for me. The radio was selling for $2.50, a huge sum for a family with kids who didn't even have underwear. Because of my incessant badgering, my mother relented and said that the only way she could buy it for me was on a "layaway" plan. It would take a year of monthly payments of 25 or 50 cents, but it was better than nothing. I agreed to the inchworm plan. We went into the store and my mother paid the clerk 75 cents to place my little transistor radio on layaway. It was so frustrating going home without the radio, for when one has nothing and even food is scarce, delaying gratification of this sort is akin to leaving a hot iron on one's face for an extra moment in order to produce a more even scar. Postponing reward was alien to us; we had to have it when we could get it.

Nonetheless, at home I thought often about the time that I would eventually get my beautiful radio. But things were not to work out in my favor, for, having made only two or three more payments, my mother then fell ill, and could not continue making payments.

No wonder, as an adult I adore radios, I collect them, and, somewhere deep in my most fundamental subconscious, I am still desperately trying to obtain my little radio which forever disappeared into the unknown land of forgotten layaways.

A similar event occurred at Leal's Bike Shop on Relicario Avenue, a little shop overcrowded with repaired bicycles that poor kids couldn't afford. This must have been around 1953 when I was about eight years old. I had never owned a bicycle and was desperate for one, even on an empty stomach. I spotted one I liked, the one the shop owner said had been repaired several months ago but had never been picked up. If I could get it I would be benefitting from someone else's monetary misfortune—another raggedy kid who had climbed a notch above me by having this bike, but who probably didn't deserve it, I thought. I wanted it, but as with the radio, it would have to be on the layaway plan. So we began by paying one dollar towards the $13 bike. I was ecstatic! No longer would I have to look enviously at other kids with bicycles for I was now getting my own.

I never did own a bicycle while all of us kids lived at home with our mother. As was the case with the ill-fated layaway of the transistor radio, this grand project never came to fruition for the same reason: my mother's declining health. The two gifts my mother planned to get for me never made it into my hands. I still wonder what ever happened to that nice bicycle at Leal's Bike Shop—the one that had a tag with my name on it.

So we mostly floated around for about two years, going from house to house, seemingly just a few steps ahead of the increasingly hostile bill collectors—those persistent men who knocked on our doors with steel knuckles and peeked through our windows because they simply did not believe that we were not home. What motivated these guys to embark on such a confrontational career that essentially harassed poor people who did not have money to pay their bills? Did they feel that they were performing some sort of ethical or moral duty in pointing out that one has to fulfill one's legal obligations? Would it have been moral for my mother to have taken our dinner money to pay these extortionists? Or how about money for school milk? How many times did I just stare at other children in my class while they drank those wonderful glasses of milk, while I painfully waited at my desk for all to finish. Why was I the only child who had to watch because I typically never had the two cents that it cost to get the milk? Countless times I had to fake that I was so busy at my desk that I didn't even notice that everyone else was enjoying their milk. In reality I was hurting profoundly inside because I felt the reason I wouldn't be getting any milk was that I was in some way defective and not deserving. Nothing was rightfully mine. I had no right to expect food or milk. If I got it I quickly ate or drank, for fear that it would disappear or that it would be taken away. Because I know how the hurt of not having food or milk can cut so deeply into one's heart, I would never under any circumstances allow similar misfortune to befall any of my children, for I would sell whatever I had, prostitute my body if necessary, steal if I had to, in order to shield them from such a wretched experience. Chronic hunger wounds the spirit much more so than it pains the stomach.

So, these bill-collector extortionists, with their bellies full of nice beef tacos, rice and beans, guacamole, fajitas, and drink, can easily afford the luxury of invoking lofty moral and legal responsibilities in persuading poor folk to pay their bills, but when the stomach is shriveled and the spirit is distressed there is no moral or legal system of rules that is more important than the will to survive physically. Morals always come after our attention turns from our stomach towards the heavens, never the other way around.

Other misfortunes always found us, as usual it seemed. At one of these houses—the one on Relicario Avenue—a car plowed straight into our living room, missing baby Benito in his crib by only about five feet. Apparently a husband was teaching his wife how to drive, and as she was traveling down our street she had to swerve to avoid hitting a bicyclist, which caused her to lose control of her car and plow into the front wall of our house. The car ended almost completely inside our living room. Needless to say, the house was uninhabitable after this.

It was at the house on Manzana Street that I had to go to see the judge for my peeking through the windows of the landlord's home. Not only that but I also used to collect cigarette butts from the sidewalks and streets, smoking them in secret whenever I could. It is only by good fortune that I did not get tuberculosis or some other terrible communicable disease.

For a few weeks I looked stupid with one eyebrow completely shaved off. I must have been about nine years old and had befriended this oddball kid in the neighborhood. Everybody said that he was "crazy." Ha! Weren't we all? He looked very normal to me, judging by my own warped standards. Well, we used to steal chickens together, something that bonded us in crime, I suppose.

He had shaved off one eyebrow "to see how it would look." Since I somehow admired this bold guy who apparently was afraid of nothing (come to think of it, I don't know if he was brave or crazy), I emulated him and shaved off one of my own eyebrows, perhaps signaling that I was beginning to escalate from killing baby chicks to something more bizarre. My psychiatric symptoms were multiplying at a faster pace.

As we had been moving from house to house and from school to school, I knew that my mother had put in an application for an apartment at the biggest welfare projects in El Paso: the massive Jacinto Projects, stretching for many city blocks and comprised of thousands of brick and concrete apartments. Nobody knew it, but it would be at this apartment that our baby brother Benito would pay with his life for the grievous disorganization and neglect within our family. And so, in 1955, when I was about nine or ten years old, we were told that our name finally was at the top of the several-years-long waiting list, and that a welfare apartment was waiting for us. We made the move into a bigger hell.

Of course we were delighted that we were getting a four bedroom apartment, that we would finally have room for all five kids. Not that it really mattered, for most of us had been sleeping in our mother's bed for years, as mentioned previously, while El Diablo usually slept on a cot in another room, a cot that none of us kids ever played on because it represented the fiend, the tormentor, the walking corpse that not even maggots would taste. We were thrilled that the apartment had two floors, with all four bedrooms and a bathroom upstairs. There was no air conditioning, but it did not bother us since we were used to greater physical hardships in the hot Texas weather. In the wintertime we were to discover that the heating system was not very efficient, and the almost 100-percent concrete apartment would be as cold as a morgue. It would be a year from then that this heating system would cause a gruesome tragedy where an entire family that we knew well would perish in the middle of the night due to natural gas poisoning as a result of the flame blowing out at night. We were there when they discovered the bodies several days later that had exploded due to severe bloating.

We soon found out that all our neighbors were on welfare just like us, something that seemed to be the constant topic of gossip and mindless complaint throughout the day. We were all poor but yet we talked about how such and such family was *really* poor, while some other family seemed to have too much to be on welfare. And as one can imagine, there were perhaps hundreds or thousands of kids in these projects, most of whom had serious behavior problems, but which at that time did not appear too unusual. It was at The

Jacinto Projects where I first came in contact with a very visible part of the Mexican American culture in the United States, the enormously violent yet interesting subculture of the Mexican-American *Pachuco*, or gang member.

There was one gang member there whom I admired: El Rafa (short for Rafael), the Pachuco with class who was never aggressive toward anyone, to my knowledge.

El Rafa would typically hang out by himself at the edge of the projects boundary, right on Third Street, smoking his cheap cigarettes and cleaning under his fingernails with his stiletto-like dagger. I can't quite remember just how it was that the cowardly bunch that I hung out with met this guy, but soon enough we would visit him at his official corner regularly. He must have been wearing about one pound of The Parrot Hair Compound each time, for his hair was combed back neatly with not a single strand out of place. And he would always wear his standard *Pachuco* clothes, including oversize black shoes that curved upward at the tip to accommodate about four extra soles stitched together under the original. Rafa would proudly demonstrate to all of us cowards how he could kick an opponent with his massive right shoe, first raising the upper part of his right leg in front of himself while holding back on the lower part of this leg, but explosively sending this lower right leg out toward the front with such speed and force that it would produce a "pop" or a "snap" sound that duly would convince all of us each time that we would never want to be in a position to see the soles of his lightning fast shoe. We listened with awe as he bragged that he had sent many lesser beings to the hospital and that he could take on several toughs at the same time; no challenge was too big or too scary for El Rafa.

Even though he evidently had a lot to gloat about, Rafa never looked you in the eye, for he always seemed to be looking into space as if reading some kind of a script deep within his soul, a script that just urged him towards this violent front as if he really was not sure that he was mad or that the other person really deserved to be intimidated. He was a reluctant *Pachuco*.

I was afraid of Rafa, or rather, I had a healthy respect for his quick temper, although I knew that he probably would not beat me to a pulp like he did his adversaries. In the two years that we spent at The Jacinto Projects, I witnessed many fights between various factions of the local *Pachucos*, battles with chains, bricks, knives, brass knuckles, guns, and bottles; fights which confirmed for me at age nine that the world was basically violent. So violent, in fact, that I was not even sure I would be alive tomorrow or next week., Yet I could never even tell my mother that, for subconsciously I felt that she was not a source of safety or security. Maybe that is why we raggedy kids drifted towards Rafa; he represented the violence that we were growing up with within our families, although he never made good on his threats against us and never once harmed any of us neighborhood cowards. Next to him we almost felt at home, with all his talk about maiming others, but it was talk which addressed the violence we were all experiencing in our miserable home lives. It was comforting just looking at him as he tried to talk with his ever-present cheap cigarette hanging from the side of his mouth while he squinted his eyes to avoid the irritation from the smoke and compulsively alternated between combing his greasy hair every few minutes and checking his trademark shoes to make sure that they had not the slightest smudge or speck of dirt.

For two years we saw Rafa, then we saw him no more. He never again came to his usual corner, which was rather uneventful without him. No one knew what had happened to this *Pachuco* with the curved-up shoes. But even though we never saw him again, we continued forevermore to call his spot "Rafa's Corner."

The irreverent stories Rafa told us awakened in me the desire and courage to venture out to explore more of the projects, at first just one or two blocks from my house, then the entire city of El Paso. Starting at around age eight I was already walking alone several blocks away from our house, but now, at age nine I was literally walking as far away as the 344 Highway, which was about eight miles from our apartment at The Jacinto Projects. Not only that, but I would stay out until late into the night, coming home regularly at around 10 or 11 p.m.

And not a question from my mother. If I was home or if I was not, it did not seem to interest her one bit, for I knew that I could come and go as I pleased, even at age eight! Prior to that I was just too afraid to venture more than about ten blocks from the house. In fact, my mother's total passivity in the area of discipline and rule-setting was about to have even more devastating effects on me as I was beginning to seek more unrestrained freedom to engage in immoral activities.

No Rules, No Discipline, No Love

The Devil would beat us and humiliate us, not only as a pathological form of discipline, but also as a vent for his considerable rage about demons unseen to us. If he wasn't beating us he would simply ignore us, as if we didn't exist. In contrast, my mother *never* beat us, *never* disciplined us, and *never* sat down with us to teach us about ethics, morals, manners, self-discipline, respect, proper boundaries, or self-respect. In our home there were no clear rules about anything, for nobody cared about what the other person was doing.

There was no specific time to eat, for we never knew *if* we would eat. There was no specific time to go to bed, for when we were hungry we would wait for hours at night for the imaginary savior who would bring us that magical meal. In the morning there was no specific time to get up for school, for we would be exhausted from the prior night's vigil staring out the window. We would never wash our hands before eating—when we ate. We never brushed our teeth. Showers or baths were optional, perhaps once a week or less often. We would wear our clothes until they were unwashable; oftentimes we would simply throw them out. Haircuts we got only when we found a careless and half-blind barber who didn't mind our leaving behind a whole nest of crawling lice. Our birthdays were nothing to celebrate, for nobody felt like honoring anybody else. Notes from school were routinely discarded—who wants to read a complaint anyway? We never had any vaccinations for anything, and only by a miracle we didn't come down with any serious illnesses. Who ever heard of life insurance, health insurance, dental care, savings accounts, checking accounts, telephones, cars, roller skates, cameras, radios, vacations, and underwear? We never had any. And the tooth fairy? If she had ever even *dared* to come to our pitiful house, we probably would have raped her and taken her money. Smart that she never did come. And my mother didn't even mind it when I would routinely defecate in the back yard so that I would then be able to play with the swarm of white worms that would crawl out of my asshole. It amazed me that they could live inside me in total darkness and with no air. Or, maybe they were just feasting on the vast quantities of the janitor's semen which I often had inside me.

No clear rules, no discipline, no feelings of entitlement about anything. How pitiful it was. Even when people are poor, good parents can show proper love and discipline in the household, but, sadly, in our case, there was none. Where was my mother's head when this horrible whirlpool was swallowing us all? Didn't she know that children need love, rules, and discipline? What did she do all day long at home? The house was always in total chaos. Why did she let me roam the entire city all by myself, as early as age eight, and even at night? Didn't she know that small children can be abducted, raped, and killed? Why did she not even ask me where the hell I had been when I would show up at home at 11 at night? *What the hell was wrong with this fucking bitch?* Why was she ever allowed to be a mother? Did her stupid parents ever teach her anything about being a mother? Did the bitch know more about spreading her legs than about being a mother? Didn't she see that her passive, non-participatory, out-to-lunch style of being a mother would effectively condemn all her children to a life of addictions, neuroses, dysfunctions, and sorrow? *Someone should have shot this bitch* the moment she conceived for the first time. Someone that incompetent or emotionally impaired had no business bringing children into this world for her own selfish motives. It would have been a mercy killing, for it would have spared the world at least the damage that I, her wretched son, would later come to inflict.

In the case of El Diablo, I can probably dismiss his violent behavior towards us because there never was a requirement that he treat us well or even love us. The major tragedy here was that my mother shacked up with him in the first place. Never have I thought or wished that he had been better, for deep inside me I feel that it was in his *nature* to be such a monster. But, in the case of my mother, I do feel that I had a right to expect decent and proper motherly behavior from her, and that she failed miserably on all counts. It is because I am desperately trying to improve on my mother's parenting legacy that I see her grievous shortcomings, and why I have come to despise everything that she represented in our lives, for only in mercilessly condemning her can I embrace honestly a more moral code of ethics that I can use as a guide in my own parenting. If I loved my mother, or if I simply were to respect her memory now that I am an adult, I fear that this would contaminate my soul to a degree that I may fall into the abyss of her own failure and hence repeat the tragedy with my children. For, contrary to lofty moral systems and legal constitutions, a person's value in society in general is inseparable from his or her behavior towards fellow human beings, and in this regard my mother did nothing of value to make this a better world, unless, of course, we count that she merely gave birth to us all. But then, so easily could a bitch-dog have done the same thing, considering the level of parenting my mother provided.

We have all paid dearly for not having been disciplined at all when we were children, for as we grew into adulthood we all had a strong pathological character with a sense of entitlement concerning our place in society, an entitlement that represented our uncivilized, unsocialized animal self, the untamed self more characteristic of a two-year old, the egocentric self that was never mannered, formed, or trained in our childhood home. Such a self may have limited use in a society with rules and customs, something that all of us at one time or another found out the hard way—when we clashed with the superior forces of society as a whole. It was M. Scott Peck who in his 1979 book *The Road Less Traveled* referred to this condition of the untamed adult as that of a person with an "unsubmitted will." Since our mother never asserted control over us in the form of discipline, we essentially grew up with a strong sense of selfish mission; we had an evil and "unsubmitted will."

But as we entered this miserable stage at The Jacinto Projects, we were lacking in discipline and in conscience, for it was there that I was going to commit an act more terrible than the bludgeoning of the baby chick in San Antonio about two years prior.

Three Dead Puppies

Summers in El Paso were blistering, with the temperature easily reaching 105 degrees for days on end while the sun shone with such intensity that squinting while outdoors becomes second-nature, even in the shade. It was during one of my long, aimless voyages around the city that I was walking next to a large empty dirt lot populated only by diehard mesquite trees. I heard what sounded like some dogs or puppies yelping somewhere in the distance. With an eight-year-old's curiosity, I walked in the direction of the sound, discovering that someone had placed a large box with five small puppies on a large overhanging branch of one of the trees. They had been abandoned there and now they were glad to see me. Yes, they were very happy to see me... Not having my own dog and feeling that this was really a bargain because I was getting something for nothing, I opted to take all five of these critters home with me. For three of them it was to be a fatal change of fortune.

The next day I was playing outside our projects apartment by a large mound of moist dirt that some city construction workers had left on our building's back yard. I dug some caves on the side "of the mountain" and placed each one of the puppies in its own "private" cave. For some reason I felt that it would be fun to cover the entrance of the caves with dirt, effectively sealing them against all air. But this animal torture was only the beginning, for as the puppies began to frantically gasp for air and push their way through the dirt covering the exit from their premature tombs, I became angry or frightened, I cannot remember, but something came over me. How dare they not stay where I put them?! I want them in their caves! Don't they know that? It was then that I reached for a heavy green hoe that the city workers had left behind, and with all my strength I struck one of the puppies with the shiny sharp blade across the neck, severing his little head instantly. Its body just twitched there on the ground, as if he was desperately running while lying down, and dark red blood spurted from the many tubes hanging from where the head used to be. As if that was not evil enough, I then delivered two more heavy blows to the hemorrhaging body, opening raw gaping wounds that showed all the abdominal innards slithering out of the body. My raging attention then quickly shifted to another puppy that had made its way out of the cave; this one too I struck with the massive blood-dripping blade, but not as cleanly as the first.

Consequently the poor animal yelped as he felt mortally wounded by the blade which had cut his chest wide open, revealing its ribs and lungs. Quickly I struck him maybe two or three more times, I can't remember, creating a nauseating carnage that I had not planned on, but finally silencing him forever. As the third puppy made his escape, I thought that maybe I had done enough, I don't know, yet nonetheless I managed to brutally lower the blade one last time, hitting the unsuspecting animal on the back of the neck, closer to the head, and also decapitating him like the first one. This time the unfortunate and headless torso urinated profusely but stopped moving within a few seconds.

The entire brutal rampage lasted maybe one minute and left pieces of puppy bodies over a large area of the dirt mound where it all began, all covered by vast quantities of blood pools everywhere. My clothes, my face, my arms, my torn shoes, and the green hoe—they were all covered or splattered with blood and tissue slowly slithering downward toward the blood soaked ground. I have a total blackout of what happened to the other two puppies. I just know they were not around anymore.

At age eight or nine when I did this, I felt little disgust and no remorse. I quickly forgot it the next day and was ready for more sinister mischief. But today as I review this awful sickness within my soul I feel the true gravity of my actions. From breaking bottles I had graduated to wrist-slashing threats, to peeping through neighbors windows, to desecrating their Christmas trees, to setting fire to a couch, to selling my body for food, to stealing, to bludgeoning a baby chick, and, now, to brutally murdering three defenseless puppies. How sick I was. This awful act definitively changed my status from being just an innocent victim of terribly abusive parents to that of homicidal perpetrator creating havoc on his own. Soon there would be no innocents to cheer for in our wretched home.

It is bad enough that I have to think about those poor puppies who lost their lives because of my actions, yet on top of this my unfortunate fall from grace is what set my conscience against me as an adult, believing that I am no better than the vicious Devil whom I despised, that I turned into a devil myself, *that if one is around filth and evil long enough, one becomes filth and evil and loses the moral ground from which to criticize one's tormentors.* Indeed, this is one of the most bitter ironies and paradoxes of life, one that the intellect recognizes but which the heart tries desperately to reject.

After I had killed the three puppies I continued with my chaotic wanderings all over the city at almost all hours of the day and night, in many ways was the equivalent of getting drunk without the alcohol. I did it mindlessly, just roaming with no particular direction in mind, maybe as a way of getting away from the house of horrors. It was about this time that my baby brother Benito kept falling off the bed, landing on his skull. As vicious as I was becoming at this time, I still felt that it was wrong for a baby to fall onto the floor in that fashion. But my feelings didn't matter, for it continued until the day that he died, alone, at the hospital, because his mother had failed to protect him from the evil forces of the world.

Benito's death did not change anything at all in our household. The beatings continued, the nights were still bone chillingly cold, there was no food as usual, my mother remained a passive creature who had no idea how to run a household, the house was always in total disarray, with clothes thrown all over the place, the lice on every surface imaginable, and the thirsty cockroaches bold enough to crawl onto our lips to suck saliva while we sometimes slept on the floor at night. One would think that a death in the family would have created an opportunity for the parents to reflect upon the direction of their lives, but not here. There was no direction but down to hell.

In retrospect I can see that here at The Jacinto Projects I had already developed an intense desire to torture, mutilate, and kill animals, for by this point I had a history of these activities behind me. And it continued with a pair of pigeons that I had bought for 50 cents with the intent to eat them at home. Instead I took them to one of the empty bedrooms in our apartment (out of our four bedrooms, two were completely empty with no furniture) and fed them to our viciously hungry dog. I recall how I looked with pleasure as the dog's teeth sank into the pigeon's chest and crushed its bones, sapping the life out of the bird. Yet, I did not permit the dog to eat the two birds, instead opting to throw them onto the porch roof to rot. I looked at the bodies daily until they rotted completely.

Then there was this boy my age who lived close by and who happened to have a BB rifle, the pump kind that held 50 BBs in a spring-loaded chamber. He, unfortunately, taught me the art of shooting birds with this rifle, lending me the gun whenever we went "hunting" together. Over a period of about two years we must have killed hundreds of birds, shooting them out of trees, inspecting our kill, and summarily discarding the body on the spot as we prepared for our next kill. He had even invented a more bizarre method of killing birds: he would load a mousetrap, place it on the ground, and then cover it completely with bird seed. As we hid behind some tree, a bird would invariably come to peck at the small mound of seed, and the mousetrap would snap close, crushing the bird's neck with a fatal force. For some reason this did not interest me very much, but he used to delight in seeing the bird go through its last twitches under the tight metal bar.

On another occasion I witnessed what amounted to an execution of about ten pigeons. It began with a group of about four of us boys, all ages eight to eleven. We broke into a nearby chicken-coop housing pigeons and we stole about fifteen of them. As we were near the property line on the way out, the owner came out with a shotgun and fired, I think, above our heads. We ran into the creek area with our hands full, and into a large viaduct under a bridge, with the man about a block behind us. The oldest of the boys made the decision that we were not going to be able to handle all these pigeons under the circumstances, and that we might as well kill them. So we all released whatever pigeons we had while still inside the large viaduct, but the pigeons did not fly away, perhaps because they were in shock over the abduction, or maybe they were disoriented. The three boys with me all had BB rifles, and they began to summarily execute all the pigeons inside the viaduct. In all, about ten pigeons died in front of me. We then continued to run and laughed about it the next day. Pretty sick.

As I recall torturing and killing animals, I cannot help but feel sickened by the whole thing. Only God would be able to forgive me for these terrible acts of violence and injustice towards these defenseless creatures. Perhaps because of these transgressions, now as an adult I never hunt.

El Diablo was still El Diablo: farting in public, never looking at anyone in the eye, changing his clothes maybe once a week, absent most of the day but coming home late at night, just like a vampire, to suck our blood by beatings. On many occasions my sister Ana and I had to search for him literally through all known bars in the City of El Paso whenever there was an emergency at home, only to find him looking at a wall with about a dozen empty Lone Star Beer bottles in front of him. What a pitiful sight.

On some occasions this half-breed worm took me with him to help lug his tools on residential refrigeration jobs, only to spend hours in smelly bars between jobs. During one of these interim periods we were at a sleazy bar in downtown El Paso, and I was seated at a table alone while he was at the bar drinking with other low-lives. There were no families there, only depressed men feigning friendship with similar others. As usual the place was dark, smelled like old spilled beer and urine, and had the requisite cantina music loud enough to make everyone forget about life's miseries. Everybody looked at me—I was the only kid there—but I just looked at all the blinking, dazzling lights promoting Lone Star Beer. Wow, if I drank beer I would have a fun life like all those people in the pictures.

I had been sitting there for about two hours with nothing to do and nothing to drink, when an old man approached me and asked me if I wanted a soda and some corn chips. My eyes lit up with joy at the offer, but this was short-lived since the The Devil promptly came to my table and told the old man that if I needed chips he would be the one to buy them for me. Then the old man, who appeared feeble and was hunchbacked, asked why El Diablo had not bought me anything in the two hours that I had been sitting practically motionless at the table. That must have touched some awful button inside the beast's spine, for The Devil flexed his muscular arm and punched the old man so hard in the stomach that he doubled over and couldn't straighten up for the longest time. The old man supported himself against a table adjoining mine, looking down, grimacing, and barely breathing. Like nothing had happened, the bastard Diablo just walked to his stool, took a long swig of his beer, and slumped to his usual beer-drinking posture. No one in the cantina lifted a finger to defend the old man. I guess they all knew about the ferocity of the beast inside The Devil. Poor old man—he was just trying to help me. He was just one more victim of our Tormentor.

Stealing was another of The Devil's distinguishing fortes. On rare trips to the grocery store he would routinely place packages of food in his pockets, especially tuna cans in his front ones. Soon I learned the lesson and I too would fill my pockets with whatever I could stuff in them. We were never caught, but it got me started on a dishonest practice that only recently did I acknowledge and finally give up. The role modeling offered in our family placed all of us on the road to ruin.

Besides the hunger, the beatings, the animal killings, the stealing, the breaking and entering, the vandalism, the threats to the lives of others by cocky *Pachucos*, the witnessing of many brutal gang attacks, the spectacle of horrific auto accidents due to drag racing on our street, Benito's cracked skull and subsequent death, the laughing funeral, the head shaving, the cockroaches in our mouths, the 12-hour city-wide walks, and the lack of love from our mother—even with all this, there still was room for sex.

By this time it had been about a year since the janitor had had sex with me for the last time, and that had given my anus time to get back to normal size, maybe. It's not that he was being nice by stopping the abuse, but rather that we had moved to a new school district and I never saw him again. It was a relief not to have to deal with long strings of mucus every time that I wiped myself when I went to the bathroom. Yet, I must have had a sign on my forehead which read: "Please Fuck Me." Soon after we had moved into the projects the older boys in the neighborhood started asking me to masturbate them, something that I found rather odd since I did not know much about sex in spite of having had so many encounters with various adults throughout my short years. They wanted me to hold their erect penises and to move them up and down, so I just thought that they could not make up their minds whether they wanted the skin up or down. I was shocked when I saw the first explosive ejaculation that got all that semen all over my hand, but I quickly learned that they had had that in mind all along. So I masturbated these older guys in the bushes, in abandoned houses, behind trees, in cars, in their homes—just about everywhere. It was just a matter of time before they asked me to lower my pants.

With all that experience from the janitor, I knew exactly what each of these guys wanted, although I could not understand why they thought that it was pleasurable or fun. So before long many of the older perverts in the neighborhood were having sex with me on a regular basis. Some of them even had sex with me on a daily basis, some even in our own apartment while my mother was in another room! Incredible but true. I think I was the slut of the neighborhood, for word got around that I could be fucked for free, and guys whom I had never even seen would force themselves on me behind the bushes or behind shacks. My sense of personal boundaries and the right to my own body were so faulty that it never occurred to me that these acts were nothing less than rape. I felt that I had no right to protest or resist, something that my mother and the janitor had taught me so well. It got so bad that the vast amounts of liquidy semen in me was producing chronic diarrhea, but it all seemed so normal to me. Life as always. At least they didn't cut me open like the ones who resisted.

These older boys from the Projects were brutal, violent, and merciless. We all heard of the time when one of the younger kids was sequestered on his way back from school. He was found two days later with half of a broomstick driven into his anus. He bled to death. Nobody ever mentioned who may have done it, and younger kids who naively asked questions had already been killed.

By age ten I had been anally penetrated hundreds of times by several adults and maybe two dozen older boys, and I had performed several hundred masturbations. Totally perverted by then, it was not surprising that I wanted to try some experimentation on my own. This happened with a woman who was about 25 years old.

Her name was Alicia, a babysitter from Mexico. Retrospectively I wonder just why my mother would need a *live-in* babysitter when at this stage she never went anywhere and never did any housework. Well, they were cheap—maybe two dollars per week. On one of the nights when she was staying over, I sneaked into her bedroom (one of the empty ones, with just a bed and nothing else) after I heard her snoring. In a totally daring and careless manner I slowly slipped under the covers with my head towards her feet and I placed my hand inside her panties. For the first time in some years I was again feeling a warm vagina, something that reminded me of my mother. What followed next I can't quite remember, other than that I inserted one finger inside her and that she never woke up, or, that she never indicated that she woke up.

It was incredible that by this age ten I had already done so much in the area of sex. It was incredible but tragic, for it condemned me to many years of terrible sexual addictions that took me a long time to even recognize and acknowledge. That was my reward for using my body for survival.

And poor Alicia! She performed her duties at our home with enthusiasm, yet she had to *starve* along with us. We had minimal furniture, all from the charity Goodwill Store, so badly marred that there simply was no point in dusting it. Besides, we would never, ever, ever even *think* of buying dusting spray. And doing the wash? We wore our clothes for about two to four weeks before changing, so there really weren't that many dirty clothes in the beer box that doubled as a smelly hamper. Cooking? When we had any, Alicia could cook some pinto beans and Mexican rice. Not a back-breaking operation. Taking care of the kids? Not really, we were always all over the neighborhood and we came in only sporadically. And for her valiant efforts Alicia always had problems getting paid on Saturday afternoons, when her workweek was over. The Devil would always find one excuse or other to delay paying her. On several occasions he even accused her of stealing "all" our food. Other times he would claim he didn't even have the two dollars she was asking for, and would promise to cross over into Mexico on Sunday to pay her. He never did.

So one time Alicia asked her mother to come pick her up on a Saturday. When The Devil tried his tricks, Alicia's mother went into a seizure that appeared like an epileptic attack, falling to the floor and foaming at the mouth. Our Mexican *curanderismo* (folk healing culture) beliefs immediately kicked into action, so we knew that we needed some herb or strong spice to bring the woman back from the brink of death. We quickly ran to the store and brought back one garlic bulb (we had only five cents), which Alicia cut in half and then placed in her mother's mouth, jamming it with her fingers against her mother's gums to expedite the absorption of the healing powers. The lady came back to life, Alicia got paid immediately, and El Diablo never again played these dirty games with Alicia's salary.

The Maids from Mexico

This incident with Alicia serves to illustrate a very bizarre practice within our family: Many times, even when we were starving and without electricity for lack of payment, we would have a maid from Mexico who would spend six days a week at our home. Imagine being dirt poor but with live-in maid service! This started when I was about 10 and still at the Jacinto Projects. I believe that Alicia was the first of a long string of maids that, somehow, we located in Mexico. In fact, my mother used to travel just across the bridge to Ciudad Juarez, Mexico, and would spend the whole day there tracking down an available young woman who could agree to a six-day, live-in work-week for slave wages of about $2 per week. Poverty was even worse in Ciudad Juarez than it was in El Paso, so there usually were many young women who would do it at that price. All they had to do was get that valuable green card for work.

Work hard they did, even though there really was no work in the house. We kids were about as disrespectful as they came, flinging insults at the maid from all directions. And, at night, the maid would retire to her smelly, urine-soaked mattress at about 11 P.M., after enduring more insults from The Devil, if he had come home early. One thing that has always been puzzling to me is *what* my mother was doing while the maid was working. My mother had quit her job at The International Hat Company some years prior to our moving to the projects, so she was always at home. But doing what? Nothing. My mother did absolutely nothing while the maid worked from 6 A.M. to 11 P.M., a 17-hour day. Well, my mother *did* look in the mirror and adorn her face, just as she did while baby Benito kept falling head-first onto the concrete floor, inching his way to his tiny grave. Mighty strange of my mother.

Often, the maid took the brunt of our complaints when there was nothing to eat at home. Normal kids from regular families would go running home from school, hungry from a hard day at study. They could raid the refrigerator, full of all kinds of goodies. But not us, for, usually, our fridge had only beer bottles or cans in it. So our maid would try to console our hungry stomachs by telling us Mexican stories, while our mother looked passively, as if simply watching someone else's life in a tragic soap opera unfolding before her eyes.

Our hapless maids had to endure the horrific dysfunction in our family, plus our swarming lice; our unbrushed teeth; no toilet paper; no washing machine; the nightly fights between our mother and The Devil; our total lack of discipline, respect, and manners; our unrestrained foul mouths, neighbor complaints; no radio, TV, or phone; our nightly beatings, no heat in the wintertime, and, sometimes, no water or electricity. Because The Devil would typically use up his weekly wages on beer, oftentimes, we would be getting letters from the electric company and the water utility threatening to shut off services. One time, we went for a stretch of about *four months* without electricity, having to survive with no lights at night, not even candles, and, consequently having to go to bed even earlier. At that point we even had to give up the one gallon of milk that we were getting twice a month because now we did not even have refrigeration. When we got our electricity back, the utility then shut off all our water for about one month. Having no running water to flush the toilet, we had to economize by flushing only after ten uses by pouring water directly into the toilet bowl—water we borrowed in buckets from neighbors. Of course, it did not even put a dent in hand washing or brushing teeth because we *never* did those things anyway. Our maids from Mexico must have thought that they had just joined the family from hell.

Through all of these hardships, maids had to perform their duties and suffer just like we did. Our neighbors were accustomed to our maid always coming over to "borrow" beans, tortillas, salt, sugar, toilet paper, utensils, and even alcohol or iodine when one of us suffered a cut more serious than the usual, as when I accidentally (?) stabbed my brother Elizeo on the lower leg with a kitchen knife. So not only did they have to endure these dreadful working conditions, but they also had to defend themselves against El Diablo who was forever accusing them of eating "all the food" in the house. All the food? The maids became for The Devil a convenient scapegoat for the lack of food in the house and for just about everything else that went wrong. Of course, nothing could be further from the truth, for our maids were always workhorses, performing beyond the call of duty with little or no food. In this respect none was better than a very old lady who worked for us for about two years at another house.

Doña Elena and the Corn Tortillas

She must have been in her 80s—wrinkled, practically blind, skinny as a broomstick, totally toothless, with chalk-white saliva running down both sides of her mouth, hair as white and as thin as fluffy cotton, with strong facial features like those of an Aztec Indian. We ridiculed her, we starved her, we disturbed her in her sleep. El Diablo cursed her, accused her, and cheated her out of her pay. And when on occasion we had flour for tortillas, she would stand next to the kitchen table kneading *la masa*, swaying to-and-fro to keep her balance, as we kids silently got on our backs on the floor and crept under her skirt to see her white pubic hairs reaching out like tentacles through the countless holes in her panties, when she wore any. She had trouble hearing and sensing, so she rarely detected our intrusion, but when she did catch us in the act she would curse us with every known filthy word in the Spanish language. It was OK, it didn't sound as if she meant it. We could tell that her tone of voice was the same unspecific, dissociated one that she used whenever she talked to herself throughout the day.

Unlike our own parents, Doña Elena treated us better and told us stories that taught us important principle such as kindness. *Out of her own miserable salary* she would plan and pay for birthday parties for us kids, complete with *cacahuates* (peanuts), *cajeta* (caramelized milk), *dulces* (candies), *tamarindos* (tamarind candies), and a small *piñata*. She would even give us some moral and ethical advice; we never took it to heart, but it was more than we ever got from the other two adults in the house who posed as our parents. On one occasion my teacher at school gave me the job of finding the Spanish translation for "esophagus," which was difficult since we all knew only "street-" or, more accurately, "gutter-" Spanish. Doña Elena heard of my assignment and offered to buy me a Spanish/English dictionary by the end of the week when she would be going back to Mexico to be with her family for Sunday. Sure enough, the following Monday Doña Elena showed up for work with a small but shiny, brand-new dictionary for me, bought, as usual, with her own money. And I located the translation that I wanted: "esofago."

Not that Elena was a pure saint, for she taught us the rough translations of many dirty words that we, as delinquent as we were, had never heard of. "Chinga tu madre," which literally means "go fuck your mother," we used daily to express our frustrations with almost anything. Elena told us that the translation was "sanamabich." For "verga" (penis) she must have given us about one dozen alternative Spanish words, such as "viznaga" (a long, tropical fruit), "picha", "riata," "la venuda" ("the one with veins"), and "la cabezona" (the one with the big head). Vagina became "la orqueta," and the woman with the big vagina became "la orquetuda." The final lesson consisted of a description of how the "viznaga" is meant to go into the "orqueta" because that is where it belongs. But in the long run Elena was more good than bad in our total development.

One day she never came to work anymore. It is still a mystery. We took it in stride. It didn't matter. We didn't know her address in Ciudad Juarez, Mexico, and she did not have a phone. She walked across the bridge into Mexico and disappeared into the crowds with the hungry faces, never to be heard from again. She was in her 80s back in the late1950s, so I am sure that by now she must lie in some grave unknown, in Mexico. Poor Elena—she never suspected she would be working for the family from hell.

We were so out of control, so ungrateful, so disrespectful, so unmannered that we didn't know how to appreciate her noble efforts for us. Even though she was poor like we were, she used her own paltry salary to purchase things for us, the unappreciative.

Poor Elena, she thought she was getting a decent job when she agreed to work for us, but instead she got a sentence under the domination of a man so evil that she called him, "El Diablo," a name that immediately struck a chord in our hearts and stuck forevermore after that. I clearly remember the day she baptized him with that name.

It was during her first week with us and Doña Elena was taking a drink of water after having swept the house with a leafy tree branch. She was sweaty from the job and from the intense heat inside the house due to the hot aluminum roof, scorching at probably 150-degrees under the Texas sun. Never having anything good to say about anybody, the monster walked in unexpectedly and harshly criticized Elena because she was "goofing off" and making our water bill go even higher. He followed that with a ten-minute tirade about how she was stealing all our food and clothing to sell in Mexico. Doña Elena fired back and said that all he had to do was to get rid of her and no more problems. The scumbag side-stepped her offer and continued with another barrage of paranoid accusations. I don't think she took him seriously, and she did not seem afraid either, in spite of her frail body. He was cursing even as he was going out the door for his nightly cantina binges. After a few moments Elena looked at our mother and at us, with her eyes almost saying, "Why do you take this shit?" But finally she did speak, simply to say, "This maniac is not a father and is not a man—he is the earthly embodiment of Satan—El Diablo! I pray for you." We knew she was right, and from then on that's what we all called him behind his back.

Besides the tragic comedies with maids and other infractions against human decency, there were some bright moments, one of which was my work at school.

While we were living at The Jacinto Projects, all of us attended Jose Cuellar Elementary School on San Eduardo Street, a nearly 100-percent Chicano school with almost everyone speaking Spanish when the teachers were not listening. In spite of my being a terror at home, killing animals in my spare time, at school I had fun for the most part. Sure, I was hungry, my shoes had only half-soles, my pants were ripped, and I smelled like poop and urine most of the time; but I loved learning. Most of all I loved science. All my teachers were always encouraging towards me, treating me like a person, and looking at me with warm, friendly eyes. At this point in my life I was remorselessly killing animals and perhaps on the threshold of irremediably developing a heart of stone on the way to becoming a serial killer later in life. But the love and kindness that I received from all my Mexican-American teachers at Escuela Primaria, and especially at Jose Cuellar Elementary, made me feel that there were good people in the world, that knowledge and learning were noble activities, and that there was hope for getting out of the ghastly home environment I had always known. No, they could not have prevented some of the fatal spiritual damage that our poisoned situation at home was doing, but I do believe that if they had not been there with their warm words of encouragement and their ethical advice, I could have easily slipped into the sinister world of violence and murder. Only in retrospect can I appreciate the enormous value of their actions at a critical junction in my life. Little did they know then that it was not only English, math, and science that they were teaching me; their words would actually save my life and perhaps that of many others. I am eternally grateful for their warmth.

My teachers, with their dedication and encouragement, cultivated in me a fascination with science, especially chemistry. At school I would show off my concoctions of 100 different ingredients, presumably a blend that would kill even the nastiest of Texas weeds or rats, earning me the proud name of "Dr. Poison." I relished that! Even my teachers called me Dr. Poison, in jest. Then I shifted to an area of science that would become my lifelong hobby: electronics.

Voraciously, I read every book on electronics that I could check out from the school library, noting especially the techniques for designing circuits. Soon I was designing my own, using tiny light bulbs, sockets, wires, heating elements, electromagnets, electric switches, and buzzers. Since I never had any money for equipment or supplies, I had to go to the city junk yard to dis-embowel old, broken television sets for parts. Like the *pepenadores* (sifters or collectors of stuff) of Mexico City's colossal garbage dumps, I was a common sight at the top of El Paso's City Junk Yard, sifting through hundreds of pounds of metal to collect the few items that I could use in my electronic projects. Then I would construct project boards, usually old pieces of plywood, with several working circuits such as switched lights, electric motors, telegraphs, electromagnets, and heating wires. One big problem, though, was that I didn't have batteries to operate them, and when I asked The Devil for a little money to purchase size-"D" batteries, he would ridicule me, nastily saying that I was being stupid by working on things I did not know anything about. Those words were typical of the brand of encouragement from that animal who wanted to denigrate everyone around him. But with the same tenacity that I had shown during my battle with the bamboo plant/fishing rod several years earlier, I continued to search for means to obtain some batteries and was eventually able to purchase them with money that I got from selling stolen junk back to the junkyard. It was not an honorable thing to do, but I already knew by that time that if you don't have the money you can still take it if you want it. I had learned that from one of the adult role models in our home.

My teachers liked my working circuits. Mrs. Trasol, my fifth grade teacher, encouraged me to go into science because she felt that I had the ability. It made me feel good. Those were words that never came from my mother's lips, and, of course, I would never expect anything remotely resembling that from The Fiend.

At that time I may have been getting better at working with inanimate objects—things that I could manipulate with my hands and could control, but my social skills, and consequently, my social relations, were appalling. At school I was already extremely shy with all adults, and I could not even bear the thought of approaching a girl to start a conversation, especially if I liked her. My constant companion was a pervasive fear of rejection, that somehow I was so defective and inferior that of course people would have no choice but to reject me. Even one time when I was able to collect enough courage to approach the librarian at the public library, I fumbled. The day before I had asked my friend how to ask in English for a library card, and he said for me to say, "I would like to join." Well, I practiced this phrase many times to ensure that I would ask the librarian appropriately, but on the assigned day I mustered all my bravery and walked up to the pretty blond librarian and I blurted, "I would like to enjoy." She gave me a strange look, so I repeated my request. "I would like to enjoy now." Surely she must have felt I was a nine year old pervert making a pass at her, but she was kind enough to probe to determine what it was that I wanted to enjoy. She gave me the card and a big smile.

My feelings toward my brothers and sisters were definitely abnormal, manifesting themselves as some sort of schizoid detachment most of the time, as when my sister Ana was almost raped by my own "friends" one very humid night at The Projects. Four of my best "buddies" and I were just hanging out around a large boulder which marked the edge of the Jacinto Projects. I was nine, they were about 10-13 years old. My sister Ana arrived there to tell me that my mother wanted me for some thing I cannot now remember. The oldest guy there, Pancho ran his hand over Ana's butt, but she responded quickly by slapping his hand while it was still on her behind. She had innocently arrived there in her blue-and-green, flared skirt we had bought, I think, for about five cents at a second-hand store, and she was also wearing a solid yellow blouse. Well, Pancho did not like that Ana slapped his hand since he was the macho man of the group and this would be considered an insult to his masculinity—his definition of what it means to be a real man in the projects.

He grabbed my sister and ran his hand up her skirt, in the process of which she fell to the ground—almost like a signal for the other miscreants to join in like a pack of wolves. All four of them worked cooperatively to lift her skirt and started to lower her panties as Ana wrestled as best she could. And what did I do? I just stood there as if I were watching some movie. Lucky thing that a man walking his dog came upon this scene and shouted at them to stop. Their eight hands were already concentrated on my sister's pubic area like the eight coordinated tentacles of an octopus zeroing in on a prey, but the man's shout made them all stop. Ana quickly got up, raised her panties and ran home crying. I did not feel one bit of empathy for my sister, or revulsion at the four hoodlums who attacked her.

How sick of me to then join them in going to the store to buy sodas after the attempt was abandoned. I had failed to protect my poor eight-year-old sister. What's wrong with me?!

It hurts me deeply now to admit and to consider that on many occasions when I was lucky enough to obtain food somewhere in the neighborhood, I would bring it home and eat it all by myself as my starving brothers and sisters eagerly surrounded me but quickly realized that not one morsel would go into their waiting mouths. Their hollow eyes and the hopeless look of their little faces now haunt me, for they left an indelible mark upon my soul. They just wanted a little piece, their stomachs were chronically empty, they thought I would share, but they did not even complain. They just gave me that empty look of resignation, of hopelessness, of death, of desperation, of having given up on anyone really caring about them. I wolfed down all my food and shared nothing with them. In this respect I acted more like a starving dog defending his bone against all real and imagined threats, even against the innocent looks of its own siblings. How could I have been so devoid of any compassion for these innocent and hollow faces, my hungry brothers and sisters? I clearly did not belong to the human race.

The sad conclusion is that in our pathetic situation we each had to function on a survival basis with no room for love. My brothers and sisters and I acted like vicious dogs who just happened to have been born into the same litter. The damage to our spiritual siblinghood was so profound that even as adults we have not been able to repair it, in spite of earnest attempts. We cannot now put into our relationships what should have been there as we were all growing up together. There clearly is no substitute for a childhood filled with security and love.

Things just kept getting worse. Whenever all of us went out with our mother and would return to our apartment my mother would embark on a 30-minute check of the entire premises by looking under all the beds, behind the bureau, in the closets, behind all doors, behind the refrigerator, and she would repeat this about three times to make sure there was no intruder, It seemed rather odd to me at that time, but now I realize that my mother felt extremely anxious and insecure, perhaps even compelled by her paranoia. She even had the bizarre habit of always referring to my sisters as "my little virgins," which at that time I thought meant that she felt that they were close to God. Every few days she would ask them if they were still virgins; my sisters were nine, six, and two years old. As an adult I can only conclude that my mother may have had severe anxiety or an obsession related to virginity, maybe as a result of her having been sexually abused, which I suspect may have been the case.

Fights between my mother and The Devil continued unabated, as they had for years, only now police were coming to our house regularly, maybe because the neighbors called them. It became routine for my mother to request that the police remove El Diablo from our home, something that was ugly to witness several times per week. The Devil and my mother would give each other hateful looks that should have been reserved only for Satan and his followers, maybe because she felt emboldened by the presence of the El Paso Police Department in our house, and he because he felt emasculated by his humiliating and forcible removal by the police. In the very short run, the presence of the police in our house was a relief for us all, for we knew that for that night at least we could sleep without the monster coming at all hours to beat us up. Yet, in the long run this slimy mucus became more violent, more ruthless, more abusive, more drunk. Since he did not love us, and since he knew we didn't care if he dropped dead anytime, why didn't he just run away from the house and leave us alone? He hated my mother, he despised us all. We would have been so happy if the Earth would have simply swallowed him up for good. Maybe his carcass would have turned up as black coal a million years later, at last providing humanity with a benefit instead of just heartache.

And so for years we kids grew accustomed to the police coming ever so regularly to our malevolent home, wearily taking away this parasite who also had adapted to the routine. What a pitiful revolving door this had become. But, the end was near, for my mother felt she had to go to see the doctor for a suspicious feeling in her breast. Even though each of us kids had already suffered enough for several lifetimes, we would still suffer a lot more. A lot more.

Grip of Death at her Breast

I was there with my mother when the doctor told her that the lump in her breast was cancer. She was 35 years old, I was 11. It was 1956. She took me to the appointment as her little husband. The sensation that I had in my stomach was one of the ugliest I had ever felt up until then, even considering that we had lived through just about every depravity known to mankind. As we walked out of the doctor's office onto Spruce Street, right in front of Escuela Primaria, we both were silent, for we knew that walking with us was *la muerte*, the spirit of death that Doña Elena had warned us against. And why not? Everything bad was always happening to us, so this was more of the same, I thought. I blacked it out, like I did all the penises that had ever attacked me, and I felt better.

Nobody in our family had ever had any decent medical care. No checkups, no dentist appointments, no regular gynecological exams for my mother. Nothing. And I do not know how it was that my mother was able to even see a doctor for this lump in her breast, for I believe that she had delayed it as long as possible, until even by our low standards it became a matter of urgency. As we were walking east on Spruce Street, my mother stopped and looked at me with tears in her beautiful green eyes. She squatted in front of me and gave me a look that I had never seen before, almost like saying goodbye. In her heart she must have known that our days together were numbered, that she did not have much time to live, that her insufferable and agonizing life would soon be over, that all of us would soon be left essentially parentless—out in the jungle at the mercy of the wolves. This life-and-death eye contact with my mother in 1956 was probably the only meaningful spiritual experience that we both shared in our short time together. Tragically for both of us, our minimal life was also coming apart at the seams in other ways.

Midnight Raid by Social Services

It must have been just a few weeks after my mother was diagnosed with breast cancer that our family suffered an upheaval that was traumatic even for our hardened hearts. Evidently someone must have called the El Paso County Child Welfare Department (our local version of "Child Protective Services") for sometime in 1956 the Sheriff's Department came in the middle of the night to forcibly take all of us kids out of the house. The Devil was out drinking as usual, so we were there alone with our mother. As my mother let them in through the front door of our Projects apartment, I already had a very uneasy feeling that these men and one woman were not here for any happy reason but to perform some kind of duty. Their stone cold faces and business-like tone of voice announced to us that something serious was about to happen. They mumbled something about a court order authorizing them to remove all of us kids from the house, something that had to be done that night. We all understood right away that they wanted to take us away, and the wailing started. As bad as the beatings and the hunger had been, we all wanted to stay in our home with our mother. As bad as my mother had been, we would not have traded her for the best meal on Earth, nor for the most comfortable bed, nor the most beautiful bicycle, or for anything that these strange people with the unfriendly faces came to offer us that terrible night. We screamed, we wailed, we cried, we spit, we punched, and we kicked as we tried to hold on to our mother for dear life, but the Sheriff's Gestapo was obviously trained in this type of "social service," and they were able to forcibly disentangle our arms from the death grip that we had around our mother. Didn't they see that we preferred her to anything that they had waiting for us? Didn't they see that in the supposed act of ostensibly trying to "help" us that they were inflicting traumatic pain? And didn't they know in their hearts that as bad as things were, we all much preferred to be at home with our mother? We all fought them with fury, but we were too weak and too small for them. The bastards had guns, and if I had gotten hold of one, I would without hesitation have blown all of them away because in life we had nothing except the comfort of a familiar and passive face, the face of our mother, and now, these presumptuous sons of bitches were coming into our hellhouse to take us to a "better place." Fuck them! Fuck the judge who signed the order! And fuck the entire El Paso County Child Welfare Department, together with all its shitty social workers who recommended this course of action!

What's a "better place," asshole mother fuckers? If I could only have grabbed your automatic pistol, believe me, I would have emptied the entire clip into your heads. No survivors, no prisoners. You'd all be dead. Never again would you be allowed to do that, you son-of-a-bitch asshole cocksuckers. Fuck you and your mother-fucking condescension.

Those incompetent social workers! Did you mother-fuckers ever even come to see us at our house? No you didn't, shitheads. And even if you had, what was the immediate danger and risk that we were in? Did you know that we had been living in these conditions for 10 years? I bet you didn't bother to check, you incompetent assholes. Where was the emergency that required immediate removal of all of us from our home in the middle of the night? Well, WHERE THE FUCK WAS THE EMERGENCY? There was none! There was no emergency that called for immediate removal! So what the fuck did you think you were going to accomplish by forcibly taking all of us away from our mother? And did you stop to consider with your maggot brain what the DOWNSIDE was of taking this kind of action, or did you ignorantly think that there was only good in it but no risk, no downside? You incompetent sons of bitches! If you had even bothered to have done a professional social work evaluation of our family, you would have found that the biggest risk and the biggest abuser in our family was your partner in incompetence, the lowly worm Merengueno Zalmar, alias The Devil, alias Lucifer. My mother was essentially *neglecting* us, something that you could have remedied by having given her counseling, and by taking The Devil away. *If you truly wanted to help our family you would have taken The Devil away and provided our family with in-house social work services and food.* That's it. Why the fuck did you have to appeal to the Court for removal of us from our home? In your own limited understanding of things, you fuckers do not realize how much damage you did when you asked for our forcible removal from our mother. That was the *only* thing that we as children felt comfortable with. Never will you receive a "thanks" from me for the "help" that you gave our family. Instead I simply say, "Fuck you and your own mothers forever. And stay away from me for if I ever see you on the street I will kill you."

That fucking blind judge. And what the fuck did you think you were doing listening to incompetent "social workers" (euphemism for the social intruders, the family patrol, the welfare Nazis), making momentous decisions about peoples' lives? Scum like you are basically power-hungry flunkies who discovered that they didn't have what it takes to be successful attorneys, so instead they opt to just sit on their ass all day, pretending to know the "truth" and the "law." So you were in family court, eh? What's the matter, flunkie, you don't have what it takes to tackle the real issues in corporate takeovers or in constitutional law? Naw, you prefer to pick on women and children, right? When those good-for-nothing social workers (intruders) came before you with a petition for you to authorize the forcible removal of us kids from our mother's side, did you ask them if there were other, less intrusive alternatives? Did you ask them if we children could be helped while still at home? Did you ask them about the nature of the "emergency" that demanded that we be removed immediately? Did you ask them if they had talked to our family to suggest immediate corrections to our neglect and abuse, with subsequent further intervention if change was not forthcoming? Did you ask them if they were *trained* and *licensed* to work with children and families, or if they were just volunteers with absolutely no social work training whatsoever, as was the case with most "social workers" in the El Paso County Child Welfare Unit? Did you ask them about possible emotional trauma to us kids from the proposed middle-of-the-night forcible removal from our home? And did you ask them what the fuck the plan was going to be to keep all of us kids *together* after our forcible removal, so that the *separation* trauma would not be compounded? You know what? I bet that you are such an asshole that you didn't even think of these questions because you yourself don't know the first thing about these family issues. Go fuck yourself, Judge, and keep picking on defenseless women and their children, you sick fuck.

The Sheriff's Gestapo Squad in El Paso

Like the vampires, the cockroaches, the moles, and unexpected diarrhea, you came in the middle of the night to do your shitty work, or rather, your foul deed. I know you like this macho bullshit about carrying a gun to do your work, but if it wasn't for the fucking gun, your word and orders wouldn't be worth shit. You basically want to bully people, to be in control, to be in charge, to have the upper hand in all social encounters, but since you have all the backbone of a larva, you don't have the courage to admit this to yourself and to others, so you have to use the convenient front of "upholding the law" in order to do your dirty work. Well, fuck you. You came into our house in the middle of the night and forcibly pried our arms and hands, which were practically knotted around our mother. For what reason? To "uphold the law"? What's the matter, fuckheads, don't you have your own personal opinion or insight about the shit work you do? Didn't it *feel wrong* that these children you came to "help" did not want your type of violent help? Didn't it feel wrong that these children were screaming and sobbing uncontrollably, not as a result of physical pain, but as a consequence of the horrific terror you were deliberately inflicting? Didn't it feel wrong that you had to forcefully pull their little arms as they were tied around their mother? Didn't it feel wrong that you had to physically restrain my mother's arms so that she could not hold on to us? Didn't it feel wrong that you literally dragged these young, wailing children out of their house and into the night, into a horrific unknown worse than a nightmare? Didn't all that feel very wrong? I bet that, deep down, you are so fucking authoritarian that you are totally blind to the parallel of what you did to us that fateful night and what Hitler's Brown Shirts used to do to German citizens in the middle of the night. All with the blessings of the fascist El Paso Judge.

Law or no law, social workers or no social workers, the FACT is that all of you mother fuckers raped and traumatized all of us children by forcibly separating us from our mother, who, in spite of all her own faults, still gave us more familiar security than any fucking alternative home which you assholes could ever provide. You can shove your assistance not up your ass but up your mothers' asses. As I said, you were lucky that I was not able to grab your pistol, for I would have shoved it in your mouth and blown you away. And thanks for your help, you Nazi worms.

One by one, they took us kicking and screaming into the darkness, our loud wailing causing neighbors to turn lights on and peek nervously through covered windows. They put us in two vehicles which had already been parked conveniently near our apartment, while other Sheriff Nazis kept looking at the neighbors' windows. I was feeling terror and panic: Where were they taking us? Could we trust that they were not going to harm us? Were they also going to rape me and my brothers and sisters? Were we going to another city? Were we being kidnapped? Why did they come at night? Were they going to deport us to Mexico? Were they going to put us in jail? Were they going to hit us with their black sticks? Did they bring guns because one of them planned to stay behind to kill our mother? Were we ever going to see our mother again? This was a night of terror as we had never experienced before in our miserable lives. In the name of social work, they destroyed the only semblance of security that we had left in our mutilated hearts. It was an unprecedented invasion of our home—no one ever had broken in and forcibly carried us children away. Our spirits died after that.

The total blackness of that night as we were driven away by complete strangers in those two vehicles was matched by the extreme terror and anxiety which I felt in my empty stomach, my throat, my weak legs, and in my lungs, which seemed to be pumping air in and out real fast. Throughout all my years, I had been used, abused, neglected, and despised. Personal boundaries I had none, but THIS SOCIAL-SERVICES-SPONSORED TERRORIST ACT AGAINST OUR FAMILY FELT LIKE AN EXTREME RAPE OF OUR SOULS, something from which none of us kids ever recovered. In our hearts, we all felt we were on the brink of death as we were taken away in those government vehicles. All our lives we had lived with abuse and extreme deprivation. This "intervention" by the Social Services Nazis of El Paso, Texas, compounded, in a very horrifying way, the damage that we had already sustained over the years.

Eventually we came to a small house that I sensed was in the *Las Lomas* (the hills) area of El Paso, a neighborhood several economic steps above ours. A gringa lady came to meet us at the door of her house, and we all were shoved in. Still in a state of shock and terror and damp by our urine, we all were given blankets to place on the cold floor so that we could sleep on them. The Nazi Squad then left. That night, we all slid in and out of nightmares, with horrible skeletons chasing me in my dreams and quiet whimpering the only way that we could communicate with each other. Was our mother still alive?

In the morning, we woke up earlier than the lady (?) of the house but remained on the floor, asking whispering questions about our uncertain fate that day. And then it happened: *The woman who was supposed to be our foster mother came running into the room where we lay, with a big paddle in her hand, and proceeded to hit us repeatedly on our buttocks for whispering and disturbing her sleep!* Lord God help us! The Unlicensed Social Workers, the Asshole Judge, and the Sheriff's Nazi Squad "rescued" us from our home to bring us to this new house with the foster mother from hell? We cried and our bodies writhed from the stinging pain of the heavy paddle on our thinly protected buttocks, adding to our terror and panic: they didn't plan to help us—they wanted to torture us. Clearly, Lord, there is no justice on this Earth. Our tormentors—they want to kill us, so we need to kill them all first! Let's find a knife, a hammer, a brick!

By late afternoon of that first day with the gringa bitch foster mother from hell, we went from feeling extreme panic to not really feeling much anymore, and our faces were pretty blank. We couldn't even talk to each other as a wave of numbness covered the terror on our hearts. I suppose we were just shutting down from our inability to tolerate any more pain and terror meted out from these do-gooders who had no idea how to deal properly with children. We were numb, we were in terror-shock. Imagine, the bitch foster mother spoke only English, while we spoke mostly Spanish, quite an unfortunate situation that produced for us even more of a feeling of detachment and stomach-churning alienation. We felt spiritually, socially, and culturally lost. We were sick with pervasive anxiety. Who the fuck planned this shitty intervention anyway? Who was the sadistic monster who authorized it?

The next few days are a blur for me; we stayed mostly indoors, with no word about the fate of our mother. None of us knew where she was or if she was still alive, and our sadistic captors did not provide any information. On about the third day of our trauma the incompetent Nazi social workers showed up again, and they told us that it was time to "take a little ride." I know now that the only other distinct group of people that uses that line are Mafia henchmen, an appropriate parallel to these detestable social workers/manipulators. Of course we were suspicious, for these were the same tormentors who had *kidnapped* us three days prior (with the blessing of the State), and now they were practically saying, "Trust us." No thank you, but you can just go fuck yourselves. We actually had little choice here, for it was not as if we wanted to stay with the blond bitch with cigarette breath who whacked us within five hours of our arrival.

Chief of the Goon Squad was Mr. Timoteo Garza, the one who personally told me that I should get in his car because we would be going for a ride. My brother Elizeo was directed to join me, but Ana, Tencha, Elsa and Tomas were directed to another vehicle, and I would not see them again for another six months. Mr. Garza drove the car through streets which were not familiar to me in spite of my being knowledgeable from all the aimless walks that I had taken in the two years prior. We came to Park Street, drove west, and turned south on Main. Within two minutes we were in a poor neighborhood like the ones that I was familiar with, and we came to a stop in front of a modest white house with a dilapidated and sinking front porch. Mr. Garza had lied to me—this had not been just a ride. I knew immediately that this was to be our new foster home—the white house on Main Street.

Chapter Five

The Foster Home: Food, Bed, and Daily Rapes

Mr. Garza introduced my brother Elizeo and me to the couple who were now our foster parents, although I still did not know why I needed them in the first place. They seemed friendly, in their 40s, with the beefy short woman clearly in control of the house, something that was atypical in the late 1950s, and especially in a Mexican-American family. He was tall, quiet, certainly deferential to the lady of the house, and very slim. Did they have food shortages here too? She, on the other hand, appeared well-fed, was talkative, had short legs, and seemed to be directing all activities in the house as she simultaneously spoke to us. They both had very strong Mayan Indian features, thick, black hair, high cheekbones, rough facial skin, prominently curved noses, and very little facial hair. Although I did not want to be here, I sensed that this Mayan-looking couple was many times better than the puta gringa from *Las Lomas* with the heavy paddle and pungent dragon breath.

Elizeo and I were not the only kids in the house, for in and out kept coming what appeared to be maybe three older teenage boys, and another boy my age. Like us, they were foster kids. Undoubtedly kidnapped like we were, I thought. But they did not bother introducing themselves to us.

They showed us all the rooms of the house—I think there were three bedrooms, all very nice but too clean. Did they spend all their time cleaning everything in the house? Were they going to get mad at us if we made a mess? The kitchen! It had spoons, forks, pans, plates, cups, and other tools I did not even know existed! Immediately I noticed that all the forks, spoons, and knives had the same flowery design on them. Why would they want the *same* picture on all their silverware? Our silverware (?) at our mother's house had many different designs, no two utensils having the same picture, I felt. Some of the equipment in that kitchen was odd looking, and I could not imagine what in the world they would use it for. So I kept asking questions about these interesting objects, while my brother Elizeo followed me closely behind. And the cupboards! When the lady opened the little cupboard doors I saw tons of foodstuffs, cans and boxes that made me feel that this was like a little supermarket *inside a house!* The kitchen alone made me feel slightly better and made me forget, for the moment, about my mother and where she could be at that moment.

After the detailed tour of the entire house we then were taken to the backyard, where to our left was a wooden shack used for storing gardening equipment, and to our right was a large chicken coop, with maybe about two dozen fulltime resident Mexican chickens which I was told would be depending on me for daily feedings. That I did not mind, although I wondered to myself how this family had abundant chickens that were placed in a cage and not eaten right away. In my view of things, if I had a chicken I would want to eat it right away—there would be no need to build a chicken coop or cage to contain it. Through the years I had wounded and captured many, many pigeons, and there had never been time to build a cage—we ate them as we got them. I would have to figure out a way to restrain myself from eating these happy chickens as I fed them.

The neighbors also seemed friendly. Their front and backyards had the usual Mexican adornments: wrought iron burros holding pots with beautiful arrangements of *rosas, margaritas,* and *gladiolas,* plastic pink flamingos leisurely strolling on very green grass, assorted ceramic figurines in every imaginable corner of the yards, wooden pergolas from which hung numerous flowering plants surrounded by massive grapevines, nicely tended gardens for tomatoes, carrots, summer squash, peaches, figs, and pomegranates, and the traditional Mexican red-hot chili pepper plants scattered about. We all knew to respect those! I also spotted a *perico* in a cage; that green South American parrot would emit an awful squawk. Why would anyone tolerate such a nuisance, when a BB shot would silence the pest right away? But, the entire picture was nice. I am sorry now that my mother was not there to enjoy it with us kids.

Feeling that he had done his part, Mr. Garza started to leave, informing Elizeo and me that we would be living here, although I do not remember if he said for how long, or if we would see our mother again. Maybe I blocked it out. So he left and I got my chance to further explore the premises. My foster

mother showed me the bedroom that I would be sharing with my brother
Elizeo, giving me a bag with all our clothes from my mother's house. It wasn't
much: maybe two shirts, two pants, and an old calendar that I had played with
at home. Had my mother packed this bag? Did the Gestapo Social Services
treat her well? Had they threatened her about not again seeing her children?
Had they accused her of anything? I'll never know the answers to these and
one thousand other questions about my mother.

In spite of the trauma of forcible separation from my mother, I believe that
I was doing OK on this day three of not seeing my mother, maybe because
I was good at blocking out the chronic pain in my life. The foster parents
were treating us well, I liked the comfortable and clean bed with sheets and
a blanket, I liked all the nice food, especially the Mexican *galletas morenas*
(brown cookies) that our foster mother gave me with hot oatmeal, something
I had never eaten in my life. They were nice, but the older teenage foster boys
living there had already made plans for me.

Pervasive Sex at the Foster Home

The nice feelings didn't last long, for on the second day at this foster home
on Main Street, I was sitting on the porch that afternoon, when Julio, one of
the other foster teens who was about 17, must have read the "Please Fuck Me"
sign that I apparently had on my forehead, for he told me to accompany him
to the shack in the backyard because he wanted to show me the gardening
equipment. I was 10 or 11, stupid but no so stupid, so I only half believed what
he told me and went with him to the shack. Once we were inside he shut the
door and asked me to lower my pants. I knew immediately that he wanted to
fuck me, and as usual, I did not resist. He bent me over, placed some saliva
on his erect penis, and inserted it in me. It was not traumatic, I was used to
it, I expected it, I liked it, I needed it. I knew from experience that when they
fucked me they would not hurt me in any other way. But he introduced another
dimension to this sexual perversion. He asked me if I liked all the *los mecos*
(sperms) that he had just put in me. I was no stranger to sperms, having been
given gallons of it by the janitor at Escuela Primaria and maybe barrelfuls
more by the derelicts at The Jacinto Projects. So I replied to him that, yes, of
course I liked his sperms and wanted even more. What originally had been
so repulsive to me was now almost like a drug, an addiction, a necessity. It
had become normal for me to have sperms in me; it was not normal not to
have it. I was so sick. I was so desperate. I was so lost.

Just as with the violence that had been perpetrated against me throughout
all my life and which I came to pathologically embrace as part of me, as when

I killed pigeons and decapitated the three puppies, the same perverse psychological process had taken me from an innocent victim of child sexual abuse to becoming an active participant asking to be abused sexually. As an adult I could have taken the high road of moral indignation and condemned my sexual abusers, yet with so much sexual activity in my short 11 years I came to see these acts as being mine, coming from my soul, desiring them, feeling good about them. Somewhere along the way between licking my mother's slit at age four and getting dozens of penises in my anus by age eleven, I had ceased to resist and instead began to enjoy, to need, to crave. The toxic shame comes from my conscience castigating the act that my inner soul remembers only too well as having been so pleasurable. How is it possible for it to have been pleasurable if it was also wrong? And therein lies the sickness: As in violence, I am divided within myself so that I cannot present an unequivocal condemnation of the rampant sexual activity that was forced upon me as a child, for as I morally begin to condemn it, my soul reminds me of the pleasure. There is no way out, the contamination of my soul is profound. My conscience was completely compromised.

After Julio finished with me he said that he would tell the other guy, Roberto, age 19, to come and take his turn. I waited in the shack with anticipation. Roberto came and asked me to lie on the floor on my stomach, which I gladly did. As was standard procedure he lubricated his penis with globs of saliva and then rammed it in me. He said that Julio had told him that I wanted sperms, and I replied that, yes, I did. As he continued inside me he told me that he would be glad to pump all his sperms into me, for they would make me strong like him, and that I would never fear anyone anymore. I remember shamefully that it felt so good as his penis pulsated deep inside me, releasing hopefully gallons of his precious fluid. I wanted it. I wanted to be strong, as he promised. I felt protected by his strong arms. Forgive me, Lord, for I am sick. How did I ever become this perverted?

This first encounter with Roberto in the shack on day two established a pattern that would continue for the entire duration of our six-month confinement. Almost daily he would motion for me to go with him to the shack for more of the same. In fact, when I was having a bad day with too much anxiety or fear due to threats of bodily harm from the neighborhood *Pachucos*, I would ask Roberto to fuck me and for him to fill me up with his semen. It would always make me feel better to know that his penis was inside me and that at any moment it would explode, sending streams of his sperm inside me. As sick as that now sounds, it is the truth I must live with. I believed him. How disgusting, what shame, how low, how despicable. I was no longer human, I had begun my own metamorphosis into some kind of depraved fiend driven by insatiable sexual desires and a selfish, loveless attitude toward life. Indeed, I should have been killed at this time.

Sex? Not only in the shack, but in many other locations he would fuck me daily. Daily. There was a wooded field the size of one square block nearby, providing excellent cover for a cardboard mattress that he had assembled under the bushes. On many occasions when we went on errands out of the house he took me there for sperms. Over the six-month period that we were in that foster home, I suppose that Roberto must have had sex with me about 170 times, having missed only about 10 days in that period. But he was not the only one who was doing it to me.

Julio continued to want his share of my body, having sex with me on the average of about three times a week, and sperming me above and beyond the quantities that I already had in me from Roberto. Just like the situation with the men and the hoodlums who had sex with me at The Projects, here I also had chronic diarrhea from the massive amounts of semen in me, considering that I was getting it faster than I could expel it when I went to the bathroom. One time our foster mother's older daughter, who had come to the house for a visit, caught Julio while he was on top of me. She just walked away from the room, and nothing ever came of it. For sure she would tell the foster mother, we thought, but nobody ever said anything about it. It was just about that time that Julio passed me on to Kike, the 24-year old man who was the son of our foster parents and who still lived at home.

Nobody knew it then but Kike was a drug addict who regularly went to Ciudad Juarez, Mexico for his drugs. He was a burly man with incredible arms that could break anything, if he wanted. Years later he would be coming back home in the bus, looking very sick from his last visit to Mexico, and collapsing and dying in this same house. But now Julio told Kike about me.

Kike had been friendly to me in the few days that I had been living at the foster home. One day he motioned that he wanted to have sex with me, so I said yes even though he was a huge man about three times my weight. He took me to an abandoned smelting complex not far from the house, and he located a secluded area in one of the smelters. When he took out his penis I got scared because it looked to me much larger than even the janitor's: It was too thick and incredibly long. By that age I had seen dozens of penises and knew that this one was too large to fit in me. Even though I complained to him that I thought that it would hurt, he insisted on at least trying. As soon as I felt the head of his penis start sliding in I screamed in pain—as distended as my anus was from the hundreds if not thousands of penetrations, it still could not accommodate Kike's mammoth organ. Luckily for me, he decided to stop when I started crying from the pain.

I was so glad that he was not going to force himself on me that I readily agreed to masturbate him when he asked me. Since it was so large I had to use both hands to hold it and to move it up and down. Then I went to a new low, for he also asked me to suck it. I hesitated for a few seconds, then I put my mouth around the head of his penis and sucked it for about one minute. Promptly I then told him that I really did not want to suck his penis, but that I would continue to masturbate him if he wanted. Of course he said OK. In no time his organ started pulsating and he discharged massive amounts of semen all over my hands. It looked like a cup of milk had spilled all over my hands and his crotch area. I just wiped my hands with a piece of an old newspaper I found on the floor of the smelter. They were still gummy from the sperms, but there were no more newspapers. It was a sticky mess.

As with Roberto and Julio, my sessions with Kike were regular throughout the six months in the foster home. We met secretly at the smelter about three times a week, and sometimes he would even give me a dollar if I made his penis spurt more semen. He liked that. During one of our sessions he asked me if I masturbated myself. Even though I had done it for other men and older boys many times, it had never occurred to me that I similarly could enjoy moving my own penis up and down. That night I decided to try it on my own.

Under the covers I played with my penis but nothing happened. I was 11, had never really masturbated (but had started playing with my penis at around age five), and had never had an orgasm. Didn't know they were possible. I decided that the next day I would give it another try. At school I went into a stall in the boys' bathroom and proceeded to play with my penis until I got an erection. I was so proud that my own penis could get up just like the hundreds of other penises I had masturbated. But its erect size disappointed me, for in comparison to Kike's massive organ, mine looked like a pencil next to a baseball bat. For several minutes I furiously moved the foreskin up and down, but nothing happened. Yet I was not about to give up, for I knew that a penis had to be stroked repeatedly until it decided on its own that it would release the sperm. After about 15 minutes I started feeling a sensation within my body that I had never in my life felt before. My torso trembled, my legs locked around each other, and I felt a concentrated sense of tickles inside my body near my penis. I felt a fantastic wave of pleasure. My penis then pulsated, just like the ones that belonged to the big guys, but no semen came out. I was too young to have sperms, I thought. But it had been a wonderful experience that left me drained and short of breath. Finally I understood why those men and assorted punks wanted me to masturbate them. I knew then why they all had been fucking me since the first grade. In a very sick way it was my first epiphany in life.

After I had discovered that my own penis could be so pleasurable I masturbated more often, and always with nothing coming out from my penis. Once I brazenly masturbated *on a barber's chair, under the cloth, while the elderly barber was cutting my hair*! I figured that he was almost senile and wouldn't notice (he did, for he lifted the cloth to check underneath), and besides, I wouldn't leave a mess for I had nothing to shoot from my penis. Then too, the daily sex sessions with Roberto, Julio, and Kike continued unabated. Together these activities constituted a highly dysfunctional and perverted manner of relating to others, as if it was only through sex that I could relate to others in a safe and non-threatening way. Maybe the perversion had really begun with the cunnilingus session with my mother when I was four years old and we all lived on Lincoln Avenue; or maybe it began with the janitor who trained me by providing food for sex, utilizing the same principle that behavioral psychologists use in the laboratory when they provide food pellets to animals which engage in desired behaviors. After a while it does not really matter that the environment is responsible for the abuse and the pain, for in time one becomes just like the environment, and is thus indistinguishable from it. That is the compounded tragedy of prolonged suffering and abuse, especially for children.

Ironically, my out-of-control sexual behavior really intensified when Social Services placed me in the foster home. They delivered me to a gang of sexual perverts and addicts who preferred homosexual contact with younger boys. How was it that the foster parents never knew of the literally *hundreds* of sex acts that took place on their premises or at relatives' homes? Were the foster parents aware of Kike's drug problem? Was the Social Services Department, and especially Mr. Garza, aware that there were two older-teen, and one adult, sex offenders in the home they were taking me to? Were there other boys my age who had been in the same foster home who had been victimized by these same three offenders? Since Kike obviously thought it proper for him to have sex with an 11-year-old boy, does that imply that Kike himself may have been sexually abused by his parents or by other people when he was a child? Since Kike is now dead we may never know the answer.

Besides this sexual activity that in retrospect I know was damaging sexual abuse, I also had to witness, survive, and endure physical violence. Neighborhoods in El Paso at that time were organized into *Pachuco* fiefdoms symptomatic of the competition and the hatred between Pachuco gangs, resulting in fierce territorial wars. Areas like *El Puente Blanco, La Guada, El Siete, Los Amores*, and *El Cuatro* would battle it out with chains, glass shards, bricks, bats, and guns, sending many fearless and brave *Pachucos* to the hospital or to the morgue. Ruthless teens I knew suddenly disappeared, while days later I would learn that so-and-so had been *filoreado* (or fillet, as one would a fish). On many occasions I was accosted by *Pachucos* while I was walking alone, and only because I was totally submissive, cowardly, and cooperative was I let go without having been hit across the face with a heavy chain or stabbed with their trademark icepick through the heart. Many times I stood there with these criminal misfits in front of me, not knowing if this was the day it was my turn to die. As William Shakespeare wrote in *Julius Caesar*, "Cowards die many times before their deaths." By age eleven I had already learned to expect death at any time. There was no place to hide, no one to protect me. So if a Pachuco kicked or slapped me I just acted meekly and would not protest, for I had seen the ferocity of these beasts when an opponent hits back. Pachucos felt totally justified in obliterating any victim who fought back because, in their view, they were just engaged in a fair fight to the death. In effect, my small size made me a coward, but a live one. Dozens of Pachucos who were real macho are now in their graves.

Even Julio fought, for he would never back down from a challenge, no matter how outnumbered he was, or how much stronger a challenger appeared to be. Once he even fought with his entire arm in a cast from a previous fight with a *Pachuco*, threatening to split the opponent's head open with the hard cast even as his challenger ridiculed him for attempting to fight him though he was temporarily handicapped. Julio put up a fierce and vicious fight with me as the only witness, ending the whole challenge in a draw, in spite of his existing injury. I was so glad that Julio was just fucking me and not pulverizing me like he did his opponents. Disturbingly, feeling his dick inside me was preferable to feeling one of his merciless blows to the face.

While it may seem that it was all sex and violence for me at the foster home on Main Street, there were other things that were normal and pleasurable. At Christmastime it is customary for many Mexican families to do a *tamalada*, a very big event where all the women, family and friends, get together in the kitchen and carry on lively conversation while making Mexican *tamales*. The corn husks are soaked in water for a few hours in advance to make them more pliable. One group of women usually bring the pork, the beef, the beans, or whatever other stuffing to place inside the tamales, the preparation of which will take a few hours. Another happy team will simultaneously prepare the *masa de maiz*, the corn dough that will then be spread thinly on only one side of each individual corn husk. Then the stuffing is placed on the corn husk with the corn dough, and the husk is then rolled up, much as one would roll a French crepe. Now comes the hard part: the cooking. For this a large stock pot is necessary, and it must be large enough to accommodate all the uncooked tamales, unless, of course, cooking two or more batches is no problem. Usually a *molcajete*, the Mexican version of the mortar-and-pestle, is placed upside down at the center of pot, and the tamales are then arranged in a spoked pattern radiating from the *molcajete* center, piling layers upon layers until the entire pot is filled to the top. A small amount of water is added to the pot to provide steam and distribute the heat more evenly. The stock pot is then placed on low heat and allowed to cook for about four hours, during which time *las comadres* (dear friends on a gossip spree) will catch up on whatever conversation they had not finished.

In the years that we lived with our mother we never even got close to having a *tamalada*, but here, at the foster home, I was fortunate to have experienced one—the only one in my life. It was a joyous occasion with lots of friendly Mexican women talking, whispering, cackling, and laughing from the center of their souls while they all worked toward the same common goal. The kitchen was in complete chaos as plates, forks, spoons, knives, meat grinders, garlic presses, various *molcajetes*, tortilla presses, strainers, pots and pans, and perhaps a dozen more tools came out of their hiding places to assist the approximately 15 women in the preparation of the tamales. It was wonderful for me to be there to witness the warm chatter, the friendly cooperative effort, the joy in their eyes, their welcoming smiles, and best of all, the preparation of a massive meal with a seemingly endless supply of ingredients. At that age I felt that this kitchen could prepare *anything* on Earth, with a capacity to feed even an army of hungry people. I was fortunate enough to have lived through a *tamalada*, especially because I had a chance to be in the presence of 15 wonderful women whom I looked at longingly as they went about their business in a motherly way. That was the highlight of my stay at this foster home on Main Street.

For the most part we followed a routine during the week, getting up early, dressing, eating oatmeal with *galletas morenas*, and walking to the school a few blocks away. At noontime we would come home to eat lunch and head back to school after playing a bit. In the evening after hearty suppers we had to do homework, shower, not with soap or shampoo, but *with laundry detergent* to make sure all the dirt came off. Wow! That white powder felt hot on the skin as soon as it mixed with water, yet I don't believe that we suffered any long-lasting effects from it. I can't think of a reason why we had to use laundry detergent to shower, except perhaps that the foster parents felt it was more suited to cleanse the dirty foster kids that came and went through the years.

Overall we had a schedule that we had never had at home, we had a comfortable bed, we had abundant food, including tamales to spare, and there were no beatings in the middle of the night.

Throughout the six months my little brother and I were there, we never saw or spoke to our sisters and brother who had been taken somewhere else; yet, strangely enough, I did not miss them. But that should not have been the case, for the Social Service Unit *should* have arranged for Elizeo and me to have met regularly with our other siblings, especially because this intrusive separation from our home had been so traumatic. That I was not feeling the trauma of separation a few days after the raid on our mother's home may indicate two equally undesirable conditions: (1) that us kids were really not close to each other, and, (2) that I began to repress the pain of the separation almost as soon as it materialized. I know for a fact that I did not feel any obvious separation pain for years until recently when I entered psychotherapy to deal with these childhood trauma issues. As with most of my feelings, these original raw emotions resurfaced, after initial repression, in other forms that came to shape my personality for many years.

As for my mother, she was forced to be out of contact with us for these six months. I can only imagine that she must have suffered considerably even though I believe that she could not have possibly loved us in a genuine, mature, responsible manner. She was left alone with The Devil in that miserable, cold, and damp apartment at The Jacinto Projects, probably staring blankly as life just passed by.

Our foster parents had some relatives nearby who lived in the more backward, wooded area of this neighborhood, an area known locally as *La Ladrillera*, or "The Brick Factory," so called because in the old days there used to be a very prosperous brick building park in the area. All that remained then was the carcass of the dusty industrial complex, providing cover for the wandering illegal Mexicans who, like us when we were living at home with our mother, had to keep a watchful eye for *La Migra*, the Immigration and Naturalization Service, and the Texas Border Patrol. These relatives had a house with a sizeable acreage in the back, full of desert-style shrubs that could survive without water seemingly for years, tumbleweeds, Texas-style, short cacti that attracted turtles with a nondescript, depressed look, and voluminous Mesquite trees, kings of survival in the hot sun with no water. As part of this small hacienda there was the usual assortment of animals that always seemed to be part of these rural households: peacocks, pigeons, ducks, rabbits, dogs, cats, chickens, and a variety of caged birds. For the most part the fun I had with these animals was normal, except for one occasion when I took a long feather and I inserted the pointed stem in the anus of a pigeon that subsequently died as a result. That act of cruelty was equaled if not surpassed when a friend of mine and I threw lighted firecrackers at caged chickens, which immediately picked them up believing they were food. The ensuing explosions blew their beaks off completely, also bringing death. It is evident to me that I had a clear history of torturing and killing animals, something that followed me to this foster home.

Overall I would say that except for the rampant sexual activity, I enjoyed a much better life here than at my mother's home. Chief among the benefits was not having to deal with the hated Devil, slug of the night, cancerous vomit, posing as a human being. In addition, the most important spiritual benefit which I received was my discovery and enjoyment of the *tamalada* with the 15 women whose demeanor and warm faces touched my soul in a very profound manner.

A sad note concerns my brother Elizeo, who of course was living with me. As much as I attempt to recall my activities with him, I am able to remember only a few, insignificant events. Whereas in normal relationships two brothers would have stuck like glue to each other in the face of adversity, Elizeo and I really did not do much together; it was almost as if we were farther apart than strangers in the foster home. Tragically, this spiritual estrangement that we all felt as children solidified through the years, and now as adults we relate to each other probably in a fashion more distant than we do to our own close friends. This has been one of the more durable and malevolent legacies from our childhood in the house of horrors with the parents from hell.

Just as I was beginning to adjust to the new school, Mr. Garza announced to us that we would be going back to our mother, who in the meantime had moved out of The Jacinto Projects and into an extremely modest home in the same general area. It had been six months in this foster home on Main Street, a house where I for the first time in my life felt that I could sleep peacefully, and where I never went hungry. Unfortunately too, this phase in my life solidified my sexual acting out, my perversions, and set the stage for further crimes against humanity.

Chapter Six
Back to Our Home, and Our Mother's Battle with Cancer

The Red House on San Lorenzo Street

All six of us kids were ecstatic to see our mother again, proving, at least for me, that the lack of turmoil about the separation once we were in the foster home may have been due to substantial repression of these uncomfortable feelings. The "honeymoon" that we all enjoyed with our mother lasted several days, for we all were so grateful that she was back that we did inordinate amounts of housework to show her our appreciation. I even wrote my mother a poem, long since lost or destroyed, about how she struggled to feed us and take us out of the "bondage" of the welfare authorities. She, too, was very happy to see us, telling us how she had been forced to go to court and defend herself against neighbors' allegations that she routinely walked totally naked in front of all of her children. While we did see our mother naked, she never did casually walk in front of us with absolutely no clothes on. In light of the ubiquitous sexual abuse that I suffered at the foster home, this alleged act by my mother which attracted the attention of the Social Services Unit may now seem inconsequential in comparison. How stupid of them to feel that their job was to protect us against our mother's naked body! What were these social work morons thinking? The Unit should have known that at one of its homes, if not at many, there were sex offenders ready to assault incoming foster children. My mother's act may have been due to ignorance, but the Social Services Unit's dereliction of duty was also sheer negligence and stupidity.

It was pure joy being with our mother, but unfortunately she also came with the dirt bucket from the city dump, The Devil. My two younger siblings, Tomas and Elsa, about age two, were very happy to see Satan, understandably, for they were too young to realize that the motherfucker was mistreating them too. He was as ugly as ever, with his eye-with-no-eyelid still the centerpiece of his monstrous face. As usual, he still walked to all his refrigeration jobs, for we never had a car, and he refused to take the bus. (The snotface avoided people whenever he could—he thrived in the dark, like the cockroaches.) Too bad our mother couldn't have left this piece of shit behind in the same mound with the decapitated puppies at The Projects.

Our new house was nothing to jump up and down about. It was about one mile from our previous apartment at The Projects, in a neighborhood slightly poorer, since the people around here did not even get welfare assistance. It was a one-bedroom, wood frame house with exterior walls so thin, and adjacent boards not abutting perfectly, that you could see through some parts of the wood and sometimes between the boards. It was about one-fourth the size of our previous Jacinto Projects Apartment, but at least it did not have the killer concrete floors.

But something had happened to our furniture. Even though at The Projects we didn't even have enough furniture to fill two of the four bedrooms, it appeared to me that this red house with one bedroom had *even less* furniture. We basically had a kitchen table, two chairs, one bureau, two folding chairs, a few kitchen utensils, and two beds for a family of eight! What happened to the few other pieces that we had before this?

Outside, the house was painted a pitiful dull red, with wood so rough that we soon learned not to lean against it or even rub our hands across it for fear of getting dozens of splinters into our skin. In fact the house was so poorly constructed that on windy days the support wooden beams would creak, creating an eerie effect on the nights on which we did not have electricity and had to survive on burning wooden sticks for light. No, not in a fireplace for it had none, but in a large aluminum tub we brought into the house. And the back yard was large but had a huge pile of rubbish and junked wood near one corner, which we had many adventures in.

Now that we were all back home with our mother and with our tormentor, it was time to consider what, if anything, the "intervention" by the El Paso County Child Welfare Unit had accomplished. We were still desperately poor, we had no medical care, The Devil was still at home and abusing my mother and all of us kids, we had no food, we still had periodic shutoffs of electricity and/or water for not paying our utility bills, and our mother was still the same detached person who had little fortitude to teach us anything of value or to run a household with six children.

But the fact remains that the Social Services authorities in El Paso traumatized our entire family, especially us kids, for no clear, justifiable purpose: The welfare authorities had done nothing substantial to address our family's real problems, which included the presence of an alcoholic, abusive man in the house, abject conditions of poverty, my mother's inability to exercise proper parental duty and control over her children, the lack of medical and dental care, the proliferating effects of sexual abuse, general family dysfunction, and my mother's worsening condition due to breast cancer. These conditions would have been obvious to any social worker with proper training, yet the Social Services Unit simply took us children by force and did absolutely nothing to alleviate our horrible conditions at home. If conditions at our apartment at The Projects had been so bad, why did they return us kids to an essentially identical situation? Why did they approve of returning six children to a house where eight people were going to share two beds in one bedroom? Why did they not permanently remove the hated Devil from our home? Why did they not assist us with food and money to pay for the electricity, rent, and other necessities? Why did they not provide counseling to our mother who desperately needed it? Why did they not provide counseling to all of us children if they suspected sexual abuse, indicated by their accusations against my mother and her walking around naked? Why did they not arrange proper medical treatment and transportation for our mother, given her cancer diagnosis? If the welfare authorities had done their job professionally, they could have provided our family with timely assistance when we desperately needed it, for we were at a deadly junction in our life together as a (dysfunctional) family. Tragically for us, the "intervention" was instead just traumatic abuse for all of us and failed miserably to help us as we were on the brink of catastrophe. The El Paso County Child Welfare Unit, perhaps out of ignorance or maybe because of negligence, failed us at a critical time, and since we had no knowledge and no resources, we continued on our downward spiral that would come to cost our mother her life and us children unimaginable trauma and psychological damage from the events that followed. In the broad picture of things, the welfare authorities did more harm than good. Fuck them all. Fuck them all to hell. And fuck their mothers too.

As soon as we had been returned to our mother, I began again with my aimless hours-long walks throughout the city. Funny how even though I felt very comfortable at the foster home, and how I had needed daily fucks from Roberto and Julio, that I did not miss anyone personally. It was as if I just did not get too close to anyone. Yet, the sexual impulse in me found a way to express itself (the "Please Fuck Me" sign). Many days when I was supposedly at school—back at Jose Cuellar Elementary—I instead played hooky like so many other dysfunctional boys, and I roamed many miles through the ravines and secluded creek areas. I could have easily been abducted and killed in these areas with no witnesses. Yet I managed to always find another outcast such as myself and would go under some bridge for sex. These were boys who were total strangers to me, usually in their late teens or older, and I always would ask for something in return, such as 50 cents or a trinket of theirs that I happened to like. In my sickness I wanted each to fuck me, to ram his whole penis inside me, like the janitor did, and to give me spurts and squirts of sperms, the juice that would stay inside me to make me "stronger" and "more brave." What awful risks I took! For any one of these could easily have given me a terrible disease or could have just killed me afterward. At that time I didn't think about it or I simply did not care. Survive for what? For this miserable life? Fuck everything! Fuck life itself!

As I was out roaming and having sex, my mother kept getting more ill from the cancer. Pro Bono doctors had told her that she needed special treatment that was not available in El Paso, that she would have to travel to San Antonio to the famed Wickerstein Cancer Institute. As a miracle from God, someone—maybe the doctors—had arranged for my mother to receive free medical care at this institute, and while that was a major benefit, we still had no manner of transportation for my mother to go from El Paso to San Antonio, a one-way distance of about 550 miles. We had no money, we had no car, we had no friends, we had no relatives in the area, we had no contacts, we were ignorant of the geography of the state, we had no citizenship papers, we were intimidated by the dominant gringo culture, we were stupid, we were deathly afraid of the Texas Border Patrol, we were terrified of the Immigration and Naturalization Service (INS), we had no decent clothes to wear to visit someone important, we could not speak English well enough to converse with someone important, we were weak and hungry, and, besides, we weren't sure that we even deserved help in the first place. We were so totally defenseless, so completely helpless. It was a miserable situation.

I remember that I was more concerned about it than the despicable piece of shit, El Diablo, who did not have any interest at all in helping my mother with her life-threatening condition. He did nothing to help her locate suitable transportation from El Paso to San Antonio, preferring instead to continue to beat her—a defenseless woman with spreading cancer in her breast. That sounds awful, malignant, ruthless, brutal, inhuman, vicious, callous, barbarous, monstrous, savage, and purely Satanic. Beating a woman with cancer. It was his moral duty to help my mother, a dying woman, yet he did nothing but continue to abuse her and to beat her. Even if I had had the opportunity to destroy him myself, his life would not have been anywhere enough to have paid for all the crimes that he committed against our family. May his soul rot with his fellow vampires in hell, and may the wayward dogs defecate on his pitiful grave.

Poverty is a spiritual cancer that rots the soul, as I experienced in full force with my family. Yet it was my mother who clearly saw how our almost total lack of resources prevented her from making that trip to San Antonio for treatment. As The Devil was out spending his measly wages on beer, my mother and I (her little husband) looked for ways to get her to San Antonio. It was my mother who had the idea that we should approach a judge who held district court in El Paso—a kind neighbor had told my mother that if anyone in the world could help it would be him. So one morning my mother and I wore our best rags with the fewest tears and stains and we headed for the courthouse.

It was an impressive building, the courthouse, constructed of red brick with smooth marble floors and huge stained glass windows. My mother and I felt out of place, for this place was much too nice for people like us—from the backlands, the impoverished streets, the urine-stained beds, the people who ate pigeons and bricks. Soon we were in the *despacho del Juez Benavidez*, the office of Judge Benavidez. He was Mexican, just like us, so maybe he would understand my mother's desperate situation. As we waited in a large room with massive wood chairs, we heard all the commotion of busy people coming and going, bringing and taking envelopes and fat files, but nonetheless we were thinking of just how we could present the picture to the judge so that he could see the gravity of the matter. It was our turn—the moment of truth, the fork on the road of life and death.

He sure looked like a Mexican to me, with dark chocolate skin, heavy features, especially his very prominent and hooked nose, coal-black hair, dark eyes with eyebrows that looked like overgrown bushes, and he spoke Spanish! The secretary sat my mother and me in the two comfortable cushioned seats in front of the judge's massive wooden desk—it looked like a banquet dinner table, to me anyway. We were there to beg, our chief skill.

I quickly got scared because the arrogant judge gave my mother and me skeptical looks from head to toe, assessing just how it was that we raggedy and smelly vagabonds from the city garbage dump managed to get an appointment at his royal office. It crossed my mind that he was feeling repulsed, and that after we were gone he would immediately ask his assistant to furiously disinfect our seats with ammonia or chlorine, for surely they would be contaminated with bubonic plague, or at least leprosy.

My mother gathered all her courage because she knew that if she failed to convince the smug judge, there would be no other avenue to get to San Antonio for treatment. It really was a demeaning case of do or die.

Valiantly holding back a torrent of tears with a deep sigh, my mother spoke, at first quite softly, almost apologetically. But I could see that her beautiful green eyes were already sparkling, with tears.

"I know we are just like cockroaches to you, Judge. We are little people, we are nothing, we are poor, we had to ask a neighbor to lend me some clothes so that I would try to look decent coming in here to see you, but she is poor too."

The judge's face was like granite, with not even a twitch to indicate what he was thinking, one way or another. He could easily have been a statue posing as a judge.

"Very well, so how can I help with whatever it is you want?" was his cold response.

"I need your help. The doctor said I have cancer in my breast and that I need to go to a special hospital in San Antonio, and…" said my mother who was then abruptly interrupted by the judge.

"We don't have any travel services. I am sorry but you were misled by whoever told you to come here for assistance."

His face became more resolute, even in granite, as if really we were there just to waste his time since he obviously had more important things to do. My mother couldn't hold the gates of despair any longer and unleashed a flood of wailing and flowing tears that quickly covered her pretty face and her modest borrowed white blouse.

Between her sorrowful weeping she was able to blurt out a few words, asking for mercy.

"Judge, please, I am dying, what about my children, they're too young, who will take care of them? Please, I beg of you, please help me, please, I have no one else, I am dying…"

I was frozen seeing and hearing my mother plead from her heart for help. Tears started flowing from my eyes as I held her hand, for her support and mine.

The secretary momentarily opened the door into the judge's office to see what all the wailing was about, but the granite judge quickly motioned for her to retreat. My mother didn't even notice.

By this time my mother had rested her arm and her head on his desk as if to cover her face in the shameful act of asking for help in this manner. Her wailing turned to deep sobs coming from the catacombs of her broken heart.

Finally he let a sigh escape from him, as if he had been holding his breath from the moment we had walked in. Our smell, I thought.

"Come on, Señora Esperanza, please, sit up straight, look at me. I am sorry about your situation. But why do you think I should help you? Your situation is a personal and private matter, not something that should be of concern to the city government." The judge with the stone face started to come alive, even if we didn't like what he was saying.

My mother raised her head from the desk, and we all noticed she had left behind a considerable puddle of tears which she unsuccessfully attempted to clean with her bare hand. She looked at the judge, still trying to suppress her sobs.

She then said in broken fragments, between her painful sobs, "It is hard for me… to ask you for help, but… I really have…. nowhere else to go. I am…… I am not asking the… government to… to drive me… to San Antonio for treatment. Maybe…maybe you have a friend… who can take me. I feel… I feel I won't be here much longer."

Now I was almost in crisis. I knew my mother was sick, but her words about not being here much longer hit me in my soul with brutal force. It is true, it is true that my mother will die soon, I groaned in my heart. My stomach was churning in acid and panic, but I just stared at the judge. It was as if we were drowning in a deadly whirlpool of black water and were begging some uninterested and stoic stranger for help. I felt tremors in my arms and legs. I was feeling that my mother's life was one of suffering and little else. Mine was only brutal. Life in this world was savage.

He then asked a few questions in a matter-of-fact way, and said he understood my mother's problem. Maybe he is human, I thought. Well, maybe not. "I know for sure that the city government does not have any transportation programs for this sort of thing, and there aren't any special accounts either." My mother's face started to lose the bit of composure she had gained the few seconds before.

"Now, Señora Esperanza, what hospital or clinic was recommended for you in San Antonio?"

With her blotchy red eyes raised toward the ceiling my mother searched left and right for the name. "I think the doctor said Wickenston or Nickelson."

"Oh, I know, it's the Wickerstein Cancer Institute. Very good clinic for that kind of problem," said the judge, losing some of his permanent frown. Years later I learned what he did not tell us: that doctors refer patients to that institute when their cancer condition is all but hopeless, almost terminal.

My mother busily wiped the tears from her face with an overused and shredded napkin she found in her blouse's pocket, feeling perhaps a ray of hope from the judge's improving demeanor.

"So, judge, can you help me please, maybe you can pawn or sell some of the beautiful furniture in this building to help me out. And when I get better I promise to clean your house for free for one year to help pay for it. Or I can cook for you for two years if you wish. I'll do whatever you want me to do. I'll sweep, I'll mop, I'll carry out the garbage. Can you help me? I have children. Please."

Many years later I came to realize that what my mother was doing at that sad moment in time in the judge's quarters was bargaining so that death wouldn't just drag her away. She pleaded, she cried, she sobbed, she begged, she wailed. Looking back at that scene, I feel a profound sadness and empathy for my mother as a human being who was reduced to begging for her life against the forces of darkness which had her in their firm grip. She was all alone in this tragic confrontation with death—with no friends, no real family, no supportive husband, no adult she could lean on for spiritual support. What a brutal world. In the end she would ultimately lose this tragic battle.

"Señora Esperanza, calm down, calm down," said the judge as he leaned slightly towards my mother and rested his arms on his desk for the first time. "No, I won't ask you to clean my house or cook for me. That won't be necessary. And I can't sell or pawn the furniture in this building because it belongs to the city government and not to me. But I can see that your situation is desperate so I will help you..."

My mother didn't let him finish but started screaming with joy and crying again as she had three minutes prior. "Thank you, thank you, thank you, the Lord will repay you many times over, thank you, thank you, judge, you are a kind man, you..."

"OK, OK, here's the only way I can help you. I know that this sort of thing with going to the clinic will take several round trips so I will ask one of my assistants to buy round-trip tickets at the Greyhound Bus going to San Antonio. All you need to do is come pick up the ticket one day before you are scheduled to be in San Antonio. Will that help?"

"Oh, yes, angel of God, angel of mercy. I thank you, I thank you," said my mother in a quivering voice as she got up from her seat and reached across the desk to hold the judge's hand firmly against her cheek.

It would be years before I came to know that Judge Benavidez used his own personal funds to buy the several round-trip tickets that my mother would eventually come to use. That gracious man died before I could thank him for his honorable and kind deed. He was, perhaps, the only man who treated my mother with dignity and respect, for all others just wanted to use her for the moment.

After this my mother was able to make periodic trips to San Antonio for treatment. All of us kids stayed alone at home in the meantime, while El Diablo, the tumorous rat, was out drinking as always.

One time while my mother was in San Antonio at the institute, I took all my brothers and sisters for a long walk in downtown El Paso, teeming with lots of Mexican residents from across the International Bridge who had come here for better quality products and for more variety. In fact, the downtown area, immediately next to the bridge, catered to the Mexican buyers who came in droves every day. It was fun to watch the various types of Mexicans walking around and shopping at the stores. Some were extremely dark—they looked Indian, maybe Mayan, with charcoal black hair that looked like black rope. Their babies they carried in cloth backpacks—it looked like fun being in one of those. Then there were the very light-skinned Mexicans who looked almost like gringos. In fact, it *felt* funny looking at these very white Mexicans speak Spanish, for this combination was most unnatural to us. Most surprising to us were the Mexicans who came across the bridge in automobiles—nice, shiny, big, roomy, fun automobiles that we envied. These people looked super rich to us, with all those nice clothes, new shoes with soles, and nasty faces ready to spit at you if you got in their way. On previous occasions my mother had told us that "women who drive nice cars do so because they have sold their vaginas in the process." Well, whatever—it was fun being downtown anyway.

We stopped in front of a ritzy shoe store that had a table on the sidewalk advertising a contest to win a children's size rickshaw, like the ones used in Japan, Thailand, and Vietnam to transport people. It was beautiful, bright red, shiny, brand new, with nice wheels, it looked like fun! We filled out maybe 100 of the entry cards on the spot, ignorantly writing in the name of our dog, Candy, for good luck. After we filled out the cards out on the sidewalk, we deposited them in the box on the table, not daring to go into such an elegant store that was clearly too high for our social level (when you're at the bottom everything looks intimidating). Then we went home.

It must have been about a month later, after we had given up hope of ever winning that beautiful red rickshaw, that we received a notice in the mail advising us in English that we had just won the rickshaw! Woweee! Never before had we won anything, so this time we felt incredibly ecstatic at our good fortune. Our interpreter also said that the note advised us to come to the store the following week, dressed nicely, to pick up the prize and to have the entire family photographed for the local newspaper's social section. We were ready.

On the assigned day we put on our best clothes—the ones with the least number of rips, tears, and bean stains—and all of us kids headed for the ritzy shoe store in downtown El Paso to pick up our beloved toy and to have our picture taken for the newspaper. As we timidly entered the store, with me at the lead, we knew right away that even our best clothes were good enough maybe only for shoe buffers in this place where everyone looked so elegant, and the cold stares we got confirmed this for us. People were looking at us almost horrified, looking us up and down, especially no doubt at our rags, our unshined shoes with broken tongues portruding shamelessly, our matted, filthy hair, and our sunken, hollow eyes reminding them of hunger, neglect, and death. From the frowns I saw, I would say that some of them were even able to smell our urine and poop stench as we walked in. When I showed the man the card that we had received in the mail he took it and read it incredulously several times, and then motioned for his assistant to bring the rickshaw from the display window. Near the cashier's desk was the photographer with a very large camera at his side, but as he was looking at us he did not seem to be in a hurry to take our picture for the newspaper's social section, as the card had indicated. The manager who gave us the rickshaw explained to us all that the photographer was not going to be able to take our picture as his camera was not working properly. That's OK, we thought, as all of us looked happily at our new riding toy. As each of us kids grabbed a part of the rickshaw we went out through the front door and into the streets. We didn't know it then because we were socially stupid and could not read people's faces well enough, but we had just been rejected for a photo for the social pages of the local newspaper. I guess they didn't like our matted hair, our torn clothing, our ghetto shoes, or our urine smell. The store owners must have felt that their rickshaw raffle had been a total public relations dud and were very glad to get rid of us as quickly as possible before our stench made breathing in the store unbearable. Picture or no picture, we didn't care—we had a toy!

The legacy from this pervasive lack of proper clothing is that none of us grew up knowing the first thing about matching clothes properly. In our house there was no need to match anything for we wore *whatever* was available. We did not have the luxury of picking and choosing so that we could match colors, styles, or fabrics. If all I had was a torn pink T-shirt for a pair of red shorts, then that is what I wore. Plaid on plaid was OK. If a long-sleeve, flannel shirt became available in 105-degree summer weather, then that is what I wore. Shoes one or two sizes too short? No problem, for with a razor blade I would cut open the front and the sides of the shoe to make it fit my foot. No shoe laces? Use wires from an old TV set from the junkyard. Clothes unbearably dirty (which even we sometimes couldn't stand ourselves) and no laundry detergent? Use clumps of mud as an abrasive to scrub the fabrics.

Through the streets of El Paso we rode our rickshaw, each of us taking turns being the unfortunate puller between the two long handles, oblivious to people's stares, yet having incredible fun with the best, most expensive toy that we had ever had. All the kids in the neighborhood were envious of our good fortune, for neither they nor we had ever seen or even known before this that toys like our rickshaw even existed. But our dubious superiority in the neighborhood lasted at most maybe two weeks, for we hit upon the idea that we could raffle the toy so that we could raise money for food. We had to choose.

My sister Ana and I walked all over town with the rickshaw in tow, selling raffle tickets for 10 cents, not having the sense to charge a more reasonable amount. We sold maybe 100 tickets, the result of which was the enormous amount of 10 dollars—enough to buy some food for about three days. We cheated on the actual drawing of the raffle, deliberately selecting the name of a family whom we liked and who lived on the same block. Of course, it was a mistake to have selected a family so near to us, for after we delivered our unique rickshaw to them we knew within the hour that we would have to just settle for watching while they played. But at least we had food for a few days.

One night after we had run out of the few items that we were able to buy with the bounty from the raffle of the rickshaw, we were humming in the dark in our house with no electricity. The song was our usual "*Tengo hambre*" melody that we sang to suppress our hunger as we watched out the window for a miracle. My mother suggested that my sister Ana and I go out into the streets to find some food. (Wasn't that the stepfather's responsibility? Why the fuck did I have to be made responsible for finding food for the family? When there is no other way you have to do what you have to do, but that does not make it right. The fucker was out drinking as usual and my sister and I were searching for food for the family. Fuck that shit.) So Ana and I went to several small *loncherias* (taco, tortilla, and hamburger diners) asking if they could please give us seven hamburgers for our family, and that we would gladly pay them in about a week's time. Here's how our efforts fared:

"*Lo siento ninos, pero no les puedo fiar porque entonces le tengo que dar credito a todos. Diganle a su papa que ya no tome y que les de dinero para comer.*" ("I am sorry children but I cannot give you hamburgers or I'll have to give everyone credit. Tell you father to stop drinking and to give you money for supper.")

"*Pero señor, tenemos mucho hambre, ya que no hemos comido como en 3 dias. Por favor denos unos lonches para comer. Mi mami esta muy enferma.*

Esta bien?" (But sir, we are very hungry because we have not eaten in about three days. Please give us some hamburgers to eat. My mother is very ill.")

"*Ya les dije que no. Largense! Me estan corriendo los clientes. Vayanse de aqui, huercos sucios!*" ("I already said no. Get the hell out of here! You are scaring my customers away. Get away from here, you dirty bastards!").

We were used to this kind of social interchange, the kind that vagabonds, misfits, and street beggars get into in their daily lives. Rejection and sneering were the appetizers that we worked with as we searched for our wayward dinner that hot summer night.

After about two hours of endless walking—building up an appetite on top on the two-days'-worth of the old one—we happened to come across a tiny Mexican Luncheonette not far from our red house. The Mexican owner standing on the other side of the counter asked what it was that we wanted to order, so I told him that we were desperately hungry and that we would like to buy seven hamburgers on good credit, that we would pay him by the end of the week. He asked me how he could know if we would pay, for he did not know us personally. To that I replied that we were going to take some old metals to the junkyard, earning money that we would use to pay him for his favor. In retrospect it sounded like a very flimsy and weak explanation, something that makes me think that this man agreed to give us the hamburgers not because he expected to get paid but because he wanted to do us a favor. I thank him for that.

As soon as he said he would do it we all felt a great joy in our hearts, for we would at last be having supper tonight. Yes, supper tonight! Praise the Lord! Tonight we will eat. We heard the hamburger patties hit the hot grill and sizzle, and our stomachs awakened from the dormancy they had gone into in order to allow us to function. When he asked us how we wanted the meat cooked I was confused, for I thought that certainly he should know *how to cook the meat*! My reply was that I wanted it cooked on the grill, the way he already had it going, but that did not satisfy him for he asked me again the same question. Rare, medium or well done, was his incomprehensible reply. It finally dawned on him that I had no idea what "rare, medium, or well done" meant, so he flatly said he was just going to cook it his way. "What a stupid question to ask," I thought. "One just cooks the meat until it is cooked. Why does he have to ask what color the inside of it should be?" I actually didn't care what color the meat was; I was just happy that we were having dinner tonight.

He gave us a bag with seven nice, warm, wonderfully aromatic hamburgers, and I assured him that I personally would see to it that my parents would pay him within the week as promised. Our joy was uncontainable as Ana and

I practically ran home with such a wonderful treasure. It was as if we had found a precious jewel and were ready to share news of our good fortune with anyone who would listen. When we got home everyone assembled in the living room—totally dark due to the electricity being shut off for nonpayment—and we all surrounded the white bag with the hamburgers as hyenas surround their prey. The aroma alone was a wonderful gastronomical experience, since it signaled to us that in our hands we were holding the precious meal for the day. That hamburger that we ate that dark night in our living room was to be the most delicious hamburger that I would ever eat, for no other after that even came close to providing that total joy. It became an unforgettable experience.

As could have been predicted, we never paid the man who did us this favor. We had no sense of responsibility, no honor, no sense of duty, and no code of ethics, for our behavior was essentially guided by needs, desires, wants, anxieties, fears, and other animal instincts, but rarely by morals or spiritual values. In this respect we really were like a pack of hyenas.

Hungers like this were quite frequent with us, shaping our values and our sense of survival. Most of the time it was just us kids suffering at home with our mother, for The Devil always managed to be at some bar, drinking up to 12 bottles of his Lone Star per night, avoiding desperately being at home with the rest of the hyena pack. As usual he just came home at 12 midnight to wake everyone up from his or her comatose sleep, hitting everyone and terrorizing my mother. Why couldn't the bastard act like a real husband and father and bring money home to buy food? Why couldn't the bastard stay at home to fix the hundreds of things that needed fixing? That was not his style. He preferred to go to bars, fuck loose women, get drunk, forget to remove his used condom, come home, beat everybody up, dispose of his bursting-with-sperm condom in our toilet, urinate for ten minutes, forget to flush the condom, and fall asleep naked in his own shitty bed. With a life like that he should have committed suicide. Better still, I would have gladly done the job for him, to put this fucking dog out of the misery he was causing all those around him.

One of the things that desperately needed fixing in this red house were the walls, for as previously mentioned they were very thin and had lots of wide cracks in them. In the wintertime we had no heat, and bone-numbing drafts from the sieve-like cracks throughout the house made indoor life not much better than actual exposure to the elements outside. We had no winter coats, so we had to wear four or five shirts at a time, one on top of the other, trying to stay warm. As it got unbearably cold inside the house I was the one who had to concern myself about ways of making it warmer, for The Devil made no attempt to help us in anything, even if it was within his physical capacity to do so. What a wretched example of a man this piece of shit was. A fucking hornet had more sense of family duty than this asshole Devil. Piss on him.

One method that I devised was to start a large fire out in the backyard using logs from rotted trees nearby. As the fire turned into redhot embers I would transfer these to a large tub that I had located a few blocks away, and I would then take the tub to the living room, where we would all huddle around it, like hobos by the railroad station, to keep our bodies from freezing. People at school soon started to complain that we all smelled like soot, burning plastic, chimneys, barbeque grills, or burning trash heaps, but, we didn't care, for at home we were feeling a lot warmer with a burning tub in the middle of our unfurnished living room. To help our bodies conserve heat we all slept in whatever clothes we used for the day. We managed to survive. Well, biologically at least.

Two little boys, brothers, about ages eight and nine, lived nearby and seemed to be more out of touch with the world than we were. Their real names were never revealed to us, for we knew them only as Cara and Pelos. That translates into Face and Hairs. Their bizarre names foretold what to expect from them.

Both of them had incredible amounts of hair on their heads, so much that it had long ago matted into a thick, carpet-like mound that played host to even larger nests of head lice than ours. We were always dirty, but next to these two boys we appeared quite clean given that they had days' old food smears on their faces, streaks of human feces on their pants, the blackest fingernails that we had ever seen, and body odor to repel even the hungriest vulture or maggot who dared to come close. Their behavior was perfectly matched to their odd names and despicable appearance, for they played with their penises in full public view, they would make strange faces at each other, and they had the filthiest vocabulary that even we, with our low, gutter, standards, had ever heard. Not that any of these things affected our sensibilities; on the contrary, we accepted Cara and Pelos and their foul odor cheerfully into our household, for with the meager food and furniture that we had we still felt like we had more than enough to show off to them who had even less. Then at the end of the day the silence of our destitute community was shattered by the gutteral howl, heard for at least two blocks around, of the boys' father yelling for them to come home. The father himself called them by their bizarre, grotesque nicknames which have no equal in the English language. I don't think we'll ever know what their real names were.

As I think back at these dreadful experiences, with unfulfilled desires and wants, with unmet expectations, with sorry deprivations in just about every single facet of childhood, with every imaginable form of child abuse, which included death for our brother Benito, I feel that there was so much that our parents could have done even with their meager resources. My mother could have steered us in a more ethical direction, with *some* discipline instead of *none*. The best that The Devil could have done was to have just left us in the middle of the night, never to return to our sorry home. Here we were in the red house on San Lorenzo Street, freshly back from the six-month stay at the foster home, and still experiencing the same insufferable abuse and conditions. El Diablo was as vicious as ever, and my mother was still "out to lunch", not having the slightest idea of what a mother is supposed to do with her children. The Devil had not even the sense to give us some money to plan something for a holiday, as was the case on the only Easter that we spent in the red house.

My mother wanted to do something special for Easter, so we decided we would go on a picnic. But where? And with what food? Prior to Easter she had inquired at the local bus company if any city buses went to the main water attraction in El Paso, Lake Las Flores, a rather small lake on the outskirts of the city, just far enough to be inaccessible to pedestrians, which is what we were 100 percent of the time. The day before my mother asked our next door neighbor and partner-in-suffering for some sliced bread and baloney, no mayonnaise, no lettuce, no tomatoes, no cheese. Now we had our picnic lunch all packed: dried bread with baloney, slightly green. No canteen, no water. No drinks. No napkins. No other accessories. What a pitiful picnic my mother had planned. Was she serious? Yes, it flopped painfully and dramatically.

Early Easter morning we took the city bus a few blocks from our house, daydreaming about this fantastic picnic that we were to have by the waterfront, with a nice palm tree providing much sought-after shade. Our visual expectations were just running wild about the Nirvana that we were going to. Soon after getting on the bus, a rare occurrence for us, we settled in, taking in the view of the mostly dilapidated neighborhoods along the way. Reality woke us up from our daydream as the driver announced to us that he advised us to get off at that point because the bus could go no closer to the lake, and that we would have to walk a considerable distance. Having no choice, my mother got off with six of us kids in tow and a small brown bag under her arm. By that time the sun was already hot, so within five minutes we were wet with perspiration and thirst became an obsession that erased our longing for the tropical palm trees by the lake. We just wanted water and nothing else. But, we had not packed any. No hats either to protect us from the blistering Texas sun.

Mile after mile we walked by the side of the highway as speeding cars whizzed by only a few feet from us. There wasn't even a sidewalk, only cacti, rattlesnakes, hordes of grasshoppers, tall Johnson grass, a few raccoon skeletons, foxes, and skunks who didn't measure up to Darwin's dictum of the survival of the fittest, and the occasional barbed wire fence that we had to scale to avoid getting dangerously close to the speeding traffic. Our dream picnic had quickly turned into a nightmare and we hadn't even arrived yet.

But I wondered: "Why is it that all these people are driving around in all these nice cars, happy as can be, while we are the only ones who have to torturously trudge to get to the miserable lake? Why are we so terribly unfortunate? Why do we have to suffer so much? Why couldn't I have been born into a family that had the normal things in life, like a nice bed, a car, food, and shoes?" This ordeal made me think about our station in life.

Our thirst was the worst that we had ever experienced in our lives of deprivation, for it became a driving force that miserable day under the scorching Texas sun. We must have walked about ten miles and collapsed from thirst and exhaustion under a dry-looking mesquite tree with leaves so shriveled that it could only fake its role of shade-provider. Since we were also starving by that time we decided that our picnic was going to happen then and there, lake or no lake. As with everything else in our lives, we had a pitiful time eating our lunch, with no drink, under the hot sun. Each of us had only one allotted sandwich, so in three minutes the picnic was over, but we still were not at the lake, and thirst became our desperation. How we all wished to God to send us even an ambulance to pick us up and take us back to our hellhole of a house so that we could all just collapse on the floor. There was no other way but to walk.

I was the oldest of the kids, and I was exhausted by that time. Everyone else was younger so we can surmise that their pain must have been many times greater than mine. Moaning and crying, we forged ahead totally drenched with salty perspiration creating white blotches over most of our clothes. Approximately three hours later we rounded a long curve of the highway, putting us in a position to see the gates at the entrance of the lake park. Forty minutes of exhausting dodging of traffic later, we arrived at the gates, no longer caring that we had arrived at our destination. Our emotional and physical conditions were such that we could not enjoy the semi-beauty of this desert-lake, for as soon as we crossed the line into the lake park we made a beeline to the water fountain and drank like camels that had been out on a desert expedition for two weeks. We then collapsed again under a shady canopy. None of us could muster the courage or stamina to enjoy the children's playground. We barely could muster the energy to talk. We just wanted to leave. We wanted to go home to drop to the floor to sleep. Fuck the lake. To hell with the picnic.

Then the dreadful reality slowly dawned on us: to get back home we would have to retrace our steps for about 12 miles to get back to the nearest bus stop. Agony! How could my mother have planned such a bad Easter picnic? No water? No napkins? No hats for the sun? No sunscreen? No toilet paper for the frequent stops that we had to make along the way? Poor transportation. Terrible lunch with no mayo, or lettuce. It was the picnic from hell! Did my mother have a fucking brain?

We were looking at the prospect of having to walk back the entire distance the same way a the depressed person looks at having to live the rest of his life with his pain: The task seemed insurmountable. Something in us just clicked and we said that we were not going to do it; we would have to find someone to take us back. Collapsed on the floor under the canopy we, could see an old man drinking beer in his car. It sure looked like he might not object to taking us back to our house. As uncommon (for us) luck would have it, he agreed to take us when I asked him, and we all practically ran from our makeshift, lakeside bed to his old jalopy. Though reeking of alcohol, he managed to keep the car on the road, getting us to the front of our house quite rapidly. We thanked him (and God) profusely, then we collapsed again for a long sleep in various spots around the house. This truly had been the worst Easter, and the worst picnic, that we had ever lived through. We were glad it was over. No more picnics. Ever!

Despite our severe dysfunction and misery, we did have the opportunity once in a while to go to the movie theatre one way or another. The local soda bottling plant sponsored movies on Saturday mornings, with no admission charge if one brought two empty soda bottles to the theatre. Ana and I were masters at stealing bottles from service stations, restaurants, grocery stores, and anywhere else we could find them, and thus were able to go to the movies several times a month. Usually the films were old science fiction movies from the 1940s and early 1950s—some were definitely corny, but, hey, we had no standards so whatever they showed was better than nothing. It was at one of these showings that the management announced a free raffle of a kid's bicycle, something for which I must have filled out maybe 50 tickets. On the day of the actual raffle I prayed so hard for God to please grant me this bicycle, since I had never in my life had one. My argument was that we were so desperately poor that, of course, in God's system of justice we deserved this bicycle very much. I must have prayed for hours for this bike, yet in the end we did not win it. My disappointment was so great that I felt abandoned even by what I had thought was a just God, Jehovah, the God that my mother had told me could grant anything as long as you asked. I silently told God that I was very disappointed that he had not granted me the only prayer request that I had made in my entire 11 years of life. From that point on I felt that I could not ask anything of God, so I totally abandoned my faith for several decades after that. It took another crisis to bring me in contact with Him again.

Besides these free movies we also went to the regular theatre with our mother on occasion, since the admission was 50 cents for adults and 25 cents for children. Our favorite theatre in El Paso was the *Royal*, conveniently located downtown for the Mexicans who came across the border. It played Mexican films exclusively, so all the movie goers were Mexicans from across the river and the local Mexican-Americans such as ourselves. A Mexican cinema is quite different from an English-speaking one with "regular" white audiences. Here at the *Royal* people came with all their kids, irrespective of age, creating a playground/circus/playroom atmosphere where I suppose that half of the adults tried to watch the film while the other half was attending (or pretending to attend) to the children. Conversations among families were common, with people not at all shy about shouting across the entire theatre to call on someone they knew. Many people also brought their own tacos, enchiladas, rice and beans, and tortillas, so crackling brown paper bags provided a backdrop of distraction against the gossiping, giggling, and necking that occurred parallel to whatever was going on in the film. No complaints—this was the Mexican way of watching a film.

Even as these movies served to distract us from the daily grind on San Lorenzo Street, we still could not escape the basic reality of deprivation. From the neighbors next door we routinely borrowed not only the proverbial "cup of sugar", but also milk, bread, rice and beans, tortillas, water, and electricity via a long extension cord that I had rigged between both houses. Sometimes Ana and I would go to the various food processing plants in the area and would scavenge for salvageable rotten food that had been discarded in large bin containers next to their rear doors. We got tomatoes, peaches, lettuce, and watermelons that had significant rotting parts, but if we cut those parts off we felt that what remained was edible. Of course we had to fight off the millions of flies that had figured that out too and felt that in numbers they could defeat us; sometimes I thought that we smelled worse than the rotting food, and that may have confused the flies.

Good luck would sometimes strike us serendipitously, as when we stopped one time at a stranger's house to ask for water and the lady immediately said that she was glad that we had stopped over so quickly to pick up the children's clothes that she had already packed. Evidently she thought we were some other kids sent by someone whom she knew, but we were not about to argue the point when she was practically asking us to please take the two large brown bags full of used children's clothes. We felt we had hit the jackpot and left after profusely thanking the woman for her unsolicited generosity.

At home we told our mother about what had happened and showed her the two bags that we promptly emptied onto the bed for perusal. About 75 percent of the clothes were the right sizes for at least one of us kids, and all were in excellent condition. We were ecstatic. The next day the party ended, for the lady showed up at our door.

We were shocked to see her there, having no idea how she located us. She did not ask to come into the house, she just burst into our Spartan living room and demanded that we return the clothes that we had "stolen" from her. Intrusions like this had happened before, establishing for us a pattern of passivity while some other force or person would take control of the situation. This irate woman did just that, as she started to put together the clothes that were still obviously scattered about the living room. She left in an even angrier mood, mumbling to herself, not ever reappearing in our lives.

We didn't have the strength to fight her, for we had a bigger problem looming over us concerning our living quarters. As the landlord began to threaten us, as was the pattern in our lives, it was my job as my mother's little husband to help her look for another landlord who had not yet heard of our abysmal record of always paying the rent late and eventually not paying at all for a few months before eviction. The Devil *never* performed any of these husbandly duties, so my mother felt that they should fall on my shoulders. She and I would walk the city many times over, asking residents in other neighborhoods if they had heard of a house or apartment being available for rent, going from one dead lead to another in an exhausting manner. Why didn't she want to look in the "Apartments or Houses for Rent" section of the local El Paso Times? I'll never know, but eventually she and I did find a brick-and-plaster house in front of San Joaquin Church, barely a few days before the date of eviction from our red house. It had been only about nine months since we moved in, apparently enough time to have caused significant problems for the landlord. Nobody knew it, but this new move was to be my mother's last, for the cancer was rapidly eating her alive.

The White House on Morelos Street

It was on a corner lot, this plaster house splashed with cheap white paint on the outside, with a storm fence surrounding the small lot with nothing growing on it. Inside, the walls were cracked, a condition that got worse as all us kids used our junk wagon to ram the walls and gouge even larger holes in

them. We were hell-bent on destruction. The one-and-a-half bedrooms had
no doors on them; not that we needed them, for we all wanted to sleep with
our mother to avoid the wrath of the monster who came to beat us up every
night. Compared to the previous house this one was a bit larger and certainly
made of solid exterior walls that not even a determined bull could penetrate.
I checked the heating system immediately: it was a natural gas furnace, built
into the wall, with vertical bricks to retain the heat from the gas flames. Ever
since that family perished in The Projects gas tragedy, we had all been edgy
about natural gas heating systems. This one was gas, but there was nothing
that we could do about it.

In the only hallway of the house was a clothes dryer that came with the
house; we were curious just how these things worked, for we had never seen
one in person before. Besides, we did our laundry very infrequently so it
was not as if it would be a significant time saver for us. More than anything
it looked like it would be a great toy. Little did we know that in the year we
would spend there this dryer would serve as a torture chamber where we
would put cats and spin them around until they defecated from the horror.
Then on some other occasions we would use it against each other, to lock each
other up for periods long enough to cause fainting. This clothes dryer was
to be the gauge of the swift downturn in our behavior, bad as it already was,
parallel to our mother's health.

Outside was a small carport—as if we cared, for we had no car. The roof
was supported by six massive wood columns worthy of an honorable mention
for mimicking Greek architecture, but they were no match for our destructive
instinct, for a few weeks after we had moved in I climbed onto the roof and
began to furiously stomp and jump on the apex of the roofline, causing the
entire structure to collapse completely to the ground. The landlord said he
was surprised that the wind had brought it down because he had deliberately
constructed it of heavier-than-regulation wood beams to make it "hurricane
resistant," he said. Ha, we knew better.

On the other side of our backyard lived a very elderly Mexican spinster by
the name of Escolastica who relished telling us at every opportunity she got
that she was a virgin at age 88, and that no man had ever touched her. That
never impressed us, especially me, for I knew that even at my age, 11, I had
already had more sex partners than most people do in a lifetime. Besides, what
was this big deal about virginity anyway? She always wore black, had more
wrinkles than the rotting prunes we picked from trash cans, had a pungent,
cheesy smell, but also was a kind woman who never refused our calls for
assistance at her door. Time after time I was in her kitchen getting supplies

for our meals, something that she was always happy to help out with. In her own way she tried to give us advice about life, about Jesus Christ, about good conduct, but we just were incapable of grasping something so alien at that point in time. She also had immense patience, for she rarely complained to us in spite of our dumping our garbage on her property.

Right in front of our house was the massive *Iglesia San Joaquin*, symbol of Mexican Catholicism with all its shiny altars, brass tools, abundant statues, enormous crosses with Christ still crucified, figures of dozens of saints that I had never heard of before, abundant velvet coverings and cloths through-out, enormous stained glass windows, and very interesting processional services with colorful costumes and lots of incense. It was around 1519 that the Spaniards reached Tenochtlitlan (present day Mexico City) and intro-duced the practice of Catholicism to the indigenous tribes who had hitherto been pagan worshippers and fierce warriors. Consequently, the Spaniards conquered and intermarried with the various tribes, replacing most of the native religions with the dominant Catholic faith, thus producing a nearly religiously homogenous Mexican population, and El Paso was no exception. From my very limited viewpoint I would wonder then just why the Church had so many beautiful things in it, maybe even gold chains, crucifixes, and statues, while poor people like us were always hungry. It was just one more unfair thing in our ignorant world.

Around the neighborhood one could see very modest homes, some passable, some falling apart, all with the required Mexican wrought iron decorations in the front yard. As is the case with most Mexican families, these homes had many kids—lots of them unkempt, with torn shirts, uncut hair, maybe lice, and *chorreados* (very filthy kids with dirty smears on their body, usually on their faces). Some homes were abandoned, and we would soon be breaking into those to explore; our mother would never question where we had been or where we obtained certain objects that we brought into our house.

Within a day or two we felt comfortable in our new home as we started to abuse doors, windows, walls, the fence, the roof, the carport, the yard, and the neighbors, with impunity, for we did not have proper discipline from our mother and El Diablo would beat us for any reason, not necessarily because we did something wrong. Soon after we had moved in, my Aunt Sonia The Brave came to visit and locked horns with The Devil, as previously described, something that we relished in secret. Satan the vomit bag left for the day after he had gotten enough from Tia Sonia, providing an opportunity for her to give us some advice on how to deal with him next time he tried to bully us. Sonia was so emphatic, so confident, so fearless in dealing with the excrement-breath that it made me feel that, yes, I could talk back to the damned Devil to let him know that I was not going to let him push me around anymore. Next time he growled at me like the dog that he is, I thought, I am going to tell him to back off. It was an ill-fated plan.

It happened the next day when as always he ordered me to sweep the kitchen while he snoozed on the flea-infested sofa that we picked up from a street corner. The bastard was good at ordering us around, but he *never* did anything to make our house look better. With my plan fully prepared in my head I mustered all my bravery and told him in a shaky voice that I was not going to sweep the kitchen floor, a challenging refusal that never before in my cowardly life had I dared. Never before in my life had I seen the beast rise so quickly from a couch, with hatred in his piercing black eyes, one of which was hideously larger than the other. Unwittingly I had awakened the Satan spirit in him, the viciousness of his character, the savagery of his discipline, the vengefulness of his response to uncooperative others, the hatred of the father in him. All of these demons were fused together into one ugly inhuman form lunging at me with the face of hatred reminiscent of when he stomped on my mother, when *she* dared then to defy his orders. My shaky plan of defiance melted immediately from the heat of hatred radiating from his ugly face, approaching me at a heart-stopping speed. Even though I had been close to being annihilated many times by this fiend, this time I felt that death was surely coming at me, that I had unleashed unspeakable venom from the soul of this Satanic Vermin, that his single-minded purpose at this moment was to destroy me for daring to speak out against him. As my legs weakened from the terror in my heart, I thought that this was it, that finally the plot of fate against me would be revealed and that my life would end at the hands of this worthless worm. But I then remembered what my fearless Tia Sonia The Brave had told me, "*No dejes que el pendejo te pegue; corre y que no te alcance*" ("Don't let the fool hit you; run and don't let him catch you"). Just then, a mere one or two seconds from the moment that the vampire had sprung from the sofa, I found the strength and the resolution to run as my Tia Sonia had advised me. The doors to the outside of the house were closed, and with the clutches of death just a few inches behind me there was no time even to grab a door-knob, leaving me no option but to run for my life from corner to corner of the house, room to room, with the rabid cannibal's breath just behind me. Never in my life had I run so desperately, breathed so hard, changing directions, jumping on furniture, leaping across beds, running and running, urgently looking for a way out of the house as I continued to run over chairs, kitchen table, sofa, and lamps. He had longer legs and the determination of hatred, both of which kept him just a few inches behind me and closing in with his massive mechanic's hands in front of him, fingers curled to catch my shirt and then devour me. It didn't help that he was cursing me as he chased me, for it augmented the auditory threat of his imposing oil-resistant boots that made that horrendous stomping noises behind me as we raced around the rooms. I was running for my life. I was only a few inches away from a violent death. I was running out of breath, wheezing from lack of air and from the terror in the pit of my stomach. My desperate situation made me contemplate for a fleeting second slamming my body against a window, hoping that the impact would break it into a million pieces and propel my body, cuts and all, to the outside. But the screens were robust, I knew, so that if I did not make it all the way to the outside the fiend from hell would then use one of the chards of glass and plunge it into my heart. I couldn't take the risk.

By now I was screaming and crying in agony as I tried to breathe at the same time. Maybe it is better to die than to run from death in this manner. My legs were getting weaker but I kept moving evasively over anything that I could use as an obstacle and still the venomous hyena was right behind me. It was in the living room where I had a momentary slip of the foot, and the sombitch finally caught my shirt and pulled me into his firm clutch. His ugly and ferocious face with the over-exposed eye was evil enough to burn its imprint into my heart as I lay under him screaming for my life and ready to die.

Satan grabbed me by my arms and pulled me to a standing position with a violent jerk. He then got a firm steel grip with one hand on my thin upper arm as he began to use the other hand to beat me violently all over my body. As his blows landed my body began to fly in all directions, like a rag doll suspended from his one hand that kept a tight grip on me. I felt the impact on my legs, my buttocks, my arms, my ankles, my stomach, my chest, my back, my face, my soul. He cursed me—how dare I talk back to him? How dare I disobey his orders? The rabid dog was dripping frothing saliva all over me as he was trying to curse me while still out of breath. Soon I knew that again I would be very close to death but that today he was not going to kill me. I screamed because of the terror but I didn't feel the pain. A few seconds later he dropped me on the cement floor and walked away, cursing as usual, and wiping away all the poisonous saliva that had poured from his revolting mouth and had covered all his ugly chin.

Just like my mother whimpered after one of his savage attacks on her, I lay there totally beaten and defeated, spiritually raped. There was nothing in the world that I could do to defend myself. My life's pattern was set. It had to run its course. No one could save me.

Looking back at this, I feel that it is this heritage that makes me shutter at the prospects of peace if Merengueno Zalmar were alive today, for I would have to kill him too for the many odious acts of violence that he perpetrated against me, our mother, and the family in general. He was so lucky that I was only 11 and real skinny when he did this to me, for now, I would not even run if he ever sprung from the sofa and lunged at me. With courageous defiance I would meet the threat, with *Pachuco*-style icepick in my hand, and would ask him if he wanted to beat me as he did when I was 11 and defenseless. Gladly I would plunge the icepick first into his lidless eye, all the way down to the wooden handle, moving it side-to-side to enlarge the opening and compound the damage. Only then would I jerk it out and stab him right through the heart, leaving it in place while I beat his ugly face to an unrecognizable pulp with a meat tenderizer.

"Well, asshole, do you still want to chase me around the room? What's the matter, chickenshit bastard? Afraid to pick on someone your own size? Remember when you did this to me when I was 11, and when I couldn't fight back. Remember when I desperately ran from room to room, trying to get away from you? Well, today I am not running, *hijo de tu chingada madre* (you son of your fucked mother). Today I won't run, because today I will kill you, motherfucker, *pendejo* (fool). Well, fuck you, because today you die, you motherfucking sombitch. Today you die. I want you to feel this thin icepick go through your heart. Here it goes. Fuck you in hell. Die, you fucking pig."

God or some other higher power must have arranged things so that this piece of shit would not be alive when I finally found courage after all the terrors of my life. With Satan already dead I didn't have to kill him. But I thank God that as I lived with my unrecognized rage throughout the years before therapy that I did not kill someone else, someone who could have triggered the rage that I had for this miscreant who came to this world to cause misery to all. It was for the best that he croaked—all alone in a rat-infested hotel, eating a cold hamburger—for we would have been at war had he been alive when I awoke from my cowardice. I would have given him no room for retreat, no room for apologies, no chance of forgiveness, for his sins against the family are unredeemable, the damage too extensive. I would have had to kill this vermin. With no regrets, no apologies. No other option for me but to kill El Diablo with extreme prejudice.

About two days after this savage beating from The Devil all my aches and pains and bruises appeared. I had rainbow colors all over my skin as blue, black, red, brown, green, and purple blotches appeared at the locations where his fist and open hand had impacted on my body. In time I knew that all these colors would start to look more alike, blending into dull brown blotches, becoming fainter, and then totally disappearing in about three weeks. This beating made me more of a coward—I could not afford the high cost of saying anything back to him. The world was vicious indeed.

I have related some of what happened in this house, but not all: eating Catholic communion wafers for lunch/dinner, continuing to eat pigeons, continuing to roam aimlessly throughout the city, still suffering from abject hunger, no water, no electricity, hair full of lice, white worms in our feces, Lucifer's bulging condoms in our toilet, the cat who dared take El Diablo's meat, *Doña Elena* and her valiant efforts, shoes with no soles, always smelling like urine, wetting the beds, continuing to receive sperms from other older boys, stealing from people's yards, attempting to raise a pig *inside* the house, still no toothbrushes (what are those?), no medical care, no dental care, no checkups, no milk, discovering that El Diablo slept nude in his smelly bed, our ravenous dogs taking bites out of pedestrians' legs, several horrible car accidents in front of our house, the police continuing to come to our house to take Satan away for the night, only to have him come back the next day even meaner, continuing to fear violence near us, and, of course, never any money for even basic school supplies like pencils and theme paper. Life as usual, yet in our stupidity and ignorance we pressed on.

Quite naively I had joined the Boy Scouts through my school (Jose Cuellar Elementary) with great dreams of going camping, learning open water swimming, mastering home repairs, using radio equipment, etc. Even on many an empty stomach I attended their meetings and studied the Handbook which I had borrowed from a charitable fellow. At the school PTA (at that time it was the Parents Teachers Association) when the Boy Scouts were invited to do the Pledge of Allegiance, I went right along on stage, the only boy wearing rags while all the others had nice, green uniforms. Many of the merit badges that I tried for did not come through because I did not have the resources. For camping, as an example, I had absolutely no camping equipment, so I could not join the others. For home repair we had no tools, and my mother didn't know the first thing about asking me what to repair. Then I came upon the bright idea of going for the hiking merit badge. I can certainly walk, I thought. No, it didn't work that way either.

Our Troop 901—Jose Cuellar Elementary School in El Paso, Texas— started with easy hikes of one or two miles, easy even on an empty stomach. Regulations required that our hikes get progressively longer and more difficult, necessitating a bit more planning and resources. I didn't have any socks, so my feet hurt on the longer hikes. I didn't have a hat or cap. Then we went for the 12-mile hike, which took us in the direction of Farm Road 654, towards the municipal airport in El Paso.

The morning of the hike I was able to obtain a piece of boloney and two pieces of hard bread from our house—this would constitute the lunch that our troop master required for this trip. That was the extent of my preparation. About three miles into the hike everyone was hungry so they started taking out nice snacks from their backpacks: oranges, apples, pears, candy bars, small tacos, grapes, chilled juices, and tortillas with beans. I had no backpack—just a brown paper bag—and no snacks, so I just looked longingly at theirs. They were thirsty, so of course they drank from their canteens. I didn't have one. Some of the other boys were kind enough to share their water with me. They all had comfortable walking shoes, while mine had holes in them. Painful blisters brought agony on the return trip. In short, I had none of the necessary resources to properly participate in Boy Scout activities, and on top of that I was too ignorant to realize that before I embarked on these endeavors. I almost collapsed from heat exhaustion and sunstroke on the way back. Never again did I engage in any Boy Scout activities after that. I had given it my best try.

One comical aspect of our life in this particular hell-hole on Morelos Street was the living legend of Don Maruco, known by practically every child and every parent in El Paso in the 1950s. Don Maruco was a very old man with a creaky, wobbly wooden wagon pulled by a depressed burro who appeared to have serious skin problems from the look of the fur that easily peeled off. He and his wagon would very slowly creep down the streets of El Paso in search of salvageable materials, mostly returnable soft drink bottles, that children would bring him in return for the small treats that he would then toss at them. Cow bells that he had attached to the undercarriage of his wagon would signal his approach with a good ten minutes of lead time, enough for all of us to round up whatever junk or bottles we had to trade for candies. We had loads of fun as all of us always played a cat-and-mouse game with him as we brought in questionable materials which we knew he didn't like (such as a broken tricycle) but persistently tried to convince him that he *should* give us candy for our effort. As some of us distracted him towards the front of the wagon, next to the lazy burro who took quick naps every time he stopped to collect stuff, others were at the back of the wagon taking stuff off and reselling it to him at the front. *Don Maruco* must have been senile, for often he would look with glee at the stuff which we had just stolen from the back of his wagon, paying us good quantities of candy or pennies for it. He would tell us that he had been looking for these items forever.

Another thing funny about him was the enormous front bulge he had in his pants as he laboriously stepped off his wagon. Of course I had seen bulges in crotches before, yet this one extended to his knees. *I felt that the man was huge!* My God, even Kike with his mammoth organ did not have such a large bulge, so *Don Maruco* must be up there, I thought, competing with the horses and his own burro for sheer girth. My imagination ran wild with *Don Maruco*'s bulge, not realizing due to my ignorance, that the poor man may have had a serious, untreated hernia.

He was a legendary in El Paso, for he could be seen in almost all parts of the city, collecting whatever the *cartoneros* (the cardboard box collectors who came daily to our city from Mexico) did not want to take (and they took everything!). Kids would scream out in delight, "*Alli viene Don Maruco. Traigan las botellas.*" ("Here comes *Don Maruco*. Get the bottles.") Sometimes he would even throw miniature Chiclets at us, even if we didn't have junk for him. In many ways he was like a one-man circus, a portable distraction, a welcome sight in our neighborhoods. But he was very old, and one day we didn't see him ever again. We don't know what happened to his burro.

Then there was Petra La Loca, or Petra The Crazy One, who was as much a legend as Don Maruco, except that in her case it was mostly infamy as people generally ridiculed her. Legend had it that as a child she had fallen out of a car moving at high speed, which may have damaged her brain and personality. Now, as a woman in her twenties who looked like she was 50, she would roam the streets aimlessly (sounds familiar?), gesturing to unseen companions and cursing the general public. Petra never interacted appropriately with anyone, as far as we could tell, thus limiting her in the friendship department. Everyone knew Petra, walking and cursing. For us, this defenseless woman was an outlet for our need to cruelly ridicule as we were often ridiculed. May her soul be more at peace now than it was then.

So there were moments of respite from our chronic misery even if these were to ridicule others *even more unfortunate* than ourselves. I continued with my efforts at school at building electronic and wood projects, something that my teachers appreciated and praised me for. About the only positive thing in my life was my school and my wonderful teachers who ignored my chronic urine smell and unwashed body odor, and just taught me the lesson for the day.

"Nothing Has More Value Than My Breast!"

As I was going around stealing, abusing my brothers and sisters, and wreaking havoc on Escolastica and others, my mother continued to go to her medical appointments in San Antonio, all the while looking worse. She looked older, and that hit us deep within our souls, for she told us that there was a possibility that she was going to die. Those words tore at my heart like nothing ever had before, even including all the past tragedies, traumas, hungers, threats, and other abuses. In the pit of my stomach was an awful feeling of insecurity, a loneliness, a personal terror arising from within—I could not even begin to escape it. If she died, who would take care of us? Certainly not the abominable Satan, for he did not know the first thing about caring for a family. If she died, who would pay for her funeral? I asked. It was at this ugly stage of her sickness, with so much high tension in our family of animals, that my mother began to routinely open her blouse in front of me to show me her enormous breasts. She did it to show me the marks on them from the doctors' needles as part of her cancer treatment. Sick as it may sound, this had a profound impact on my life.

Deep in the middle of puberty, I now had pubic hairs and was producing voluminous amounts of semen. My mother showing me her pink, bouncing breasts made me sexually excited, and as an adult I would still think of her pendulous breasts in my forbidden fantasies, imagining that I would suck on them forever, drawing unlimited amounts of milk, becoming totally immersed in them as their massive size would completely engulf my face and my soul. I wanted to *merge* with her breasts, to *disappear* in them, to eat them so that they would forevermore be mine.

I came to realize that deep in my soul the true relationship that I had with my mother was really with her breasts, for my mother *the person* never developed a true and genuine relationship with me or with any of my brothers or sisters. Somehow, in the terrible misfortune of my birth in Mexico, my mother may have begun to give me her breast—just long enough for me to make some connection—and then mercilessly yanked it away from my mouth as she discovered that she did not want this dependent parasite to suck away her precious milk or deform what she saw as her breasts' perfect beauty. She may have just given birth, but that did not mean that she had to be a mother to this thing that tenaciously clung to her nipples. "Let go of my fucking nipple, you little bastard, and go suck on some dog's tit instead, you squirming parasite!" is what I envision she told me when I was an infant. Of course I would not have understood her words, but my budding soul would have read her eyes and the tone of her voice, and be forever damaged beyond repair. She subsequently disappeared for maybe two years, maybe to keep a safe distance between my sucking mouth and her perfect breasts.

So, showing me her breasts at a time when my adolescent hormones were breaking through all my psychological defenses of childhood only served to awaken this specific symbiotic force, present in all babies, forever sentencing me to be fully aware of this infantile need for my mother's breasts. No normal adult son should ever feel this way about his mother and her nipples.

Yes, she adored her breasts. My mother told us that the doctors had recommended several times that the cancerous breast be completely removed in order to prevent the cancer from spreading, but almost in the same breath she said that she would never agree to that, that she had a different solution.

La Curandera, the Faith Healer, and Black Magic.

All throughout our lives as children we had lived with the ever-present Mexican subculture of *curanderismo* (the practice of healing by belief, and by using certain herbs, weeds, and amulets), *espiritismo* (the practice of dealing with the spirits of the unborn and the departed), *hechizos* (the practice of casting black magic spells on one's enemies, similar to voodoo), *sacrificios* (animal sacrifices either to appease God or to cast bad luck on an enemy), *mal de ojo* (or "evil eye" whereby one can bring someone misfortune by deliberately admiring the other's possessions, including relatives), *caido de moyera* (the drop of an infant's fontanel from the top of the skull to the roof of the mouth), *yerba buena* (all purpose herb, boiled and drunk as tea, that supposedly would cure a variety of ailments including upset stomach, rheumatism, cancer, and mental illness), *hechar la mala suerte* (willing someone to have bad luck), and *corazonadas* (unusual palpitations of the heart foretelling that something is about to happen). It was quite common for my mother to speak in conversation about the spells that a neighbor had cast through a witch against a troublesome enemy. Or about how a woman who had wanted her estranged husband back had successfully recited a few lines every night as per the recommendations of the local *curandera*, the neighborhood witch who was held in considerable esteem because of her powers to deal with the supernatural world. In fact, in everyday life we encountered the culture of spells and witchcraft as we met people who threatened us with black magic, who said that they could tell if we were lying by consulting the stars, or who claimed to be in touch with the spirits and could obtain information about the future. Some years later I also stumbled first hand as a witness into a black magic animal sacrifice.

I was already living at another foster home as a teenager, and upon walking out the front door in the morning to open the grocery store that I was working at, I discovered that a large turtle had been hacked to pieces on our front porch, creating a large mess of turtle parts blood that was smeared all over. Quickly I informed my foster mother who upon looking at the gory scene said, "Don't worry. I know what *they* are trying to do. Help me pick up these turtle parts; there is something that I need to do." She took them to a shack that we had in the back, and she didn't come out for about 30 minutes. She explained later that she had to counteract the evil spell that someone was trying to cast on our home. I had full confidence in her ability to fight these unseen demons.

But back to my mother and the witch. My mother said one night that I should get ready because I would be accompanying her to visit to the local *curandera.* She knew where all the *espiritistas, curanderas,* and *brujos* were, and there were plenty in our neighborhoods. We didn't have to walk for long as we came upon this small, wooden house with uneven curtains and all the shades drawn. Even though it was night-time the house was completely dark—we couldn't see any light coming from any of its dirty windows. It had a fence around it, broken in many places, as if the owner really didn't know what was happening to the outside of her house. Our suspicion of neglect was also supported by the numerous potted plants which seemed to have withered a long time ago. There was no sign outside indicating that this person engaged in the business of curing all sorts of incurable diseases, or of connecting with spirits from the other side of reality. One would have to *know* that this was the house of supernatural powers in order to obtain her services, for appointments were only by invitation and only to the ones who strongly believed in the power of the dark world.

I had already asked my mother why we were visiting *la curandera.* She replied that she needed someone who could really help her with her breast problem. She said that she had lost faith in the doctors, especially after they stupidly suggested to her that she permit them to cut off her breast. It would take me years to properly realize that my mother had been intensely proud of her body, especially her shapely breasts, and that to have had one of them completely severed would have dealt a perhaps fatal blow to her misplaced self-esteem, to her definition as a real woman. I recalled too how she used to preen herself pretty while my baby brother Benito kept falling off the big bed (his death bed). Her looks were more important than her life, a psychodynamic that would take her away from us, and leave us at the mercy of foster welfare homes.

We knocked on the door a few times, wondering if the witch was home. The door had some poorly done etching of what looked like a half-horse, half-wolf, and we were about to touch it when the door finally opened. It startled us. The frail-looking and hunchbacked Mexican woman in the red silk dress and black veil spoke first.

"Good evening. Leave your doubts outside. Just let the power of the spirits guide you. Come in and don't speak until we are seated." She motioned us in.

Inside was very dark, with the strong odor of mildewed clothes or wet wood, I wasn't sure, but it reminded me of the many abandoned homes I had broken into. She had almost translucent curtains or cloths hanging across doorways—good thing because it allowed my mother and me to get a glance at the witch's large collection of bottled teeth. Hopefully they were from animals. All over her walls were odd-looking ornaments or figurines in the shape of animals—maybe wolves—and crosses with sharp ends, as if they could be used as weapons if needed. Whatever those ornaments were, there were lots of them, making the wall appear like a display at a store, only darker as if the intent was for the customer not to be able to see the objects. She also had about a dozen Catholic symbols and saints, dimly lit with small incandescent light bulbs. In one of the corners on a bookcase was a skeleton on display—a raccoon, I believe. Immediately the thought came to my mind that maybe she too liked to kill animals for fun. *No doubt she stabbed them with those Catholic crosses made from stiletto knives. This was an angry witch!*

She led us into her parlor, the floorboards creaking as we formed a line through the narrow hallways. In the middle was an unassuming square table with four chairs and a bright red cloth cover, illuminated by the maybe 25 candles she had burning throughout the room. She motioned for us to sit down, then she sat herself. She looked very intently at my mother, removed her veil, and then she spoke.

"I understand you have a problem and that you need help."

"Yes, Señora Carmelina, the doctors said that I have this thing, this cancer in my breast. They want to cut it—to take it out, the breast I mean, but I will not let them. And that is why I came to see you. The people say you are very good at solving these kinds of problems."

With the veil off I could see the witch's face, and she wasn't pretty. She looked about maybe 65 years old and had a lot of wrinkles and a bulbous nose with pimples or some other stuff growing on it. Her lips were very thin—she almost didn't have any. Oh, but her eyes were sharp and expressive—she looked at my mother with such intensity.

"Yes, there are no problems that cannot be solved with the power that God has given me. Let me see your breast," the witch told my mother.

At that point my mother partially opened her blouse, exposing her bra, and the *curandera* slid her hand inside it. I knew exactly what she was feeling, for a few days earlier my mother had asked me to squeeze her bare breast, and I felt a horrible hard lump inside. I'll never forget that ugly feeling, even though I enjoyed squeezing my mother's other, normal breast.

"Oh, yes, I see. How long have you had this?" she asked as she removed her hand from my mother's bra.

"About a year, maybe a little bit more. Do you think you'll be able to do something about it—to make it go away? I really do not want to let them cut it."

"OK, close your blouse. I'll let the spirits take care of this. They will dissolve the lump and you'll be able to tell those ignorant doctors *que se vayan a la chingada*" ("to go fuck themselves").

The hunchback woman took out some cups, some odd-looking utensils, and mixed some powders and liquids together. She was talking to herself, or rather, to the spirits that she was addressing to enlist their assistance with this difficult problem. As my mother looked yearningly at this woman, I looked intently into my mother's green eyes, watering with tears and reflecting the dancing flames from the two-dozen burning candles in the small parlor. Little did I know then that at that very moment in time, my mother's demise was being prepared in those cups that contained this witch's potions. My mother's eyes, innocent now in the face of death, reflected merely the candlelight, not the more sinister delusion that was to cost her her life. They were eyes full of hope, full of despair from the intransigent cancerous vulture that had established residence in her breast. These were the eyes of desperation, of a woman driven to the edge by a horrible life devoid of normal pleasures, happiness, security, and love, and she seemed unable to make any changes for the better. Of all the mistakes that she made in life, of all the bad choices that she felt were good, of all the wrong turns that she took, of all the instances of poor judgment, this session at this parlor with this hunchback witch was to be the last junction in my mother's life where she could have made a right choice for life, for after this regrettable decision, nothing else would matter—my mother would be on an irremediable, irreversible road to her own death. Nobody knew it then, but as my mother was placing her full trust and her life in the hands of this wolf-woman, there would be no more junctions in her life. No more mistakes. No more bad judgment. The implacable forces of nature would then take over so that further decisions would be irrelevant and superfluous from that point on. My mother was innocently choosing death at that table.

La curandera finished mixing the powders, then she passed her hands over the mixing container, mumbling something about some Catholic voodoo spirit guiding the healing powers so that this "healing" would have God's full blessing. With a dark spatula adorned with a bone handle she transferred the pasty white stuff to a small jar, capping it tightly and kissing it as she looked upwards toward her ceiling, and I guess the heavens. Then she looked at my mother again and placed my mother's hand around the jar. She asked her to repeat after her:

"The spirits have blessed this *pomada* (pomade)."

"It has the power to remove any disease from any body."

"Bless the spirits of the light."

"Bless the spirits of darkness."

"Take the evil spirit from my breast, spray it with holy water, and watch it burn."

"May the spirits of the light and the darkness assist me forever and ever."

"Amen."

The witch then told my mother, "Rub it on your breast at night before going to bed. And your lump will disappear."

"But how long do I have to keep doing this?"

"Do it until you run out of the *pomada*, and then your lump will be gone. The spirits are never wrong. Never!"

I was an unwitting witness to this fateful meeting, ignorant myself, to the cultural ritual that is the misfortune of so many. If I had only known, if I had only been wiser, if I had only been older, I would have protected my mother, I would have driven her to any hospital on the face of the Earth, I would have told her that losing her breast would not lower her value as a person, I would have comforted her, I would have wiped her tears, and I would have brought her breakfast in bed like all mothers deserve. But, the unseen and depraved Demon of Death had been sitting all along on that fourth chair with us at that parlor table that tragic night, secretly manipulating events so that it could enter the momentous decision of life and death which my mother was making. When my mother accepted the pomada jar from the witch, her death was almost guaranteed.

I don't recall if my mother paid the witch. In any case, with trembling hands she placed the pasty stuff in her purse and we left, full of fatally false hope.

My mother had already made up her mind that she was going to disregard whatever the doctors at the Wickerstein Institute were suggesting, and she neglected to go to treatment, opting for a few months to rub the pomade on her breast to try to save it. It was in these few months in early 1958 that the cancer had spread from her breast to her inner chest, although we did not know it then. As my mother finished using all the pomade that the witch had given her, she began to realize that the lump was bigger and harder, and not smaller. She again decided to resume her medical visits to the Institute in San Antonio.

In the past every time she went to San Antonio for treatment she would stay for two or three weeks, while I handled all household duties. The useless Satan was never home, so as best as I could I would have to get all the kids off to school, sometimes without breakfast, and chaotically manage them when they came home in late afternoon. I was so bad myself, what was I doing managing a household? This time it was no different.

She got her Greyhound Bus round-trip ticket ahead of time. It was sometime in May, 1958. All of us kids were playing on the floor of our white house on Morelos Street. As usual, the cockroach Satan was nowhere to be seen, even this day, when his very sick wife was going to San Antonio for treatment. How vile and despicable of him. As I said before, this vermin needed to die. It was about 7:00 in the evening when my mother announced to us all that she was ready to leave the house and walk to downtown El Paso where she would then board the bus for the grueling ten-hour ride to San Antonio.

She had a small bag with some clothes, her purse hanging from her forearm. I think she kissed us all—but I can't remember—and went through the front gate. As she rounded the corner of the lot we waved to her and she waved back. She looked sad and tired. I never saw my mother alive again.

A few years ago, my Uncle Felipe from San Antonio gave me the horrifying details of my mother's last few weeks in San Antonio. He had first-hand knowledge because my mother stayed at his house while going to the cancer hospital during the day. He said that when my mother arrived at his house that May in 1958, she was already looking very sick. The next day he took her to the hospital for her appointment, and the doctors immediately performed a series of extensive tests and took numerous X-rays. He had the unpleasant duty of being the family member called in by the doctors who told him that my mother's breast cancer had spread to almost every organ in her chest cavity, affecting her lungs, stomach, liver, kidneys, esophagus, and bladder. They said that the situation was hopeless. There was nothing they could do; there was no treatment for a cancer this advanced. The doctors then told him that it would be up to him to decide if he wanted to tell my mother that she only had a few weeks left. He said through tears that he agonized over the decision, especially because all of us kids were back in El Paso, writing letters to our mother to please come home soon because we were all alone. We had no idea that our mother was almost dead.

Uncle Felipe took my mother back to his house, and as per the doctors' instructions began to administer medications for pain. Felipe's wife, Tina, who was about 18 years old at the time, had the unenviable task of injecting our mother daily with morphine to ease the pain of the ever-spreading cancer, a task that she performed with responsibility and honor, as Uncle Felipe described to me. It hurt me so deeply down to my core to hear my Uncle Felipe tell me that my mother kept asking him, from her deathbed:

"Felipe, how are my children? Are they alright? Are they eating alright? Felipe, how are my children? Will they be OK? How's the puppy doing? Felipe, am I going to be alright? Is everything going to be OK just as the doctors said? Am I going to get rid of this cancer?"

Uncle Felipe had already made the decision to lie to my mother about her condition, telling her that she would eventually be cured. He said that he did that because she was already suffering too much, that she was in extreme pain from the massive amount of cancer in her body. Sometimes she would foam at the mouth. Sometimes she would gasp for air. Sometimes she would empty her bowels in her bed. She no longer could eat. My mother was so close to death.

Back in El Paso we went on with our disorganized lives, fully abandoned, surviving as well as we could. I then received a letter from my mother in which she said she wanted to let me know that the previous December (1957) when she had been staying briefly at the hospital in San Antonio she had heard these carolers singing Christmas songs just outside her hospital window, and that her all-time favorite was "The Little Drummer Boy." She said she thought of me. At that time this did not mean much to me, but now as an adult it is a warm thought from my mother who must have suspected that the end was near.

Early June 1958. I should have known something was up. We received word in El Paso that some of us kids should immediately leave for San Antonio. El Diablo made the decision that the three girls should go to San Antonio, and that the three boys, including myself, should stay behind. They had been gone a few days when the devastating news came to us.

Sunday 16 June 1958. It was about 10:00 in the morning, and I was alone in the house with my brother Elizeo and my brother Tomas. El Diablo had not spent the night there—whereabouts, unknown. Social Worker Clara Barrientos, with whom we were familiar, knocked on our door, so I let her in. She had an unusual look on her face; she asked us to sit down. For the next several minutes she rambled about God and about how things sometimes don't work out the way we want them to. Then, there was no way around it—she had to say it:

"*Les vine a decir que esta mañana su mama se fue con Dios.*" ("I came to tell you that early this morning your mother went to be with God.")

Was there no end to our suffering? We looked at the floor, numb. None of us three boys cried. I was 12, Elizeo was about 6, and Tomas 3. On top of our other misfortunes, now we were also motherless. And I thought about it

again: "Who will pay for her funeral?" "She'll never see the doghouse I built."
I can't seem to remember much of the rest of that fateful day. Now we really
were all alone in a shitty, hostile world.

Uncle Felipe recently told me about the horrible events of the early morning of June 16, 1958. My mother's gasping for air had apparently woken up
Tina, who immediately picked up my mother and placed her head on her lap.
Felipe said that he had never seen a human being gasp so horrendously as my
mother did that morning. The cancer was everywhere, growing relentlessly, as
if on a mission to make itself supreme above all other natural forces on Earth,
stopping at nothing, compassionless as all diseases are, and choking her lungs,
turning them to black, gooey sponges. Yet, even in the final clutches of death
my mother again asked Felipe if everything was going to be alright, and Felipe
answered affirmatively. Our poor mother gasped one last time, foamed at the
mouth, and then released all tension in her body, exhaling one last gutteral
rush of air and dying at last in Tina's arms. Our mother's insufferable, short,
and tragic life was over. She was 37.

How many times have I reviewed this tragic death in my heart? How
many times have I cursed my mother, expressing a wanton desire to kill her?
In light of her terribly sad and tragic life, I feel like an ogre and a despicable
human being for saying such terrible things about this woman who suffered
enough for ten lifetimes. No matter how neglectful she was, she suffered along
with us, for her life was also a living hell just like ours.

As I mentioned earlier, my mother herself came from a horribly abusive
and dysfunctional family, her father having been an alcoholic who beat up his
own kids regularly. I suspect strongly that my mother may have been sexually
abused by her own father when she was a young child or a teen. Why else
would she exhibit such dysfunctional behaviors and sexually inappropriate
conduct so early in her life? She eloped at age 15—with a 45-year-old man—
only to be forcibly brought back to the house. Apparently she had sex with
several family members, one of whom may have impregnated her. She then
went on to marry again—Arnulfo Alameda—divorce, and marry again, this
time the lowlife of all lowlives on the planet, Merengueno Zalmar, alias The
Devil, alias El Diablo. Her life with this scumbag Demon was all hell.

My poor mother deserved a happy life, but somehow it always eluded
her. She did not deserve the chronic pain, the abuse, the beatings, the stomp-
ings, the starvation, the insults, and the neglect that were very much a part
of her daily life. And this was on top of the other abuse that she suffered in
her parents' home. How can life be so horrible for a human being? Where is
justice and fairness? Where was God throughout all this? Her death, too, was

horrifying, premature, lonely, and, in my view, unnecessary. It could have been prevented had regular medical care been available to my mother so that she could have had regular checkups that would have uncovered the lump much sooner. And the *curandera*? Damn the fucking witch! She exploited my mother's poor judgment in switching from medical care to magical pomades. That worthless, phony session that cost my mother her life! Such a tragic waste.

After all that my mother endured, she then paid with her life. Then, I, her oldest son, in reviewing my past declared that if my mother were alive today I would have to kill her. Is that fair? Her own son would have to kill this woman who suffered so much? After her own father abuses her, after she suffers from poor choices in husbands, after her own monster husband abuses her, stomps on her, and despises her, after she gets sick with cancer, then her own son kills her? There is something despicably wrong with this. This mother, who wrote me in her last letter from her deathbed that "The Little Drummer Boy" made her think of me? This mother whose life was cut short at age 37? No! It wouldn't be that way! If my mother were alive today, I would have to love her, to help her find the comfort and happiness that she never had but so rightly deserved, to treat her with dignity and respect as all mothers should be treated. I can think of no other woman on the face of the Earth who would be more deserving of a little respect, caring, and love for the innumerable injustices that she endured, only to eventually die away from her home, away from her children.

There is no other road to human dignity and righteousness but the road of forgiveness. I would have to forgive my mother for her terrible mistakes and the pain that we felt as a result. As a parent myself I know how easy it is to make mistakes with one's children, thus putting my mother's terrible parental judgment in perspective. I forgive my mother forever for everything she ever did that caused me pain. Her own suffering was a sign that there was no malice.

"Mami, forgive me for the terrible things I said about you. I was so angry at the awful things that happened to us. Our life was terrible, terrible, terrible. Did you leave me when I was a baby? Where did you go? Why did you leave me? Who is my father? You told me when I was ten years old that Arnulfo was my father, but when I asked him he said he wasn't. Why did he say that? Did you really have sex with the relatives? Whom did you see when you took me to The *Hotel Central* back entrance? Why did you leave Arnulfo? Why did you shack up with El Diablo? He was so vicious to all of us. I am so sorry, Mami, that you got sick with cancer. I wish I could have been bigger so that I could have helped you make the right decisions. We should not have gone to that *curandera*, mami, she steered you wrong. I would have sold everything that I ever owned, even now, to have gotten you proper medical care. You wouldn't have had to worry about your value without a breast, for you would always be our beloved mother, you would always look pretty to us. I wouldn't have let you take the Greyhound Bus to San Antonio, Mami, for I would have driven you there as many times as necessary.

Uncle Felipe told me how much you suffered in your last week. I am so, so sorry that you had to suffer. No human being should suffer like that. I wish I could have been there to see you one last time. I am sorry. I would have wanted you to stay with us forever, but even I could not have stopped what happened. I would have kissed you, Mami, one last time. But you know what? Before you go I need to tell you that I am going to miss your not being with us everyday. Who will see me in the play at school? Who will go to my graduation? When I got married (then divorced) you were not there. I envied the other people who had mothers. I wish you had been there, Mami. And you need to know that one of the greatest sources of pain for me as an adult is that my children never got to meet you. I could never give them a grandmother on my side. That was you. They had only the other grandmother. But you are their grandmother in spirit at least. I wish so much that you and they could have had a relationship. That is a great pain in my life.

I would have loved to have fixed our problems so that we could have had a normal mother-son relationship as I became an adult. I just want you to know that I feel so sad because of how you suffered. Don't worry about the things I said concerning your mistakes. I was angry. You are my mother. All is forgiven. Just rest in peace. You will always be in my heart. I love you, Mami. Bye…"

The Funeral

Soon they arranged for us to travel to San Antonio by Greyhound Bus, as my mother had done on so many occasions. El Diablo came with us, and we all arrived late at night in the heart of San Antonio's downtown section. I recall very clearly that as I got off the bus at what must have been three o'clock in the morning, I was dazed and it just didn't really feel that we were here for our mother's funeral. Where was my mother's body? We are now in San Antonio, she is somewhere in San Antonio. Where is my mother's body? Will we see the body right now? Is the body stiff? Where are we going tonight? Where are my sisters? What will happen to us after the funeral? Are we living in El Paso with El Diablo? As depraved as our life had been in El Paso with our mother as the passive body and El Diablo as the Great Tormentor, it still had some perverse *predictability and familiarity*, which had evaporated with my mother's death. Our inner sickness had adjusted to this tormented life, finding some sort of wicked comfort in preferring the predictable depravity to the uncertainty of a new life.

Uncle Felipe was there at the Greyhound Bus Station; everybody exchanged a few words, nothing meaningful, just maybe his asking if we were all OK. He drove us in the deathly still of the early San Antonio morning to his house, where everybody was asleep, and I gathered that my mother's body had already been removed, taken somewhere to spend the night. We were so tired but managed to find the energy to eat one doughnut with milk, then all of us went to bed on blankets on the floor. There was no time to cry. Life was moving too fast to understand anything at this stage. I passed out as soon as my body was horizontal on the floor, the same floor that my mother had walked on in the last days of her life. I could almost sense her footsteps—now gone forever.

In the morning we woke up and saw my sisters Ana, Tencha, and Elsa, but I don't remember being excited about seeing them. We all ate a quick breakfast. It was time to go to the funeral parlor to see my mother in the box. I had wanted to see her for so long, but I never had imagined that I would be seeing her lying down, asleep forever, in a coffin. We left the house with knots in our stomachs.

Along the way everyone was quiet. There was nothing to say. Who would be paying for my mother's funeral? I felt responsible for the expenses. I had an idea that as her brother, my Uncle Felipe, would be taking that responsibility. I'll have to pay him some day for my mother's funeral, I thought, because right now I only have six cents in my pocket. As her oldest son it was my duty to at least pay for her funeral expenses. The car made its way through some of San Antonio's poorest neighborhoods. I kept looking at the pitiful houses with broken windows; at the countless dead mattresses that people threw on the sidewalks (did they urinate on them just as we did?); at the dismembered cars that littered the streets, abandoned and ravaged by perhaps kids just like us; at the dirty, filthy Mexican kids who played with old truck tires on trash heaps, unaware of the unforgiving cancers lurking just below the surface. I knew that El Paso was not the only city with poor kids like us, that life was hard elsewhere on the planet.

We arrived at Salamanca Funeral Home and entered through the wide front doors. My other aunts were there, plus some strangers whom I had never seen before, but, that was OK, since we never had any rules about strangers or about safety. We were seconds away from seeing my mother's cadaver in the box. I wasn't sure if I wanted to see her. I could still see her waving goodbye at us as she turned the corner last time she left for the hospital.

My Uncle Felipe asked all of us kids to sit down. I thought of my brother Benito's funeral—now my mother's. We were on the front row of the chapel, so my mother's death-gray coffin was squarely in front of us. I was afraid to ask if I could look at my mother because Felipe would say yes. I was afraid to look inside. Felipe must have known what was in my mind, for at that moment, just seconds after we sat down, he asked me if I wanted to take a look at my mother. "Yes!" I said.

As my line of vision slowly reached the edge of the coffin I came face to face with my mother's dead body. I had thought earlier that I would scream, or cry, or vomit, and tremble, and turn my head away, but none of that happened at that moment that I laid eyes on my poor mother's cadaver. Where's the cancer? I thought. Did it eat all of her insides? Is the fucker happy now that it ate my mother up? Does it die along with its victim? My only consolation for my anger against this unseen and silent killer was that it too would be buried along with my mother, so it could never get out of the box. As I stared at my mother's face I did not feel anything, I could not feel sad, or sorry, or angry—I simply could not feel. My brothers and sisters, too, could not cry. In fact, nobody cried, or even whimpered at this funeral. At that moment my Aunt Julieta asked all of us to line up against the coffin, but to not obstruct a clear view of my dead mother's face, for she was about to take a photograph, for posterity. After the flash of light we all went back to looking at my mother's face, not knowing what to do next.

It was years later that I first saw the photograph of all of us next to my mother's coffin, and I was aghast at the terrible look that all of us had on our faces. Even though none of us cried, we all had the hollow look of long-term trauma, as if we had been hostages all our lives, real hostages—of fate, of nature, of family disorganization, of depravity. To my surprise, even the hated Devil had a look of grief on his ugly face. He had needed a woman to be ugly with, as much as she had needed a half-man, half-dog who was a "real" man in her jaundiced view of things. The venomously pathological relationship was over, so the Fiend no longer had a victim to suck spiritual blood from. Perhaps my mother represented to The Devil his *own* mother, with whom he had had a similarly caustic relationship, and in feeling some grief for his own dead wife he was actually feeling the loss of his own emotionally sick mother. It cannot be said ever of The Devil that he shed a genuine tear of love for my dead mother, for his behavior and the look in his eye while she was alive was not the look of romantic love but rather of contempt, hatred, hostility, disrespect, and dishonor. On one occasion he said of my mother as she related to him how she had had severe trouble breathing while en route to the hospital in a Greyhound Bus, "She should have choked to death to get it over with." This savage dog did not have the capacity to shed a genuine tear for anything.

There was no point in staying around looking at the body too long, for we were not going to cry—we were in shock, as I knew from the infamous photograph. My Aunt Julieta took all of us kids to a small coffee shop across the street. She told us that from there we would be going to the cemetery. I guess we were ready.

After they closed the lid of my mother's box at the chapel, I never saw my mother's face again. Her eyes were closed, she could not smile. My mother was gone. Then at the cemetery we waited by the open grave as these burly Mexican cemetery workers brought the casket and placed it above the hole. As the pastor read Psalm 23 ("The Lord is my shepherd, I shall not want...") from *La Santa Biblia*, my Uncle Felipe's wife, Aunt Tina, leaned over to me and said, "*Victor, si quieres llorar llora, llora por tu mama. No tengas verguenza. Aqui todos te entendemos.*" ("Victor, if you want to cry, cry, cry for your mother. Do not be embarrassed. Here we all understand you.") With those words Tina welded her image in my heart forever. Those were kind words from someone who had just spent so much time with a dying woman, time which she could have been spending enjoying her young marriage to my Uncle Felipe. But I did not feel like crying as they lowered the casket into the hole. This was it. My mother was in the ground. The Mexican gravediggers were now reversing what they had done yesterday. Soon we could not see the box. The days of terror were over for Maria Esperanza, 37, our long-suffering mother.

The Shame of Death

Within a day or two after the funeral all of us kids were back in El Paso at our white house on Morelos Street, although I have absolutely no recollection as to how we got there. Then it started. I noticed that when I would see some of the kids and familiar adults of the neighborhood, people I talked to regularly, I would be terribly ashamed to talk about my mother, and about my mother's death. I remember vividly the consuming feeling inside my chest, as if a cement block had been placed on my chest when I was lying down, and the churning motion of my stomach, all coming together as people approached me and asked me about my mother's condition. The shaming of my soul was pervasive, painful, unforgiving, unrelenting—I felt that I was a leper, a worthless animal, an outcast, a pariah, a misfit, a loner, a renegade from society, a reject from the junk pile, a kid on the block not deserving of having a mother. Somehow the universe had deemed me unworthy to have a mother. At a time when our pain was the greatest, we actually did not have the other parent to ease the pain. On the contrary, the hated Devil kept on abusing us, compounding the damage many times over. We desperately had needed counseling all our lives, but more so now. But there was nothing. Where was the El Paso County Child Welfare Unit? Had I had the courage I would have ended my life at this point; too much raw pain from a viciously hostile world.

I couldn't even be honest with the neighborhood kids I regularly played with. I visited them as soon as I got back to El Paso after the funeral, and they knew that my mother had been desperately sick. Yet upon my return I was terrified that they would ask me about her, so I just avoided the subject. When one of their mothers looked into my eyes without saying anything I was so afraid that she knew the truth about my mother but was just not admitting it. I was so afraid that she knew that I was no good, that I was a piece of junk, that I was inferior to the rest of humanity, that of all the kids that we all knew I was the only one who did not deserve a mother. Would they laugh at me? Would they ask me why I did not have a mother? Did they know that I did not deserve a mother? Would they want to make fun of me about my dead mother? The shame inside me was sickening and unbearable—as if I was being squeezed around my chest by a satanic cobra, a serpent I could neither see nor name. I couldn't get rid of that horrible toxic feeling in my soul. Worse, I didn't know what to call it. Nobody to talk to.

The heartburn, or "hot vomit," that I had had since I was two years old became even more pronounced, making me feel that my meals would stay just below the throat on most occasions. And, concerning my better friends, I never did tell them that my mother had died—I never talked about my mother to them ever again. They must have figured it out and were gracious enough not to bring up the subject.

Through the years the shame stayed with me, influencing me sometimes in very subtle but toxic ways, but sometimes not so subtly. Of course the death of a mother doesn't mean that the surviving children have no value, but, on the other hand, a living mother serves to validate their existence, their life, and essentially their value. And since The Devil served mainly to degrade us in every imaginable way, our budding sense of self-esteem had no external support, no social validation. We were left at the mercy of our own internal demons, defenseless and defeated by hunger, abuse, neglect, and the loss of our mother.

Final Breakup of the Family

Being in the house all alone, all of us kids, with no loving and supporting adult, and no mother, felt eerie. The Devil was his usual ugly self; nothing had changed for this beast, this vermin from the toilet bowl, for he would leave us all alone for the entire day, and I, at age 12, was still desperately trying to maintain a household on my own. Social Worker Clara Barrientos kept constant contact with the family, and she told me that the child welfare authorities in El Paso had indicated to her that they felt that all of us kids would have to be removed from our (despicable) household, but that the unit did not have money for my foster care support. In other words, there were funds to provide foster care for everyone except me, the oldest. She told me, however, that she knew of a middle aged couple who were looking to adopt a boy between 10 and 13 years old, and that they were interested in talking to me. Imagine that: I was now for sale! If I said the "right" things when they came to see (interview) me, then possibly they could adopt me. It would mean leaving my brothers and sisters behind, for the couple would want to adopt only me. I thought about that for a while, wondering if this middle-aged couple, who had plenty of money for vacations, nice homes, and a college education, would want to adopt a boy with head lice crawling up and down his shoulders. Shamefully, I concluded that if they asked me to go live with them I would definitely go. It is sad to say, but my brothers and sisters and I did not enjoy a normal sibling bond, instead behaving more like snakes which came from the same batch, but essentially needing to go their own ways without looking back. We really did not have a normal closeness; we just happened to have come from the same womb, and to have suffered together.

When the husband and wife showed up I immediately saw the obvious: they were gringos! That was a plus, the way I saw it, since we all knew that gringos had more food, more money, and better houses. We sat them by the kitchen table and they began to talk to me, telling me how they were looking for someone like me to be their son. Never mind that my mother was just recently dead in the box; here I was "interviewing" for a possible adoption by this white couple who appeared nice, and were looking at me very intently, and whom I wanted to go home with. I was sick of the hell with Satan. Looking back at this meeting I am surprised that this man and woman did not just walk out of our house without looking back, for the entire house was in total disarray, and we kids were absolute terrors and utterly without manners.

Mrs. Barrientos was there acting as a mediator, which brings another thought to mind: Legally The Devil would have been notified of this attempt to adopt me, and apparently he must have given them the OK to begin adoption proceedings. As despicable as our situation had been in the company of this maggot-face, it still does not feel good to know that he readily agreed to put me up for adoption, for it is such a tangible sign that he just wanted to get rid of me, something that I suspected in my heart all those years of hell. For all I know, he may have come a lot closer than I ever suspected to carrying out a plan to kill me, for when the time came when his services would be needed as the only parent at home, he opted instead to put me on the market for adoption. As I said, this anal tumor did not deserve to live.

Many years later the thought hit me as to why none of my aunts or my uncle adopted us kids who were left without a mother at the mercy of The Demon and on the verge of going to foster homes. No easy answers. They fumbled their explanations, and it was all bullshit. I can only conclude that they had very little love to give after barely taking care of their own families. Besides, was it their moral duty to take care of us six kids too?

Nothing ever came through with this white couple who wanted to adopt me, for Mrs. Barrientos later said that they had changed their mind. Apparently they were also looking at some other kids, and I lost out by a few "points." So the leech-bitten Devil did not want me, and now this couple had second thoughts. It did not make me feel good, right after my mother's death.

All along I think that Mrs. Barrientos had had a backup plan, for she told me at that point that she would welcome me into her home even if the Child Welfare Unit did not have money to pay her for the foster care. I agreed.

It was late July 1958. It had only been a few weeks since my mother's death, but our family was about to complete its disintegration. On the appointed day Mrs. Barrientos and other social workers from the Child Welfare Unit came to pick us all up. We did not even pack any clothes—we hadn't thought of it. El Diablo was not there but was out drinking his life away, as usual, and the message was that he simply did not care that all of us were about to exit the house and never come back. When he left that morning I did not know it then, but fate would have it that he was actually walking out of my life forever. No more torture, no more beatings, no more humiliation, no more terror. This horrendous monster was out of my life for good. Elsa, Tomas, Elizeo, Tencha, Ana, and I did not cry, did not hug, did not kiss, did not say goodbye as we exited our white house on Morelos Street, that fateful house where we last saw our mother alive. In fact, we did not even look at each other; we felt like leaves being blown away by the winds of social forces too great for us to comprehend or to resist. With hollow eyes and with our hearts in a fog, all six of us kids were divided, separated, and put into four separate social work vehicles destined to go to four separate homes. Never again would we lay eyes on the filthy, flea-infested furniture we were leaving behind. Never again would we touch all the rags that we called "clothes." Never again would we see the two starving dogs that had the misfortune of being our pets. Never again would all of us be in the same room at the same time. Never again would we be together as a family. Never.

Mrs. Barrientos locked the doors of the house and got into the car with me. The house was now empty, except for the skinny cockroaches and the lice that fell off our matted hair. This tragic house knew the horrors we lived through, of the blood-curdling screams of terror and agony in the middle of the night. Of the chilling nightmares that tormented our damaged souls. Of the merciless beatings and depraved sexual abuse that were part of our lives. Of the violent and neglectful manner in which the adults of the house parented us. Of the chronic hungers and deprivations that killed our sense of brotherhood. Of the wretched disintegration of this pack of worthless hyenas that called themselves a family. The closing doors kept the wailing spirits in their proper tomb. In a way our life, our souls, our experiences, our suffering, our losses, and our terrors in the night, condemned this poor house as the place where a highly toxic and irredeemable subhuman family once lived. The karma alone would make it uninhabitable.

The four vehicles drove us away in four different directions, into the unknown, far from the house of horrors, closing this terror-filled part of our worthless and tragic lives, and opening a new life, yes, a new life now full of alarming symptoms, for we all carried deep within our souls the dormant seeds of serious emotional disturbance.

Chapter Seven
Six Years at the Barrientos Foster Home

To my surprise, Mrs. Barrientos was driving in the direction of the foster home where just recently I had done some time, so I started to wonder if indeed she had been truthful about offering her home to me. About two blocks from the previous foster home we turned into an unknown street and made our way to her house, a wooden structure attached to a small, brick storefront called *Barrientos Grocery*, located on the West side of town. I did not know it then but this would be my home for the next six years, and henceforth I would work in that store in the early mornings and after school.

All my brothers and sisters had been taken elsewhere to three other residences, so I was the only one who was accepted by the Barrientos on a nonsubsidized basis since the Welfare Unit claimed it had no money. Mrs. Barrientos showed me into the house, which was modest but very clean with four bedrooms and a garage in the back that had been converted to a tool shed. Next to the garage was a massive *mesquite* tree with bark split in so many places that it reminded me of so many heavy Mexican men who had gained so much weight while still keeping their old shirts, causing the front of the shirt to stretch at the buttons right at the belly line. At the base of the tree was a large but neat stack of boxes full of empty soda bottles, undoubtedly from the store. I immediately thought of the Saturday morning movies that we had been going to with just two empty soda bottles as the admission price. And here in front of me I had well over 500 bottles—enough for 250 free movies, I thought.

At the very corner of the lot, physically attached to the house, was the cubic concrete building, painted white just like the house, that was home for the grocery store, which, I found right away, belonged to this foster family. Mrs. Barrientos took me inside the store, through the back entrance that connected to the porch of the house, and she introduced me to her husband, El Señor Fausto Barrientos. He was a slightly heavy man, friendly, who had very strong and prominent facial features and a dark brown tone to his skin that reminded me of an Aztec Indian from the interior of Mexico. I knew right away that I would get along fine with him.

Inside the store I could see the basic groceries that it carried: canned goods, basic toiletries, some fruits and vegetables, assorted candies, a wide selection of soft drinks, pinto beans, fresh corn and flour tortillas, some luncheon meats, and, of course, beer and cigarettes. A very small section on the counter was reserved for "Electrical Appliance Repair," as a sign read, a sideline of the store—this caught my interest right away because of my experiments in electricity and electronics. There were some irons, toasters, waffle irons, and a wide assortment of appliance parts on a peg board against the wall. It was beginning to look very interesting.

Mrs. Barrientos soon introduced me to the three other kids in the house and also to a young woman who appeared to be about 20 years old. Berta was her name—she was introduced as Mrs. Barrientos's daughter and was soon to be married. I made the mistake of assuming that the other three boys in the house were sons of Mrs. Barrientos, but I was promptly corrected: "We are foster kids just like you. They brought us here." At this point Mrs. Barrientos suggested that it might be a good idea if we called her *Tia*, and that we should call Mr. Barrientos *Tio* (Aunt and Uncle, respectively. Everyone spoke exclusively in Spanish). I sort of liked that, for it implied some kind of family connection. So from that moment on that is exactly what I called them.

That first week I spent mostly on getting to know where everything was, what the rules of the house were, and what my duties were going to be in helping out at the family grocery store. Of greatest value to me was that (1) there was always food in the house, (2) I did not get beat up, (3) I did not have to worry about what would happen in the middle of the night, (4) there were no fierce fights between the adults in the house, (5) there appeared to be some order and direction in what we were doing, something that prior to this had been alien to my life, and (6) I did not have to submit to rapes for food or other necessities. I stopped wetting my bed (at age 12), and it felt so good to have a nice, clean, warm bed every night. No more urine smell, no more disgusting looks from others because of my repugnant body odor. They de-liced my hair with the strongest full-strength dog flea-and-tick shampoo that they could find (we used to call it *El champu del perro*), and even then the job required several applications in addition to hundreds of strokes from a very fine-toothed lice comb to remove every last firmly embedded egg. With strong medications they de-wormed me, and the antibiotics got rid of the several chronic infections in my body. Soon enough I also got eyeglasses and marveled at the brilliant colors of the world around me. The Barrientos couple also gave me my first toothbrush; the entire first week I used it my gums bled profusely from the relentless assault of the bristles upon sensititive gums and teeth. That brushing force was totally alien to my mouth and my gums—they were protesting the intrusion. Then they also surprised me with underwear: brand new T-shirts and briefs. It felt so nice to feel tight under my pants! I had gotten used to the idea of having my testicles banging around all the time, so these tight briefs were a welcomed change for the better. Yet in spite of all these nice things that were happening to me, there were still some demons tormenting me in the middle of the night.

On several occasions in my sleep I "accidentally" half-strangled our little dog, a Chihuahua named Chiqui who used to sleep in the same bed with me. It was Mr. Garza of the Welfare Unit who had come to the house specifically to address this problem, asking me what prompted the strange attacks. I replied truthfully that I had been dreaming that The Devil had been chasing me and that he was about to catch me when I woke up in terror. Somewhere within those dream sequences I had squeezed Chiqui's neck. He advised that in my sleep I should take a gun and shoot El Diablo as he was chasing me so that I would never again have to worry about his attacks. I accepted his suggestion, and the premise behind it, but never again had the opportunity to shoot the scumbag Satan in my dreams, for his tormenting influence just disappeared after that. Maybe at some other level, more profound and more sinister than in these dreams, or even than in real life, his legacy would come back to haunt me in the form of deep subconscious conflicts leading to the formation of numerous neuroses which I later developed in adult life. It was not going to be easy to separate myself emotionally from the years of trauma and torture that had already consumed a major portion of my psyche, leaving me with undiagnosed conflicts and pathologies that would slowly surface in the years ahead. Only time would tell what horrible symptoms would come to the surface, or, worse, influence my behavior surreptitiously—that is, without my being fully aware of why I wanted to do certain things. I should have gone into psychotherapy as soon as I began my new life, and spared myself and others untold anguish, pain, and suffering.

As I was adjusting to the new, more normal life, I did not bother to think much of my dead mother, in the ground only a few weeks. Who knows, was it that I just buried the pain, repressing it because it was too uncomfortable to think of how alone I was even when I had numerous relatives? I remember very well: After I was brought to the Barrientos foster home I never again shed a single tear for my mother, I never again thought much of her, I never spoke of her, until in recent years I underwent extensive therapy, and then the colossal dam burst. Then too, in those years in this foster home, I never missed my brothers and sisters, even though it would be two years before I ever saw any of them after we all split up at the Morelos Street home. There must have been very poor familial bonding, or, rather, maybe there was no family bonding at all.

Right from the start Tio started showing me the ropes at the store; my assigned job there was to wait on customers and to ring up their purchases at the cash register. It tickled me no end to handle so much money; I used to get excited at the sight of a mere nickel. Shy at first, I quickly learned the skill of asking customers what it was that they needed, totaling up their purchases, and giving them change from their dollars. I was happy with this arrangement.

Not that I was going to make much money here. By the end of the first week, on a Saturday night, Tio approached me as I was watching TV, exhausted, and he handed me my first week's pay: a total of $1.25 for 30 hours. Of course it was small, but I did have money to spend, and I was so glad to get experience with sales.

Soon I had the opportunity to observe Tio as he accepted small appliances for repair, mentioning to him that I would like to try my hand at it. He readily agreed, showing me how to disassemble toasters, how to diagnose problems, and the techniques he used in the repairs. In less than two weeks I doing all the repairs, earning extra money for my effort. It made me feel great that I was doing something constructive, something that was challenging.

As I was learning new things at the foster home, I was also learning about rules—there were *rules* at this home. We were supposed to take showers at night, go to bed at 10:00 P.M., get up at 6:30 A.M., go next door to the store and prepare it for opening for 7:00 A.M., get dressed, go to school, come home for lunch at 11:30, wait on customers at the store for about 20 minutes, eat lunch, go back to the store for another 20 minutes, go back to school, come back to the store at 4:30 P.M., work there until 8:00 P.M., do homework, shower, and back in bed by 10:00 P.M. It was a full day, every day. It was what I needed. God, it was what I had needed all along!

Tia and Tio seemed to like me from the beginning, and I liked them. It was clear to me that Tia was in control at this house, quite the contrary of what had tragically been case in our own family. But Tio did not seem to mind—he was good natured about her suggestions, making his own needs known in a variety of ways. I liked them both, but Tio became special for me right away maybe because he was a nice man—a father figure so different from the Demon who had posed as our father when we lived at our own home. Soon I started following Tio around the house as if I were a dog, even waiting for him right outside the bathroom! I quickly learned how to roll Bugler cigarettes for him, and how to fix him one or two drinks per day (mostly Tequila Cuervo with Coca-Cola). He would talk to me, unlike the Satan fiend.

Many times in the evenings Tio and I would just sit on the patio of the house, after the Texas sun had gone down and the oppressive heat of the day was replaced by the welcome dry and cool air of the evenings, he drinking his Tequila, and Coke or Pepsi for me, talking about politics, Mexican culture, history, jazz, women, or about electrical repair techniques. Not that Tio was an intellectual, for he had gone only to about eighth grade, but he did have common-sense and well-thought-out opinions. Jazz, for example, he said was *puro pedo* (not real, not written, all "gas"), that jazz musicians play free style, playing whatever notes or musical sequences come to their hearts at the moment. I thought that the concept of someone playing jazz was outrageous; how could one repeat the performance the next night if one had played "at random" the previous night? It was mind boggling. Most of the time, though, I just listened as he talked, learning new things, things that children normally learn from parents, but which had never been discussed at our own home. In fact, as I look back, I do not think that in our mother's home we ever had a decent conversation, or that we ever sat together at the dinner table as a family. That never happened. That never happened!

One interesting thing about Tio was that he made only intermittent eye contact with whomever he was talking to, including me. As we sat outside he would take a deep drag from the cigarette I had rolled for him, a non-filtered job made from the harshest dry tobacco imaginable, and as he would release the smoke from his lungs he would talk at the same time, the smoke emanating from his mouth perfectly synchronized with the syllables and the linguistic emphases of his stories. I was mesmerized by this feat of talking and smoking at the same time. At The Projects, Rafa had performed similar feats, but this time with Tio it was different, there was somehow some wisdom behind his talks, as opposed to the raw vulgarity and anger of Rafa. Tio would puff and look in the direction of the sky, as if searching his mind's catacombs for lost information, relating to me some deep truth about the universe. One of these was about the relationship between the white, gringo culture, the dominant political and economic force in El Paso, and the subservient Mexican culture.

"The gringo is very smart—he's always trying to figure a way to make more money, Victor," said Tio. "Just look at how the gringo designs the hundreds of parts that we use for repairing appliances, and look at the prices of these parts. Sometimes the separate pieces cost more than a whole iron. So he gets you by selling you the iron first, then by selling you expensive parts when it needs repairs."

"So why can't we buy some of these parts in Mexico where I am sure they would be cheaper?" I naively asked.

"No, Victor, it does not work out that way. The gringo *no es pendejo* (is no fool); he keeps the best stuff here in the country and ships to other countries, like Mexico, parts that are of inferior quality. Why do you think we have so many Mexicans from Ciudad Juarez coming here to our store to buy these parts? They are not fools either, for they know that what they buy in Mexico will not last one-third as long as the American parts. It is the same all over the country."

This belief was often expressed when we worked together in fixing an appliance. Knowing only that "It doesn't work; I want you to fix it" as ordered by the customer, we would test an appliance, such as a waffle iron, to determine what it would do or not do. In a series of progressively more complex testing sequences we would oftentimes determine the *symptom* of the appliance, zeroing in on a subsection of its hardware as the potential source of the functional problem. As we would disassemble the waffle iron we could see its inner components, making it easier to visually inspect for irregularities in the functions or appearances of individual components. Sometimes, though, we would be stumped, unable to locate the precise nature of the problem, even though we could determine what the symptoms were. On these occasions we would further disassemble the appliance, only to discover some *new* components inside, parts which had specific functions related to the manifestation of the symptom. As Tio would lay eyes on these new components, he would sigh in relief, but would add, "These gringos are always trying to confuse me. Look here. They have added an overheating sensor to this waffle iron, a sensor that will shut down the entire appliance if it gets too hot. Of course it will prevent a meltdown of the grille areas, but now we have one more component that can go bad. In fact, this one is defective. That is the problem here."

Tio's philosophy of the gringo was not confined to manufacturing and distribution of products, for it seemed that he had thought carefully about other issues as well.

"Since the gringo controls all of the political machinery here in El Paso, as well as all the major employers, you would do well to join a union when you grow up and start working. *La union* will get you a dentist, a doctor, some sick time, and a good paycheck. I should have done that myself, but I had to run this grocery store for my mother. Most of my friends, like Chago Villarreal or Earl Reed, joined the Union-Pacific Railroad many years ago and have done well for themselves. There is no substitute. If you join the union you will do well."

Tio held this opinion very strongly, yet I was not persuaded. Something in me had already been awakened and I was hungry for knowledge, science, electronics, words, classical music, philosophy, and discussion. For the first time I even thought of going to college.

Yet what Tio was saying was of vital importance to my identity, even though I would not know it for many years. Even though the Mexican culture was pervasive all over Texas—in El Paso, San Antonio, Corpus Christi, Houston, Galveston, Dallas-Ft. Worth, Amarillo, Lubbock, Zapata, Cotulla, as well as in hundreds of other cities and towns, it was the white gringo culture that had all the political power, relegating the Mexican-Americans like myself to a sense of inferiority, despair, and fatalism as a way of life. I recalled that my mother had said to me many times when I complained to her about a particular injustice that I had suffered that I need not concern myself with justice or fairness, that in God's eyes all evil-doers, extortionists, and criminals would have to pay in the future. "*Dios los castigara*," she used to say ("God will punish them"). Meskin, greaser, wetback, spic, bean boy, tamale kid, and illegal alien—those were the names gringos called me with hatred in their eyes and venom in their voice. Didn't they know that I had already suffered enough? Didn't they know that my self-esteem was almost non-existent from the years of spiritual, sexual, and physical abuse?

Besides the obvious verbal daggers, there also were the subtle messages that were molding my view of the world and of my culture. All the advertisements depicted beautiful gringa girls or women with blue eyes and blond hair. And, of course, with a beautiful Texas twang accent, a la Lady Bird Johnson, when they appeared on television or on radio. My black hair did not seem too valuable next to photos of these beautiful blond girls. In 1958, at age 13, my own sense of cultural identity was already mortally wounded, for I had seen very little of Mexican family pride in my short years, but whole mountains of organized and consolidated white cultural influence that made me feel that it was indeed superior, that its people were cleaner and more morally sound than my own, that somehow there was something terribly wrong with the

Mexican culture because it had so many problems, that my goal in life was to be more like a gringo, and to eventually marry one of those beautiful blond, blue-eyed girls with the clean, white skin. In contrast I was already feeling that the Mexican culture was ugly, dirty, ignorant, and stupid. These conversations with Tio about the gringo culture simply served to reinforce my belief that the gringo was indeed superior, a belief that Tio had not intended to instill.

As much as Tio was aware of the slight-of-hand in the political and cultural domination of our Mexican culture in Texas, his affective attitude was not belligerence or hostile indignation, but rather it was more like my mother's, except more lucid. He felt that the system was stacked against the Mexican-Americans (all of us!) and that the best you could hope for was to get a good laborer job (for example, a railroad yard worker) while keeping a low profile away from the gringo. Even at age 13, I could tell that Tio was not a fighter, that he had already peacefully adjusted to the harsh realities of two cultures clashing head-on. That is why Tia was the dominant one in this foster home.

Then at other times in the evening air, with Texas-size crickets and moths inviting themselves to our meetings, Tio and I would simply discuss the events of the day at the grocery store. Did we have enough potatoes, onions, and bananas to last until Friday, when the next shipment was scheduled to arrive? Were these items selling faster or slower than usual? Had I filled up the refrigerator with an assortment of sodas? Had I dusted all the shelves? We had fun just talking about some of our silliest customers, like Pelona, the matronly chain-smoker with the personality of a pitbull. She would always complain to no end about our products, services, appearances, and just about anything that did not suit her tastes.

"I want three dozen corn tortillas. And hurry because I have the beans on the stove. You wouldn't want me to eat burned refried beans, would you?" she would bark.

"Sorry, Pelona, but we just ran out of corn tortillas. We had a kid who just took five dozen. Would you care for the flour tortillas? They are warm, soft, and fresh," I would answer.

"What do you mean you ran out? You know damn well I like only the corn tortillas."

"Señora Pelona, I am sorry, we did order about 24 dozen, but they are all gone. Try these, I am sure they taste good. You can make nice bean tacos with them."

"What kind of a *rascuache* (cheap, low quality) store is this anyway? Every time I come here you are out of this or that. Don't you already know the things I like? Why don't you order enough of everything so that you won't run out so frequently. *Chingada madre!* (God-damn it!). OK, I'll take three packs of the *tortillas de harina,* and you might as well toss in five packs of cigarettes. I'll be cooking for a while."

After she got out her frustrations on me she would change her demeanor right away, and would be a friendly person on the way out. Everyone in this foster household knew about Pelona and her foul mouth.

Tio and I talked about others as well. "Did Chago come in today?" Tio would ask.

Oh, yes, Chago had come in. He was a legend in the neighborhood. Chago (nickname for Santiago) was an elderly man of about 80 who was suffering from Parkinson's disease, yet he would walk all over the neighborhood with his cane. Almost every day he would come into the store, a sort of ritual for him since Tio and I would listen to his never-ending stories. He would always buy the same thing: a soft drink, some tortilla chips, and maybe a few slices of American cheese. This was a store, not a restaurant, but Chago got special privileges and was allowed to eat and drink at the cashier's counter. Even though I had spent my first 12 years of life with no morals and no manners, I did feel a certain sense of respect for this old man. As his very jittery hand picked up the soda bottle to bring it to his mouth the liquid inside would slosh and swirl from the considerable involuntary movement of his hand, often spilling about one-fourth of the entire contents. I enjoyed looking at his huge and rugged hands, marked by countless lines and wrinkles, but wrapped in tough, leathery skin, as they held on to the soda bottle, which looked puny in comparison. Poor Chago, his soda would run down the sides of his mouth as the jitteriness made a secure connection between lips and bottle very difficult to achieve.

He would stand there at the counter, eating, drinking, shaking, and deferring to all customers who happened to be there. When I was not busy waiting on someone, he would start up again on his old stories about his life, his many jobs, his tough life as a laborer, and his current problems with his grown children. How incredible that this man, born in the 1870s in the high plains of Mexico, had been to almost all parts of Mexico, regions I never even knew existed, had met maybe thousands of people in his life, was still alive and settled here in this small city of El Paso, Texas. In his conversations with Tio and me, Chago was always polite and friendly, which endeared him to us and we respected him for having lasted for so long in spite of his tremors. I was glad he felt comfortable talking to us, every day.

If it happened that Tio had been temporarily out of the store and had maybe missed the daily visit, at night Tio would ask me about Chago. He would ask me how Chago was and what he had talked about. It was almost like the gossip hour, because Chago too wanted to know how other customers, mutual friends of everyone, were doing. Similarly, if I missed the Chago visit I would ask Tio about him during our evening chat.

So while I was already on a roll with my duties at the store and with my evening chats with Tio, Tia was doing her part to make the home a little better for everyone. Her cooking was excellent, comprising dishes of tacos, tamales, caldo (soup), guisado (fried meat), pollo con mole, chiles rellenos, migas (fried tortillas), bistec con frijoles (steak and beans), and capirotada (Mexican bread pudding). There *always* was food in the house! Hallelujah! Thank God! Food! When she was not cleaning the house she was at the store helping, or, she was on the road as special deputized social worker for the Child Welfare Unit, under direction from Mr. Timoteo Garza. She alone in the family had excellent social and communication skills, for she could start up a conversation with literally anyone, assuming full control right away. No, she was not intrusive or overbearing, for she knew exactly how to do this without anyone knowing it. I admired her confidence.

She was firm with all of us, a side of her that I had not seen as she had been visiting us at our mother's house. Her main weapons, I found out, were (1) her refusing to speak to the misbehaving kid for days or weeks, and (2) her refusing to set a place at the dinner table for this same kid. I found out the hard way about talking back to Tia about anything, for she would simply clam up and refuse to talk to me, or even have eye contact with me, for weeks. Tio would advise me to make up to her by admitting that I was wrong, but on many occasions I felt that I was right, so consequently I did not "make up to her." Needless to say, it was very painful for me to be in this situation of having no verbal contact with Tia who, after all, controlled all the commodities and privileges in the house. Some years later it even got to the point that when I complained to her about this problem she retorted, "*Si no te gusta, largate.*" ("If you don't like it, get the hell out of this house.") Her refusal to talk to me, as well the invitation to leave the house made me feel insecure about what I thought at the very beginning was a very secure homebase.

But I have no complaints, since overall she was a positive experience in my life. Her shortcomings and mistakes are more akin to the ordinary ones parents commonly make in raising children, and certainly not at all comparable to the catastrophic parenting failures of my own biological mother. Tia never sat down with me to give advice, but I, an uncivilized teenager, just absorbed whatever rudiments of ethics and morals I could simply by living in an ethical environment at home, and I credit her and Tio for providing the atmosphere that prevented me from going down the criminal path of destruction during my teenage years. Certainly I had the rage in me, right from the womb of my mother, but apparently it had gone underground, perhaps to resurface later in some other form not readily identifiable.

But Tia had another, more mysterious side to her personality, for she was well versed in the art of Mexican *hechiceria* (what the West would call "witchcraft"). In Mexican culture, religion, witchcraft, superstition, ignorance, hope, hatred, spirituality, voodoo, and science all blend together in various practices that comprise family culture and the social fabric. I was very surprised the very first time I saw this. I had told Tia that I had an ear-ache, that I could not go to school, and she asked me to sit down for the "cure." She got a large, brown paper bag which she cut to make one square piece of paper. She then rolled up this paper to make a large funnel, the small end of which she inserted in my afflicted ear. To my concern and almost horror, she then lit a match to the large, open-ended part of the funnel, while the small end was still inserted in my ear. In no time the entire paper funnel was in flames shooting up towards the ceiling, sending black smoke and burnt particles all over the room as I cowered. I was trusting her with my life here, for I had no idea how long she was going to wait, or how close she would allow the flames to get to my ear. As I was serving as the human base of this towering paper torch, Tia was reciting some words or phrases that were incomprehensible to me, something about getting all the bad spirits out of my ear. At the moment when the hair on my head started to smell from the singeing, she pulled the remains of the funnel from my ear and deposited it in the kitchen sink. After that first time I was not sure which was preferable: to live with the earache or with this fiery ritual.

Of course the earache was gone, but probably because the concern about the flames became the focus of my attention. What's an ear ache when one has a rapidly approaching torch in one's ear?

Then she taught me about the *apretones*, the quick cure for the flu, the common cold, and general bodily malaise. In this procedure the sick person assumes a standing position with fingers of both hands interlocked and placed directly behind one's neck, immediately below the base of the skull. The practitioner then goes behind the sick person, and locks his arms directly in front of the sick person, ensuring that the forearms of the sick person are included in the lock. Finally, the practitioner then lifts the person off the floor with a firm shaking motion to ensure that the individual vertebra of the spinal column are spread apart to release the evil poisons causing the sickness. Successful exorcism is accomplished when one hears the spinal column crack. Victim and practitioner both feel a sense of relief upon hearing the tell-tale crackling of those vertebra. I went through dozens of these *apretones* myself, both as the patient, and as the practitioner. At least it made all of us feel that we were doing something together to combat the misery of the flu.

The time that I found the dismembered turtle on our porch I certainly felt glad that Tia knew something about the occult, for I did not know how to interpret this ghastly event. As I said before, she took the remains of the turtle and performed a neutralizing ceremony so that the evil *hechiceros* (witchcraft practitioners) in the neighborhood would not succeed in placing a hex on the house or on the family. She thought that the hex had been placed by a person jealous at the fact that we had a store.

She also put dollar bills in bottles with a certain kind of *agua bendita* (holy water) to bring better times to the grocery store. The dirt and metallic dust from the cash register coin bins (*marmaja*) were also supposed to have a special significance, so she collected those too.

Yet nothing came close to Tia's *curanderia*, for it was the center of everything else that she did. These healing powers, as bestowed on her by God and Christ, were meant to be used only for the most strictly ethical purposes. On many occasions I was witness to her extraordinary workings.

Typically an unknown person would call Tia over the phone, telling her that he or she had a certain medical ailment that doctors were not too optimistic about (I believe this sounds familiar), and that a third person had recommended *La Señora Barrientos* because of the fine healing work she had done in the past. Tia would ask the person to say no more, offering some initial descriptions and evaluations of the problem. Then a home appointment was made.

At home Tia used her bedroom as the parlor for this kind of healing and required absolute silence from all of us. She would greet the visitor at the door and very formally lead him or her into the bedroom where the visitor would sit while Tia sat on a recliner stretched all the way back. I often sat totally mute in a corner. With the room very dimly lit, she would say a few prayers, asking God to help her make the correct diagnosis, while providing her with the wisdom and the strength to be able to rid the body of this terrible disease. Then she would close her eyes and begin the stage that she called "*ponerme en trance*" ("get myself in a trance"). She would grimace with eyes closed as if seeing something unpleasant. I could even see her eyeballs behind her eyelids, moving around rapidly as if they were following some unseen object. Soon she would begin to speak about the ailment, addressing the anxious visitor by name and giving the details of the disease.

"Señor Treviño, I see a dark spot somewhere in your lower abdomen. It's fading but I'll have to try harder. Let me clear the skin and the muscles away so that I can see underneath. That's better. I can see there's something wrong with your left kidney."

"Si, Señora Barrientos, I have something wrong with my kidney. What do you see?" the visitor would ask nervously but obviously impressed that her words were corroborating what he already knew.

"It's a growth of some kind. No, it's a stone. Wait. There are two stones. I see two stones in your left kidney. God, Almighty, I pray that you give me the strength to see better. Lord God Jesus, give me the strength to see this man's problem better. Clear my vision, Lord, clear my vision! Thank you Lord God in Heaven, Almighty."

I sat there mesmerized by this effort at healing that went far beyond what the other *curandera* had done with my mother two years prior. The room was deathly quiet as Tia spoke in very strained and deliberate phrases, as if these words came to her from the deep recesses of her mind or beyond. The flickering candles illuminated her as she reclined, producing eerie shadows on the walls in the bedroom decorated with numerous figurines, similar to the parlor of the other *curandera*, the one who steered my mother wrong. Typically the visitor's eyes would be glued to Tia's face, hungry for positive signs and terrifyingly afraid of negative nuances in her expression. Often they cried from the magical and spiritual quality of this experience.

"You have had these stones developing in your kidney for the last five years. Something else was here. You drank something that was not good for you. But the other kidney, I see it, it is clear; you don't have to worry about the right one."

"*En el nombre de Dios, señora, por favor deshaga esas piedras. Se lo suplico.*" ("In the name of God, madam, please dissolve these stones. I plead with you.")

It was usually at this stage that the visitors would get very emotional, showing their full dependence on the laws of nature, of God, and on whatever Tia could do to help them. People would shed rivers of tears as they listened to these accounts of their medical conditions.

As the afflicted visitor pleaded with Tia, she would ask for more silence, raising her arms in the air while beginning to move her hands and fingers in a motion that indicated that she was handling some unseen objects—body organs and diseases, in this case kidney stones—in the air. There was no question in my mind that the quality of the movement of the arms and hands indicated that Tia fully felt at that point that she had something in her hands, and was moving it accordingly. The addition of the outstretched arms in the air added more eerily dancing shadows to the walls.

"Lord help me help this man. Give me the power to rid his kidney of these ugly stones. These stones from the devil—*Satanas*—who goes around destroying good lives. Give me the strength in my hands to crush these stones."

Her hands would open and close as her fingers rubbed against each other in a motion reminiscent of someone trying to break up clumps of dirt into fine particles. Her eyes were seeing her hands inside the man's kidney.

"I am inside your left kidney and am breaking up the two stones. They are not too hard. Yes, they are breaking up. I think that I will be able to break them completely."

From where I was sitting it looked very difficult. Beads of sweat would form on her forehead and upper lip, indicating fatigue that periodically forced her to rest her arms from the outstretched position. Not once would Tia open her eyes when she was "in trance." As she finished her work she would tell the visitor if she had been successful in alleviating the problem—sometimes she would say that she could not get herself in the proper "trance," and so had been unable to cure the ailment. Whatever the outcome, all visitors were very generous with Tia.

Her fame reached all the way to Spain, for she had several clients in Madrid who would call her frequently for consultation. Most, though, were from El Paso, and from just across the border in Mexico.

As for the other kids at the foster home, I can say that they had some problems but unlike me were not real criminals. They had all come from terribly dysfunctional families that could not care for them. I had met the mother of one of these kids; she was a woman who looked old, even though the kid was about 11 years old. I had heard Mr. Garza and Tia talking about this woman who had a habit a frequenting Mexican bars, getting real drunk, passing out, and then turning up pregnant without even knowing who had had sex with her and who the father of her baby was. She had six kids born under identical circumstances. None of the six fathers ever came forward or had any contact with the kids.

Two of the other kids at the foster home were brothers, one very slow in learning, mispronouncing almost all of his Spanish words, and the other extremely cunning, selfish, and shrewd. These two kids created so many problems in this foster home that Tia requested that they be sent to another home, where several years later the cunning one was caught dealing drugs and was sent to prison. Another kid that I became friends with lasted only a few months there, was transferred elsewhere, and died a few years later in a fall from the international bridge onto the concrete embankment below. And finally, there was a cocky kid from Mexico who somehow ended up at the foster home, also only for a few months, and a few months after that died in a drunk driving accident in Ciudad Juarez.

A lot of these kids were from families who lived on the edge of human decency, families who took risks as a matter of course in every day life, families like mine who existed on the purely biological and animalistic level and had no real appreciation for the ethics, manners, compassion, and empathy in relationships with others. These families were on a self-destruct course, each subsequent year bringing more misery, more alienation, more depression, more hatred, more dysfunction, and a deepening sense of futility. As many used to say: Fate has already determined your course in life, so it is useless to try to change it. Your time is already marked; when it's your turn to go, you go. God will punish evil-doers, extortionists, and criminals.

As had been the case with my family, the families of these children had almost no skills for coping with the frustrations of life, the lack of which then subsequently brought what psychologist Martin Seligman called *learned helplessness*, that despairing feeling that one need not try to improve one's lot because the lot is already cast. Feelings of futility create their own momentum, subsequently requiring a stronger counter-force of optimism to arrest or reverse it. These people were definitely no optimists.

For the most part all of us kids got along well with each other, cooperating with and assisting each other with our duties at the store. Most importantly, we all knew that this foster home was better than what we had had prior to coming here, the realization of which made us feel grateful.

Towards the end of that fateful summer of 1958 when my mother died and I ended up at the the Barrientos foster home, I was already re-adjusted to this new life with food, rules, and productive work. Thoughts about my brothers and sisters just did not enter my mind at all; it was as if I had erased them from my heart for good. In reality what was happening was that my heart and mind were setting up defenses against the painful traumas I had endured, creating the stage for more serious problems later. For the time being, though, things were working a lot better here at the foster home than they ever did at home with my mother.

Sex And My Damaged Self

One problem I had to deal with as I entered Ferrer Junior High was that I was extremely shy, almost overanxious in my social relations. Fortunately

I was not so delusional as to completely misinterpret reality, for I saw that in comparison my peers, both boys and girls, enjoyed a great degree of self-confidence in relating to, and interacting with, other people. I watched helplessly and enviously as other boys easily struck up conversations with girls and established friendships I desperately longed for.

In retrospect I can see how the series of sexual encounters from about age four had a profound impact on my life, for by the time I got to the Barrientos foster home in 1958 I was already deep into a masturbation addiction which I indulged several times per day. Prior to coming to this residence I had masturbated just to get an orgasm and not for the concurrent fantasy that so goes along masturbation. But as I turned 13 and entered junior high, I discovered that I felt an attraction towards girls, thereby adding fantasy about sex with girls to my masturbatory sessions.

I was very shy, especially with the prettier girls, so I had almost zero chance of developing a relationship with any of them. Even if I did have a chance, would my behavior towards her be normal, or would it be driven by evil and disgusting impulses? As I mentioned previously, children who are abused can later claim the high moral ground of victimhood, but if they are abused beyond some dismal point, they lose the torn remnants of their soul, and like their abusers they become fiends who in turn inflict damage on innocent others. These young abusers, like me, deserve no pity, no forgiveness.

I so desperately wanted to relate to girls. Well, by sheer luck the welfare department brought a foster girl to the Barrientos residence. Oh, my God. We lived in the same house—she had to talk to me!

Carmela was about 13 and I was 14 when we began to discover that we were attracted to each other. Even though I felt drawn to her, I had not the slightest idea of how to approach her. How could I know? Nobody had ever taught me any proper manners for dealing with people in socially appropriate ways. I do not recall how we got started, but we soon began to touch each other sexually, a new experience for me with a girl, for a change. Touching soon escalated into digital penetration, and finally into intercourse, although to this day I cannot recall clearly if I actually put my penis inside her vagina or not. I thought I did but then again I did not know how it was supposed to feel inside a girl. One rather odd thing about our sexual relations was that I never opened her blouse and I never touched her breasts, even on the outside through her clothes. In addition I also used to put pencils inside her vagina, which I enjoyed and which she apparently did not mind. We did this maybe four or five times, and she eventually moved away. Never again did we cross paths.

As I think back at this initial sexual contact with a girl, I feel sorry that it ever happened—well, that it happened in this manner. I feel bad that my contact with her was purely sexual and also rather odd: I can't understand why I found the need to insert (unsharpened) pencils into her, or what sad motivation she may have had to have agreed to such act on several occasions.

As I started exploring my sexuality, things did not look pretty. These sexual acts with Carmela were not all that was going on at the time. I was now being driven by an intense sexual desire I did not fully understand. Masturbating five times a day was not enough—I had to do something, but I did not know how to approach girls. I began to think, and then I began to explore, the area of bestiality—sex with animals. My soul was so lost that nothing in the area of sex was too low for me.

It began as an innocent outing to a small ranch that Tio and Tia had access to in north El Paso—a *rancho* with about 20 acres of wooded land. This land belonged to the Barrientos in conjunction with an associate. As Tio stayed in the farmhouse talking to the ranch keeper, Gerardo, I went about all over the acreage exploring, soon coming to the chicken house. Inside were about a dozen chickens, all egg-laying hens neatly arranged in rows of nests equipped to handle the egg production. As I saw the chickens' anuses expand to release the egg I got the idea that my penis could also fit in there. It was then and there that I took a chicken and forced my penis into its anus about half-way in, getting a very hot sensation. From there I graduated to sex with the goats and with a frog, through its mouth.

Of course, I now feel sickened and ashamed that I resorted to such unnatural acts with animals, but at the time I did not even give it a second thought, providing me with the orgasms which I so desperately sought in unnatural sex acts and in masturbation. Reflecting upon it now, it would appear to me that when I was in my teen years I may have had a good rebound intellectually as we were taken away from our dead mother's home and placed in this foster home; yet emotionally I was very much damaged, and these highly inappropriate sexual acts were merely a window into the sickness of my soul, the damage to which would not be fully known until many years later.

At the time that I was engaging in these acts I *knew* that other people felt these kinds of behaviors were wrong or inappropriate, yet I did not have that internal guide to make me *feel* that they were wrong. Now that I know better and am fully aware of the internal psychodynamics that influence behavior, I can see how my own situation in my teens and thereafter resembled more that of common criminals and other deviates who do not have a properly developed conscience (or *superego*, in Freudian terminology) and who therefore function almost purely as a consequence of raw impulses from the *id*, that source of desires, wants, and needs within us, with very little reflection before action. My only saving grace here was that I was not a common criminal transgressing over the rights of others, except in the area of sex, where my feelings and my boundaries were damaged, pathological, or otherwise not healthy for me or for those around me. It is the very real similarity between my mind and the criminal mind, especially that of the remorseless serial killer, that makes me feel that even though I did not turn out to be a common criminal—robbing, stabbing, and maiming, or a serial killer, methodically abusing and killing people—I feel that spiritually I came from the same cesspool of abuse and neglect, and that therefore whether I like it or not I have a common brotherhood with these dismal representatives from the world of pure evil. That is, we came from the same bowels of hell, so it distresses me to think that in a sense somewhere within my soul are some seeds of evil which I can never eradicate because they are at the center of my being. For some reason unknown to me these more sinister and monstrous ones have never sprouted.

Unnatural sexual desires and behavior, poor boundaries in the area of sex, extremely shy and avoidant of people, with no desire to see my estranged brothers or sisters, no grieving for my dead mother, addicted to masturbation, no desire to see my aunts and uncle in San Antonio—these were some of the symptoms that were prominent at the time, although, of course, I did not even know them as such; I thought that these things were natural parts of life. Sex is what feels good, I felt, even if others don't approve. It would be many years later when the floodgates would open up in psychotherapy that I would realize just how sick my soul had become in the course of my evil childhood, and how much pain I in turn had caused others in my life.

At about age 15, for some reason I stopped all forms of sexual contact with animals. In fact, for the next three years I did not have any sexual contact with anyone. It appeared that my desires were becoming more normal as I simply wished to find a nice girl I could date, love, and maybe even have normal sex with. No pencils, nothing strange. But, no luck, since my shyness made it very difficult for me to confess my attraction to any girl, for I had a profound fear, even terror, of rejection. I envied so much the other boys who had the skills, even the charisma, to chat leisurely with the pretty girls at our high school, getting dates by the dozens, while I concentrated stupidly and defensively on intellectual pursuits such as my electronics, music, model cars, and even some philosophy. In this respect my personality (if I had one) resembled that of a schizoid to some degree, not knowing how to properly interact with people. It was horrifyingly similar to the mindset of perverted sex killers.

This fear of rejection effectively ruled my life, for it encroached on just about all aspects of my contacts with other people. But especially in my relations with girls. Deep inside me I felt that I simply was no good, that I had so many defects, that I was totally incompetent, that my body was very ugly, that my face was clearly inferior to those of other boys, and that if I tried to start a serious conversation with a girl she would immediately realize how damaged and useless I was. Of course, she would just turn around and run the other way. There was this girl in high school whose hand I desperately wanted to hold, to hold her in my arms, and to kiss her lips gently. In fact, I did not have a fantasy about having sex with her, for I felt that sex would "ruin" the relationship. I would not want to contaminate my "nice" and "respectable" relationship with her with this evil thing called sex. How sick I was to have felt this way, not knowing that the effects of the years of damage that I carried around had pathologically affected my feeling for what normally is a beautiful and spiritual act for most people. And so it was that for all of high school I never had the courage to ask her out. God, I expected she would laugh at me for even thinking that she would go on a date with me. I was sure of that. Well, when I masturbated I just buried the deepest terrors and insecurities of my worthless carcass, my worm-infested soul.

One Friday evening a group of my friends from high school came over to my house and invited me to join them on a trip just across the Mexican border into Ciudad Juarez, to the red light district. I couldn't miss that, so I jumped into the car.

La Zona de Ciudad Juarez

In order to clean up the downtown area of freewheeling prostitutes and pimps, the city government of Ciudad Juarez in Mexico had created a special prostitution zone in the southwestern part of the city Also required were periodic checks for venereal diseases which were rampant at the time. That area came to be known as *La Zona*, *El Zumbido*, or *Boys' Town*.

Ciudad Juarez's red light district was legendary all over West Texas. There was not a single boy at our high school who did not know about all the young girls and the women who would do anything you wanted for as little as two dollars. The hottest item that absorbed the imagination of all of us had been the blowjobs that one could get for only 50 cents! These rates were possible because of the serious discrepancy in the purchasing power of the Mexican *peso* in contrast to the American dollar. One could go across into Mexico and buy literally several bags of groceries for about two dollars, a monetary reality that transferred to the fees of the prostitutes.

We talked often about going to *La Zona* to "get a blowjob," and someone would invariably say that he would ask the prostitute to swallow his sperm after he ejaculated in her mouth. These types of discussions provided us with hours of amusement.

There were five of us guys in the car as we drove across the international bridge right into the heart of downtown Ciudad Juarez, the border city congested near the bridge by hundreds of wall-to-wall stores and shops peddling everything from furniture to Mexican parrots, to street tacos with meat of origin unknown, to *aguas frescas* (those delicious citrus fruit drinks; my favorite was *la limonada*, made with Mexican cane sugar and lime), to homemade figurines, to leather and wrought iron goods. As we drove that evening through the very narrow streets of the city of sin and deprivation, I felt rather safe inside the metal shell of the car, for outside, just a few feet from my window was a world that seemed so chaotic, so animalistic, so destitute, so filthy, so sorry, and so incomprehensible. These people that I was looking at, like the man overburdened by his heavy load of *sarapes* (heavy shawls) as he staggered along the sidewalk attempting to sell them—where would they go after this night's chaos was over? Did this *sarape* man do this every night? How does he manage to be on his feet with such a heavy load, yet without any socks? Do his feet hurt? Where are his children? And what about that Indian woman sprawled on the bare concrete sidewalk with three young children clinging to her as she attempts to look at passers-by with an open hand for a *limosna* (any handout from a stranger)? Does she even have any diapers for the baby? If she wanted to go to the bathroom, where would she go? Do her children get medical care? Where is her own mother? Did she consult a *curandera* just as my mother did?

About a hundred feet down from the woman and her children in this tragic state was a little taco cart, most obviously home-made from recycled plywood and wobbly bicycle tires. The cart itself looked pitiful, since the plywood had many ugly patches and no paint to cover the numerous blemishes from use and abuse, yet the warm glow of the kerosene lamp gave it a romantic gleam that attracted unsuspecting customers. We in El Paso had already been warned to avoid the Ciudad Juarez street taco stands since there was no public health regulatory agency that could oversee the hygiene and quality of their food. In such a destitute situation the cart owners typically resorted to serving dog and horse meat blended with some beef, but even the beef was questionable since these street merchants could afford to buy only sick and cancerous cattle. Hey, but maybe I should not complain about this stuff, for not so long ago it would have suited me perfectly.

Children were all over the streets, children as young as maybe three. How can a three-year-old child walk the streets alone selling Chiclets? How does this work seem to the heart of the child? Is it play for him? Or is it a total resignation to the brutal and unforgiving forces of abject poverty? Their clothes were mostly rags ready to fall off, only to be picked up by the next more unfortunate creature who would then wear them even longer. And so on. Their faces, hands, and feet were as filthy as if the kids had slept on the dirty streets, allowing the mud to cake right on the skin and thus producing rough patches with long cracks that resembled elephant hide. I could identify with the empty, hollow look in their eyes, those eyes that hauntingly seemed to be saying to me at the moment, "Don't criticize—you are one of us." Yes, it was I who was out there, with nothing in life besides the hollow look and the rags I wore. No, it was not I, for I had already left that world. I wasn't sure.

A few blocks later we saw a long row of storefronts with absolutely no space between them. The electrical wiring coming from the telephone poles attracted my attention, for it led into the electrical meters in a most haphazard and careless manner, exposing live wires and live bolts that could easily kill any innocent person who may happen to brush up against them. The heavy gauge wires were tacked onto the facade of the store as an afterthought; I imagined the incompetent or careless contractor saying, "You know, it might be a good idea to try to get this wire out of the way of these pedestrians." But all the stores were like this, suggesting a gross disregard for the sensible management of electricity. Or it could be, as I well knew, that the forces of poverty and ignorance take precedence to those of sensibility and even ethics.

One block up ahead we saw a man near a parked horse-drawn carriage who (the horse, too, looked destitute; I am sure he would have preferred to have been bought by someone who could pet him and give him hay instead of hell) must have seen our *TEXAS* license plate, for he immediately tried to stop us with his cry of *"Boys' Town, Boys' Town!"* He wanted to lead us to the destination where many Texas cars went, for a small fee. "No thanks," I thought, "we already know the way (to hell)."

Soon we were right there next to *Plaza de las Rosas*, the one-square-block plaza area where I knew that my mother had met the worm of the earth, The Devil, 15 years earlier. Who would have guessed that when my mother was looking for a man—any man—in this area, that 15 years later she would be dead in the ground and her son would be traveling by? Who would have guessed that her life would be a living hell if she teamed up with the vomit that was making a pass at her? Who would have guessed that both of them, after establishing their mutually ruinous relationship, would fall back dead into the unforgiving earth that spawned them, leaving behind the miserable children who had the grave misfortune of having been born to these random combinations of eggs and sperms? Yes, I was next to a historic monument in my life, the very place where two terribly incompetent and sick individuals had decided to join pathologies, assuring their mutual destruction and the spiritual damnation of the children of the house.

It still was the same. Was another Devil there tonight, prowling the plaza, looking for someone to be ugly with? Was there another dispossessed woman here, scouting the throngs, looking for a man—any man—to be father to her children? Yes, there were practically hundreds of men and women of all ages walking slowly around the perimeter of the plaza, making eyes at each other, not knowing if the glance was being returned by a true lover or a Demon. He's out there somewhere. He prefers the night. You don't know it is Him until it's too late to save your life. The nightmare comes so easily—it just creeps into your heart.

We finally passed all the slow commercial distractions along the way and found ourselves in dark, unpaved streets full of crater-like pot-holes that could swallow up an entire vehicle. Dimly lit houses doted our way there, providing guiding posts in an otherwise dark area. After a few miles of this zigzagging, we came to a very long and tall concrete wall, about 20-feet high, that had imbedded glass shards on top to cut up any intruder. This was the mile-long perimeter wall that totally enclosed the red-light area. We were now at *La Zona*. Nirvana for all over-sexed young men.

As we drove through the only entrance into the fortress-like compound, two paunchy Mexican policemen gave us a quick, cynical look and motioned us to continue without stopping. Once inside we felt that we had entered an eerie world, for Mexican cantina music (mostly *corridos* (ballads) and *polkas*) permeated the entire area while scantily-clad women walked everywhere.

We parked our vehicle next to a long row of small, one-room apartments, all very dimly lit, but most with their doors fully open, welcoming us. I remember clearly my apprehension at the idea that here in front of me were women who were ready to have sex with me if I so wished. This was it. The five of us walked together along the broken sidewalk that connected all the rooms, visually inspecting the Mexican women who stood by their doors displaying their breasts, legs, or buttocks to entice us to choose them. I was so in awe at all the female bodies that I could not decide if I really wanted to have sex or not, for simply looking at these women was a feast in itself. The more experienced guys in our group were the ones who fielded questions for these women: Can you give us a special price for all five of us at once? What do I get for one dollar? Can two of us do you at the same time? Do you swallow? As we walked farther along the sidewalk, I noticed a peculiar pattern. The women near the entrance where we had parked were prettier than the ones farther away. In fact, as we went past the half-way point in this very long row of rooms, the women got to be simply ugly, I am sad to say. Some were very obese, with folds of skin cascading down their exposed chests and legs, reminding me of a very large candle with waves of molten wax slowly dripping down its sides. Others just did not have pretty faces or figures, and the fact that they were situated far from the entrance into this massive bordello may have meant that some administrator thought the same thing. But it did not matter to us for we were having a good time talking to the ladies.

We all stopped by the door of one particularly aggressive woman who was short, thin, and wore lipstick well beyond the outer edges of her thick lips. Did she deliberately do that, or was she simply sloppy in applying her makeup?

"Hey, boys, you come over here; I have something for you. Yes, for you, Papi. All of you come over here now. Which one of you wants to have a good time with me?" said Belina, who appeared to be about 40 years old, opening the slit in her skirt as she enticingly spoke to us.

"All of us want to have a good time tonight, baby. Do you think you can take on all five of us at the same time?" asked Robert, only half seriously since we *had* talked about this on the car ride here, and none of us wanted to have sex in a group.

Robert was the master at buttering up girls, so we all looked up to him, hoping to learn some of his techniques. As we were there right at her doorstep, literally one or two feet from her, we could get a very clear view of her room lit up only by three candles, all bearing the symbol of the Mexican *Virgen de Guadalupe*. A Spartan room it was, with a twin bed, obviously caved in at the middle, in the far corner of the room, and at another corner a small dresser with a dented lavatory bowl on it. Apart from this there was nothing else for the candles to illuminate.

She coquettishly ran her eyes up and down our bodies as we sheepishly stared at her generous, bulging bosom, beautifully displayed in a blouse mostly unbuttoned and a brassiere perhaps two cup sizes too small.

"Not at the same time, boys. But four of you can watch as I take care of each of you individually. How's that? Wanna fuck? Which one of you is going to be first?" she offered as she propped up her breasts with her cupped hands.

Then Joe, not being the shy one, went one step farther.

"Can I squeeze one of your tits to see if they are firm? We need to know what we're getting."

"No, cabron (asshole), you pay first and I let you squeeze them all night if you wish. OK? Come on, now, are you guys just little boys not knowing what to do or do you want to get down to business?"

With that statement we felt she was growing tired of our oogling her with no real commitment, so we opted to move on as we told her that we would look around and then maybe come back later.

"I'll be here, boys, waiting and ready for you. When you get hard, come to me. I'll take care of all of you," she half shouted as we were three doors down already.

The other women in rooms close to Belina's didn't bother to ask us to come to their doors, for they had been watching as we focused all our attention on Belina. Perhaps they thought we weren't serious. But there was one who did call on us.

Her door was near the end of the long, depressing line of small rooms that we had been walking along, and her hair was grey. She had not bothered to wear something alluring, preferring to adorn herself with an old, conservative looking, shift dress that simply covered her but did not reveal if she had any curves at all. But I took a closer look and realized that it would not have mattered to me, for this woman with the crinkly grey hair, wrinkled skin, and slurred speech looked to me to be about 80 years old, a rare oddity in the world of prostitution where firm bodies and youth are one's commodities.

"*Muchachos, vengan aca. Quien de ustedes me quiere meter la verga?*" she queried. ("Young men, come over here. Which one of you would like to put his dick inside me?") We were all taken aback by her vulgarity, especially since we thought that at her age she could not be serious about being a prostitute. She looked more like a grandmother. Besides, none of us would ever even consider having sex with this woman who by anyone's standards was ancient. Just for fun we stopped at her door.

A closer look at her readily revealed that indeed she was a very old woman, with considerable wrinkling of her face, arms, and hands. Her slurred speech was maybe due to her not having teeth nor dentures, for we could see that her lower jaw closed in against the upper jaw, leaving no room for normal lip placement and producing the doubling of the lips that is so common in people who have no teeth and no dentures. Besides, at her age she also had no breasts to speak of, for they hung mostly flat against her chest and belly—they actually looked more like deflated skin bags.

As I think about it now, I feel sorry that this old woman found it necessary to sell her body and her dignity at an age that is commonly revered in Mexican culture. Surely this woman had grown children of her own, and probably grand- and great-grandchildren. Where were they? Could they have helped her to get out of that hell hole? I certainly feel sorry that I was part of that party that behaved in this manner toward these women, but especially toward this old woman.

None of us wanted to stay there long, so we started to drift away. Then, just as we were about to leave, Javier, a rather thin guy with a mustache, decided that he wanted to go into the room with the very old grandmother. We knew Javier as the one with the gumption and courage to take on any dare, any assignment. Once he surreptitiously placed a lizard in a teacher's purse when she was not looking. In class she opened her purse to get some tissues, and the ugly lizard poked his head and tongue out of the purse. The teacher, who was so strict that she was not well liked, let out a loud scream and ran out of the class to the principal's office for refuge. Her blood-curdling scream paralyzed practically all classes in our building, so much so that school was dismissed at that point.

Meanwhile, tonight, the ancient grandmother was overjoyed that one of us was showing an interest in her—we were dumbfounded—and after a brief discussion with Javier we left the row houses heading for *El Papagallo*, the most popular bar at *La Zona*, where we agreed to wait for him. Why in the world would this young guy of 16 want to get in bed with grandma?

Walking back we stopped at an old cantina, the kind that I was used to seeing in the old Mexican movies that my mother took me to occasionally. It stank heavily of old beer, with the average customer a beefy Mexican man wearing a regulation straw hat with sweat rings around it. About half of these guys had equally heavy and sweaty women sitting on their laps as they enjoyed their bottles of *Carta Blanca* beer, shamelessly caressing the women's bodies, oblivious to the presence of the general public. Oops, come to think about it, there was no general public, only people who already wanted to be in that decadent atmosphere. The musicians by the corner played *Mariachi* music as best as they could, yet it seemed to me that they were either drunk or had been kicked out of the better night clubs in the city. Nevertheless, the lawlessness there attracted me like a magnet, seducing me to think that this was my natural environment, the milieu familiar to me from the many *cantinas* that The Devil had taken me to when I was a young boy. The uglier the better, the more lawless the more I liked it, the raunchier it was the more I *said* I detested it, yet in my heart there was a secret and profound admiration of the dark side of human behavior, the underbelly of the cultural fabric, the raw reality about human values and ethics.

My friends and I sat down, they ordered beers while I, as usual, ordered a soft drink (Thank God I never developed an alcohol addiction!). With great amusement I watched the many immoral melodramas that were unfolding at the various tables all around us. That fat guy to our right, the one with the pimples and the enormous chest, had his face buried in the woman's chest, periodically asking her if she could come home with him because he felt lonely. Her face showed no sympathy—and I suppose that none should have been expected—as she instead continued to indulge his oral desires while she simultaneously scanned the surroundings to determine if a better deal was forthcoming. Even in the world of love-for-money, market forces determine who gets what. Nothing personal, you know.

To our left was a couple who was laughing from the heart, probably because the man would periodically sneak his free hand up the woman's short skirt, a minor transgression that she would have to feign indignity over, at least to maintain the illusion that he was conquering her, an arrangement that both parties had entered into quite subconsciously, each for his or her own sick reasons. Of course, this did not explain why she never did complain about his other hand which was already fully inside her blouse.

Since it was a hot, sweltering night, my friends guzzled their beers and wanted to head on to *El Papagallo*, hopefully before Javier got there. We all knew from legend and gossip that the prostitutes here knew techniques on how to make a man ejaculate within a minute after insertion, even against the man's plan to prolong the act to get more action for his money. I glanced quickly at the entire scene one more time, and we all then stepped out onto the street and made for our goal.

After a few minutes of walking slowly down broken sidewalks and pot-hole infested streets, we arrived just outside the famed *El Papagallo* that was the centerpiece of the entire redlight zone. Glittering neon lights atop and in front of the structure announced to the world the existence of such a place, wonderful, fun, and joyous to some, and a symbol of human perversity for others. I knew that, but I was on the threshold of new vistas, so I did not care what others thought; I was going right into the cauldron of sin and decadence.

At the dark entrance we were greeted by an attractive woman, maybe 20, in a very tight and very short skirt. Innocently I thought that she was to be our waitress, but two minutes later I found out that she was assigned to sit with us at a very private table. As usual, I was shy with this woman, as with all women, so I did not know how to respond when she asked me if I wanted a blowjob. Privately every guy that I knew, and myself too, felt that a blowjob was like the nirvana of all sex, yet I was terribly embarrassed to say "Yes!" to this woman. In fact, I really did not want her to perform oral sex because I would not know how to respond to her while she did it.

The truth be known, I had never gotten a blowjob, but I said it would be great because all the guys in our group said it was. If this beautiful woman were to perform oral sex on me, would I hold her hand, or tell her I loved her, or tell her she was great, or what? I was full of sexual desires, but I had more questions than ideas about the whole thing.

So I wanted it but I did not want it. In the end she quickly figured that I did not know what I wanted. Shit, even when a woman threw herself at me I still did not know how to proceed. Did I subconsciously see my mother's eyes behind hers? Did I fear the infantile rejection I must have experienced from my mother in my first two wretched years of life? Did I somehow feel it was my mother asking me if I wanted a blowjob? What sickness. We had left the house of horrors, but the demons had already gotten inside me and eaten my soul. What sickness. Lord, what sickness.

But how I envied my friend Roberto when she shifted her attention to him. I could see her hand firmly grabbing his penile bulge through his clothing while he negotiated a price somewhere between one and three dollars. Within a minute or two they were gone. I felt like a fool for being so stupid, cowardly, and gutless in dealing with women. Why was he so successful in getting what he wanted while I agonized? So I promised myself that I would not back down if another woman came and sat next to me. It had to be done. Otherwise, on the way back home they would have stories to tell while I would just have to say I enjoyed sipping soft drinks!

Didn't have to wait long. About a minute later this short woman of about 25 came and did just that. I remembered what I had just told myself, and I had to fight every instinct in my body to speak about sexual services with this woman. Quite simply she told me that we should go to her room so that she can make me happy. She asked me for $5, but I told her that I had only $2. She grabbed the money from my hand and motioned me to follow her. I hadn't clearly said "Yes!" yet I was now in some way committed at the very least to go to her room.

The club had a long corridor through the back door that led to various private rooms where the women could service their customers. As she led me inside her tiny room, she asked me matter-of-factly to unzip my pants because she was going to first inspect my dick and then wash it. Again I felt so awkward, so stupid, and almost like a little boy who was being asked to undress by his mother. I had been talking tough for so many years about our high school girls and how to kiss them, how to touch their breasts, even how to make love to them, but now, confronted with a real-life opportunity to do what I'd said I'd do, I was chickening out. Then even more horror struck me as I realized that I was about to be undressed by a woman for the purpose of having sex and my penis was nowhere to be found—because of my apprehension, it simply refused to get up and shriveled away! What if she laughed at me? I had never dreamed that sex with a woman would be this difficult and this exhausting. At that moment in time I would have preferred to have been 100 miles away, but I did not have the courage to stop her at this late stage of the game. Events had acquired a life of their own and were moving forward with little effort.

As I awkwardly stood there by the side of her bed, not knowing if I was supposed to suddenly feel passionate about her, I contemplated walking towards her and kissing her with all the fiery ardor of a moose in heat. That is what should happen, right? That's what we guys said happened as you were about to have sex with a girl. But I did not *feel* like kissing her, at least not in the same way that I felt like passionately kissing the girl I admired at our high school. I was on the threshold of having sex with a woman, yet I had all the doubts in the world about it. I started to shiver even though the temperature in that sweaty room must have been 105 degrees. Any moment now she will laugh at me and push me out the window, I thought. Why in the world did I think she would want to have sex with me, the lowest worm on earth?

In my plain view she began to undress, or, rather, finish taking off what already was half off inside the club. In a very methodical manner she placed her blouse neatly on the dresser, along with her skimpy bra which covered very small breasts, and finally her skirt. As I saw how she undressed and took care of her clothes I could not help but wonder how many times she had gone through this routine in her life, how many penises had entered her chambers. I also wondered if *she* expected *me* to kiss her. But I didn't want to kiss her. Wearing only pink bikini panties she walked over to me in a very unembarrassed and confident manner and began to unbuckle and unzip my pants; my anxiety level increased ten-fold, but not enough to cause me to run away screaming in hysterics. Given that we had already gotten this far, was I supposed to have an erection? Was I supposed to embrace her as she tugged at my pants? I was totally lost, totally at her disposal. When she finally lowered my underwear she took my penis, more limp than a wet noodle, in her hands and proceeded to pull the skin back, visually inspecting it for some signs of deformities, diseases, filth, or other misfortune. Her warm hands and gentle motion on my penis and my testicles must have awakened some primordial reflex action, for I knew immediately that my penis was about to rise to the occasion, providing me with a much needed sense of relief and a boost for my manliness. It was a good thing that she did not laugh at me when my dick was down, when I was feeling that even a hamster had more to show his partner than I had to show this woman. I must have passed the first test, for she asked me to sit on the bed as she finished pulling off the rest of my clothes and then promptly led me into the bathroom where she motioned me to place my now-triumphant organ over a bowl of warm water. With soap and water she then washed my penis, causing it to get even bigger because of the massaging. After she dried it she led me by the hand into the bed, fully directing this choreography in all respects.

She promptly maneuvered my body so that I was on top of her, causing me to remember that I had promised myself that I would use a condom if I ever had sex with a prostitute. Very meekly I asked her if she would mind if I got off briefly to place the rubber over my penis, but she showed some resistance.

"Why do you want to wear a condom, Papi? I want it like this. I want you to come inside me. OK?"

"Well, my friends told me that it would be a good idea if I wore one. I already bought it anyway, so I would not want to waste it. It will only take a few seconds."

Her tone changed as she conceded and said, "*Pues si te lo vas a poner pontelo ya y hay que seguir.*" ("So if you are going to wear it, do it now and let's get on with it.") A few seconds later I was back in bed with her and our intercourse lasted at the most three minutes. Was I supposed to enjoy this? Was I supposed to kiss her? Should I have at least looked at her face or said something nice? I was still shivering from the intense cold in the sweltering room when I went to the bathroom to clean up and get dressed, while she did the same after me. As we walked back to the club together, a total time period of less than one minute, we spoke meaninglessly, and then parted upon entering. This was not what I thought sex with an adult woman would be like. I had years of experience with sex, yet I did not know anything about it. Or, rather, my feelings about it were all wrong. This clearly had not been a macho victory for me. Worse, I started feeling, "Did I just fuck my mother? Did I just fuck my mother? Oh, God! Oh, my God!" My stomach was churning but I didn't let my face show it.

Back at our table we guys started arriving one by one from our escapades, comparing notes on our relative successes. Of course I bragged about how I had rammed my "enormous" organ into her, causing her to writhe in ecstasy with every inch I put inside her, eventually releasing what surely must have been three pints of grade-A sperm deep inside her. Joe the extrovert even claimed that the woman had screamed in agony as he had to force his massive tool into her, going ever so slowly so as not to rip her insides. Well, we all had to talk big, to make sure that we were seen as real "macho" guys by the others, something that was an unspoken rule between us all. Yet even though I *knew* very well what my own emotions had told me during my own sex episode with the woman, I disregarded these and reflexively made this peer version the only reality to go by. Oddly, it appeared that I was aware of the non-correspondence between what I was feeling and what I *wanted to believe or to feel*, yet at some subconscious level I must not have thought it necessary for external behavior to reflect inner emotional life. Perhaps this was another manifestation of the strange emotional and spiritual realities which I had grown up with.

After about one hour Javier showed up, strutting with his usual blend of conceited blowhard and Mexican macho cowboy. We were all dying to hear about how he had done with the octogenarian he had gotten the "hots" for. He had a big smile but said that it had gone only "so-so" since "she really did not put much effort into the whole thing." He continued with the tale and said that as he was on top of the woman with his penis furiously working inside her, she had her head turned to the side, reading a newspaper at the same time! At that point the woman had turned to him and said, "Please, honey, don't mess up my hair. I want to be ready for the next guy." Like me, Javier just wanted to finish and get back to the group.

Javier could not articulate what bizarre emotion had prompted him to seek sex with this very old woman. It was clear that none of us, not even Javier, found her physically or romantically attractive, although he did concede that she made his "dick hard." Poor Javier—we learned several weeks later that he had gotten a bad case of gonorrhea from her. In his usual unabashed language he had informed us that his dick was leaking pus from the old lady, and that he might visit her again so that she could suck it all out. We were so repulsed by this, we never talked about her again.

Now that the fun was over we needed to start heading back to El Paso, for we had had enough for one night. On our walk back to our vehicle we had to pass near the entrance to the compound, where we arrived just in time to witness a police shootout. All we saw was a car that exited from the gate at a speed higher than normal, after which the two Mexican police, typical with their the voluminous paunches and cynical looks, drew their .38-caliber revolvers and fired repeatedly at the rear end of the speeding car. The two final clicks we heard produced no gunshots, so we knew they had each fired all six rounds. Then they leisurely reloaded, walking about and joking as if this was routine for them; not in the least did they appear concerned or distressed over what had just happened. As we continued to walk to the car, we wondered if we would get shot at on our way out. We got in our car and very carefully drove towards the gate, ready to stop docilely at the slightest sign from the beefy police, but they gave us a quick, cynical look and motioned us to continue without stopping. Even as we drove past them we were ready to duck on split-second notice, for we feared that we would get shot in the back of the head as suitable sacrifices to re-establish the authority and macho-quality of the Mexican police. Only after we drove for a mile and around a curve did we breathe easily again.

What a night! I did not again visit this hellhole for another five years, and never again did I ever have sex with a prostitute here. I felt dirty, but could never admit it to my companions.

My Tio and Tia never found out that I had gone to *La Zona*, although I know that Tio would not have condemned my going and would probably have recommended it as a "growing experience" for he was easier-going than Tia. It was Tio who always encouraged me to try new things, to discover new vistas. About two years before, he had encouraged me to get another job, when I was about 16, so that I could earn extra money for clothes which I desperately needed for school. The El Paso County Child Welfare Unit still was not paying them anything for my foster care, so the added burden of their buying school clothes was more than could be supported on the minimal income that the little grocery store was generating. For several weeks I looked and looked but could find nothing. El Paso, as always, was in an economic depression, and there was a scarcity of jobs, certainly none available to teens like me. But something did come up which I reluctantly accepted because I had no other choice. At the age of 16 I became an agricultural worker, picking cotton and cantaloupe in the lush Texas fields.

The Cotton Fields of Texas

It was during the summer of 1961 that I became a cotton-picker by fate and not by choice, an experience that taught me more about people than it did about earning a living.

Typically I had to get up at around 5 A.M., prepare my lunch, and then venture along the still-dark streets to wait for the flat-bed truck to pick me up. Many times, as I sat at the corner I wondered just how long I would have to do this because I simply hated it. My self-introspection and self-pity would invariably be interrupted by the familiar roar of a diesel engine just around the corner, a sound that signaled the arrival of the flat-bed. It would only stop momentarily in front of my corner, so I had to be ready to hop in, As I climbed on, I had to quickly find a spot to sit next to the other cottonpickers, a varied lot of very dark-skinned Mexican-Americans, both men and women from about age 15 to 60, who wore light-colored clothing, long sleeves, heavy collars, and straw hats. After the first few times in the very hot sun all day long, I, too, wore the same type of clothing as protection against the sun. All of us had brown paper bags with our treasured lunch and drink, another common link that united us against the hardships of the job. As the truck made its way along the poorer sections of El Paso, more people would come on board to join us. Santiago, an old man of about 60, had been picking crops for Texas agribusiness all his life. No family. No sons or daughters. Father and mother dead. He told me that life is hard, but that there is no use complaining about it; he just did his job and went home at the end of the day to watch television. That was his job—his life. Pick cotton all day long, go home, have dinner alone, watch television alone until 11:00 p.m., then go to bed, alone. Get up early. The Mexican will never progress, he said, because God has willed it that our people will forever be poor and ignorant. Santiago was one of the spiritually dead people who had given up on life and hope a long time ago. This brand of fatalism one finds among Mexican agricultural workers was more virulent because a great portion of these disenchanted workers were among least skilled of workers and consequently had the lowest wages known anywhere in the United States of America. Santiago's spirit had apparently died a many years ago.

Some were a bit more upbeat, like Teresita, the single mother built like a truck whom one would never want to doublecross. She got into the truck and sat next to me, asking me cheerfully how I was doing. I think that she liked me because I was relatively new at this business and she could explain things to me. Our relationship was mutually satisfying, for I liked the idea of a coworker helping me to learn the ropes about the business. Teresita had two young children in school and no husband—he had left her for a younger woman in Mexico, and was never heard from again. That sounded very much like our culture, where men are given praise for having a wife, several kids at home, and at least two pregnant girlfriends on the side. The macho thing to do is to impregnate as many women as possible, for the number of children that one sires is somehow indicative of the value one has as a real macho man. Even at the ripe old age of 16, I was already feeling that same macho urge, yet when the bubble finally burst for me many years later—in the form of painful consequences for myself and others—I had to confront this macho philosophy. I had to acknowledge the destruction that sexual immorality had caused in my mother's family and in my own personal life. My discussions with Teresita certainly started me thinking about the social and personal aspects of our cultural beliefs.

Soon we were all on our way up the old Santa Clara Road, north to Farm Road 2972, feeling every bump and pebble that the truck ran over, for we were sitting on the solid wooden deck of the truck, with none of the customary cushioning to absorb the considerable shocks from the frame of the vehicle. Anyone with a weak stomach had already quit the job long ago. Then, too, we had to hold on for dear life as the truck made sharp turns, breathing the heavy diesel fumes that always managed to get sucked into our area by the vacuum created by the truck's forward motion. We then drove west until we came to a vast field of cotton, all beautifully adorned with very white cotton balls which dared us to pick them. To the uninitiated the area from a distance looked like a huge plateau covered with snow; it was an awesome sight to behold. It also presented a huge task.

The truck pulled up next to the field a few feet away from the endless rows of cotton that we would pick today. Even in the very early morning hours the air was already hot. As heartlessly required by the plantation owners, I had bought my cotton collection bag for $20, a cylindrical canvass sack, about two feet in diameter and 15 feet long, with an over-the-shoulder strap, that we lugged around all day long collecting cotton balls. All of us claimed various locations within and underneath the truck and placed our bagged lunches there as markers for our lunchtime territory. There were no toilets there, so we had already learned to go to the bathroom, whether we felt like it or not, at home, just prior to the truck picking us up, for we had to endure the entire ten-hour day without facilities. Of course, if the urge was really uncontainable, both men and women knew that we could always go behind a bush and simply hope that the driver had brought along some toilet paper or old newspapers. Leaves were not an acceptable substitute since they caused *rosadura* (anal rash) due to pesticide contamination. We all lined up at the beginning of the rows, one row per worker, and began our picking, moving forth in parallel lines.

Mature cotton plants stood about five feet tall, with the cotton balls spread about evenly from the top to the bottom of the plant, making the harvest of the top ones less difficult. It was this dispersion of the product that made it such a back-breaking operation, since every few seconds, for about ten hours a day, one would have to stoop, straighten up, then stoop again. Thousands of times per day! Then there was the bulb that originally had housed the cotton blossom completely enclosed; upon ripening its hard, dry shell would split from the top, allowing a cotton ball to emerge and to expand. But the hard shell would remain, like a small cup, under and around the bottom half of the cotton ball, with jagged points and edges where the original blossoming rupture had occurred. It was these sharp edges and barbs that cut into one's fingers every time we reached for a cotton ball; and this happened thousands of times per day. Those of us who were new went around with hundreds of fresh cuts near and around all ten fingernails; the veteran cottonpickers had leathery hands which were impervious to the barbed assaults.

We all know how much cotton weighs; we would have to harvest many cotton balls to notice the cumulative weight in our hands. The amount that I got paid was two cents per pound! I would agonize by the minute thinking how much cotton I would have to pick to equal one pound! As our hands got full from the harvested cotton we would then quickly place it into the sack we dragged via the shoulder strap. Of course, as time passed the sack would get heavier and the harvesting would get more difficult. Eventually it would become next to impossible to drag the cotton sack due to the increasing friction of the fabric on the dry earth, so each individual would then skillfully turn the bag around and head back to the point of origin so that the bag would get weighed and the amount credited to that worker's weekly account.

Our field supervisor, another Mexican by the name of Gonzalo, remained with us in the field all day, mostly in his truck reading *El Diario de Ciudad Juarez* (the Mexican newspaper—how boring!), but he was clearly a "company man" whose surreptitious goal must have been to cheat us all. The scale that he used to weigh our harvests for credit towards our accounts did not seem to us to be a "true" scale; for one thing the needle would go back beyond zero with no weight on it. We complained to no avail, getting only the standard response that his bosses had said that it was "true," so it was. Heartless to the bone, he would even deny water to some of us who ran out during the day.

Within a half-hour after we had begun, all of us would be drenched in perspiration, but we could not take our shirts off due to the Texas sun which burned almost instantly. Needless to say towards the end of the day we all smelled pretty bad, and if we left our wet shirts at home hanging over the back of a chair overnight, in the morning they would be dry but stiff from the starchy quality of dried perspiration. After a few days of this I became accustomed to the new standards of hygiene.

Even though I was always hungry by 9:30 in the morning, I would have to wait for the official lunch break at 12:00 noon. There were absolutely no tables anywhere, and oftentimes no shade of any kind. Cotton fields, like other fields, did not have trees near the cotton rows simply because the owners wanted to utilize as much of the land as possible for planting cotton. Having no trees, our only oasis in the scorching sun was the diesel truck, or, more accurately, the place *under* the diesel truck. Even the most reluctant of newly hired *piscadores* (pickers, harvesters) would soon overcome their pride or anxiety and recognize that there simply was no alternative to eating lunch under the vehicle, sometimes right next to the smelly diesel fuel tanks, for this was the only place with shade. We would sit on the hot ground, hopefully against some part of of the truck as support for our aching backs. The less fortunate sat and used one arm to eat and the other to form a brace against the ground to support their bodies. Either way we would have to daydream about something pleasant to forget the misery of our current condition.

But there were some happy times, for lunch break gave us an opportunity to talk with each other about our lives. Most of the workers I met there had made a career in agriculture, often moving from state to state, following the harvest seasons across America. All of the people there were residents of El Paso. The one common thread was a sense of fatalism about the world and a strong undercurrent of feelings of powerlessness in the face of the events that shaped their lives. "I guess that God wanted me to work as a migrant; that must be the reason why I can't seem to do anything else," would mumble one middle aged woman, Migdalia, about her life. "And these *malditos patrones* (damned bosses) will be severely punished by God when their time is up. The more they mistreat us the more exacting their punishment will be." Yeah, sure, I wasn't convinced.

These same words had come out of my mother's mouth numerous times many years prior when she was referring to how she was treated as a cheap Mexican (-American) worker at the International Hat Company. No doubt, the privileged upper class in Mexico had no such attitudes about the forces shaping their lives. In contrast, the gravely dispossessed lower class—the Mexican "middle class" is minute compared to the bulk of the population— has a fatalistic view of society and the world, a characteristic that is both a defensive reaction towards their pitiful condition and a personality trait that contributes to it.

Reasoning along these lines, Mexican psychologist Samuel Ramos said in 1934 that the Mexican's deep sense of inferiority has led to pervasive feelings of low-self esteem, suspiciousness, a penchant for violence, and a supreme failure to believe in the future. Charles Ramirez Berg's 1992 study of Mexican movies, *Cinema of Solitude*, echoes a similar idea in that Berg asserts that the desperate state of the lower classes in Mexico was accurately reflected by films with fatalistic subthemes in Mexico's golden age of cinema, the years 1940 to 1965.

But as I talked to my coworkers under the massive frame of the diesel truck, fighting off the suicidally aggressive Texas fire-ants, I could not understand why they felt that all of us were being controlled by forces from the outside, that we were merely puppets of fate, that luck and black magic and voodoo and secret plots and the will of God had already determined our station in life, with very little room left for individual initiative. I rejected that. On the contrary I felt that we could rise above whatever sewer "fate" had dropped us in, that our final "station" in life was mostly determined by how well we worked from a "plan" to get us what we wanted.

Yet, my own rejection of this fatalistic view so characteristic of the dirt-poor classes which were part of my own soul (Remember my eating bricks and pigeons?) did not indicate that I had a superior ability to understand the forces of nature. I did not know it then, but my thinking patterns, while they appeared more intelligent on the surface, were actually symptomatic of a more serious deviation than the supposed defensive nature of the fatalistic orientation of most of my poor cohorts. These were thinking patterns that would take me along a certain path—a path that later proved to be problematical.

As with all philosophical discussions, we never got anywhere with these interpretations of our lots in life. "When your number is up, it's up. It does not matter what you do for a living, or what kinds of risks you take. If God has not willed your death, you will be protected even in the most dangerous of environments. There's no need to worry about when you will die," asserted Pancho, a lifer in the migrant trade, who chained-smoked with a cigarette always hanging from his mouth. I admired his manner of talking out of the side of his mouth, but not his philosophy. It was more fun when we talked about Mexican films.

Lunch break did not end with an abrupt signal from our supervisor, but an increasing number of fire-ant-bitten workers just spontaneously began to emerge from underneath the truck to get back to the harvest spot where they had left off prior to lunch. It was that time of the day when the sun radiated the most intense heat and light, bright enough to cause chronic squinting (which in turn painted those "crows' feet" on our faces). It was just about this time when people needed to go to the bathroom but had to do it a little way from the area where the truck was parked, always anxious about who might catch a glimpse. Soon we were all bent over again, battling the barbs at the base of each cotton ball with our defenseless fingers, collecting the practically weightless cotton. We simply knew by faith that if we picked enough of these weightless balls, that by sheer numbers they would eventually amount to something. Some of us, even one hour after we restarted after lunch, could not easily stand up straight from our hunched position. Even if we could, the sudden positioning of our head at an elevation higher than our hips brought on a mild dizziness. Or maybe it was the hot sun. Or the pesticide powder that mixed with our perspiration to add to the starchiness of our clothes. This was a rather physically harsh life that tested the limits of the body's endurance. As I despaired over my miserable physical condition, I would tell myself that this was only temporary, that I would study hard to get an education, as I had thought about in the last days before my mother died, so that I could have a better life. But the others were just resigned to their station. They took comfort and gained stamina from their belief that God had happiness waiting for them in heaven and not on this unjust earth. The lifers had smiles, so maybe there was something to be said about this blind faith.

By mid-afternoon we were all like zombies from the repetitive work, but perhaps more from the constant dissociation that accompanied our physical movements. Throughout the day I would think of pleasant things not associated with my current work—I would daydream about music, my secret crush at school, my electronics projects, and even some philosophical issues such as the nature of God in an essentially cruel world. A particularly nasty prick from a cotton barb would usually bring me back to my harsh reality.

Quitting time. We would all drag whatever we had in our long sacks back to the truck for the final weigh-in of the day to get cheated of our wages. Almost as a rule we would calculate quickly how many pounds we had done for the day: my average was about 200. At two cents per pound that would mean four dollars per day. Pitiful slave labor. There was nothing else I could do.

The trip back on the cushionless flat bed served to connect us back to reality, in a way, for I still spaced out by thinking about other matters more pleasant than this painful reality. The unobstructed wind from the movement of the truck cooled us rapidly, and soon even our previously drenched clothes appeared more dry, but with large white stains from the considerable tonnage of salt that had oozed from our pores during the day. Maybe we were driven biologically to sprinkle our tacos, beans, and tortillas lavishly with salt because of how much we had lost in the course of our working lives.

At my stop I would say "*Adios!*" to all my fellow workers, who like me, just wanted to get home and change into a clean set of clothes. Tomorrow the cycle of stooping, picking, sweating, and dissociating would begin anew.

This torture on the Texas cotton fields was not what I wanted my life to be, especially now that I had come to know the joy of playing in a symphonic band at school and of working on electrical repairs, two activities I enjoyed tremendously and which I would consider as careers. Fortunately for me, Tio had sought out a job working for a local electrical contractor, to supplement the small family income coming from the grocery store, and he asked me to help him on difficult assignments. I gladly accepted the challenge. Tia took care of the store.

It was a very small electrical repair company; in fact, it consisted of the owner, Tio and me! Typically, customers would call about problems with electrical switches, baseplugs, fuses, or breakers, and we would drive to the client's location in the company's beat-up Ford Econoline truck to diagnose the source of the problem and hopefully to make a repair on the spot.

Over the two summers that Tio and I spent working for the electrical contractor, we had a lot of adventures and I learned a considerable amount about electrical wiring and electronics. It also offered Tio and me the opportunity to chat, as always, about many different topics, including about girls/women, and about my plans for the future. As I had said before, I had even thought of going to college to make sure that I would not live the same wretched life that my parents had. But another, less honorable, motive of mine was that I felt that I needed to get well educated so that I could be more valuable to the gringa girls when I would begin to date them—whenever that would be. My feelings of inferiority were as strong as ever; my admiration of the gringa girls on TV and on the streets was ever increasing.

In fact, even without any conscious effort on my part, many aspects of my life were normalizing. Since coming to the Barrientos foster home I had not had any sexual contact with boys, and had not used the safety pin which I began to use at age two to inflict pain on myself. And for several years I had refrained entirely from bestiality (how disgusting!). Most importantly, I am glad I never got into any drug use and criminal activity as a teenager. On the other hand, I still had some strange symptoms. Every night I masturbated as if there were no tomorrow, letting my mind run wild with fantasies about having sex with numerous girls from our high school. Retrospectively, I can say that this may have been an addiction as much as a reaction to my hormonal stage. I suspect that the memories of my painful childhood would awaken in the darkness as I contemplated going to sleep, and they would prepare themselves for a night of torment to remind me of the hell which I well knew existed within my soul. I just avoided thinking any more about it, since it was all in the past. Then, too, I still had no desire to see my brothers and sisters; it was as if I intellectually knew they existed, that we all had come from the same womb, the womb from hell, yet my heart did not feel any connection to them, and I could go on forever without seeing them again. Maybe they were just a painful reminder of a hellish family that I had known in the past. Sadly, in retrospect, my heart just did not feel I had any brothers or sisters.

Whatever the reason for my not seeing them, I did not feel the need to reflect morally or intellectually about it. My own life was improving at the Barrientos residence, I had plans to improve myself even more, so I did not want anything to stand in the way. That is certainly sad, because my mother had once told me that if she did not make it to live until all of us were grown up, we should all make the effort to stay together. When she was alive and we were under the absolute domination of the scum of the earth—The Devil—that seemed desirable to me. But after our mother died and I saw at the Barrientos' what a better life looked like, that idea seemed irrelevant, even if I had considered it merely a dying woman's last wish.

Tio certainly felt that if I wanted to go to college I should give it a try. Although he did not know the first thing about college, entrance exams, transcripts, applications, dean's lists, letters of recommendation, tuition, scholarships, etc., I felt that Tio was a good support for me in my quest. Mrs. Jacobs, my genius physics teacher, had already given me her blessing, so, in my senior year in high school I made the decision to apply to what I believed was the best school in the state: Renwick University in Houston.

My grades at the high school had been good, mostly "A" and "B" averages throughout my sophomore and junior years, and now, at the beginning of my senior year I had mostly an "A" average. So I applied to Renwick with no other thought than that I was interested in learning more, and that I had good grades in high school. By the end of the fall Semester 1963, I had submitted the application and all documentation to the university.

Then I also had to think of The Senior Prom. Time to panic! I felt that this was a once-in-a-lifetime event that I did not want to miss, yet I did not know how to dance, and, worse, I did not know how to ask a girl to go with me. I was torn inside and panic-stricken as the deadline for registering approached. Yet this was so typical of me: always secretly longing to do this with or say that to a girl I liked, but at the same time extremely insecure and terrified at the prospect. What a coward! That is the reason why I did not date in high school: I was the schizoid loner who had minimal social skills—almost autistic I would think. I preferred to work with inanimate objects such as switches, Tesla Coils, electrical tubing, and antennas, objects which I could *control* and which would not reject me or ridicule me. Yes, loner, maybe, since I would spend literally hours pondering the mechanics of certain objects; I was fascinated by mechanical movement. Thinking about it now I feel grateful that by some miracle from Providence, I did not go into the bizarre and reprehensible world of crime and killing, since I know now how close I was psychologically to men who eventually just start killing girls and women for sport.

Going against all the panic, fear, and anxiety in my body I forced myself—literally forced—to invite one of the prettiest girls at our high school, Isabella Cuellar. In fact, I feared so much having to ask her face-to-face that I procrastinated until the very day of the deadline then had no choice but to first register and get the tickets for the Senior Prom *before* I even asked Isabella if she wanted to go. Of course, within minutes after I registered for the Prom the news spread like wildfire, and the entire school knew about it since never before in the history of the world had I been known to invite any girl on a date. Why would I? I was just schizoid. Even Isabella knew about it before I asked her, although I did not know that when I finally mustered enough courage to do it. My stomach was in so many knots that I felt like throwing up, which greatly exacerbated my panic. But without any hesitation she said, "Yes!" I could not believe my ears. This pretty girl, this goddess, did not turn me down. My elation lasted several days.

So the plan was now set for Isabella to go with me to the Senior Prom of 1964, as I nervously awaited a response from my college applications.

It was in the Spring of 1964 when I was a senior in high school, and when Texas colleges were sending out letters of admissions or rejections. I remember clearly that it was a Saturday and I was working at the grocery store when the mail came in. As incredible as it was, I had been accepted at Renwick University, and with full scholarship—the biggest triumph of my miserable life, ever—ever! My biggest opportunity to make my own life.

But back to prom night. I can honestly say that never had I forced myself so completely to do something my heart so feared with panic and physiological apprehension. The dancing went well even though I just pretended, and Isabella graciously followed along, herself pretending that all was OK. But the requisite dinner at a restaurant later that night was something else. My fear of rejection was all consuming; I could hardly eat from the nausea that enveloped my soul. Several times I had to excuse myself to go to the toilet to vomit profusely from the intense panic. It took every ounce of fortitude I had to return to the table to be with Isabella, whom I think suspected something but graciously pretended not to. Afterwards I just took her home without even kissing her—how could I even think about kissing this pretty girl when my nausea was consuming me. When I got home I was totally exhausted from containing the sheer terror of possible rejection. I just dropped into bed and passed out.

The anxiety had been debilitating, pervasive, and paralyzing. I simply did not feel confident about holding a conversation with Isabella, so I expected that at any moment she would reject me for being a jerk, a zombie, a schizoid, a loner, a foster-child with not a real mother but a foster mother. I hated myself, I hated myself, I hated myself—only I did not know it. Yet.

My graduation from high school was uneventful, and in the summer of 1964 Tia and Tio drove me to Renwick University in Houston for the next stage of my life. I certainly was much better than in the days when we lived in the hell house with our depraved parents. Well, maybe "better" is not the right word. Intellectually and functionally I was performing better, yes, but my insides, my soul, my spirit in relationships had never been fixed. I mean, who knew it needed fixing? No one knew it, but I was full of maggots eating me from the inside…

Chapter Eight

Katherine's Green Eyes

The drive to Houston from El Paso had taken about ten hours, giving me plenty of time to get all nervous about leaving my home of six years to live in uncharted and unknown territory. Along the way Tia and Tio told me they felt I would do well, that I had the "brains" to do just about anything that I wanted. Insofar as "brains" were concerned I guess I already *knew* that I could handle all the undergraduate work, so I expected to do well at any university. What I did not know and was about to learn was that different environments require different social and personal skills for survival, coping, and navigation, this university environment being one of the toughest from the point of view of a very insecure Chicano foster child.

As we drove into Houston that late August in 1964, I could see the Renwick University main library building from a distance. As we got closer to the students walking on campus, I could see that my skin was several income levels darker than that of the sons and daughters of the Revolution who were arriving in their graduation-gift automobiles and sporting wide smiles, white skin, and moving trailers which brought their home amenities. As I compared their advanced modes of moving their belonging with my homely brown cardboard boxes, I knew that I was not even in contention for a legitimate comparison. Their confident smiles and their overloaded vehicles bespoke of the unquestionable superiority that they enjoyed in almost any sphere of life. At least when I lived in El Paso, we were all in the same boat of misery, differentiating ourselves quite doubtfully only by the nature of the pain that defined our lives. Even under the best of circumstances *inside* the Mexican culture, I had trouble relating to people, bronzed people with poverty, ignorance, cotton fields, and pain as the source of our unity in destitution and misery. But here, among the blue-eyed elite of Texas, I could see not a single brown-skinned, dark-haired, brown-eyed Chicano with whom I could feel solidarity and a heart-warming linguistic brotherhood. From the relatively safe Mexican milieu of my high school in El Paso, I had taken the plunge into essentially alien and hostile territory at the non-Mexican Renwick University, clearly a galaxy outside of my league with respect to my socio-economic status, and, more importantly, outside of my self-esteem comfort zone. I was already beginning to doubt the wisdom of my decision to expand my intellectual horizons at the "best" school I could find. I began to shiver and I felt nauseous.

My acceptance papers indicated that I was to live at the Pebblestone Center Complex, a high-rise co-ed student dormitory that rose many stories above the frenzy at ground zero. In due time we had parked and taken my "Falstaff Beer" cardboard boxes with my clothes into the lobby, where again I was surrounded by blue eyes. Tio and Tia helped me with the boxes all the way to my room, then Tia asked me to kneel down so that she could bless my education at this school. In her best *curandera* dialect and prose she recited some *cantos* as she laid hands on the top of my head; I desperately needed some supernatural power to assist me in coping with the culture shock which was beginning to envelope me in a whirlpool of anxiety (as if I didn't have enough of this in my "normal" mode) and even greater self-doubts. What am I doing here? This is not my culture. I can't communicate well in English. When these gringos see my brown hair and brown eyes, will they tell me to my face that I am ugly? I know that Texas gringos despise all of us Mexicans. How can I defend myself if I'm all alone? That's 40,000 to 1.

My Tia and Tio left. I was now truly alone. Due to my ignorance I did not know it then, but nonetheless on this Day One I was already starting to show the unmistakable signs of culture shock and panic attack: increased pulse, pounding in my ears, hot flashes, increased level of respiration, restlessness, and a few days later, chronic vomiting in the mornings from my fear of attending classes. When my alarm clock rang in the mornings, I would wake up with a sense of dread, of doom, for I knew that I would have to *force* myself to go to classes where *nobody* would even talk to me. All the white students would jovially talk and joke with each other, but not with me. I assumed that they must have known each other since at least the days of Christopher Columbus, for I detected an enviable confidence and smoothness in their social intercourse. Some weeks later when I read Ralph Ellison's 1952 novel *The Invisible Man*, a story about a black man's search for identity, it struck me right away that I was in exactly the same nightmare as the story's main character: I, too, was essentially invisible to the dominant white culture. Their secret strategy must have been to simply ignore me for I was not worth engaging in conversation. But even if they had, I would not have known what to say, for my conversational English was not even at the functional level. And so every morning as I used every ounce of spiritual strength to combat the feeling of doom within my soul, I would walk along the campus sidewalks dutifully en route to my classes but stopping periodically to vomit behind the bushes. To minimize this problem I stopped eating breakfast altogether, but the result was that then I would vomit only green and yellow bile. My body was perhaps trying to expel the alien forces that were making me so spiritually and physically ill. If I had only known that there were things such as counseling centers and minority student representatives! No, this was more than just a case of my being outside of my culture for the first time in my life. Unknowingly I had placed myself in a very hostile environment, which was unfortunate in itself but further compounded by the severe underdevelopment of my coping skills.

The gross difference between my poor Mexican culture and that of the prevalent white, Anglo-Saxon culture at Renwick University was a constant threat from the very beginning. As I filled out endless applications at the registrar's office I noticed questions asking for name of "your banker, your attorney, your doctor, your internist, your dentist, your travel agent." They also wanted record of inoculations, an estimation of vacation expenses, etc. This was so alien to my way of thinking and living. No, I had no attorney, no banker, no internist, no dentist, and no travel agent! And vacation? Never in my life had I ever gone on vacation! In our culture of poverty one was lucky to eat and be alive. When I was living at home (if we can call that snake pit "home") with my mother and The Devil, we *never* went on a trip anywhere as a family, for as should be clear now we were just glad to be alive, to catch some unfortunate pigeons and devour them at night. The term "vacation" was alien to our life, our family, and our culture of ignorance and destitution. An attorney? Ha!—one needs an attorney only when one has the will and the means to fight some legal battle against an aggressor; but our last ounce of will went into surviving against hunger and against the spiritual and physical assault from the master-snake, The Devil. Attorneys were totally irrelevant to our lives, much as a barber would be to a drowning child. And I scoffed when I noticed that they wanted the name of my "banker." What in the world would I do with a banker? Of course I knew that there were banks and that these banks were run by stiff men in death-gray suits, but why would I ever need to talk to one of those cold corpses personally? Even when I lived with Tia and Tio, we never dealt with bankers. "That's for the gringo folks," Tio used to say. "They use lawyers to try to figure a way to cheat you. *No son pendejos.*" ("They are not fools.")

So I began classes and sat as inconspicuously as possible, listening to the instructors as they provided us with erudite interpretations of exciting topics that I had only recently begun to think about. Soon enough I was getting a broad perspective on sociology, psychology, linguistics, mechanical engineering, English, philosophy, anthropology, and the history of music; I was in awe at the sheer volume and scope of the knowledge that was out there. My classes, like the typical student's, were spread over the entire campus, so that I had to practically run after each class to make the next one on time. Between the vomiting and the panic attacks, I enjoyed very much the *knowledge* that was being made available to me, but I cowered under the intense pressure from dealing interpersonally with other students and with teachers and staff. My greatest fear soon became being asked a question by a professor in class, for I had significant difficulty in speaking conversationally in English, a deficit which made me stutter and stumble through my answers. I just knew that it made me sound like a barely-functioning moron. To further compound my misery I was terrifyingly afraid that all the white students in my class were surreptitiously making fun of my very strong Spanish accent, for in most of my classes I was the only one with brown skin; there were very few ethnics with whom I could feel solidarity in this socially hostile environment. Nonetheless, in spite of severe anxiety and self-doubts, I was determined to triumph over the seemingly insurmountable odds of getting my education in this difficult environment so that I would never have to relive the hell that my mother and The Devil (that sociopathic hyena) had provided to us under the disguise of a home. In spite of the unbearable distress, I knew that I would not permit myself to quit, just as I had struggled with my hands dripping with blood against the bamboo stalk when I was four years old. Whatever the pain, whatever the terror of rejection, I will not quit. Never!

As I began classes I also noticed that the well-heeled white students would wear *different* shoes and belts almost every day. To me that seemed rather peculiar, for I could not comprehend why it was necessary to wear different shoes on different days. By my estimate these students each owned about 10 to 15 pairs of shoes, while I had my *one and only* pair and was happy with it. All my life I had survived on one pair of shoes at a time, or no shoes at all. What is the logic of *owning* more than one pair? Isn't it only possible to wear one at a time? Why the waste? If we can wear only one pair at a time, couldn't we wait until that pair wears out to buy a new one? Given my background, the gringo logic of owning multiple pairs of shoes was beyond comprehension.

And the belts? Why so many belts? One is enough! Wear it until it practically falls off, then buy another one if you have the money. That is how I survived. One day my English teacher (a rather nice looking white female graduate student) was complaining to us students that she was tired of her "wardrobe" (what is that?), that it was the same that she had worn last semester. My God! Now we are supposed to change all our clothes every semester? How wasteful, I thought. She was feeling dejected because she had "only" 22 pairs of shoes, and was lamenting how she felt she was at the "poverty line." Poverty? She is poor because she has only 22 pairs of shoes? She is poor because the several thousand dollars she spent on clothes last semester represent "last semester's fashions"? Did I come here to get an education or to witness a fashion show? Of course, now that I know the white culture really well I realize that these practices are not at all "odd" but rather typical of the ethical and moral consciousness of our civilization in general. At that time, it was I who was embarrassingly out of touch with society in general but especially with the gringo culture.

In 1964 the first two lessons that I learned from the gringo culture at Renwick University were: (1) poverty is relative, so I should feel solidarity with the white students with 15 pairs of shoes, and (2) clothes are not just to protect and cover one's body, but are an individual statement of one's sense of fashion and class. That clothes could be used for "fashion" was also alien to my "culturally deprived" background.

When I heard white students say that another student's clothes "matched," I thought that they were just stating the obvious: that to "match" something was to select the same color. That is, a blue shirt will "match" only with a blue pair of jeans. That was my concept of "matching." Only when I found the truth in the course of conversations with another student did I come to the full shocking realization that clothes "matching" meant that the colors of the various items we wore had to complement each other in a visually pleasing manner. The lightbulb lit up in my head and then I realized why white students were always looking at me rather peculiarly: As per their standards, I *never* matched my clothes.

Typically I wore plaid on plaid, mixed red and orange, as well as pink and purple. I felt OK, but the white students must have felt that I looked like a colorful Mexican parrot, consciously attempting to wear all the colors of the rainbow simultaneously. Yet to all this I was practically blind prior to my discussions on "fashion" with some students. Deep inside my soul the voice of necessity and poverty had grown to feel that a shirt is a shirt, with color being totally irrelevant when one has no other shirts. That is, *whatever* color my shirt was, that was the correct color for my body, for it shielded me from the sun and covered my nakedness from others. If I had a pair of shoes, I was happy. I dared not even look ahead and contemplate a second pair, for fashion was irrelevant because I was not trying to look my best or attempting to impress others. Back in my old neighborhoods, we all knew that everyone was in the same sinking boat, and with hungry stomachs, so why look at another person's shoes or at the color of his shirt? As the sea of poverty and destitution engulfs you, the wetness turns all shoes and all clothing into the same drab colors, thus making fashion an essentially irrelevant luxury. Since I had lived in that sea all my life, and even to a great degree at the foster home, I already had the culture of poverty deep in my soul. Prior to my fashion encounters at RU, nobody had ever told me that certain colors and styles went nicely with each other. This cultural perspective on my part, along with other obvious differences between my Mexican culture and the RU white culture, made me a student that was seen, even officially in university publications and courses, as being "culturally deprived."

Being culturally naive and interpersonally stupid, I accepted this "cultural deprivation" model that was the rage of white liberals on campus. From their perspective these white students and well-meaning administrators saw all ethnic students' customs and beliefs as vacuums indicative of a lack of "culture" (i.e., we did not have the white culture in our souls) that could be ameliorated by the proper "cultural training" (i.e., we were to be made aware of the wonderful cultural heritage of the dominant culture—the white culture). I already felt that my Mexican heritage made me an inferior member of the human race, given the thousands of abuses that I had suffered, the numerous knifings and killings that I either saw or knew about, and the economically desperate condition of my fellow *Mejicanos*, so I really did not need for the white students to now tell me that I was culturally deprived for I wholeheartedly accepted that tenuous premise even before I arrived at Renwick University.

This kind of attitude was pervasive in what I was reading in my general classes at the university, for Lyndon Johnson's *Great Society* programs were getting started while the counterculture revolution was taking campuses all over the country by storm. In retrospect, I think that there actually may have been two distinct forces on the political left: the more paternalistic mainstream liberals who sought then to include more ethnics into the political arena but who felt that we needed "education" to help us out of our "cultural deprivation," and the more radical "New Left" that had purportedly lost all faith in the workability of existing political structures and which sought through violent confrontation and even revolution to replace these with new ones which could operate with complete honesty, integrity, and with availability to all citizens. I had come to Renwick University to get a quiet, orderly education, but instead I found myself vomiting every morning because of anxiety, and in the middle of a sociocultural revolution led by the counterculture with a vicious force that I had not seen in the gringo culture ever. My values and skills were already abysmal, so this social, moral, and political upheaval only served to confuse me even more.

In my classes we typically would talk about moral and political issues, of dilemmas that fired up the imagination while at the same time illustrating an important point. Being politically involved was the last thing that I wanted, for I really did not have a strong view about anything at that time, except perhaps that Mexicans were inferior to the white culture. I agreed whole-heartedly that my "cultural deprivation" was a real problem, that I would have to take many courses here and observe the gringo students so that I could learn about the correct way to do things. I did not even know that one shook hands only with the right one! I discovered that in embarrassing ways. How pitiful I was! I was so fucking stupid—a complete moron! The gringo students must have thought I really did come from under a rock in the desert of El Paso. In a sad way, they were right.

As odd as it may sound, I was having a hard time with the idea of "rights," for I did not comprehend what all the confrontations were all about. Quite simply, I had not grown up with any rights so I thought that they were unnecessary, given my very primitive personality and my even more regressive political understanding. Most of what the "establishment" was saying to me made a lot of sense, like working hard and keeping our noses to the academic grindstone. But the New Left and the counterculture spewed complex concepts and philosophies such as "military-industrial complex" and "the illegitimacy of the Vietnam war". What I was seeing was a student population with an unmitigated passion for political discourse, richly endowed with an enviable sociocultural vocabulary and a dogged, almost religious, belief that they were right. How I admired their confidence and strength of conviction; I did not, however, admire their actual political positions.

These counterculture students certainly had strong convictions, if only in the anti-parent, anti-authority direction, so it is surprising to me now that I did not embrace this philosophy promptly, which would have made sense given the degree of anti-mother and anti-stepfather sentiment that I carried within me but which I did not come to feel or acknowledge until just in the last few years. But on the other hand, these students may have been rebelling against the authority of discipline, something which had negligently been left out of my childhood.

In very real terms most of these politically involved undergraduate students were light years ahead of me, for they were functioning at the sociopolitical level of moral understanding, what psychologist Lawrence Kohlberg later came to identify as the "morality of abstract principles" in *The Philosophy of Moral Development* (1984). I, on the other hand, was still at the relatively primitive level of integrating my anxiety-contaminated personality, struggling with fundamental personal issues such as how to engage others in conversation, how to keep my involuntary vomiting at bay, how to answer questions in class, how to cope with the chronic siege from within my soul that sabotaged my efforts at feeling competent at tasks and within my person, and how to understand the values and competencies of students around me, for in a very real sense everything appeared surreal to me. Looking back, I think that at that time I was physically 18 to 20 years old, but my personality at that point was probably at the level of a very immature five-year-old kid (I've gotten a little bit better since then). It was through the grace of having a very weak sense of self-esteem that my primitive moral development did not get me in trouble at that time, for the rigorous and polemical intellectual environment was prompting me to question the very few morals or ethics that I did have. I was realizing that I was a moral relativist, or so they said. Given my primitive personality, that was a dangerous opinion to hold.

Those Beautiful University Women

By the end of my first year in college, the symptoms of panic had subsided, a welcome relief that allowed me to have breakfast in the mornings. I have no idea how I survived one year of constant panic, vomit, and internal siege. My course grades were in the A and B range, with a few Cs here and there. I still needed to learn much about the dominant culture, for the more I interacted with white students the more I realized how little I knew about the important and proper things in life. For example, I was horrified to learn from others that there were other vegetables and fruits besides tomatoes, onions, lettuce, green peppers, oranges, lemons, bananas, and watermelons. I had no clue what green beans, zucchini, okra, eggplant, summer squash, cauliflower, broccoli, artichoke, parsnip, radish, rutabaga, apricots, raspberries, and turnips looked like. Nor did I know anything at all about currants, gooseberries, blueberries, huckleberries, or cranberries. Quite simply, these had never been part of my life. My God, I was an idiot but was too stupid to notice it.

As things improved I was able to appreciate more the predominantly blond female students, by far the most beautiful women that I had ever seen up to that time. From my culturally damaged perspective, I knew in my heart that these gringas were far superior to the Mexican women I knew or had known, for they had golden yellow hair and the bluest eyes that captured my imagination in the most profound, ecstatic yet painful manner. For even though I was absolutely mesmerized by their radiant beauty, deep inside me I felt that such gifts from heaven were strictly reserved for persons better than me. In retrospect I can see that the subconscious or unwritten rule that seemed to be operating in me was that if I felt that a woman was pretty or beautiful, by default she was not for me. That was the rule of the universe. That was my destiny. God had so declared. My mother must have carved that rule in my heart when she gave me disapproving stares in my infant years. Yes, I was doomed to be a cockroach.

Even in listening to their strong Texas accent (the *twang* that rings out in "Y'all come back now, y'hear?"), I would simply look longingly at these beauties secretly wishing that someday I could marry one. Interestingly enough, if her face attracted me I would fantasize mostly about her being my wife, while sex was not really part of the overall daydream. This pattern of mine just had begun in junior high as I started to take a great interest in girls but subconsciously left sex out of the picture. Somehow I felt that the girl I liked was a "good" girl, so of course she did not do such dirty things. How unfortunate that I was already on this good-girl, bad-girl track from such an early age.

Predictably, I could not easily strike up a conversation with these women, especially with the ones whom I secretly admired because of their facial beauty. My feelings of inferiority and my expectation of rejection were intense, so intense that I could not effectively override the defacto veto that these had over my desire to walk up to a pretty woman and simply introduce myself. A fully confident and more normal guy would have correctly perceived that the worst that could have happened was that the woman could simply have said that she was not interested and we would have been be no worse off than we were at the beginning. I clearly did not aspire to be a Don Juan like the one in Tirso de Molina's *El Burlador de Sevilla*, but rather I wanted simply to find a nice blond, blue-eyed girl and develop a loving, long-lasting relationship. Even in my failure, I always held out hope that someday I might meet a nice blond girl who wouldn't mind dating a skinny, ugly, stupid, and insecure Mexican-American abused foster child cockroach like me.

But there also was a powerful yet separate sexual dimension to my admiration for the college women. In 1965 at Renwick University there were approximately 20,000 women on campus, most, if not all, wearing short shorts, revealing heavenly thighs, and very low-cut blouses or tank tops, accentuating their shapely bosoms. To make matters even more tempting, thousands of these girls walked around with no bra, thus providing a voy-euristic feast as we guys just stared at their pendulous 36-D breasts showing pointed and erect nipples through the fine fabric of their flimsy blouses. For those who did not wear shorts, there were the ever-popular miniskirts, again by the thousands across campus, providing rubber-necking men with clear views of panties as the women sat on benches or on campus steps, or, when they walked up flights of stairs. From every direction, left and right, up and down, day and night, in the classroom and in the cafeterias, I was bombarded with views of the skimpily-clad bodies of blond beauties by the thousands; I walked around with an almost chronic erection. It appeared to me that the gringas were entirely careless about how they sat, for almost everywhere on campus one could see fully-exposed cleavage and colorful panties between legs that were nonchalantly (?) left open. For the first time in my life I felt an unending heightened level of sexual arousal that soon fueled a voyeuristic impulse that was with me almost 24 hours a day. I felt almost like a moth drawn irresistably in a thousand directions by the lights all around it—the heavenly breasts and thighs of the most beautiful women on the face of the Earth: those Renwick University gringas.

While my hormones were raging from the overwhelming temptations of the Texas beauties, my sense of self was so poor that I could not do what most of the other men on campus were doing: asking for and getting dates. Deep in my heart, I felt that any girl I would ask for a date, admittedly a date based primarily on raw sexual attraction, would turn me down if not laugh outright. My sexuality wanted to approach, yet my self-esteem was crushed by self-doubts and anxiety. It was a classic and painful approach-avoidance conflict.

This impasse was intensely painful, and it fueled fantasies of my simply taking a woman into the bushes and just raping her, raping her because she was parading her exquisite wares in front of me as if she knew I couldn't have her. Somewhere deep inside my soul lay the paradoxical state of feeling admiration, awe, and hostility towards these objects of beauty and tempta-tion. Sexual admiration within me produced tension, then frustration, and finally aggression or hostility. Moreover, it was as if logic did not matter, for how could I feel admiration and hostility simultaneously? Certainly I was not consciously choosing to feel hostile toward these women who attracted me because of their physical and sensual beauty. Well, I was torn inside because of the complexity of these emotions, yet I am grateful to whatever forces in the universe intervened and prevented me from acting out such rape fantasies, for I know too well now that such emotional forces are similar to those typical of rapists and serial killers, that is, forces such as frustration, anger, sexual dysfunction, poor social skills, and an inability to relate properly to women. Even though I was hot all the time I am so glad I never crossed the line.

And so it was that within this framework the stage was set for the events of the Fall of 1965 when I met Katherine and my life was forever changed.

During my second year at RU a friend of mine, Pedro, asked me to stay at his apartment for one hour while he was in class because a fellow student would be coming to pick up a book Pedro had borrowed in class.

"Sure, I'll do it. What's his name?"

"Katherine," he answered with a smirk.

Oh, my God! It's a gringa and she's coming to pick up a book here! My stomach started churning acid and my arms began to tremble. Can I really handle this?

I heard a firm knock on the door. I said, God help me, I took a very deep breath and opened the door. It was Katherine, it was fate. Standing there in front of me was a Texas-Tennessee-Louisiana gringa with light brown hair and the most beautiful green eyes that I had ever seen. I was meeting a goddess. "Hi, I'm Katherine. Is Pedro here? I'm supposed to pick up a book."

Her smile and friendliness captivated me from the moment I heard her heavenly voice, so I began to tremble as I was coming to the realization that she was talking to me willingly and that the minutest error on my part, either through cultural ignorance or stupid negligence, could very well bring this joyous beginning to an abrupt end. I asked her to come in and we both sat at the kitchen table, next to a mountain of garbage that could easily be mistaken for the aftermath of a colossal college drinking party. Katherine looked at me in the eye as we spoke, something that I immediately had mixed feelings about; her face was truly a work of art, especially her eyes, so green, so clear and bright, so friendly and romantic. But her friendly look made me nervous, for if I was looking into her eyes she obviously was looking into mine, and therefore she would soon know that I was really just a stupid Chicano from El Paso, and a foster child at that. Besides, also a miserable and motherless insect.

But no, our conversation quickly entered the arena of Chicano politics and the antiwar movement. To my surprise Katherine was extremely well versed in Chicano history and was fluent in Spanish! Can this be true? A gringa who speaks Spanish?! Here is a beautiful gringa—a goddess really—who understands my culture almost like an insider, and she even speaks to me in Spanish! Yes, it was true. She was a history major at RU, came from a very liberal Houston family, and had a father who was a history professor in Houston. But best of all, she liked the Mexican culture! Oh, yes, before I forget, she did come for that book, but I told her what Pedro had asked me to relate: that he had left the book with me here in the apartment, but that he would like to keep it longer.

The gleam in her eye was telling me something, although I was not too astute at interpreting body language or facial nuances. As she told me that she had to go to catch a class, I knew that I had to do something to make sure I'd see her again, but how do you ask a girl for a phone number? That was a tough job. My anxiety level by this time was near nuclear proportions, and it got even worse as we approached the door. This was the second time in my life when I had to make the decision to be brave—the first was asking Isabella Cuellar to the high school prom. So I used all my energy to keep my vomit down and I asked her for her phone number. She said, "Sure!" so we exchanged numbers as I promised Katherine that I would call her in a few days to take her on a motorcycle ride. After she was gone and I closed the door, I jumped up and down with the joy of a little boy being told that he was getting his first bicycle. Never before had I had such a conversation with a girl as pretty as Katherine, so I was simply overjoyed by my good fortune as I ran back to my apartment to get ready for my own classes. For the next several days the only thing on my mind was Katherine's beautiful face and gorgeous Texas-Tennessee-Louisiana-Mexico accent. I was in heaven. Nothing else mattered. I had actually spoken to a goddess!

After missing her several times when I called her at home, we finally made contact and went out for the evening. For me it was a new experience to be going out on a romantic date with such a beautiful girl, and Katherine made it so easy by talking about things that were dear to me such as Spanish, Mexican culture, tacos, sociology, history, and the university culture. We ate, we laughed, we joked, we giggled, we looked at each other. Nothing else mattered as I was falling in love (I think that's what it was) with her; from the way she looked at me I knew that she also was feeling something. After that first date we went out 12 consecutive days immediately afterwards for a total of 13 back-to-back dates. Our dates were blossoming out into a heavenly romance.

Soon we were doing everything together: going to classes, studying, eating, watching movies, shopping, and kissing, by far the most wonderful activity that we did together, in my then-ignorant opinion. As with all lovers enthralled, we would sit at *Capital Cafe* on the main university drag, Sussman

Street, and sip coffee between the long silences when we would simply stare into each other's eyes, something that I had only read about and which I had secretly envied when I saw other love-struck couples doing it. But here, with Katherine, it was really happening to me. It was real. It was passionate. It was all-consuming. It made my body tremble. It altered the normal chemistry of my body. I could not eat or sleep or concentrate as my mind obsessed about her image, her figure, her legs, her face, her eyes, her accent, her expressions ("*Ni papas!*" (typical Mexican expression meaning "No way!")). And as we became fully intimate with each other, I knew that this was about as close to heaven as anyone could get, for I felt like merging with Katherine, something that was not logical but rather passionate and inexplicable. Whereas, before I met her, I could continue being dysfunctional without the need for any particular person, after we met I felt that if we were not together the world could not turn, the rivers couldn't flow, and the stars could not shine—unless I held her hand. It was a wonderful yet painful feeling, for I wanted to possess Katherine, this priceless jewel who walked into my wretched life, more so because I felt that she might just leave or disappear in spite of the many times that we confessed our romantic love for each other. She won't leave, right? I can trust her, I think...

As our relationship grew I felt in my heart that I had fallen in love with her and that I wanted her to marry me, something that I feared discussing with her. Her playing Beethoven's *Für Elise* on the piano for me regularly served to cement more strongly my heart to hers. One night as we were parked in Katherine's old Volkswagen somewhere in a dark cubbyhole on campus, I asked her.

"Chata, do you think that maybe you and I could one day get married?" My heart stopped, my blood ceased to flow, and my breathing came to a standstill as I had just forced that question out of my lips, waiting for the universe to disintegrate if she no.

"Oh, I think that it is possible," she replied slowly and pensively, as if she was quickly assessing the possibilities, benefits and risks, and revealing an underlying concern or doubt. As my heart was racing with excitement and my breathing doubled to catch up, she revealed the nature of her concern: "And if we do I think we will have a stormy marriage," she added, expressing a doubt that she phrased in words that were so on the mark and so prophetic but which in my initial excitement I chose to ignore. Little did I know that Katherine was far more astute about relationships, and that she was in effect predicting what came to be the most glorious and the most gut-wrenching times of my adult life.

While on campus we did all our studying together, and our relationship quickly moved forward. There was very little friction, really—nothing that would signal that we were not made for each other—so in December of 1965 we became engaged. I was in heaven knowing that this beautiful girl, this goddess, was my girl and would soon be my wife. Never had I known such bliss, joy, happiness—never had I seen eyes that did not make me feel like a cockroach. Yes, a gift from heaven for all the suffering I had already gone through.

Interestingly, as my romance with Katherine blossomed my purely sexual interests in other gringas diminished by about 90 percent; all my energy, my attention, my daydreams, my aspirations, and my obsessions went to Katherine, so I did not have much left for the other pretty women who strutted around campus with see-through blouses and crotch-splitting jeans. When I was not with Katherine I would still turn my head to catch a glimpse here and there, yet even as diminished as my impulses were, they were still there, strong enough for me to ask myself if I was supposed to have gotten over that "stage" now that I had my dream girl. I wasn't sure. My heart belonged totally to Katherine, I felt, yet my lascivious inner self still had something to say to me—that there were other pretty girls out there worth looking at. Is this normal? How do I know? Had I been wiser I would have interpreted this much more prudently, for years later this impulse contributed significantly to the disastrous unraveling of our relationship, an event of major proportions in my life. In our state of bliss after our engagement, dark psychological forces were readying themselves to destroy our dreams, and even the dreams themselves already contained the seeds of conflict and ultimate destruction. Only now with the benefit of hindsight and a bit more wisdom, can I say that the path we were on had to play itself out—its unfortunate and painful conclusion could not have been easily avoided.

But there was one early signpost that I missed. Katherine was quick-witted and astute in political discourse and debate. She showed a fervor for the New Left philosophy, with the exception of the abortion issue on which she was clearly of the old conservative pro-life school, just as passionately as her parents. So when we discussed political issues I typically would just say that all political and moral issues are relative and that nothing is right or wrong. Her passionate response was that I had "no backbone" as far as political thought was concerned. And even though I held steadfastly to my view on the relativity of all political and ideological opinions, I still participated in the debates but without much passion. Whatever. Indeed, the "no backbone" critique went over my head as I believed that no political system was worth fighting for; it would be years before I would finally realize what my true love meant when she leveled that charge against me. Developmentally I was eons behind Katherine, only I was too naive and too stupid to know it. It was not that I believed in the total relativity of morals, it was that I had no fundamental moral structure in my soul. Tragically for us it was an undiagnosed weakness that in conjunction with my other character flaws served to sink this God-given relationship very painfully several years later.

In 1966 Katherine and I were married, and we held our reception at her parents' home afterwards. Katherine looked so beautiful in her Irish white gown, her arms gracefully moving by her side as she looked at me with those gorgeous green eyes. If there was any redemption for all I had suffered in my life, this was it. Nothing else could come close to it.

After a brief honeymoon in New Orleans, Katherine and I returned promptly to RU, I to my studies and Katherine to a job as a teacher. She was a year older than me so she had already finished her studies. As close observers of the human condition would have predicted, reality then set in. We were very happy with each other, but the normal arguments began—hostile fights as differing views about household matters clashed. Especially acerbic were the confrontations centered around my relationship with Katherine's parents whom I perceived as being rather intrusive in our marriage, an opinion that Katherine did not share. At least that was my surface-level feeling and opinion. These fights were so intense that on several occasions I left the house and Katherine had to go driving around looking for me. Had I been wiser I would have recognized the severity of the conflict and sought assistance, but my eyes were pathologically blind to the folly of my heart, for I fear now that what was really happening was that I had married Katherine to possess her totally. I wanted to own her completely with no one else making claims to her attention or love. Only in retrospect can I clearly see the uncountable instances where I wanted her all for myself, with no friends around, with no parents present, with no one to share our lives with. Somewhere deep inside my soul I wanted Katherine to forsake all other relationships from her life, yet amazingly enough I was not sufficiently astute to even recognize this subconscious desire of mine. The possessive force was real, but it operated as a hidden hand within my soul, directing my actions, reactions, and attitudes towards Katherine in a smothering, unloving, selfish manner, irrespective of what she wanted or what may have been good for her spiritual wellbeing over the long-term. I remember clearly how in almost any group situation I would feel intensely jealous when Katherine would show pleasure and joy in interacting with other people—friends and family. It was usually a major event just to plan for us to go visit her parents, for I would typically feel that we visited them too much, even when it was once a week. And, to make matters worse, Katherine would say that when we argued my voice would get threateningly loud, something that intimidated her. I should have listened to her. But I couldn't. My dormant demons were waking up and taking over major parts of my personality.

Of course, Katherine had been right when she foresaw that we would have a stormy marriage, yet I do not think that either of us knew just how bad things would get. In my loving her so strongly I wanted to possess her, to own her, to consume her, to merge with her, and to control her. As I look back, with more accumulated wisdom, at this early stage of our marriage and reflect upon how I felt about and acted towards Katherine, I get an uneasy feeling that my *love* for Katherine may not have been a healthy one with genuine concern for the other person and guided by proper moral and ethical principles. Lurking deep inside my soul undoubtedly were pathological forces unknown to me yet operating in the shadows behind my eyes, with their own set of eyes, their own power, their own mission. I consciously felt that I loved Katherine very much, that she unquestionably was the best thing that had every happened to me. I yearned to be with her. I loved her kisses. I was in heaven when we held hands. I lusted after her body. I was enthralled by her beauty and her face. I admired the way she moved her arms, her legs, her hips, her mouth, her lips. I wanted her to be with me for the rest of my life. I simply wanted her. I loved her. As far as any human being can *know* anything, *I knew in my heart that I loved Katherine.* Yet, I can see from my *behavior* that whatever it was I felt inside, that it was *not* an honest, ethical, mature, genuine, and caring love. In a most surreptitious manner the sinister emotional forces inside me had preempted my ability to correctly identify what I was feeling, or rather, they obscured behind a veil of repression the real nature of my attachment to Katherine. I believed delusionally that I was deeply in love with this wonderful, gorgeous woman. With pain in my heart I see now that what I felt for Katherine was not true romantic love, as much as I would like to label those wonderful feelings as such, but rather a set of feelings centered around *symbiosis and attachment similar to that which a young child has for his mother.* In a very real sense my inner soul must have felt that Katherine was a mother-substitute, a female figure who brought me comfort and pleasure, who could serve me and attend to my every need without requiring much reciprocation for her acts of kindness, love, and service. That needy little boy who lived at the center of my soul threw tantrums fueled by strong feelings of entitlement, symbiotic possessiveness, and an extremely egocentric and self-serving view of the world. I didn't really love Katherine in a mature, responsible manner—I *needed* her as a child needs his mother. I loved her as a child loves his mother: I was attached to her because she provided security in some way, and like a child, I was able to take love but unable to give it. Nor was I aware of this ethical and emotional need for full reciprocity in mature, romantic love. Fundamentally I was a five-year old boy in a man's body with adult intelligence, and quite delusional about my feelings for Katherine.

Had I undergone through psychotherapy when I was initially placed in the foster home, I would have had a more mature understanding of my feelings, especially those associated with my mother. Maybe I would have loved Katherine in a more genuine manner. But, no, all the garbage in my soul was being stirred up, and it was setting us up for the tragic failure that was in the making even in the first year of our ill-fated romance, by far the greatest romantic experience I have ever had.

Given the severe disturbance which I suspect very much I suffered as an infant, and given my general lack of individuation, or, as Katherine had put it, "no backbone," it made sense for me to think of my case as arrested emotional development. In other words, because I had a significant disturbance in my relationship with my mother when I was an infant (recall also my passionate sucking of my mother's toe when I was about four years old), I concluded that at the time that I met Katherine I could not have been capable of entering into a mature romantic relationship with a woman. As I see it, I needed a mother *first*, then I could transfer feelings *later* to another woman as romantic love. Having missed the first, the second was theoretically impossible. Even now I still have my doubts about my capacity to love.

When, many years later, I became more familiar with psychological analysis, my suspicions about the genuineness of my love for Katherine were aroused when I finally noticed *the severe discrepancy between what I believed I was feeling and how I was behaving presumably as a result of that feeling.* I *believed* that I loved Katherine, yet my behavior *was not loving* towards her. If I had been a child my behavior would have been characterized as a special case of "oppositional-defiant disorder" whereby my anger, defiance, and selfishness would have been directed not generally at others but specifically at Katherine. But as an adult this behavior was simply abusive towards the woman I loved, albeit as a child loves his mother. My first real romance, and I had already failed from the start.

Along the same line of analysis, I came to discover that this whirlwind romance and marriage to Katherine represented for me the very first time that I had *attached* myself emotionally to a woman who was not my mother, and that in the development of this relationship some very peculiar traits of mine came to the surface: that selfish, demanding, and controlling little boy inside me had been awakened when Katherine unsuspectingly opened the door for him with her dedication and her love. The emotional bully had been kept at bay behind the door of rejection, abuse, and indifference, the door that my mother had built and shut herself. But, in my view, once the bully surfaced and gained strength, a greater and stronger door would be needed in the future when the only support for his living out in the light, Katherine, would opt to leave, thereby reopening once more the original soul-deep wound that only a mother could have inflicted. The setting in place of this greater, more unopenable door of the future would come at the tragic price of profound spiritual sickness that would in turn inflict untold emotional pain on innocent others. Whatever my coping defenses had been that assisted me throughout my relatively isolative junior- and high-school years, they were now penetrated and could not be propped up. Newer, stronger, more sinister ones would be needed soon if I was to keep on functioning. It was just a matter of time.

So Katherine and I continued to have friction, but in spite of our increasingly caustic fights we still felt a passion for each other, and I still thought that she was the prettiest girl on campus. When in Katherine told me in 1966 that she was pregnant I was overjoyed, but her parents were not. "And how are you going to support this child?" they rightfully asked with the proper adult authority which I did not have. Money was not the first thing on my mind, it was the thought of my wife having *my* baby. My macho Chicano cultural traits kicked into action.

Countless times in *barrio* conversations with other Chicanos and with adult men as I was growing up, I had come to learn about the relationships between boys and girls, men and women. Boys and men were strong, brave, courageous, active, fearless and born leaders, while girls and women were dainty, soft, maternal, coy, weak, beautiful, pure, and obedient. Girls should wait for a boy to ask them out for a date, since the boy determines what direction a relationship should take. In fact, for me one of the most interesting concepts in these gender rules was the idea of a Chicano man's duty and obligation to "make the woman fall in love with you." As a boy I had been told by many adult Chicanos **and** Chicanas that if I liked a girl that I should go to her with the purpose of *enamorarla*, that is, to do whatever is necessary to make her fall in love with me, for love depends mainly on what the boy does, not on what the girl wants. Furthermore, to cement that budding relationship I needed to *conquistarla*, and, *hacerla mia*, which meant that as soon as I deflowered the virgin girl she had no choice but to be mine until I said otherwise. In fact, many grown Chicana women told me over the years that a particular man *"me hizo suya,"* which meant that "he succeeded in sleeping with me, so I became his." For the longest time I have had trouble understanding these teachings, although as I grew up with them, I believed that they were part of the order of the universe, that boys and men were the natural leaders in any relationship. This was something that I lamented very much since I lived the hell of my childhood in my mother's home where The Satan, The Hated Devil, that spineless phlegm, was the unrivaled malignant leader. In secret under the covers at night I wished that God had made women—my mother—the leaders in the household.

Not only that, but even after marriage the man of the house, the Macho Chicano, was supposed to have several clandestine girlfriends—secret only from his wife—and hopefully he would impregnate several or all of them to show to his fellow Macho Chicanos that he was *puro hombre, puro macho*— pure macho man. The more children that the Macho sired outside of his legitimate marriage the more "status" he acquired—real or perceived—in the eyes of his peers. Little wonder that I soon learned as a small kid that "real" boys and men do not wear condoms when they have sex with a girl or woman; the sperms should not be wasted inside a condom but rather deposited deep inside a woman so that "they can do their job." Other phrases of wisdom along these lines were:

"Cuando te cojas a una vieja, hechale los mecos." When you have sex with a woman, give her all your sperms.

"Metesela hasta el tronco." Sink your penis into her all the way to her spine.

"Le di sus vergasos." I whipped her with my penis.

"Si tiene cara de tren, ponla a mamar." If her face resembles a train, make her give you a blowjob instead.

"Metesela toda hasta que le duela." Slide all your penis deep into her until she squirms with pain.

And the list of Macho sexual maxims went on and on about other vulgar facets of sexual intercourse, all of which served to show that the man was in charge of the woman's body and destiny, and that with his actual penis he could beat, conquer, impregnate, and control the woman for eternity. It was thoroughly incredible what a man could do with this meaty organ!

Through the years I was very much indoctrinated into the Macho philosophy, adopting it wholeheartedly without much critical thought. I saw no contradiction, no hypocrisy, for I knew that when I grew up that I would find a nice wife and fill her up with my sperms to impregnate her. Yet, there were other sides to this philosophy, most notably the image of a fearless warrior, the vindictive protector of the home.

If the sexual facets of the Macho philosophy served to give the Chicano man the unfair advantage in a relationship with a woman, then maintaining the position of the "fearless protector of family honor" served to place him at inordinate and unnecessary risk, for in mindlessly accepting this role millions of Mexican and Chicano men have perished needlessly through the years. This defense of personal and family honor did not necessarily involve physical or verbal threats against the Macho's self or family, but rather consisted of real or imagined slights which could conceivably devalue one's honor in the eyes of one's peers. Growing up in the Mexican communities of El Paso I knew of or had personally seen how Chicano boys and men would be assaulted, maimed, or killed for looking at someone else's girl for more than the duration of an unintended glance, an act which was seen as a violation of the "honor" of the boy or man accompanying the female. In its greatest absurdity the Macho way of life required a real man to never back down even from a convincing threat that was clearly too formidable to neutralize, resulting in a senseless and tragic faceoff in which there were no winners, only dead bodies and fugitives from the law. Consider this scenario:

In a Mexican cantina Cleto looks for more than a moment at the woman who is accompanying Benny, known for his raging jealousy. Benny, Macho man that he is, is ever vigilant in a place like this, for he knows that *all* the men here would like to fuck his woman and get her pregnant, an act that would earn them prestige and him humiliation. Metaphorically he has just brought the hen into the cage with the foxes, so it is inevitable that what he secretly fears the most will happen. Benny notices the hungry look that Cleto is giving his woman.

"So what are you looking at, pendejo?" Benny asks menacingly as he struts over to Cleto's spot at the counter, walking as if his testicles were too big for the limited space between his legs. Now Cleto has been put on the spot, for he was caught doing what a good Macho man does, but caught by someone very unhappy that *his* woman was the object of it. In the philosophy of the fearless warrior, Cleto cannot let this challenge go unanswered, much in the same manner that Benny did not see a choice after he noticed that someone was salivating over his woman.

"Nothing. I was just admiring your woman," responds Cleto as his soul gets ready for a further escalation that will require a blanket denial of his fear. Even as Cleto answers the direct challenge from the chief rooster, he straightens up and faces his opponent squarely so as not to imply the slightest deference, the most minute amount of fear, lest the opponent gain courage.

Since another man has now openly acknowledged that he has been visually undressing his woman, Benny sees no choice but to humiliate him in front of his peers, the only way a Macho man can teach a lesson to another man who affronts his manhood or his honor. "I did not give you permission to look at my woman, so you had better get the hell out of here before I break your face," says Benny in a probably subconscious effort to confront the other man publicly while simultaneously creating a way out of escalating things further. But the subconscious attempt at de-escalation is outwardly still much too strong and menacing for Cleto to accept, for it still reeks of a Macho rebuke for his having done what his Macho soul naturally yearned to do. By this time both men are hopelessly locked in a headstrong Macho challenge and standoff which will carry them to the brink of tragedy if not beyond.

"What's the matter, pendejo? Are you gonna make me leave?" asks Cleto in a self-assured and provoking tone, raising his Mexican nose higher into the air and now looking only obliquely at Benny, implying that Benny does not deserve full attention or a direct presentation of Cleto's face, an affront that Cleto felt he had to give and which Benny now cannot ignore. All the eyes in the Cantina want to know who is the more Macho of the two strutting peacocks.

Since words do not seem to be winning the battle for Benny, he sees fit to meet this newest challenge by taking from his jacket pocket a .357-magnum revolver that he normally carries around to show others that he is to be respected and feared. In a terrifying escalation of the verbal duel, he points the weapon at Cleto and admonishes him.

"I told you to get the hell out of here before I blow your fucking head off!"

The latest round of escalations has placed Cleto in the most unenviable of positions, for he is staring at the barrel of a very lethal weapon, a threat against which he has no defense, at least not in a physical sense. But as the Macho war of words escalates into absurdity, Cleto finds a "face-saving" counterattack, for in his heart he knows that the whole world is watching him defend his Macho honor in front of the woman that he so admired. He will save face but will lose his life.

In a terrifyingly desperate act that is repeated very often in the cantinas of the Macho world, Cleto finds words of defiance to attack his opponent.

"So you think you're gonna scare me with that piece of shit? I'm not afraid of that popgun, man. Shoot me, pendejo. Go ahead. Shoot me, you asshole!" screams Cleto in an aggressive tone more typical of a military sergeant hollering at his troops. "Come on, right here, right here! Shoot right here! Andale, pendejo, tirale," says Cleto as he motions with his index finger where Benny should point his gun at Cleto's chest. Maybe beneath the surface Cleto is afraid as he stares into the lethal cannon of the .357, but his defiant and fearless challenge serves momentarily to anesthetize him from the horrible situation he's in, and it also serves to show others that he cannot be easily intimidated. Cleto is a Macho man—he does not know fear. The other machos in the cantina admire Cleto's balls. Unfortunately, this also ups the ante for Benny.

As others watch, Benny correctly sees himself as the object of a challenge from another Mexican who would probably be seen by all of these spectators as "more Macho," an intolerable humiliation for Benny. As Cleto defiantly repeats his challenge to shoot, Benny knows the ball's in his court and he must act. He cannot let Cleto get away with it, so he blasts him once in the chest, the bullet going in and coming out the back, killing him instantly. The killer has reaffirmed his honor and integrity, the dead man has saved face. They are both Macho men. It's a draw, and they both win.

The above example is not theoretical or conjectural, for sadly it happens every day in Mexican, Chicano, Puerto-Rican, and other Hispanic communities as boys and men must live up to the Macho standards of their peer groups and communities. It was precisely this absurd view of the world which ended the lives of many of the kids I grew up with, young Macho boys who felt in their hearts that they had to intimidate others to prove their manhood; boys who in the dead of winter wore only a thin T-shirt outdoors to prove to the admiring girls just how tough they were; boys who drank beer and straight alcohol to show that they could "hold" their liquor; boys and adult men who should have known better but who felt slighted on the highway if another vehicle driven by a male passed them, and who subsequently had to regain their lead position at any speed, creating in the end some of the worse highway carnage I have ever witnessed anywhere in the country; men and boys who never admitted to having an emotion that implied weakness of any sort, who worked hard at the presentation of self as a concrete machine with little emotion other than near-homicidal aggression towards opponents and unrestrained lust for any female in the immediate vicinity. The Macho philosophy left little room for thoughtful reflection—his inner soul guided the Macho's behavior quite spontaneously and with no apologies.

On the aggression side I never did fit in, for I was a certified coward all the way, refusing all challenges and backing down from all confrontations, whether I was right or wrong. In fact, many of my peers who never backed down and who rode the Macho stallion every day of their lives are now dead, having found a more-Macho (or luckier) opponent who had to teach them a lesson. In its most virulent form the Macho personality does not allow comfortable co-existence, for there are always other Machos who feel that they are more Macho and are itching to prove it. Another contest is always around the corner.

But on the sexual side I feel that my behavior with women up to the time that I married Katherine was, in fact, quite dysfunctional in its own way even without the contaminating influence of the Macho philosophy. With Katherine my behavior was of the Macho variety, even though I did not *consciously* endorse the positions of the Macho men. I recall well that I expected her to do all the housework and to serve me at every opportunity. In a way the Macho man expects his wife to serve him in much the same fashion that his own mother did when he was a young child, only now the grown up little boy is very much in control of his mother-wife, who must also submit her own body unconditionally to him, whenever and wherever he wants, irrespective of her own mood or desires. It appears to me from this perspective that there are undertones of the *oedipus complex* in the Macho personality, that have their basis in the original desire to possess the mother sexually when the son is about four to six years old. In fact, most Hispanic men call their sweethearts and their wives "*mami,*" while the corresponding term that women use is "*papi.*" That it is a cultural trait may attest to the pervasiveness of the confusion over the overlapping roles of wife and mother in the Hispanic Macho culture.

In my case I can see that I clearly treated Katherine as a mother, yet I was also very proud that she was pregnant, that she was carrying *my baby* inside her. Secretly I said to myself that I, Mr. Macho, had been the one who *made* the baby inside her. I was the designer, the engineer, the architect, the stud, the walking penis, the million-gallon sperm producer, the one who can make babies inside the wombs of women. It was almost as if Katherine had no part in creating the new life inside her, for all that was needed to make a baby was my penis and a few gallons of sperm. That was it. This Macho perspective has its counterpart in the Hispanic female, for it is very common for Hispanic women to admire the baby sired by a man with another woman, and then to complimentarily mention that "*el pinta muy bien.*" Literally it means that "*he* paints very well," but conceptually they are saying that "*he* produces very beautiful babies in the women he selects to impregnate." Even the women attribute the admirable qualities of a newborn to the sperm of the man, while the baby itself and the mother are hardly mentioned as significant factors.

Notwithstanding my newfound pride in having impregnated my wife, I still fought in the usual manner with her, and for the same old reasons. The down-to-earth demands of the relationship were perhaps too much for me—I certainly did not know how to properly execute my role because I had never seen a proper role as a young child.

But, several weeks after Katherine got pregnant we lost the baby. The doctors never gave us a definitive cause for the miscarriage. She was heartbroken, while I was confused. Were my sperms defective? In a heartless manner all I could think about was just to get her knocked up again to reassert my manhood, my macho self-image. Soon enough Katherine was pregnant again. This time I told her to take it easy at work. Now I realize that I did not say that for her benefit but for mine: a second miscarriage would almost be positive proof I just could not get a woman pregnant and make it stick. I was having none of that.

This time it did stick and our baby girl Sarah was born in March of 1967. Still feeling quite "embarrassed" about my role as a father, I was ambivalent about telling people that I had a daughter, not because of Sarah but because the word "father" was alien and "suspicious" to me. I found myself in the role of a father without knowing the first thing about fatherhood, for my intellect knew about "fatherhood" from books and movies, but my heart understood the concept only in the darkest and most painful manner: All I knew about being a father came from the savage lessons I had learned from the The Devil, certainly not a role model of decency and unfit to father even wild dogs. But I was ignorant and morally and spiritually blind at 22, so while my intellect may have recognized some general principles of decent fathering, it was my inner soul, damaged as it was, which without question took over as my hidden guide in my pitiful attempt at fathering. Yes, demons and more demons in my soul. They really came out and guided my hand, but I was blind to them.

Sad to say, but I do not believe that I loved my daughter Sarah when she was born even though at that time I believed with all my heart that I did love her from the beginning. For years I labored under this delusion, lacking the proper knowledge and perspective to reflect on the inconsistency of my belief and my non-empathetic behavior. As in my relationship with Katherine, here too I was out of touch with reality for I very much *wanted* to believe that I loved my daughter as all fathers are supposed to love their infant daughters. And then I spanked her.

Meadow Apartments were wooden structures apparently from the World War II era, and they showed it in their paper-thin walls and creaky floors. We had a separate bedroom for Sarah, which Katherine had decorated with all the warmth and enthusiasm of a new mother. From the very beginning Sarah used to cry a lot, I don't know why, but I had a feeling of torture and frustration when I heard her cry. It was not as if her cry would trigger an empathetic and nurturing response from me, as should be the case with a normal father, especially with a newborn infant. *But I was not normal, and, worse, I did not know I was not normal.* One day I was changing her diaper and she kept on crying in spite of my efforts to make her comfortable. Almost quite reflexively I hit her on her bottom two times, which produced some purple marks by the next day. This shocked me so much that I never did it again. I should have known that this inauspicious beginning to my role as a father indicated that I did not take to the responsibilities in a natural manner, that within me were not the archetypes of a decent and responsible father; on the contrary, there were bad memories and other pathologies on standby to produce inappropriate and dysfunctional fathering. Unfortunately for my poor daughter Sarah, fate had placed her with a father who knew not a thing about caring for and loving a child. That was me. It would take me many years and countless dysfunctional and inappropriate interactions for me to finally realize how woefully inadequate I had been as a father, as a husband, and as a person. "Inadequate" may be too mild, "personality-disordered" and "neurotic" may actually be closer to the painful truth. I was unraveling as life presented me with new challenges.

While all this was going on I received news, after many years, about The Devil. Finally, The Devil, El Diablo, The Worm of Worms, Merengueno Zalmar, King Scum of the Sewers, died in El Paso in 1967, reportedly of a heart attack while eating a hamburger alone in the rat-and-roach-infested motel (quite befitting) where he ended up spending the last useless days of his worthless life. The sombitch was about 41 years old. When I heard the news I was not impressed either way, neither feeling elated nor sorry for the passing of El Diablo, for in a very real way I had simply set aside the memories of what he had done to us, and especially to me. Nope, it was a non-event because I had not thought of him—at least not consciously—for many years, or at least for the nine years since Mrs. Barrientos had gone to our Morelos Street house to pick us all up. It was many years later in therapy when I rejoiced at the passing of this scum of the Earth, this beast who terrorized all of us, who assaulted us, who beat our mother, who abused us, who neglected our basic needs, who violated our spiritual integrity and our basic human rights. Even if I think hard about it, I can find no redeeming qualities about this dog. He came to this planet to cause misery to all, and only to take for he had little or nothing to give to others. El Diablo was worse than a parasite since his presence was enough to cause spiritual decay in those around him. It was best that he died before I became fully aware of the seriousness of his transgressions.

No, wait. Stop. Now I am wiser and I can see my illness. I have been mercilessly criticizing Merengueno Zalmar for his evil deeds. But I too was doing terrible things when we all lived together in my mother's house, and after I started living with the Barrientoses, when he was not around me any longer, I kept doing dastardly things on my own. Clearly, I was not any better than The Beast whom I so despised. And now I was ruining Katherine's happiness, and a few years of her life, and then I heartlessly spanked my infant daughter. How could I do these things? What kind of monster does this? I was becoming a Demon on my own. I was becoming other people's El Diablo, sucking away their integrity and their happiness. Horrible. Horrible. I did not want to do that, but I did it. I should have been executed before I married Katherine, but certainly before she got pregnant, to spare innocent people the further spiritual damage that I would do. Better still, my mother should have drowned me the day I was born, or at least should have had an abortion when I was but a spineless larva in her wicked womb. I can't think of a more moral solution.

Countless times I have processed with my therapists the knotted threads of feelings that The Devil left me with, and even though the Monster may be dead in the ground, his legacy in the form of permanent scars, neuroses, and other undesirable personality traits is repugnantly part of my soul, a disgusting contamination of my spirit that I am still coping with. My soul was in its formative years when The Devil came into our lives, and to my misfortune his wretchedness placed its imprint on it. As I see it, the general goal of my years of therapy has been for me to learn how to recognize the pathological footprints of abuse in the mud of my soul and, at best, to fill in the imprints, or at the least, to walk around them so as not to follow down their dark path.

As Sarah got stronger and bigger I concentrated more on my history studies at RU, deciding that I would want to go to graduate school to earn my master's in the same field. My grades were good so I applied for the M.A. program at The Graduate School of International University in New York. Soon enough I was accepted with a fellowship, so Katherine and I jointly decided that New York City would be a more exciting place for us. Given that we had been arguing a lot, we felt that a change would be good for us. So in mid-September of 1967 we packed all of our belongings and we headed for NYC in search of intellectual enlightenment and cultural diversification. We found both plus the painful end of our "stormy marriage." (As she had said.)

Chapter Nine

Intellectual Vigor and Spiritual Death

We traveled for several days in our moribund car and finally got to see the New York City skyline from the fume-infested New Jersey Turnpike, an experience that started me thinking about the wisdom of what we were doing. What were all those refineries and smokestacks producing? I wondered. For the fall sky did not look blue as it did in Texas but had a rather definite brownish tint even in the middle of the day. The 16 lanes of the Turnpike were a sight to behold with thousands of cars, trucks, and buses busily racing in all directions. Where were they going? Were they getting *away* from something or going *to* some place?

As we neared the George Washington Bridge that connects New Jersey with upper Manhattan, we were in awe at the splendor of the magnificent steel artwork of the geometric girders and cables which suspended this steel behemoth over the Hudson River. Driving over the upper deck we were right next to the suspension steel cables with a thickness of a tree, yet each was composed of perhaps dozens of smaller strands intertwined into one colossal cable that seemingly could hold up the Earth if it was asked to. And there were hundreds of these.

As we drove south on Broadway that fall day, I could see that the sun was *trying* to shine through the cloudless sky but was being obscured by the same brown tint that we had seen just across the river in Jersey. The malodorous smell of the buses' diesel fumes added to the Los Angeles-type smog that we were to inhale daily for the next two years. I asked Katherine where all the houses were since we could see only buildings in Manhattan. Could it be that all of Manhattan was really a business district and that people lived elsewhere? How naive I soon discovered these questions were, for soon we were directed by the International University residence office to our married student apartment on Candle Street, a nice building like most others in Greenwich Village. No, there weren't that many houses in Manhattan; people lived essentially stacked by the thousands inside these very tall buildings by tacit contract with fate given their desire to live among the throngs in an area surrounded by water on all sides. I didn't know if they liked it that way, but my own dislike for it appeared irrelevant since we too had given in to our desire to study in a "cosmopolitan setting," going against my better judgment that these conditions were not human.

Within a few days we were fully settled into our little apartment, giving me more opportunity to make contact with the Graduate School at International University. Very soon I was doing my coursework at the U.

As a general rule I would leave the apartment by eight in the morning, leaving Katherine behind to care for Sarah who was still under age one. Katherine had gotten her B.A. in history at Renwick University and had voiced aspirations to continue on with her Master's degree at some point, yet this desire of hers got lost in the considerable upheaval trekking across the country to New York. Not that it mattered to me, for the added stress of the different cultural environment of New York City plus the tremendous overload of academic responsibilities at IU were combining to show more of the limitations of my personality and my integrity. Soon I was very demanding of Katherine, feeling entitled to "extra" domestic services because of my vigorous efforts in graduate school. My frustration level was already very high when I came home from school, high enough that I had no more coping power left when I had to engage Katherine in communication. She would justifiably ask me to talk to her about what I had learned at school that day—what new historical theories I had uncovered, what new themes I had read about. But I would bark at her and tell her that I did not feel like talking about history since that is what I had been doing all day long. My demanding attitude towards Katherine had gotten out of hand, so much so that I was literally forcing her to go out at night so that she could get me the kind of soft drink I wanted. On some occasions I even demanded sex when she clearly had told me that she did not feel like it. In my view then, I felt that she had to comply when I needed something, and her feelings were generally irrelevant. Slowly and unknowingly, I had turned into a tyrant towards the woman whom I believed I loved, the beautiful woman with the pretty green eyes. The goddess who had captured my heart.

To make matters worse, the manic preoccupation with women which I had had at RU in Houston in the year prior to my meeting Katherine had returned with a vengeance in the morally loose environment of New York City. On a daily basis I would see women without bras wearing see-through blouses, short shorts, or other revealing attire. My eyes were always glued to their breasts, their crotches, or to the portions of their buttocks which stuck out of their shorts. There was also the "singles" circuit which advertised ubiquitously about the "exciting world" of singles that were having fun with hundreds if not thousands of other "eligible" people all over the city. Singles clubs, "swap" clubs, singles bars, singles yellow pages, sex advertisements, lonely heart columns, and offers of "no strings attached" liaisons—they all made me feel that I had committed a major blunder in having married so soon after I entered college and before I could enjoy going out with many women to sample what was available. Not that I saw anything lacking in Katherine; on the contrary, I always thought of her as a wonderful and beautiful woman whom I enjoyed being with. With her I felt comfortable, secure, and happy, or so I thought. Yet, there was a growing force within me that seemed to be totally blind to the fact that I had a good woman at home, a force that was capricious, independent of logic, and increasingly assertive in its hunger for lewd contact with women. It was all part of me, but if I had recognized its pathological nature in time I might have gone into therapy at that point (not that I had not needed it much sooner, probably as early as age two) and averted a tragic and painful unraveling of our marriage.

Left, right, in front, and in back—all I could see was the enormous crop of women in New York. By the thousands they rode the buses and subways, displaying their generous bosoms to the men who could only ogle in secret. Of course, I did not know for a fact that these beautiful women were indeed consciously and deliberately displaying their wares, but in my heart I *felt* they were. They crossed their legs so that their skirts would creep up to reveal shapely thighs that could cure the worst case of impotence that could ever be imagined. Or, more simply, they would just sit with legs left carelessly open, revealing tantalizing panties that covered what I imagined was a feast for the tongue. Such were my thoughts as I traveled back and forth between our apartment and the various libraries at International University.

In spite of my feeling these strong forces of attraction towards the women in school and on the streets, I consciously refrained from acting on these impulses since I did feel a loyalty towards Katherine—I felt that it would be wrong for me to surreptitiously have sex with another woman behind Katherine's back. In fact, even the simple act of my having coffee with an innocent female colleague at school would trigger feelings of guilt and self-doubt because I felt at some level that I should not be having this type of contact with another woman besides my wife. So while I was honorably attempting to refrain from acting on these feelings, the urges were becoming increasingly unmanageable due perhaps to the stresses at school and at home. Our fights were getting nastier, mainly due to my unfair feelings of entitlement towards Katherine (my immature tantrums), and to my unfortunate inability to treat her fairly and honestly, among other things. And at school I was discovering that some of my classes were boring and my duties unmanageable.

This daily stress was making me very irritable, so consequently I had no patience left when I went home to be with Katherine and Sarah. In spite of the problems I was having with Katherine, I still managed to *behave* towards Sarah in a semi-loving manner. I fed her, I changed her diapers every day, I bathed her, and when we went out shopping I would carry her, giving her kisses every few minutes. Overall I had a *loving* feeling towards Sarah, so at this stage I can say comfortably that I had corrected in some way my lack of patience which had caused me to spank her when she was a few months old. But as we shall see later, simply having a "loving feeling" is no guarantee that the loving parent's behavior will continue to be authentically loving under changing conditions as the child grows. In my case it just so happened that Sarah was at that stage that did not trigger many pathologic reactions within me; but, again, it was just a matter of time.

Another facet of my personality which was becoming more solidified around this time was my overriding cynicism about human relationships and about the world in general. Very clearly I recall how I would have discussions with Katherine and others about the "futility" of social philosophies such as democracy, communism, federalism, Christianity, Judaism, and even common federal laws and statutes, which, in my view, were all "relative" and thus had no basis "in reality." How odd of me to have felt that all laws were valueless because they were based simply on "human bias" and not on strict adherence to logic, rationalism, and empirical verification. That is, whatever desirable behavior it was that was legislated into law was simply an "opinion" of those in power and their constituencies, and did not necessarily have any basis in "fact." I based this opinion of mine (which I felt was the "truth" and not simply an opinion) on a historical perspective of how laws are routinely changed depending on circumstances, and on how different cultures—in fact, even different *states* in this country—have differing moral opinions on similar behaviors. How can a specific behavior, say having multiple sex partners, be absolutely morally wrong when some cultures treat it as such and some see it as desirable? Isn't it true, I asked, that my view on this issue would depend on which culture I was born into? And where is God when we have so much evil in this world? Maybe there simply is no God. I was a moral relativist, an agnostic, a cynic, an existentialist. I did not believe that there were *any* absolutely immoral acts in the universe, for there is no reliable system of moral values. Anything goes. Combine these intellectual views with my tragically deficient moral training and the stage was set for the deepening of my inner spiritual and moral crisis. I can see now that because of my experiences as a child with little moral and ethical training, that my inner sense of values was so weak that my intellect, driven by a terror of woefully deficient self-concept, became the supreme and reigning facet of my personality, a process which served me well to physically survive the hellish conditions of my childhood but which was quite pathological in dealing with the normal frustrations and social relationships of adult life. What was happening, only I did not know it, was that my intellectually relativistic views on life could not serve as a moral counterforce against some of the aberrant desires that were making themselves more frequently known to my consciousness. In other words, if I felt an impulse to do something I would probably do it if my intellect concluded that the risk was not too great. That is not how a parent should feel, not how a spouse should behave.

Quite justifiably, Katherine was very much alarmed by the opinions I discussed with her, especially my nihilistic and amoral attitudes towards people and life in general. Unlike me, she had definite ethical and moral standards based on a liberal democratic interpretation of the world. As she said countless times, I had "no backbone." This emerging ethical gulf between us served only to widen the emotional estrangement that she was beginning to feel, further weakening our bonds and perhaps irreversibly damaging the romance which had glued us together in the first place. For me though, these arguments and developments did not lessen my "bond" with—or dependence on—Katherine. I still could relate to her in the same fashion whether or not we agreed politically on an issue, perhaps due to the fact that my "political" views did not come from the heart but from the emotionless intellect. In contrast, Katherine's political and moral views did come from the heart, and any attack on these went deep to her soul, something that took me years to comprehend. So, now that our romance was under siege due to our serious ethical differences, the underlying personal traits and values that normally hold a relationship together for the long term and which she saw as unsavory in me were not enough to maintain the closeness and affection that we had both shared and enjoyed in the beginning when we stared into each other's eyes at *Capital Cafe* at The Renwick University campus. We were holding on by a very thin thread indeed.

I finished my first year of graduate work at the university with good grades, so for the summer we decided on going back to Houston to take a break from the harried life in New York City, The Big Apple, or Sin City. In September 1968 we were back in New York and ready for the second year of graduate studies. The stage was set...

So as I was exploring intellectual issues at school during that first part of the 1968-69 school year, Katherine was beginning to do sporatic baby-sitting at our apartment to supplement our very low income. There was one very small child I did not like, for he irritated me because of the way he moaned and groaned for food. My dislike of him got so intense that on occasion when Katherine was not looking I would first sneer at him, and soon I was also stepping on his hand as I passed by where he was sitting on the carpet. On one singular occasion my revulsion of him was such that I momentarily placed a small electrical battery on the bare skin of his back, giving him a shock that made him cry. After that for maybe half-dozen times I deliberately made him worry that I was going to drop him by letting my arms drop down fast for about one foot while still holding him well enough not to drop him. And, finally (forgive me, Lord), I stuck a small comb in his mouth to make him gag.

Of course this was a very shameful episode in my life, and I realize that I physically and emotionally abused this young child. But at the time for some reason he had become some sort of scapegoat in my wretched emotional life, serving as the target of my frustration and anger at the environment. I suspect now that I was subconsciously reacting aggressively to his needing attention from Katherine during his sporadic visits to our home. How dare he do that? Katherine was mine! It was a sick way of subconsciously perceiving the meaning of this child in my own home. Then too I already had the unseen hand of El Diablo directing my inner emotional landscape and consequently my evil behavior.

I only hope that this child went on to a better home and that my abuse did not cause much permanent damage.

While I studied, pondering philosophical and historical issues, I contin-ued to obsess about women at school and elsewhere. Even though I fantasized about them I never did anything or planned to do anything sexual with a woman behind Katherine's back. Not that I was that moral, but I did feel that it would not be right to do that to her. It was quite by chance that a situation took me over the edge when I least expected it.

It was at an evening get-together for history graduate students at the university where this stunningly beautiful blond girl with radiant blue eyes struck up a conversation with me. Where did she come from? I had never seen her before. It didn't matter. Almost immediately I knew I was in trouble because I sensed my rabid macho spirit come to life as my eyes feasted on her gorgeous face and her sex-goddess figure. I started to tremble with her by my side as I sensed that this was the most sexually attracted I had felt to another woman after having married Katherine. I was speechless when she asked me to dance to a very slow song, but I could not force myself to say no. As I had her in my arms I could smell her heavenly body and the moist vapor heat radiating from her chest against mine. I thought about my duty to Katherine, but I could also feel my ravenous macho instinct already fantasizing about opening her blouse right there on the dark corner of the dance floor and feasting on her voluminous soft breasts. Oh, my God, a goddess has been delivered to me! How can I refuse her?

I then said to myself secretly: Fuck it all—I am going to do it. I don't give a shit if it's wrong, and I don't care if I'm betraying Katherine! Fuck everything! Fuck everything!

My animal, my beast, my demon, my dick, had won the tug-of-war and pushed me to the next step. I then asked this beauty if she wanted to walk outside for a while and she readily said yes. Soon enough we were kissing passionately in a dark area, soon deciding that a classroom would definitely be more comfortable. And that's where we went. It was night. It was dark. The classroom was empty. That's where I undressed her on the floor of the classroom and had incredible sex. No protection, I was in macho heaven as I pumped all my semen deep inside her. My macho man spirit felt so proud, proud like a rooster—proud like a big, fucking rooster who wakes up the whole countryside, announcing to the world that *he* just woke up!

Yeah, I was proud, but only for a few seconds. What followed made me sick.

She was dressing up in the dark classroom when I excused myself to go to the bathroom to pee. In reality I went there to vomit profusely. "Oh, my God, what have I done?!" I could not stop vomiting into the sink—that's as far as I got before I threw up. More and more contractions of disgust and severe regret hit me in waves for how I had betrayed Katherine. I felt dirty, very dirty. More dirty, more vomit. I took my dick out of my pants and I must have washed it with soap and water about a dozen times, and still it felt unclean. God, my dick felt unclean—no amount of washing could remove the sin from my dick. No amount of rinsing or gargling could remove the taste of her nipples from my mouth.

I had never thought of myself as a righteous guy, so I had a hard time understanding just why I felt so supremely guilty at having cheated on Katherine. Total confusion. I had spent about thirty minutes in that bathroom, cleaning the immorality from my body, but it was worse than that. I was in shock, I was scared, I was in a panic. In a way I was terrified. This was not just about betraying Katherine, it was as if I subconsciously knew I had unchained one of my big demons. God help me. He is now on the loose, roaming freely somewhere inside my soul.

I went back to the classroom, just as a courtesy, but she was gone. I never saw the blond girl ever again.

Walking slowly back to our apartment I contemplated how I was going to inform Katherine about what I had just done. At the last minute I opted to delay telling her until a suitable time arose. It certainly did not help our mounting problems since I became even more irritable towards her, perhaps since she was the visible embodiment of the moral and spiritual values which I could not live up to and over which I was in constant battle within myself. That conflict was making me sick inside. Without the benefit of insight into my own emotional conflicts and pathologies, I continued to send our marriage into a painful downward spiral, watching almost helplessly as the beautiful romance which had flowered between us on that fateful day when we met in Houston had now withered, only to be replaced by strife, hostility, demands, counter-demands, and a cold bed. The flower of our marriage was dying if not already dead. It only needed to be put away, forever, in my book of regrets.

The full crisis arrived with a rage that summer of 1969. My guilt was no longer containable, so, in what I thought was the best possible moment I confessed to Katherine. I innocently and naively had imagined that of course she would be legitimately angry at me, but that she would find it in her heart to forgive me. It was a gross miscalculation, for I had not taken into account the truly sorry condition of our relationship. For Katherine it was the last straw.

She gave me the cold shoulder for two days and on the third she announced to me and to her parents that she was opting to leave me, something that sent my stomach, my soul, and my heart into panic and crisis. "No, it is not possible," I thought. "This is not happening. We are married. She is my wife. She cannot leave just like that!" But, as decisively as dry sand swallows up a drop of water, Katherine left with no hesitation. I felt my life had come to its wretched end.

The usual symptoms of separation and divorce took over my body: couldn't eat or sleep, loss of concentration, jitteriness, feelings of distress and gloom, heightened awareness of other couples, loss of interest in normal activities, and a new-found desire and strength to "work on the problem." Of course, it was too late, so my ready willingness to bend in all directions to alleviate our tensions and long-standing differences was irrelevant, for Katherine said that she had taken enough and had made up her mind. I begged her as I had never begged in my life; I even offered to drop out of my own graduate program so that she would get her Master's degree. I naively offered to "change" my undesirable "traits," the ones that had bothered her so much. Never before had I cried so much. She refused to reconsider. Oh, my God, abandonment again.

We also had to think of Sarah, then about age two, and how this would impact my relationship with her. I knew that I wanted to continue being her father in as many ways as possible, and fortunately Katherine agreed that we should both co-parent her. That was the only thing that kept me from going over the edge on this most painful of losses up to then. I was ready to throw myself on the subway tracks because the loss was monumental. She had opened my heart, then she plunged a dagger into it when she left me. Now I can see she really had no choice—I was not worth much as a husband.

The rest of the summer of 1969 I limped along in a semi-comatose state, not knowing if I should continue to plead with Katherine or to resign realistically to the facts before me. How I regretted having confessed to her my transgression! I blamed myself for having been honest but stupid, for several of my friends had told me beforehand that one does not confess momentary weakness, especially if it was just for one night and was not a drawn-out affair. And in the moment of pain I said to myself that never again would I commit the same stupid mistake, ever. For in trying to be honest I delivered what amounted to the final blow to our marriage.

With the added benefit of many more years of pain and reflection I now look at that painful episode and try to make sense out of it, so that I may learn from what happened. As I said before, it is my belief now that I may have married Katherine because in some way my heart fundamentally yet subconsciously felt that she could be or was a mother substitute for me, something that I believe I may have yearned for without knowing it. Even though I delusionally believed that I loved her romantically, my *behavior* towards her more closely resembled that of a small boy acting out and throwing tantrums in front of his mother. I wanted to possess her—I wanted exclusive right to her attention. When she disagreed with me I would sulk, shout, or push back in some way. I would ask her to do things for me and expect immediate service—I would throw a tantrum if she failed in any way. I felt that she had no right to refuse service or even her body to me. In fact, the sexual act itself was not too romantic, for I never did make the connection between foreplay, romance, sexual play, intercourse, and afterplay. I simply wanted to get right down to intercourse as if it was a physical function, with no genuine love and romance. In this respect it may have felt like an incestuous relationship, for the romance did not extend into the marriage bed, just to the edge.

Hence, if in my heart I felt subconsciously that Katherine was my mother substitute, I can only surmise that her physical presence and her emotional connection to me opened up hidden chambers of my heart, those compartments which had been slammed shut and closely guarded due to the emotional abuse and neglect that I had suffered from my mother. For years prior to meeting Katherine I could not relate to girls or women; I would only fantasize about what I would do with them sexually, yet I did not have the social skills or the spiritual courage to approach girls in an appropriate fashion. In the psychiatric world this may have been thought of as a case of semi-schizoid personality, indicative of an inability of relate properly to others (in my case, women in particular). Yet Katherine opened these infantile chambers of my heart, penetrating my long-standing defenses against the pain of the distant mothering which I had experienced. Somehow in subconsciously behaving as a child in Katherine's presence I was demonstrating that I felt "safe" with her—that she was a "mother" that could be trusted. Unknowingly I had revealed to Katherine my true inner self. Unfortunately for her, this true inner self was just a frightened, incestuous little child with no idea of mature romantic love, a child that nonetheless was being operated by superior intellect that twisted all needs and desires in such a way so as to make them "logical" and more reasonable to regular adults. It was the intelligence facet of my personality that overshadowed the fundamentally damaged and immature nature of my soul, and which thus made it difficult for even close friends or observers to see the tantruming child behind the massive intellectual curtains.

With my child's heart open to Katherine, it once more came into the light and became vulnerable. Then Katherine did what she had to do, and I cannot morally blame her. Yet, by her leaving me she inflicted wounds that I believe felt more grievous than the ones that my mother had inflicted, for I can say that it took me about five years to get over the loss of Katherine. More importantly, I believe that the old defense which my relationship with Katherine had penetrated—that of the distant, schizoid personality—could not be reinstated or resurrected, and that a more powerful one would have to take its place to cover up the pain. My new defense—my coping mechanism—would help me survive physically in New York, shielding me from the inner-core wound and the resulting pain, but would essentially require spiritual death. My soul gladly welcomed it with open arms. It was a deal with the devil.

Even though Katherine had already made it clear to me that our relationship was over, I continued to hope that she might reconsider and decide to make an effort to repair our relationship. But all my efforts were in vain; she clearly was adamant about her decision to leave. In her honor I lit a small light in my apartment that I kept on 24-hours a day, nonstop, until it was time to put it out five years later. Symbolically it came to represent my lingering feelings for her, and my undiagnosed inability to simply mourn the loss and get on with my life. I became emotionally stuck.

Soon I began to exhibit more sinister symptoms, behaviors which I interpreted as simply part of my free, liberated, and macho character, for at that time I knew little about normal personality development and did not have the wisdom to recognize serious neuroses in myself. How I wish that even at that late date I would have thought of getting myself into therapy. Instead I began to exhibit more egomaniacal symptoms and went on to engage in regrettable behaviors.

Most regrettable of all my pathological mistakes in life at that point was the totally inappropriate manner in which I parented my young daughter Sarah when she was with me half-time as part of our joint-custody agreement. Delusionally, I was believing that I was a "progressive" father with none of the "hangups of the previous generation." No, we have to be in step with progress, so why hide our bodies and why have the old fashioned, conservative attitudes about sexual behavior? It is more "sensible" and "healthier" to embrace the "free love" philosophy, right?

Well, because of these perverted delusions I essentially broke every normal boundary that a father must respect so that his child can achieve proper emotional development. Routinely I would walk around stark naked in our apartment, even when Sarah was in her teens. A normal practice that we began when she was a baby—bathing and showering together—continued beyond the age of propriety, perhaps to about age seven, and I allowed, if not encouraged, Sarah to soap and scrub my penis in the shower. On one occasion she spontaneously kissed the tip of my penis in the shower. I never had any boundaries for her vocabulary, so routinely she would use four-letter words which I reinforced because they sounded so "cute" coming from her child's mouth. No sleeping schedule; we'll sleep when we get sleepy. No eating schedule; we'll eat when we get hungry. No moral or ethical training: "If they hit you, hit them back twice as hard." Burping, belching, farting—I encouraged it all. I even brought out my favorite pornographic magazines to show Sarah, as young as age five, about "how the human body looks," including very graphic photos of men and women in gross acts of sexual intercourse.

We even developed jingles and songs using vulgar words, and we sang them together. And I thought that it was such a great education that I was giving her. One time I had masturbated and ejaculated onto a cloth towel near my bed. Later on that day I showed Sarah my semen and "explained" to her that this fluid is what makes babies. How ugly and tragic my skills as a father were. How regrettable. How sick.

After I had been in New York for about seven years and was ready to move to another city, I stopped at Katherine's house in New Jersey, and spent the night there in preparation for the long trip the next day. Sarah was seven years old at the time, and she decided to sleep on the floor with me. In one of the sorriest and most depraved episodes in my role as a father, I stripped naked and placed Sarah on top of me with the intent to have sex with her. Fortunately she blurted out, "Daddy, be careful or your penis might go into my vagina." Those words stopped me immediately and I did not proceed. However, the next morning as I was getting ready to depart I touched Sarah's private area through the panties, and kissed her goodbye.

The incidents continued after we had all moved to Kansas City in 1974. There I continued to "pinch" Sarah's private area, through her clothes, and continued to give her my pornographic magazines for "educational purposes." I believe that I even asked Sarah at that time how she felt about having sex with me, or about watching me having sex with my girlfriend. She was not interested (Thank God!). All, or mostly all, of these boundary and abusive violations stopped when I got a new girlfriend, Geena, in Kansas City, as she wisely pointed out to me that it was not normal to do that; I promptly stopped.

The last incident which occurred with Sarah was when she was about 16 years old, and she asked me to rub her foot because it was sore after some sort of physical exercise. I shamefully but clearly remember that as I rubbed her foot I got fantasies about having sex with her, and I started to rub her ankle and then her calf, getting progressively more excited (God, where does all this perversity end?). Fortunately, Sarah's better sense interfered and she said that her foot was feeling better. I stopped. That was the last incident with Sarah, my poor daughter who ended up with a wretched father like me.

From my recollections of my parenting efforts towards Sarah, I can see that my fathering philosophy was centered around the themes of sex and perversity, and not much else. In New York after the divorce in 1969 Sarah was only two years old, but soon afterwards I began to have problems with inappropriate boundaries (e.g., letting her touch my penis) and almost a total lack of structure (e.g., no schedule for sleeping, eating, etc.). Why did I enjoy walking naked around Sarah, knowing that she was staring, mostly at my penis? A more fundamental question might be: Why was I an exhibitionist in front of my daughter? What was the underlying psychodynamic *motive*? Was I subconsciously replicating what my mother did many times before me? Does the perversity and the scum repeat itself on the innocent children? Here I was being a horribly abusive father to my daughter, yet my soul was so sick, delusional, and blind that I did not even realize the extent of my perversity. It would take many years and a resurfacing of some of these behaviors with my second child before I finally realized how far I had fallen into moral and spiritual sickness. I knew nothing about being a father, and to make matters worse, I did not know that I did not know.

Part of the real tragedy is that my own parents had been terribly abusive, as were others in my life, and that by the time I came to fully realize their shortcomings and mistakes, I had done other things to my own children that were equally abusive and repulsive. The lessons I learned from my years of psychotherapy were valuable indeed and did prevent me from exacting even more grievous damage upon my kids, although these lessons came too late to prevent abuse altogether.

So why did I do it? Why did I not behave as a normal father with normal boundaries who had genuine and ethical concern for his children? My therapists have told me that I simply did not have the appropriate role model for fathering and consequently I had no idea of how to be a father. In fact, until recently I also had no idea of what a "good" mother was supposed to be like; I had pathological ideas about the roles that mothers and fathers play in the family. But I believe that my problem in the area of fathering went much deeper than that—that it was not just a case of my having been ignorant of normal fatherhood. Ignorant, yes, but also disturbed.

I had no business being a father. I believe now that you first have to be a good and moral person before you can be a father. But that's just wisdom and not a requirement. The same goes for being a good spouse. But I was not a good and moral person when I met and fell in love with Katherine. My idealistic and romantic feelings got ahead of my personality development, and I did not have the wisdom to know that I first needed to address my mental illness before I could even consider a serious relationship with a woman. And I did not have any adults near me who could advise me of my situation.

It's easy to make excuses, but I am merely trying to understand how it was that I became a monster just like Merengueno Zalmar. Ultimately all parents have to take responsibility for how we treat our children, for if we don't, the little ones will keep on suffering, and all we adults can say is, "Hey, don't blame me." It is a parent's moral duty to improve himself and correct his deficient parenting behavior, even if he can legitimately claim that his own parents threw him under the bus. Children don't care to know how we adults suffered, they just need security and love.

And so, in those early years after my painful divorce from Katherine in 1969 I became the father from hell, lost in a spiritual decay which spread to my efforts in parenting. Yet, my spiritual cancer was even worse in the area of sexual voyeurism, for I was also deep in the perverted grip of pornography. I was getting worse.

Nothing in my post-therapy life makes me cringe as much as my recalling my extensive history of pornography consumption in New York City in the years right after my divorce, for I was so deep into every known variation in pornography, yet all the time feeling great because I knew more about the subject than anyone else, except, perhaps, the porno dealers themselves. At every opportunity, at any hour of the day or night, I would peruse through my extensive "library" of porno magazines, ogling with a smile the photos of countless variations of sexual intercourse, and the just as numerous combinations of persons and animals engaged in sexual perversions. I used it, I enjoyed it, I loved it. Pornography was my "hobby." Pornography was my toy. Pornography was my drug, for I desperately needed it.

Like I must have done hundreds of times on the anonymous streets of New York, one hot summer night, in June, in 1971, I left my apartment on Candle Street with the purpose of visiting my usual sleazy porno shops in the Times Square area of midtown Manhattan, the porno capital of the East coast. As I walked from Greenwich Village north to Times Square, mind and soul were already hot with anticipation of the many wonderful things that I would be seeing and touching once I got there. The people around me on Candle Street were mostly students, professors, and others connected to IU, so I could say that they looked decent, but I was a seasoned New Yorker with a healthy paranoid impulse that made me look over my shoulder often while staying a cautious distance from anyone who looked in the slightest way suspicious. Soon, with the change in location, the aura surrounding my fellow pedestrians would change for the disgusting worse.

At the subway token tollbooth one level below the street, I asked the clerk for two tokens and handed him my money through the small slit in the bullet-proof glass which completely enclosed the small booth which measured about 10' by 6'. As usual the dog-faced clerk shoved the tokens back through the slit, frowning like he was thoroughly disgusted with life in this cage but getting his kicks simply by treating all token-buyers with disgust, as if all of us were mere interruptions in the course of his dejected, resigned life. Almost always in the thousands of times I took the subway train in New York, I felt that the job of tollbooth clerk was inhuman, created by bureaucrats sitting in some dark cavernous office—like the sealed-off subway station between 86th and 96th Streets on Broadway—because it was a job that needed to be done. Oh well, in time I came to see hundreds of subway clerks in New York, and they were all nasty and probably chronically depressed because their career consisted of spending eight hours a day in hell. "Fuck them!" I thought, as I hurriedly got my tokens and inserted one in the turnstill. By habit I rushed down one more level, in expectation that the IRT #1 subway train would soon be charging through the platform. Other similarly neurotic riders were apparently feeling the same way, for swiftly I was consumed in a running crowd of anonymous but recognizable strangers, all concerned about their chances of catching the #1 train and a seat, hopefully not next to a vomiting alcoholic or other smelly derelict.

Soon enough the steel monster came barreling at 50 miles per hour into the subway station, and as soon as the doors opened human logic and courtesy fell dead on the tracks: the human sardines that were already packed into the train struggled to exit through the doors as an anxious and ruthless wave of newcomers was forcing its way in, creating oftentimes momentary impasses. While it is *logical* to wait for current passengers to exit so that seats become available, one would have to be a fool to follow that logic when one's fellow travelers are rushing in against the tide and claiming seats about to be vacated. It is animal and mob logic that allows for physical survival in the subway (and in New York generally), but which simultaneously robs the soul of the brotherhood of all people.

As usual the subway car was defaced with the mindless spray paint of incorrigible hoodlums whose need to express their inner feelings was stronger than their sense of respect for property rights, something that many New Yorkers mistakenly and generously wanted to interpret as "the artistic urge" but which I saw as nothing less than an expression of their unsocialized animal instincts. That most of these graffiti artists were juvenile offenders did not seem to bother those bent on praising their antisocial behavior. Intellectual rationalizations aside, I had already become immune to the visual assault from the unwelcome graffiti, so my main task was to satisfy my own desire to get a seat at the expense of all others; that is, when the doors open it's every person for themselves, even if you have to push and shove a little. Everyone knows the fundamental selfishness of the game.

I managed to get a seat next to an odd, slightly overweight, middle-aged lady with clammy skin who felt rather too comfortable about pressing her bare arms against mine. Even as I unsuccessfully tried several times to reposition my arms and shoulders so as to avoid contact, I was able to peel my skin—like one peels plastic wrap from a flat, moist surface—only momentarily as the natural arrangement of our bodies on the long seats brought us in contact again. Was the perspiration that she was transferring to my arms "contaminated" with something? She didn't bat an eyelash at my discomfort though, and busily pretended to be having deep thoughts, rolling her eyeballs around looking into space and pursing her lips as she pondered some dilemma. When she detected several times that I was looking at her, she'd intensify whatever expression she had at that instant, the same way people in an almost empty elevator find the little numbers above the door much more interesting as another passenger comes on board. This lady was obviously strange but fit right it with everyone else on the subway.

Seated in front of me was the sleazy-looking "telephone man," about 40, dressed in a cheap, wrinkled, three-piece suit and talking out of a black house phone stored inside his suitcase, which I hope he did not intend to pass off as a briefcase. As he made a big show of talking to his pretend associates over the phone, he'd stare at other passengers to see if they were looking at him with admiration. At that time there were no portable phones, so he must have felt very proud of himself in this pitiful attempt to impress us. Well, at least he did not appear to have a clammy face, maybe just a sorry personality.

As the subway raced to my Nirvana, I began to detect the pungent and acrid stench that was very familiar to subway riders. It could mean one of two things: (1) a vagrant had defecated on the short platform between the subway cars, as they frequently do for lack of toilet facilities in the city, or (2) a derelict was onboard, probably lying down, full-body length, on the long steel seats. It took a little bit of rubber-necking on my part, but I finally spotted the source of the offensive odor: On the corner of the subway car was sprawled a very tall man, apparently sleeping or passed out from alcohol or drugs, wearing several layers of winter clothing—it was summer and hot in the subway—that themselves bore several layers of caked black dirt, mud, or vomit. As much as he revolted me, I thought of how I used to sleep in street corners myself, roaming endlessly throughout the city when I was a young boy. That was my innocent equivalent of "getting drunk" at that age. I guess he was doing it too, but at a later age. There was nothing we could do but breath less (or at least try to). As I said, par for the course.

Every single time that I went into the catacombs of the massive New York City subway system I would become philosophical about the "meaning" of the visual extravaganza before my eyes, wondering about the lives of my fellow passengers. In my first year in New York I actually (naively) enjoyed the subway, for it provided so much to see and interpret. But now I detested the impersonal system that herded people like ranchers herd cattle during "roundup." Not only that but there were many obnoxious people, by the hundreds or thousands, that I had to deal with or at least tolerate in some manner. Or maybe it was me. Maybe I was the problem.

My level of tolerance was painfully low, for I disliked traits that most people do not find bothersome. Odd hair styles, strange hair colors (purple+green+orange, etc.), ornamental rings on nose, navel, cheek, or tongue, real boa constrictors worn as neckties, men in tutus, lesbians tonguing each other, homosexuals patting each others' crotches, old ladies with pet parrots on their shoulders (and parrot doo-doo down the front of their blouses), "macho" men with no shirts and tight bikini-style shorts, people eating lasagna in the subway and getting the tomato sauce all over their faces, thousands of people with strong body odor, fresh, cheesy vomit on numerous places in the subway cars, thousands of panhandlers telling their ridiculously tragic stories and asking subway riders to place their "generous" offerings in greasy cups that looked like they came from a cesspool (at one point I felt so much contempt for these smoking vagrants with wine bottles that I thought that they should all commit suicide to end their life of misery), and the usual assortment of conduct-disordered teenage hoodlums who terrorized the unfortunate riders. I always felt that there was a very thin line between the organized chaos in the subway system and outright anarchic revolution. That is why I was always vigilant in all parts of the City, but especially in the subways and most especially in Times Square, my stop.

As the train barreled into the 42nd Street/Times Square Station, I stood up to see the several-blocks-long passenger platform pass by our windows in a dizzying blur, coming more into focus as the train's high-pitched brakes further assaulted my senses but brought the train to a perfect stop. Not a few hundred, but thousands of people exchanged places in about 20 seconds, those of us who just arrived at the hot and humid station hurrying up the urine-puddled walkways and steps, ready to tackle and dodge several more hundred people along the way. Being New Yorkers we learn to move at this fast pace, subconsciously running away from the mayhem and not realizing that we all are part of it, that we carry it with us no matter how fast we walk.

If there were two distinguishing characteristics of the Times Square Subway Station, they were these: (1) It was and is an undisputedly massive feat of concrete and steel engineering, with several interlacing levels and stories of subway tracks, leading to all directions of the city. Sometimes to make connections from one subway train to another the harried rider literally has to run up and down long flights of stairs, walk down tunnels several blocks long, and again walk up and down stairs to a specific point on a platform, never seeing the light of day because he is several stories deep below the street level. It took me a long time before I felt comfortable changing trains at Times Square without the essentially unreadable map supplied by the system. And even if one knows the pathways, at night evil lurks in stairwells, on platforms, in the long and lonely tunnels, and in the subway cars themselves. (2) The second distinguishing characteristic of the Station was and is its filth. My guess is that the walkways were essentially unmoppable and uncleanable, for they incurred an almost interminable assault from the thousands of riders who passed through daily, many of whom apparently found it natural to discard almost any refuse and body fluid on the floor. The thousands of vagrants who milled around the station urinated behind pillars, in stairwells, behind benches, in phone booths (as I did on a few occasions to test my courage (how stupid!)), or right in front of other riders. Garbage, spit, vomit, and urine—the four spiritual muggers that attack hapless riders 24-hours a day. Governing so many millions of people in New York might be impossible, so in the underbelly of the beast—the subways and the slums—anarchy seems to run supreme.

Walking, almost running, up the last flight of stairs I felt my heart pounding from the anticipation of the visual extravaganza which was only seconds away; in a very real sense I was acting like a junkie, a porno junkie. Up the last few steps from the subterranean cesspool, and then I stood right on 42nd Street and Seventh Avenue, in Times Square, the Porno Capital of the East Coast! What a glorious place, I thought! I had arrived at the place of real life—nothing compared to this high.

The entire Times Square area was ablaze with what seemed to me several billion watts of flashing, glittering, pulsating, oscillating, glaring, streaking, twinkling, glimmering, sparkling, and colorful lights, of billboards or marquees. I imagined that in the several square *blocks* that comprised the main section of Times Square that there were more lights than in some entire towns in the United States. The patterns of light and the colors commanded my attention, making me feel that I was *alive* and enjoying some fantastic spectacle on this planet, something that every person had to experience to be able to say, "I am alive! I saw the lights! I have been somewhere! This is where real life begins!"

Usually in the *hundreds* of visits I made to the porno areas, I would walk around first on Seventh Avenue and on Broadway, enjoying watching the kamikaze driving style of the hundreds of yellow taxis that bullied all other vehicles on the road; maybe that is why these cabs were dented all around—they had to make good on their threats. All around me would be the slime of the Earth, and that night was no exception. Drunken derelicts, drug dealers by the dozens at each intersection, con artists soliciting unsuspecting tourists to play quick card games, store fronts screaming "Liquidation-Bankruptcy Sale, Everything Must Go!" continuously for the 4th year in a row (they discovered that going "bankrupt" is good for business), street peddlers hawking everything conceivable including designer clothes and watches, roving gangs of hoodlums harassing meek-looking pedestrians, religious evangelists screaming at passers-by to "Repent!" but refusing to answer legitimate questions from those who were naive enough to stop by, porno versions of the old village crier yelling "Check it out, gentlemen, check it out. Complete Service in One Location. Check it out!" as they handed out flyers with information on where to get a blowjob for six dollars (swallow was extra), brazen prostitutes who would pull single men by the arm and offer a free sample, and despicable pimps in their flashy cars who hurled a steady barrage of insults and reprimands at the cowardly women who worked for them—all around me in one gargantuan spectacle of sin, perversity, and moral decay. And I was loving every minute of it! This is heaven!

Block after block, that night I walked, searching for street filth and degradation to amuse myself, enjoying whatever it was that someone was doing to another human being in a spiritually degrading manner, violating basic human trust and propriety. The filthier, the better. The more degradation I saw the more I enjoyed it. The more outrageous the longer I stayed at the scene. A disoriented man walking *totally naked* down the street? Yes, I gawked at him for blocks while many turned in repugnance at his filthy nakedness. Only because the police finally came and gave him a pair of pants did I lose my interest. But even the police were not impressed or shocked, calmly asking him when they arrived, "Hey, buddy, what happened to your clothes?" They were matter-of-fact about the incident, and left him alone after he struggled to put the pants on. Hundreds more to go, I suppose.

It was time to turn to my favorite part of this modern Sodom and Gomorrah, so I headed south on Seventh Avenue and turned west onto 42nd Street, the largest single concentration of hard-core pornography anywhere on the face of the entire planet. Besides war, this was the closest thing to living hell on the face of the Earth, only no one knew it, including myself. On both sides of 42nd Street, there were row after row of hard-core porno theatres with blazing marquees announcing the tantalizing titles of movies direct from hell: "Ramrod Stud," "Wet, Wild and Ready," "Juicy Cunt," plus hundreds more, overwhelming the eye. Now my pace slowed down to a crawl as I had to take time to feast and enjoy just the *outside* of these establishments which always seemed to have dozens of creepy-looking men just milling around the entrance, smoking, drinking from bottles camouflaged in nondescript paper bags, and occasionally sniffing white stuff from their elongated and filthy pinky fingernails. They were revolting, yet I enjoyed the sight of these shifty worms, these men who probably had families somewhere and took the spiritual cancer home to their children. Passing just two of the dozens of theatres, I had already gotten about ten offers for drugs, five from cancerous-looking pimps, and five from very assertive prostitutes who spoke to me in coded language such as, "Are you going out today, honey?" Lining almost every linear foot of storefront were other creeps who appeared to be torn between remaining in their comatose state or raising hell by shouting, urinating on the sidewalk, or threatening the other worms who happened to step into their storefront territory. The marquee for the "Live Sex Show on Stage" caught my eye, so I bought a ticket from the emaciated female ticket clerk with the sores on her lips. The man inside who took my ticket was not much better-looking, but at least he appeared to be fighting whatever fungus his face was suffering from.

Once inside the theatre I had to select a seat away from the weirdos—it was filling up with mean-looking men who appeared paranoid, shifting their eyes and heads in all directions as if expecting some "spiritual police" to come after them for the wicked things that they were doing (as for me, I *did* expect that some policeman would come and force me out at some point). There were no women in the audience, only irredeemable perverts like myself who came to get hot over some sex act on stage.

Soon the show started, with actors and actresses wearing very revealing attire, and attempting to act out a plot that was essentially irrelevant, for all of us had come here only to see a big penis get inside a juicy vagina. No plot needed, thank you! Well, I was not disappointed as the "plot" suddenly required the "actress" to cry and permit herself to be soothed by her "sensitive" boyfriend who asked her gently if she wanted to stroke his massive organ. "I know it will make you feel better." Of course she said yes, and one minute later the man had put his penis inside her and was pumping furiously to the delight of all us degenerates in the audience. My penis was hard from the voyeuristic feast, but it was only a prelude to the real stuff that was to come.

Now that I was good and cranked up sexually, I was on the prowl for more good stuff on this strip of sin and decadence, where the God to worship is the God of Sex and Orgasms and Blowjobs and Ejaculations. Soon enough, just about 20 feet from the talentless sex act show, I came upon a porno bookstore and Peep Show, combined for my pleasure and enjoyment. Inside were hundreds of tables and shelves shamelessly displaying thousands upon thousands of very hardcore pornographic magazines from around the world. Even the New York Public Library would have envied the worldwide connections that the sleazy owners must have had to be able to locate almost any magazine, book, or other sex-related media from any porno shop in the world. And I am sure that they would not come up with excuses such as, "Sorry, but it's been checked out." Like a child in a candy store, I was in awe at the *treasures* before my eyes, these wonderfully photographed magazines in glossy, expensive paper. Men having sex with several women; men ejaculating on women's faces; a woman with facial expressions of ecstasy as a man's huge penis was shown entering her vagina; a different magazine with the *same* woman showing an expression of extreme pain as the same man with the mammoth organ was entering her again; women proudly showing their enormous breasts; women performing joyful fellatio while other men were entering them from the rear; women doing women; homosexual men inserting their entire lower arm into the anus of their beaming partners; several adults happily giving enemas to each other; a woman defecating generously onto a glass table under which her lover watched; women urinating on men and vice versa; women piercing their nipples with needles and pins; women in spiked heels chaining and whipping men into submission; women seen in vaginal contact with the penises of horses, dogs, and pigs; old men having sex with prepubescent girls; the same old men having sex with young boys; and various versions of "snuff" films where the female protagonist gets disemboweled after her lover has sex with her: these plus hundreds more I relished that night. Nothing was too dirty or taboo. No picture was too ugly or obscene. No sexual act was too repugnant. No amount of pain on anyone's face was too great to elicit empathy. No combination of races or ages was inappropriate. No animal was safe from being included and perversely enjoyed in sexual acts with people. The more perverse, the better. The more wicked, the more evil, the more immoral, the more unnatural the act the more I loved it. Necrophilia, pedophilia, sado-masochism, fetishism, bestiality, exhibitionism, fetishism, voyeurism, coprophilia, klismaphilia, and urophilia—they all attracted my attention and fed the now-ravenous and immensely evil pornographic addiction deep within my maggot-eaten soul. Morally outrageous acts made my blood boil with wicked delight and perverse enjoyment. In fact, the more kinky and uncivil, the better, I thought. Kiddie porn was a special section, as was "snuff" with cutting of organs and disembowelments. I even went through the homosexual and the sado-masochism shelves to make sure that I did not miss anything special that I "should know about." In those days I had pride about the extensive "knowledge" which I had about sex practices, sexual mores, and cultural factors in sexual expressions, so I frequented Times Square to stay current with the prevailing practices in the field. After all, this was part of history, and as a historian it was my duty to know about it. Right? What a sick delusion!

In this porno shop I had to keep an eye on the other perverts like myself, for I never knew what to expect. Some were slimy, cheesy, sleazy, unshaven, with shifty eyes that made offers in glances to other similarly-inclined men in the same section. Yet others looked quite respectable—on the outside—with their London Fog raincoats (were they wearing anything underneath?) and their expensive-looking TuscanyLeather briefcases. It really didn't matter: We were all very sick and rotting with maggots in our souls.

At the "sexual aids" section were the plastic penises in several sizes ranging from maybe two inches to some that seemed to be modeled after horses. Who would want one of those things? Will some of these men here tonight buy one for their wives at home? And the life-size inflatable doll with a big, open mouth as well as "anatomically correct" orifices? Many men buy these sorry substitutes for a real woman, perhaps wanting something that will respond to their every command. Is foreplay recommended?

Towards the back of the sizeable shop was the Peep Show, a completely enclosed round stage surrounded by about 20 private booths in which voyeuristic men deposit money into a machine which raises a small black curtain, allowing the peeping Tom to see the completely naked women dancing on-stage. Of course, more money is required periodically to keep the curtain in the raised position. I went into the very private booth and inserted 25 cents into the slot machine which promptly raised the black curtain, allowing me to see two totally naked women fake dancing on the round stage in front of me. One wriggled and squirmed in front of me, touching her genitals in what she intended to be a sexy fashion but which I felt was sick and revolting. That is why I loved it. Since all our little booths were arranged in an almost perfect circle around the circular stage, I could clearly see the ogling eyes of the other male sickos in most of the booths in front of me, watching her every move with the attention and unremitting focus of a snake about to strike its prey.

"These guys look so sick watching these women," I thought to myself as I continued to feel repulsed by the open genitals which left nothing to the imagination. Just then the familiar odor of fresh sperm hit me and I had to remind myself not to touch any part of the inside of the booth since from experience I knew that all the walls would be dripping with several quarts of fresh semen from the masturbation of the many peeping Toms who used this viewing booth ahead of me this evening. After about one minute of seeing her private parts, I was ready to leave this sperm-sprayed booth. Quite poetically, as soon as I left the booth the sperm-cleaning janitor arrived with an industrial-size bucket and mop and proceeded to clean the floor and walls of my booth after giving me a sneer which insinuated that I too had added to his burden that evening. As he went through the motions of cleaning the uncleanable, I wondered about the nature of his job. What did he tell his children when they asked?

"Hey, dad, what do you do when you go to work?"

"Well, I mop semen from the floors and walls all day long. It really is not as bad as it sounds."

"But what happens when you rinse the mop in the bucket?"

"That's the tricky part. I have to keep reminding myself not to forget to rinse it, or it will be solid starch the next day. Then I have to soak it in pure ammonia for 24 hours."

As I finally left the porno shop I thought about all those sleazy men in there and how they had secretly gone into the booths to sperm the walls. By day they may look respectable, maybe like me, but by night they are sleazy sperm-shooters. It was the evil dragon of pornography inside each of us, ready to finish consuming whatever remained of our wretched souls.

Out on 42nd Street again I was feeling even higher on the sickness which I had just consumed, so I started on the prowl again, searching for bigger and better pornographic experiences, something more outrageous and immoral than necrophilia or disembowelments. Unbeknownst to me, of course, my addiction was escalating, requiring progressively more depraved representations of human sexuality, or whatever it was that was depicted in those glossy magazines and behind those little black curtains.

I entered other shops which specialized in animal acts, on S&M, on Golden Showers (peeing on each other), getting my kicks from those too. About two hours later I then turned the corner on 8th Avenue, heading north and dodging the drunks, pimps, and other miscreants (like me!) who typically got into altercations with the repugnant shopkeepers along the street. Who, but who, would ever want to manage or own a shop in this hellish, depraved neighborhood? Only another degenerate soul could ever survive among the spiritual filth and moral decay of these wretched streets. As for me, there I was willingly among the throngs of the spiritually corrupt, *looking for someone to be ugly with.* Up on 44th Street I found a brightly-lit shop advertising "complete service" (was this the eight-dollar job?), and I decided it was time to "check it out."

As I went in I knew that I wanted some kind of a session with a woman, but I was not sure what specifically I wanted to do with her. The beefy female cashier with sloppy lipstick and the cheap, crooked wig asked me what "service" I wanted. I imagined that she had been put out to pasture after many years of "servicing" street scum like myself. She had made a career out of the maggot infestation I was carrying.

"I don't know exactly. What do you have?" I asked meekly, fearing that she might throw me out for not wanting to simply have sex right away.

"Listen, honey," she said, as her open mouth revealed badly decayed teeth and a tongue with some growths on it, "we have everything here from A to Z. How much do you want to spend?"

"Well, what can I get for ten dollars?" I nervously asked.

"OK. Give me the money. Now, when I buzz you in, turn to the second room on your left and go see Sheila. She'll take care of you."

With much trepidation I went through the fortress-like door into a dimly-lit area adorned with raggedy hanging laces, locating the target door on my left. A cadaverous-looking Sheila was waiting for me with a business-attitude smile. Shit, did she have some sort of horrible disease?

"You want me to suck you?" was her abrupt way of beginning our illicit relationship, which caught me off guard. Sure, I was not expecting a pristine maiden with a bouquet of flowers, but neither was I ready for this vulgar greeting.

"Yeah, I guess so," was my unmanly response. She motioned for me to follow her to a corner of the room as she continued to direct the whole operation quite adroitly.

"I'm gonna have to wash your dick. Drop your pants, honey." There I was, the *expert* on human sexuality, but not knowing what to do with this woman who was very willing to suck my dick. It was out of character for me, but I embarrassingly did manage to slowly lower my pants, and she began a furious scrubbing of my penis. About a minute later she led me to a table covered with a thin mattress and a sheet, motioning me to lie on it, which I dutifully did. Then she began to perform fellatio on me, apparently bent on finishing the job as quickly as possible for she did it quite furiously. While she was doing it, I was feeling embarrassed because I did not know if I was supposed to touch her or not, creating a rather tense situation for me in spite of the physical pleasure. Soon it was all over and she motioned for me to go to the bathroom to clean up. I thanked and told her she was very good, although I am sure that she could not have cared either way. A few seconds later I stepped back into the night, looking for the next opportunity for more depraved social interaction with other walking corpses devoid of a human soul—like me.

It was already past midnight on Times Square although one would not know it from the large crowds of sexual perverts, transvestites, pimps, prostitutes, scoundrels, swindlers, perpetrators, malefactors, and other reptiles milling around porno shops and spit-floor eateries. It was so ugly, so vile, so vulgar, so wanton and so without respect for the human spirit; but I was loving it! I felt alive (!) looking at and mixing with these dregs from the spiritual toilet—who the whirlpooling water hadn't yet sucked into the sewer. As I saw the hundreds of sex-, drug-, and sin-transactions made that night, I felt that I was at the epicenter of what really mattered in human relations. Forget the intellectual acuity of the study of history; that's just study, this is *life!* The lights, the shops, the large storefronts, the magazines, the shameless sexual offers, the indecent manner of dress, the contemptible lack of manners, the disgraceful lack of warmth about the face, the scandalous display of body parts and orifices, the green spit on the sidewalks, and the almost total absence of human civility—that is what I liked and loved about the filth on Times Square. The shameless decadence and carnality of human social relations in the Times Square area reflected the moral state of the disintegration of my soul: I was being attracted to the external personification of the putrefaction going on in my soul, the center of my being in social relations. It was all-consuming and not available to critical introspection. In a very real way I had a vicious vampire in me—it was the Satan of Pornography. And he was unrelenting.

As much as I wanted to spend another three hours in this spiritual excrement, I began to feel that it was time to go back to my lonely apartment. Already I had extended my visit as long as possible, maybe because subconsciously I dreaded going back to that quiet, lonely apartment full of terrifying demons of the night. It was time to tackle my other demons.

Going to my empty apartment at night when Sarah was at her mother's was always very difficult for me. I dreaded it with a passion. From experience I knew the chain of events that would transpire every night: As I meekly entered my apartment the silence hiding behind the door would lunge at me and attack me mercilessly, going on a rampage through all parts of my body and my soul. My arms, my teeth, my legs, my fists—they were all useless against this wicked and shrewd tormentor who moved in with me when I started living alone. Worst of all, the silence in my apartment had an unseen accomplice who moved from room to room, corner to corner, or, most dreadful of all, waited in my bed for me. Yes, my agonizing loneliness. As I put on my pajamas I could not see it lying on my bed, but from experience I knew that I would sense its presence as soon as I laid down on the mattress: yes, a pervasive and insufferable sense of loneliness would begin to consume my soul and spirit like a wave of ravenous maggots, eating my insides while I lay there helpless, almost totally paralyzed by the ubiquitous anxiety. I was essentially defenseless against this ruthless accomplice that nightly tormented me, for I had to come to my apartment and I had to get into bed, where it always waited for me. It would attack my soul from within. Silence The Tormentor, and Loneliness The Ruthless Accomplice. It was a desperate situation. There was terror in the night, terror in my loneliness. There was nothing I could do. I was defenseless and it was unforgiving. This was a most sickening feeling, almost like waiting for certain death, a death hiding and waiting to spring at me at any moment.

At that time I did not have the words for it, but I know now that my soul was under siege by the allied forces of silence and loneliness. The most insidious enemies are those that strike from within to weaken resolve, spiritual cleanliness, and personal integrity, the very personal qualities that had become alien to me due to the manner in which I chose to hold my tormentors at bay. My weapon of choice was furious masturbation. Even though I had begun to play with my penis almost daily at the age of around five (not real masturbation, though), here in New York after the divorce I went deep into this spiritually degrading practice, often masturbating three to five times per day, mostly at night. I had found out a long time ago that the enormous high of the orgasm would effectively mask the effects of the tormenting loneliness on my soul just long enough for me to fall asleep to avoid my sadistic tormentors. Of course, the masturbation had a progressively more difficult job, for it was going against a cumulatively longer line of internal tormentors dating back to my infancy and to the then-current pains of divorce. Apparently the pains of my infancy and childhood had overwhelmed my budding capacity to process them appropriately, leading to a survival defense of blocking them either by repression or addictive intoxication (e.g., masturbation), which worked well as a method of last resort of emotional and psychological survival in the hellish conditions of my childhood but which in time became maladaptive as I got older.

So while in bed I masturbated to feel better, and I found in time that the silence lurking behind the door as I would come to my apartment could be compromised by having music playing continuously. That is, to mask the fundamental desperation of my life I would have almost 24-hour music in my apartment, even when I was not home, so that the silence would have to go away. Oftentimes I would also have the television on just for noise, in order to trick my soul into thinking that there were other human beings who actually wanted to live with me and who were talking in the other room. It was a pathetic part of my wretched life.

My private orgasms helped me to sleep. That night it was no different, as I felt desperately lonely in spite of the thousands of people which I had been near that night—the night of the porno feast—like many others. Masturbation made me feel good, even if only temporarily, and afterwards I had a relaxed feeling which lasted long enough for me to close my eyes to this filthy world and my nihilistic life. But the fantasies needed to be fueled by real-life material to be valid. The other lurid part of my sexual aberration was my shameless promiscuity. It was a sad story.

It had been maybe two or three years since Katherine and I had split up, but the pain of the divorce was still in me, causing me periodic bouts of crying and sadness I could not control. My addiction to pornography was in full swing, as was a pattern which at that time I mistook for my Macho Chicano prowess. I was always on the prowl for women I could approach for meaningless conversation to assess the chances of getting them into bed after a brief and cheap dinner. Candle Street, on Fifth Avenue, in Greenwich Village, at the Soho, on Broadway, at Central Park, in restaurants, on subways, and at women's shoe stores, I would visually assess an attractive prospect and approach her if I thought she was alone and might be receptive to some Machiavellian flattery. Of course, I didn't get very far with many, but with dozens of women I was able to get a first date, which greatly increased the chances that they would jump into bed with me. That was the extent of my interest in these women, for I did not care at all about their personal histories, their personalities, their virtues, or their moral values. All I wanted was their bodies. I had a ravenous addiction to raw, impersonal sex.

Typically I would try to get as far as possible on the first date, inviting the woman to a relatively inexpensive restaurant maybe in Greenwich Village. During dinner I would gather as much information about her as possible so that I could determine if she had weak points which I could exploit for my own selfish motives in getting her into bed. To this end I would employ deceit, flattery, manipulation, distortion, fakery, and persuasion to increase the chances that she would agree to come to my apartment. On many occasions the woman was very willing to come to my apartment for sex, quite possibly because she may have been a sex addict just like myself! Once she was in my apartment I would proceed with the usual foreplay until she was ready for sex, or, if she still did not feel like it after about 30 minutes of foreplay I would promptly get up from the sofa and announce that we should go out again for coffee. That is how I would unceremoniously end an "unproductive" date. "She did not want to open her legs," was my private assessment of the wasted evening. But then after dropping her off I would try to go out to pick up another woman if the evening was still young. It was a pathetic attitude to have towards women.

During the several years after my 1969 divorce from Katherine, I must have had sex thousands of times with dozens of women in New York. Sometimes I would have sex with three to five different women per week, sometimes with two to three per day. It was as if I was in some kind of sexual marathon where I was being judged on how many women I could have sex with in a week. In fact, I felt compelled to keep my numbers high, for if I had not "conquered" a new woman on a specific week I would feel depressed, sensing that I was losing my Macho Chicano power. For instant relief I knew that I could always count on the vast list of women in my little black book, that famous list of "trophies" under my belt. Oftentimes as I went on the prowl on the streets of New York I would end up empty-handed even after considerable effort at singles bars, parks, and restaurants, but I would console myself by calling one of my predictable standbys, even at 1:00 in the morning, inviting myself to her apartment to have sex and leaving promptly afterwards. By the time I got to my apartment the high of the orgasm had already worn off so I would have to masturbate in bed to relieve the disgusting feeling of being alone in a sea of women. It was a disturbing way of life.

About midway in my infamous sexual career in New York I started noticing a pattern that had been there for a while but which I had failed to detect. Typically I would take the woman to *her* apartment because I could then leave much faster than if she was at mine. Once there I was driven with an obsessive-compulsive desire to have sexual intercourse, even if I didn't think that she was pretty or attractive. In bed I would kiss her body all over, but I would not hold her hand and I would not kiss her lips, the only two things I considered sacred and still had respect for. Of course, in the heat of passion two lovers want to kiss and hold hands and caress their bodies tenderly, and it was no different with these women. It made me feel very uncomfortable when her lips moved closer to mine, and my wretched soul was secretly pleading, "Please don't ask me to kiss you. I can touch you, I can suck your breasts, I can kiss your legs. But please, please, please don't ask me to kiss your lips!" Yet I wanted so much to have my penis deep inside her, giving her every last ounce of my full load of semen. It usually worked out that way, and then it was all over. The pattern was that my compulsive and irrepressible desire to have sexual intercourse was instantaneously and almost magically replaced by a wave of despair, disgust, guilt, and depression. It was a disturbing case of Jekyll-and-Hyde: One moment there was no other motive in my life besides achieving full orgasmic climax inside her, filling her with as much sperm as I could ejaculate. Even if my life had been at risk at that moment, I would not have cared, for the only purpose in my life was to complete the sex act. Then the next moment I was a different person with a more realistic outlook and a damning guilt over the repulsive manner in which I had just had sex with this woman. *Immediately* after orgasm I felt that the woman's body was "dirty," that she was "ugly." Because of this nauseating feeling I absolutely did not want to touch her body at all, feeling almost like vomiting for having gone to bed with a woman I felt was so repulsive. As I lay there next to her naked body I would ask myself: "Why am I here? I do not want to touch her skin! Why does she want me to 'cuddle' her? I hope she does not hold my hand. And I do not want to kiss her. I need for her to simply disappear. Oh, God, save me, take me away from this wicked bed!" But I could not say these things outright to her, so I had to lie in bed next to her, fighting against the vomit which wanted to shoot up my esophagus. Lying there next to a naked body which I did not love, I felt very much like a prostitute. The prostitute within me was my soul, for it was being compromised into doing what it fundamentally felt was patently disgusting. And my damning sexual addiction was my *pimp:* it cared about nothing but its own agenda. It would pimp my soul to these women who honestly took all my conversations for genuine acts of interest. Neither I nor they knew at that time that they had been talking to my pimp all night long up to the point of orgasm, and that then the coward fled into the subterranean recesses of my mind, leaving the prostituted and violated soul to fend for itself in a compromising position in bed with a naked woman. The addiction pimp was tearing me apart, almost as if I was at war within myself.

So after a few minutes in bed I mustered the courage to get up and leave in a hurry. All the way home my soul was under attack by the tidal wave of repulsion, disgust, guilt, nausea, and a sense of failure. If I had any morals, these were it, for it was my underdeveloped conscience that was now lashing out at the prostituted soul for what it had done. My soul was under siege from two fronts, and it was losing the battle. In bed alone, I would then masturbate to forget it all, and the cycle was again ready to repeat itself. I could almost hear the maggots and the larva gnawing within me. It was a deplorable sickness. I should not have been born.

In spite of the torrent of disgust, the next day I was ready to play Jekyll-and-Hyde again. Actually, I had very little control over the two personalities which took over my life: The first was an insatiable, tyrannical sex fiend; the second was a despairing, depressive, and reactive personality that lamented the sins of the first, more powerful one. In hindsight I can say that my two personalities probably had a symbiotic relationship with each other, for my despairing self would depend on the sex addict to create a sexually euphoric mood, while the sex addict needed the despairing and depressive soul as its host, akin to a parasite sucking blood and giving it a high in the process. Even though I never got into drugs or alcohol, in a very real sense I was an addict who could not function without sex with different women every day or week. Sexual intercourse was my drug. Despair, depression, terror, and panic were my constant companions. I had no one to talk to. Indeed I was all alone in the universe.

One very ominous component of my sexual addiction was a strong feeling of entitlement when I was on the prowl—when my addiction was activated. Within me I felt *that I had a right to the woman's body* once I decided that I wanted to have sex with her, and that her unwillingness or hesitation was merely an obstacle to my goal of getting her in bed. Of course I understood that her body was hers and that we should all respect each other, yet a very powerful part of me just felt that it was my right and my duty to have sex with her, and this component of my personality did not listen to reason or to whatever conscience I may have had at that time. It was this odious force which gave me enormous motivation to be persistent and persuasive even when the woman would say that she really was not ready for sex. Because of this relentless persistence I was able to exhaust many women who initially said no and who hours later finally gave in. In fact, on two occasions in New York City I brought a woman home and I literally kept my hands on her and my leg between her legs for about three hours while she kept saying no, until I was finally able to maneuver between her open legs and have sex with her. Afterwards she shocked me when she cried, "You raped me!" Her words numbed me for several minutes. It never occurred to me that I was raping her. In spite of that we continued with our sick relationship for about one more year.

Then in Kansas City years later it happened again, with one of the dozens of women I dated and had sex with. She had come to my apartment after we had gone for a soda at a restaurant, and we started to kiss on the sofa and were soon undressed. She appeared to be enjoying all the foreplay, including her opening her legs with me on top of her. But then at the last minute she said she was not sure if she wanted to have sex, yet I did not listen to her and proceeded to enter her. In retrospect, even though our relationship similarly continued for about six months, I should not have had sex with her when she was clearly saying that she was not sure she wanted it.

It was only in recent years when I entered therapy that I told my therapist of the above questionable behavior on my part, and she informed me that what I had done was referred to as "date rape." In spite of having previously been told that by the woman in New York, this shocked me again, for I had never thought of myself as a man who committed this terrible act. It was a shocking testament to how low I had sunk, how evil my behavior had become.

It is horrifying for me to look retrospectively at the pervasive disorder of my being and my soul, at the gross desperation that was my life. During those years I spent in New York working on my history degree, I was so spiritually sick and full of undiagnosed psychiatric symptoms, which, when viewed with my now-better understanding of personal psychology, make me feel that I really was so close to having engaged in horrifying serial transgressions or murders. I do not say this lightly; I do so only because my intellect has seen the discomforting resemblance between the "profiles" of wanton and remorseless serial killers, and my own history and background. As I said before, the similarities are bone-chilling.

The height of my sickness occurred on the streets of New York when I was devouring women sexually almost every night as a matter of necessity and looking for increasingly more ugly and depraved forms of pornography to stimulate me. Even after a night of wanton pleasures at Times Square, I still went home to masturbate compulsively to the arousing effects of powerful fantasies of women under my sexual control who writhed with pleasure as I introduced my powerful organ into their bodies. With all this ugly history and sexual madness, I don't know how it was that I did not start hunting in the pattern of a serial killer. I thank God that even though I did do many deplorable things, I never crossed the line and started depriving people of their lives, for I definitely was on the frightening path of a sexual sociopath. All the childhood ingredients for a terrifying sexually-based killing were already in me, and were being stirred by the hands of despair, loneliness, depression, and the original rage from the womb. I was like my step-father, The Devil. Yes, I was a sexual Satan on the streets of New York. El Diablo was driven by a rageful need to control and subjugate, I by a totally narcissistic desire to use women as sources of sexual euphoria. Both of us used people in a heartless manner with no regard to their personal and spiritual integrity.

Pornography, wanton and meaningless sex, kleptomania, date rape, exhibitionism, pedophilic tendencies towards my daughter Sarah, fascination with the perverse and the filthy, child abuse against one of the kids in our care, and interpersonal manipulation: I was a sorry and dangerous character among the anonymous throngs in the streets of New York. *What was going on inside my inhuman soul?*

In spite of my unusually painful childhood I had managed to do well in high school, with only a minimum of unnatural activities and no crimes or drug abuse. My schizoid-like personality made it very difficult for me to approach girls I liked to introduce myself and ask for a date, but in spite of this I did not feel any unusual antagonism towards girls or women. But when I arrived for my first semester at Renwick University in 1964, I started feeling a considerably heightened level of arousal because of the feast-like abundance of blond women on campus, a sight that connected directly with my predisposition to admire and desire blond, white women. It was at this point when I was in a sea of blond beauties that I first started feeling a *reactive* hostility towards these women, because somehow in my soul I felt that it was their fault that I was feeling frustrated at the sight of them. Quite possibly, this hostility may have been a very immature defense mechanism whereby the internal anger I felt against myself for not having the courage to approach women was instead directed outward at the object of my attention—women. Or it could have been the psychologically simpler process of scapegoating: I directed my anger at a convenient object that was the center of my attention when I started feeling my internal frustration. This type of inner defense is usually more typical of two-year-old children who batter a toy that they are not allowed to play with. If my analysis and analogy are correct, I was responding to the normal frustrations in romantic relationships (e.g., feeling anxiety about approaching someone) with the heart of a two-year-old child, and was subsequently reacting with the hostility of the two-year-old. But this immature reaction in the strong, fully alert, mobile, and knowledgeable body of a 20-year old could have been lethal in other circumstances. More mature men would have interpreted the frustration, if they had any, as a natural result of legitimate boundaries or limits in the situation, and would have moved on to explore other, more promising alternatives.

When I met Katherine in 1965, I believe I fell in love with my mother, for in treating me with kindness, love, understanding, and in looking intently into my eyes, she unknowingly penetrated years-old defenses that had bottled up my desperate need for the closeness and physical comfort which I never received from my own mother. In doing so she started a chain reaction within me which emotionally regressed me to about the level of a two-year-old child, an angry child who threw tantrums and had a typical egocentric attitude where he felt that the world revolved around him and his desires. My poor wife Katherine was married to a two-year old masquerading as a 20-year-old university student. That was a very sorry and sad chapter for her. I spoiled several years of her life—this wonderful and pretty woman who gave me all her love.

When our marriage inevitably broke up,, the now-totally-defenseless toddler within me felt an apocalyptic motherly betrayal that drove a spiritual dagger deep into his soul, causing immense emotional pain and intense abandonment anxiety, both for the second time in his wretched history. Intense abandonment anxiety. Intense abandonment panic. I felt like a little boy whose mother had invited him to go with her to see the animals in the park, and as she asked me to look at the lions she quietly sneaked away leaving me standing there all alone, forever and ever. There are no words that can describe the profoundly sorrowful feeling of maternal abandonment in the life of a child, and the resulting despair and anxiety of a life spent looking for her in every woman's face, heart, and bed.

Providence had granted me a beautiful, wholesome, loving woman—a goddess, really—but I had no idea about how to take care of her. My stupidity and my sickness destroyed what I had longed for in my life, and now, in front of me, lay the wreckage of the best I had ever been granted in life. Like heavenly water she had just slipped through my fingers, gone forever.

Losing Katherine was catastrophic not only because it inflicted insufferable abandonment pain, as is usually the case when romances come to a tragic end, but also in the sense that it left me exposed without any supportive systems at a time of unbearable pain and sorrow, a situation which quickly exacerbated my dormant pathologies and personality weaknesses. The pain of this I could ameliorate, at least momentarily, by reluctantly succumbing to my treacherous demons who offered quick relief, those that drove me to regrettable promiscuous behavior and insatiable consumption of all forms of vile pornographic materials.

So not only did I lose Katherine, but I also lost the small, residual value I had left as a human being. I became a vile sexual addict, only I did not know it at that time because my resident demons had their hands over my eyes.

After Katherine left me I cried like a child, I cried and cried, I waited and waited, I looked and looked for my mother who never came back, becoming ever more consumed by deep existential and abandonment pain that made everything else in life seem worthless and meaningless. My emotional regression included endless walks through the hundreds of miles of streets in New York City, just like I had through the streets of El Paso as a child and living in the house from hell. In El Paso I was suffering from the pain of abandonment and abuse; here in New York I was suffering from the sudden departure of the only woman with whom I had found some real albeit immature emotional connection. The child had lost his mother, again. Years later this child was still begging and hoping that his mother would decide to come back, even agreeing to change everything else in his life to entice her to return and to love him again. It was this most profound infantile abandonment-betrayal that set the stage for the drastic defenses that my inner soul subsequently set up so that it could ameliorate the pain of the sorrowful wound, a self-defense move which would by nature impair my proper functioning as an adult in the future.

I was not promiscuous at Renwick University in Houston nor when I married Katherine, but in the first few years after our divorce, I was relentlessly so. *Why did I engage in such an unethical and spiritually degrading practice?*

My memory is very clear about the fact that I had very little personal interest in all these women whom I took to bed, preferring instead to rate them according to breast size and the fit of my penis inside them. I recall vividly how I would be immensely energized as I was going out with a new woman, inspecting her bosom size, her hips, her legs. My imagination would run wild, full of fantasies and expectations of the glory, the ecstasy, the joy, and the exultation that was to come when I would have her in bed, preferably as soon as possible. I literally would salivate at the prospect of getting her in bed and devouring her completely, sucking her breasts dry and driving my penis deep inside her to deliver a full load of sperms which she needed and deserved. Yet almost without exception, I secretly felt like crying a few seconds after we had finished intercourse. I felt sad. It was some very mysterious process which took place between the sheets. Invariably the woman would want to touch me afterwards but I would feel repulsed because, after all, I hardly knew her. She was a stranger to me, so how could I be spiritually intimate with her? Don't touch me! Please don't hold my hand. Paradoxically, as the abandonment panic returned hours later, I was ready to take a new woman to bed for more meaningless and sick sex. In a way I was like Dracula—I needed new blood almost every night. How different it had been with Katherine: I always wanted to touch her and hug her in bed and hold her hand. Even after sex, I always wanted to hold her hand. But she left. Forever.

It was one of the most disgusting phases of my spiritual illness, this perverted and sick desire of mine to mingle with the decaying spiritual corpses of the similarly sick zombies of the night, stalking the unwary and raping them, and myself, spiritually. The sickening stench of human urine in the countless corners of the Times Square Subway Station was for me both a stink and a perverse aphrodisiac which prepared me for the impending descent into the bowels of hell, a trip which I was too happy to make on a regular basis.

We were all in the same spiritual coffin, carrying the ravenous demon which made its demands clear: It was the unquestionable ruler of our soul, perverting all other drives to the service of raw, decadent sex, allowing no ethical or moral considerations to delay its immediate gratification. It did not matter that persons in porno magazines or in peep shows were merely objects for the satisfaction of another. It did not matter that some of these persons were children or animals or handicapped or cadavers or the elderly or women who were tied to a hot water pipe. It did not matter that tenderness, caring, or love were never part of the sick plots which sleazy editors sought to paste onto the basically raw sex. It did not matter that a basic theme through-out most of the magazines was a forceful subjugation of women, with men inflicting the pain with oversized penises, forceful penetration, humiliating ejaculation upon the woman's face, or the standard S&M practices which no longer raise an eyebrow.

Most of the acts were ugly, vile, immoral, evil, unnatural, criminal, irreverent, and highly disrespectful towards the human body and the ethical relationship which should exist between the two human beings engaged in sex. Now that I have seen and enjoyed the *entire* range of pornography that our culture can produce, I can say unequivocally that pornography is a spiritual and vile sickness indicative of a lack of inner compassion for, and an inability to identify with, other human beings. In pornography the reader or viewer lets loose the sexual hatreds within his soul, *with little or no moral reflection*. It is highly satisfying because pornographic materials tap into a very profound and perverted desire which the pervert may not satisfy in real life, not because he has ethical qualms about it but because his intellect warns him of the potential risks of getting caught. Contrary to current opinion, I believe that pornography does not corrupt the soul, but rather is the *outward manifestation of an already very sick and disturbed inner spirit*. That is, it cannot corrupt what is good, but will attract those who already have the maggots inside. And my insides were already thoroughly rotted out from the maggot infestation.

When I read in the New York Times that a controversial film from Brazil had arrived in the city, I felt the urge to "check it out." The porno film had to be made in Brazil—"where life is cheap," they said—because apparently a novice actress in Sao Paulo had been lured by the pornographers with promises of a great film career, only to be brutally disemboweled for real in front of the cameras after the obligatory sexual scene. Because the film distributors admitted that the sex murder was the real thing, the police authorities in New York got involved in the case and the showing was quickly shut down. But not before I got to see it and feel sickened by it. In my relentless pursuit of ever-more-ugly forms of brutalizing sex, I had finally reached the outer limits of my inhuman sickness and pulled back. If it hadn't been for the stabilizing routine of my history studies at International University I fear that my consumption of pornography would have eventually destroyed whatever redeeming values I may have had. In my Jekyll-and-Hyde life, I was spending more time at the library. That probably saved my life. And maybe that of some women.

My changing moods and my impulsivity caused harm to the many women whom I deceived, to my daughter Sarah, to my ex-wife Katherine, and to the many creditors who had financed my very expensive college career. As I finished my studies at International University I immediately filed for Chapter 11 Bankruptcy to get out from the crushing weight of ten years of student loans. I felt no moral compunction in doing so; it fit with the many years of financial irresponsibility in my life—I would impulsively spend money I did not have, even rent money. Some women fell in love with me (why?), yet I trampled over their love and took advantage of them. At least one that I know of got pregnant and had an abortion because our relationship was nowhere near stable. I had no family and no friends to speak of. My usual social connections were the women whom I took to bed. I stole small items from department stores and motels. I urinated in phone booths. I still consumed pornography as ravenously as the maggots eating away inside me. And my language was as filthy as ever, even in front of my young daughter. I was a pathetically unbalanced and sociopathic schizoid by the time that I finished my studies at IU.

During the Summer of 1974 I was already getting responses from the many job applications I had submitted all over the country for history teaching positions. One very good offer came from East Kansas State University—the salary was $21,600. I was already getting tired of the New York scene and decided that I wanted a radical change, maybe even to the plains and cornfields of Kansas. And so it was that in August of 1974, at age 29, I rented a truck and loaded my broken furniture (I should have left it there), kissed Sarah goodbye in New Jersey where she was staying with her mother, and headed West towards Kansas City—just my maggots and me.

Chapter Ten

The Cornfields of Kansas and Geena's Blue Eyes

It was a very pleasant experience driving West along Interstate 80 to Kansas City, thinking about my new teaching job at The East Kansas State University, yet feeling sad because I had left Sarah behind with Katherine. During the many hours of silence on that trip, I reviewed in my mind the many women whom I had known and slept with in New York, feeling that with the exception of one, none were attractive to me as marriage partners. I did feel that I was going to miss Amornpan, a loving Thai woman whom I had gotten pregnant and who subsequently got an abortion. One big hurdle in our relationship was that her family insisted that she date only within her race. Even though she had been good to me I had disrespected her and failed to truly love her, something that she justifiably felt was the downfall of our relationship. "As soon as I get into Kansas City I will give her a call," I thought as I floored the pedal on my rented truck to keep up with the high-speed traffic.

After two days on the road I finally arrived in Kansas City. Would this be my new hunting ground, or is all that in the past? I asked myself.

My first thought was that I was thankful that it had something like "skyscrapers," for I had been getting an uncomfortable feeling the whole day after seeing endless miles of cornfields. But in spite of the tall buildings, I found out, Kansas *did* have seemingly endless miles of cornfields and plains, while the local radio stations played no New York Philharmonic concerts and instead offered me the "local hog and seed report." Another thing that struck me right away was that Kansas City was not a "walking town" like New York

City; rather, people preferred to drive their cars everywhere. Besides, the neighborhoods were not seamlessly connected like New York's but had gaps where there weren't even any sidewalks. But it looked clean to me and I was overjoyed to be in this new city.

In no time at all I unpacked all my decrepit furniture and pitiful belongings into my apartment on the west end of town. No cockroaches! No peeling paint. Brand new carpeting! Central air conditioning (I had had none in New York)! I loved my apartment which was in a very clean residential area.

But, again, this was not a "walking town"—and I had no car! The subways in New York City, despite all the human vermin they hauled around, did have the unquestionable virtue of getting you to just about any part of the city at breakneck speed, so there really was no need for a car there. But here I needed one rather fast. Using my bicycle I was able to do my errands in the first few days, but eventually I found a foreign student who wanted to sell his ten-year old Plymouth, with 160,000 miles on it, for $500. At last I had a car!

Within the next several weeks I had the opportunity to meet my fellow teachers at The East Kansas State University, and we began the semester quite uneventfully with my teaching some history and sociology classes.

What to do during the evenings and on weekends? The maggots were stirring. My evenings were agonizing as I again found myself tortured incessantly by the silence and the loneliness of my apartment, the same as in New York. I would sit on my couch pretending to read, but the silence would attack me from all directions, especially now that I lived in this very quiet area. At night in my bed I felt that I was the only person left on the planet Earth, that there was no one who wanted a connection with me. The monsters of silence, loneliness, and abandonment desperation were everywhere: in every room, in my closets, under my bed, in my lonely kitchen, behind the shower curtain, behind every open door. It was worse than in New York because there were fewer people here who served as bodies and as noise-makers to scare away my tormentors. All I could do to defend myself against these unforgiving tormentors was to leave all my lights and radio on at night to make believe that there were other human beings in my life, people who perhaps were just in the other room talking. That's right, they're relatives, and they are having a good time talking. But there was no Sarah. No friends. No family. I was desperately alone in the Midwest. And I always turned to my drug of choice: serial nightly masturbation. It helped me at least until the sleep blacked out my consciousness for the night.

It did not take long for me to make connections with some women in town, going down the same lecherous path that I had taken in New York. While at the University I helped students during the day, by night I would do my Jekyll-and-Hyde transformation, roaming the streets and finding women to deceive into inauthentic relationships so that I could improve the probabilities of their going to bed with me. In this fashion I was able to have sex with several women during that first year in Kansas City. One that stood out particularly was Stella, a Black nurse I met in the parking lot of our apartment complex.

Stella was attractive, slim, pretty, and best of all, she lived alone. When we went out on our first date I already had made up my mind that I would try to romance her if she invited me to her apartment that night. She did and I did. In the heat of passion I opened her blouse and I kissed her bountiful breasts like I never had done before with any other woman, proceeding slowly to taking off her skirt and her panties. And then, in a moment reminiscent of my joyful, illicit, and eventually fateful affair with the blond woman at International University, I entered Stella and was lost in an ecstatic union that I had not felt for a very long time. Indeed, our lovemaking that night was wonderful in a way that I had not known for many, many years. Later that night, when we were still in bed, Stella shyly and quietly asked me if I had deposited all my semen inside her, something I thought was rather odd for no woman had ever asked me that. Nonetheless I told her, "Yes, all five gallons of it." She looked at me rather coyly, smiled and fell asleep with her naked right leg across my thighs. Amazingly, I did not feel like crying at being naked and in bed with Stella. I did not mind her touching or kissing me. Most importantly, I liked holding her hand. I could not explain it. This was our first date. I had not been fantasizing about a great romance with her, but my inner spirit obviously felt very comfortable with Stella, for reasons unknown to my awareness. I obviously liked her, it seemed.

It did not take long to figure out what the coy look was all about, for about six weeks later Stella told me she was happily pregnant with our child, something that she had wanted for a very long time. In fact, the first night of our passionate lovemaking had not been at random but was carefully chosen by Stella when she figured she would be ovulating and had the maximum chance of getting pregnant if I took her to bed. She purposefully had not insisted on us using any contraception, so her plan had worked rather perfectly. I had not been the only one with a hidden agenda that night. It would appear she had seduced me into seducing her.

I liked very much that Stella was carrying my child in her womb, for I liked Stella and was very pleased with our relationship. Besides that I had the lion's feelings of a Macho Chicano whose sperms still could do the job of getting a woman pregnant. But I also had to think rapidly of what the pregnancy meant for our relationship. Did I want to marry her? Did I really want another baby now? Would she want to raise the baby all by herself? Then the critical question came to my mind: If our baby turned out to be a boy, his being half-Black would mean he would have dark features and crinkly hair—an unfortunate and terrifying constant reminder of how The Devil looked—that hated Devil! I would then come to hate that innocent baby!

Too many uncomfortable and unanswered questions were overshadowing my feelings for Stella, and in the end I decided that I did not want her to have our baby. In a move that I now regret, Stella reluctantly had an abortion after I told her that I would not feel right about her bringing the pregnancy to term. It was a bigger misfortune for her because as it turned out she was not able to conceive with another man after we broke off our relationship several months later. Stella, the pretty, kind nurse with a heart of gold, was never able to have the baby she desperately wanted.

It had been less than a year since I had been in Kansas City, and I had already broken several hearts and pressured Stella into having an abortion, all out of my relative disregard for common decency and for the feelings of these women. This, however, was in sharp contrast to the image that I had at the university and in the community.

At the university I participated enthusiastically in all faculty programs to help students with academic, social, or personal problems, often going out of my way to contact families and involve them in the students' programs at school. My demeanor with my students was always cordial, encouraging, respectful, helpful, and academically challenging. With my colleagues I was for the most part polite and also helpful by participating in many academic committees to serve the faculty and the university as a whole. As recommended by the Board of Regents, I often presented academic papers at invited State and National conferences, and I wrote and published several professional papers in history journals. In addition I had a vigorous community-liaison program whereby I made almost weekly presentations in community centers to help residents with local problems. Many of these presentations were in fact workshops geared towards promoting empathic caring of our community resources and residents. I soon was given the responsibility to produce and host a Spanish radio program geared for the Mexican community in Kansas City, a weekly duty which I enjoyed and carried out for about one year.

Not surprisingly I was well regarded at the university and in the community, for within a two-year period I was given awards by the Mexican Community in Kansas City for "Outstanding Community Service," and I was promoted to Associate Professor as well as awarded tenure by the university. I was indeed a pillar of scholarship, ethics, and morals. Wasn't that ridiculous?

Retrospectively with the wisdom of time, I can see the sharp contrast between my generally ethical behavior with my students at the college and in the community, and my sexually deviant practices elsewhere. While I was executing my public service duties and doing my volunteer community work, I actually felt and believed that I was such a great person because of the good deeds that I was doing, not finding any discordance with my manipulative, deceptive, and dishonorable behavior in other areas. Colleagues would routinely say that I was a very "caring" professor who did everything possible to help disadvantaged students. People in the community would call on me frequently because they knew from experience that I was "an honorable man intent on helping the Chicano community." It is not at all in question that at International University in New York and at East Kansas State University, a lot of what I did in academia and the community was very helpful to others, but I now question my underlying psychodynamic motives. At that point I was still too deep in my spiritual illness to see the truth.

The last year at IU and these first two years in Kansas City made me feel real good about myself, for I had this image of the erudite and caring professor who would do just about anything for a student or community member in need. On the average I would engage in about 15 community-service projects per year, all on a volunteer basis. In addition, my publishing efforts were indeed successful, and I was being invited to present history papers at local, state, national, and international conferences. Then ,too, a professional journal invited me, for a term of one year, to be a special reader for them, critically reviewing the professional papers that other academicians submitted for consideration for publication. Besides the academic side, I also had a personal penchant for exercise, for I had already been jogging for about eight years in sleet, rain, and cold, something that I felt attested to my superior endurance and dedication to excel in my chosen endeavors. So, in spite of my being under siege at night when I was all alone, I still felt positive and proud of all my academic and community achievements. I loved helping people and exceling in academic and community affairs. What a fraud I was.

My dark side lived a life independent of the honorable me, but at that time I did not have the insight or the wisdom to recognize it. I cheated, I cursed, I tricked, I mocked, I stole, I cajoled, I betrayed, I deceived, I seduced, I defrauded, I corrupted, I deflowered, I irresponsibly impregnated. These behaviors were just as much a part of me as the "caring and empathic" behaviors which had earned me such a good reputation in the first two years in

Kansas City, only I did not see how this dark side patently contradicted the image that the community and I had of myself as "good and honorable." My introspective blindness was near total—almost as if I had no basis in reality when it came to the evaluation of my own impulsive behaviors vis-à-vis an ethical system. Years later I learned that this sickness has a name: narcissistic personality disorder.

That is, a person is very likely to have a narcissistic personality syndrome if he or she exhibits on a regular basis behavior patterns consistent with a selfish outlook on life. And, generally speaking, the disorder is more severe the more numerous and severe the symptoms. I am sure I also had other forms of mental illness.

During that first year in Kansas City I was deep into having meaningless sex with many women and had already gotten two women pregnant and both had abortions. Katherine and I still had the shared-custody arrangement concerning Sarah. She was spending more time with me in my apartment, while I had my porno magazines all over the floor. In fact, I believed with all my heart that she should know as much as possible about the techniques of sex, so I regrettably encouraged her to read and to view the disgusting photographs. Delusionally, I believed that I was intellectually teaching Sarah about the world, the sex world, but behind the scenes it really was my depraved sexual aberrations that were guiding my hand and permitting me to introduce the inappropriate concept of sex into my relationship with Sarah. She was only eight years old. I had no idea whatsoever about the ethics of parenthood. Worse, I was becoming increasingly more delusional about my life and my relationships with others.

One day I was out on my daily jog on the college track when I spied this gringa with flaming red hair, blue eyes, and nice legs—also jogging. When we were both cooling down after the run I approached her and struck up a conversation. She told me that her name was Geena and that she was a student in sociology. I was 30, she was 23, a young chick, compared to what I was used to. Little did I know that when we spoke our first words on that jogging track we were opening the fateful door on a relationship that would span many years and have the most beautiful highs as well as the most gut-wrenching and suicidal lows. Without knowing fate, we both got on the train of mutual sexual attraction and *disastrously compatible pathologies*, quite in the same vein as my mother and The Demon at the *Plaza de las Flores* 27 years earlier in Mexico. Can I now understand how my sick mother teamed up with the piece of shit, The Devil? Do I have a moral basis for criticizing my mother with such venom?

From the very beginning I felt sexually attracted to Geena, but I also liked her more than any of the other women I had gone out with up to that point. In fact, I liked her so much that I *feared having sex with her* because I knew from experience that my attraction to a woman would evaporate magically as soon as I had an orgasm inside her. Then I would be forced to pretend that I enjoyed lying in bed with a repulsive and essentially anonymous naked body. I liked being with Geena; I enjoyed talking with her; I enjoyed looking at her face, and especially her bright, blue eyes. Contrary to the personal policy I had at that time, I made no attempt whatsoever to seduce her or in any way to deceive her into having sex with me. That was new to me. In fact, I believe that it was the other way around, for she appeared more ready than I to get into bed, the bed that for me was a whirl-pooling sea of bliss and horrors, filled with sperms, orgasms, masturbation, empty physical contact, repulsive naked bodies, sticky body fluids, as well as my unrelenting tormentors of the night: the silence, the darkness filled with fears, and my ever-present and painful loneliness.

We had our first date at the Dairy Queen, and soon we began holding hands, which also signaled to me that I truly felt different with Geena. I loved just holding hands with her—no need for sex—I didn't want to spoil it. I just wanted to hold her warm hand. With every conversation and every subsequent date we got closer to my bed, much to my anxiety because I did not want to "ruin" a relationship which I felt positive about. Besides, Geena had told me that she was in the middle of a divorce, and I felt that I didn't want to complicate matters for her. Much to my surprise, I wanted to behave honorably with her. In spite of my apprehension and my reluctance, we did finally make love in my own apartment. Geena told me some years later that she thought that our *first time* had been a lousy experience for her; in contrast, I did not feel afterwards that I was lying next to a disgusting naked body. That was a positive for me, although it is pitiful that I have to describe the experience as the absence of a negative.

She was a farm girl from rural Oklahoma and had gotten married very young to a local boy. They had moved to Kansas City to study at East Kansas State. That is essentially how she ended up in the area. From the very beginning she struck me as unusually intelligent, for she could argue a philosophical issue with me to the point where I could not win. That fiery redhead was capturing my heart. But her spunk also signaled that she was much like me and would never stop until she won an argument. Good for her, bad for us. As always, I did not see this dangerous point at that time.

It was about two months after we met that Geena announced to me that she was pregnant with our child, and I knew immediately that I would not ask her to have an abortion for I wanted her to have our baby. My ecstasy, however, was short-lived, for within a week or two Geena told me that she had done some soul-searching at the advice of her mother, and had decided to go back to her estranged husband to give the marriage another try. She broke my heart with that announcement, and when I was alone I cried for the loss. It was especially painful because both of us had enthusiastically already given a name to our unborn baby: Jasmine if it was a girl and Bentley if it was a boy. I recall vividly how I had to prepare myself for Geena's departure, and telling her to take care of our baby whom I'd never see. We tearfully said goodbye, and she was gone.

It took me a while to stop crying over her, but to ease the pain soon I was back with my old standby women, meaninglessly romping in bed as usual. One of these was a 30-year-old Chinese woman I had met on campus and with whom I had a most peculiar sexual arrangement. From the very beginning we established a pattern whereby I would visit her at her studio apartment for sex and nothing more. In fact, we never even went out on a regular date, for apparently she was willing to come to my apartment the very first time for sex and thereafter I always went straight to her place with no need for a meaningless date. The routine was always the same: I would softly knock on her door, she would open it; I would make some small talk for about one or two minutes, then begin to play with her breasts; I would remove her skirt, make love to her, go to the bathroom, say "goodbye," and leave. It was pretty routine and pretty sick. That routine went on for a while, and we used contraceptives all the time. But for some reason one day as she lay naked on the bed she told me that she wanted me to make love to her without using any contraceptives. I thought she meant that she wanted me to "pull out" just in time, so that my sperms would not go inside her. But no, that is not what she meant. She said she wanted me to release all my sperms deep inside her because, she said, "I want to give you a son." Those soft and innocent words from her delicate mouth activated my powerful Macho Chicano soul, making me feel like a lion in heat with an irrepressible urge and pride to impregnate and reproduce, to fill my bedmate with as much reproductive fluid as possible so that she could bloom with the fruit of my effort. It was in this spirit that I entered Meifen and passionately made love to her as I never had, releasing millions of my sperms inside her, hoping that they would reach their destination deep inside her and thus bring her to the new frontiers of motherhood. For the first time ever, she did not get up from the bed, but just lay there with only a thin sheet to cover her fully spent body. For me it had been a wonderful experience.

About four weeks later I received an unexpected call from Geena; she said that the situation with her husband had not worked out and she wanted to come back to me. I was both joyful and apprehensive, for I did not want to get hurt again. And even though I was happy to have her in my arms again, something was missing from my soul this time around. It was not the splendored love I had felt for her at the beginning. Besides, now I had Meifen to contend with. I did not know if she was pregnant too.

Since Geena's belly was getting bigger we decided to move in together into our own apartment, but the problems began right from the start. As much as I loved to kiss Geena and to have her in my arms, I still felt a need to visit my old contacts for sex as usual; I did not kiss or hug them—it was just sick, impersonal sex. In the beginning I felt a moral duty to inform Geena about my desires, so I discussed this issue with her in spite of my having promised myself in 1969 after the fiasco with Katherine that I would never again confess any sort of infidelity, no matter how short or unimportant, to a significant woman in my life. So Geena and I discussed the problem, and I recall very painfully how I struggled with the issue: I am now living with this woman I love and whom I love to kiss and to hold. She is having our baby. We are practically married. Our union should be monogamous. Can I forsake all these other women forever? This time around just the *thought* of not ever being in bed with my other women again was enough to make my body tremble with panic—the panic of an anxiety attack. Regrettably, I did not have the wisdom to recognize the unmistakable signs of what I was experiencing: the terrified panic of an addict with a perceived threat of loss of the object of addiction—casual serial sex with unengaging women. I had a severe addiction to many forms of sexual aberration. It was on this lamentable footing that I began my romantic union with Geena.

A short time later I told Geena that I would be willing to go with her to see a counselor about my sexual feelings for these women, although I truthfully did not see what the counselor could tell me to convince me that I should give these women up. Much to our surprise—and our misfortune—the marriage counselor said that he did not see anything wrong with the husband going to bed with other women once in a while—that it added "spice" to the marriage. In spite of my strong addiction, I nonetheless felt instinctively that his advice was morally wrong. Tragically for us, this issue went essentially underground—not to be talked about again—but remained within me as a spiritual cancer; it became a malignant tumor that compromised the integrity of our romance.

Undeterred, I continued to visit other women about once a month for casual sex, always without Geena knowing it, but always knowing it. Meifen had refined her technique for getting pregnant. When she knew I was coming that day she simply would leave her door unlocked. I would enter her dark apartment and would find her already naked in bed. We never again spoke about contraceptives. We just shared a crazy passion—no dates, no promises, no questions, no requirements, no strings, no serious conversations, no love, not even friendship. Her slender body and her long black hair were a feast for my eyes—I relished them. I think it was one of those relationships where our needs were complementary yet simple: She wanted a baby, I wanted to feel like a Macho man who could give her one.

Besides the fatal problem of my sexual infidelity, Geena and I also started having caustic and bitter arguments, oftentimes over insignificant matters. These were not the common differences of opinion that ethical couples experience, but rather were vicious fights where we showed corrosive disrespect for each other. I suspect that I was to blame for this more than she, for in all other areas of her life Geena was friendly and ethical, never known to have shown any malice toward another person. That pattern, of course, was the moral antithesis of the history of my life and my wicked behavior towards the human race. If there was a God, He had sent Geena to try to clean up the degenerate nature of my soul. But maybe I had already walked far too long with Satan, that is, with The Devil we had had at our childhood home.

Geena was shocked when she first saw me pinching my eight-year-old Sarah on her crotch through her clothes, something that I did as a "loving" gesture, as I said previously. She said that I should not be doing that—that it was not appropriate to be touching my daughter in that fashion. As incredible as that may sound, this was probably my first instruction on how to be a better (and appropriate) parent. She said it with such conviction that I did stop it immediately and completely. In a similar fashion, Geena convinced me to put away my hardcore pornography magazines, and to refrain from showing these to Sarah. That was in '75 or '76.

Geena and I were now living together as husband and pregnant wife, fighting battles almost every day, yet also feeling romantic towards each other. But the bitter arguments hurt me to the core, for I felt "betrayed" every time that Geena understandably withdrew her love during and after the battle. It felt almost like a new abandonment, for my heart was open yet she was cold to me. I remember clearly that after almost every vicious fight I would feel an urgent need—a panic—to visit one of my standby women for quick sex, for it would somehow relieve my misery and anxiety. A terrible loneliness closed in on me when Geena was angry. It killed me every time she withdrew her love.

As usual I went to visit Meifen at her apartment after one of my arguments with Geena. On this particular occasion I noticed that she was visibly distraught about something, and it looked like she might not want to jump in bed with me. After rebuffing me twice she said, "I think I am pregnant with your child." Of course I had expected that she might end up pregnant since we had not used any contraceptives for a while, but after she spoke I felt both a Macho pride in knowing that this Chinese woman was now carrying my baby inside her, and an uncertain fear since I had a woman at home also with child. Meifen added, "I am four weeks late with my period, and I am never late by more than a few days. My breasts are very sore and in the mornings I feel like throwing up. I would say that I am definitely pregnant. I think it's a boy." I was just a ball of convoluted emotions as we sat together and she placed my hand on her abdomen, that abdomen that I had intimately connected with on many occasions. From the look on her face I could tell that in spite of her apprehension Meifen was happy to be with child. That is what she had wanted all along.

Notwithstanding my obvious delight in having Meifen pregnant, I told her that perhaps the best thing to do was to have an abortion, since I could not be a proper father to this child. Had she followed my advice this would have been, I believe, the fourth or fifth abortion I would have been responsible for. I selfishly regarded the women who had them as fodder for my narcissism and addiction. Fatefully, Meifen refused and we broke off contact that day. Apparently she had been serious all along about having a baby out of wedlock and with no father. About three months after Geena gave birth, my baby with Meifan was born—a boy, as she had predicted. I recall I saw him only once, and then he and Meifen left for Beijing and I never saw either of them ever again.

In Mexican culture it is very common for men to have children with many women, spanning several cities and states, and the more the better. It is an intrinsic part of the Macho culture to show one's virility by impregnating women and especially by producing sons. Of course, it is still a patriarchal society where women are seen as serving the needs of men, a philosophy that I had wholeheartedly embraced since my junior high school days when I started noticing girls and the older boys told me about the "facts" of life. This cultural trait was further buttressed by my addictive and narcissistic tendencies towards sex as a drug to numb the pain of loneliness and pump up my ego.

It felt good having sex with Meifen, and even better to know that she had my baby because that validated my macho man status. It had to be this way. That may sound callous and selfish, but it was the truth at that time. For me it was just sex and macho ego. For her it was a way of getting the baby she wanted. It was, as one of my former women put it, "A fucking relationship."

All philosophical mumbo-jumbo aside, I feel I should not have impregnated Meifen in the first place, and that I acted gravely irresponsibly by agreeing to have sex with her with no contraception. I feel as if my moral and spiritual obligations towards Meifen and our child were not fulfilled. It is very unfortunate that I replicated the same type of tragedy for which I wanted to kill my mother—the irresponsible and unethical behavior on the part of the parent that produces an innocent child under insufferable conditions such that in the future this child will have shame about his parentage and will go through life asking, "Mama, who is my father?" I know only too well how this shame and uncertainty works like a virus within the soul, spreading into all areas of the psyche, infecting almost all facets of human functioning. I committed that unpardonable sin by fathering Meifen's son and by not having been there to be a father to an innocent child. If my son with Meifen ever felt like he wanted to kill me for having abandoned him, I would not argue with him or defend myself against his rage. He would be morally entitled to have feelings of spiritual betrayal from his father. He would be morally justified in saying, "If I knew who my father was, I would have to kill him." I am sorry that it turned out that way. Somehow I lost my moral license to condemn my own parents when I started doing the same shit they did. Now I am just as lowly a maggot as they were.

During the period when Meifen was pregnant, I was always nervous but managed to act normal in front of Geena so that she never suspected anything. Of course, this was a grievous betrayal on my part, but my only concern at that time was to keep things under control so that I could continue with sick sex somewhere else. I am sure that deep inside Geena must have known that I was wandering, something that contributed to the bitter arguments that were always escalating.

One other peculiarity that came to the surface during Geena's pregnancy was her neediness and my response to it. She had a severe case of morning sickness and consequently needed me to help her with a variety of personal things. While in the beginning I was able to do it with little effort, towards the last trimester I found I could easily not care if she needed me, for I felt angered by her constant demands. She needed backrubs, she needed for me to be constantly moving and cleaning her emesis bowl, she needed and required lots of understanding for her groaning and moaning about her miserable condition. In her subsequent pregnancy my anger intensified as her true medical neediness increased, resulting in her understandable bitterness about my lack of sympathy. She was right. I failed to show proper empathy for her medical problems.

At that time I simply thought that she was just too needy, but now I can understand the dynamics much better. It all goes back to mother. My own mother had made me her little husband when I was about six years old, requiring me for years to give her rubs; to anoint her belly with olive oil for one hour every night to "relieve the stress"; to rub her navel while terrified that if I did not do a good job that the "hernia" underneath would rupture and she'd die; to serve as her confidant and listen to her endless stories of woe; to act as the hapless "lookout" while she went into the Hotel Central on her escapades. The Devil was busy fucking women—too busy to be a husband. So my mother grabbed me instead. During my childhood my mother absorbed all my energy so that it seemed I had none left for my own wife. Maybe I didn't have anything left to give. Maybe subconsciously I was feeling angry at my mother when Geena was asking me for help and assistance during her hours of greatest need. Or maybe I was just irresponsible and am trying to find a lofty excuse for my reprehensible behavior. Nonetheless, I failed this test too.

By July 1976 Geena was big enough to deliver, so I took her to the hospital where she continued laboring for about 12 more hours, an unusually long time that alarmed the doctors. As per her instructions to me, I furiously rubbed her lower back with my fists, hard enough to produce black and blue bruises the next day. This I kept up for many hours but it only minimally alleviated her discomfort. Eventually the physicians in the birthing room declared "pelvic insufficiency" and ordered a C-section to avoid any more "fetal distress." I accompanied Geena into the operating room with my camera and witnessed the doctors make an incision across her lower abdomen, reach into her belly, and pull out a very robust Jasmine, screaming and kicking right from the start. I was really in awe and distress in witnessing this C-section, so much in fact that I could not tell Geena that we had a baby girl, in spite of my promise to be the first to tell her the sex of the baby. A few days later we left the Kansas City hospital with Jasmine, and we went to the Dairy Queen in the Leawood section of Kansas City to celebrate our new baby. I was happy.

But at home a new demon materialized in my soul. I felt an intense jealousy when Geena would breast-feed Jasmine, so much so that I would pressure Geena into terminating the feeding sooner than she wanted. My God, what a lamentable thing to do! A baby knows when to stop nursing, but, no, I was there to tell Jasmine when to stop. I was sick in my soul. At that time I did not even question why it was that I was feeling this way; it was a natural feeling, I thought, that had to do with the "real" situation in front of me: in *fact* our baby was sucking too much milk. Too much milk, clearly. I felt strongly that my objection was legitimately based on a justifiable concern that Jasmine was spending too much time at Geena's breast. I had no intuition and no introspective need to ask myself why I would feel this way when my own infant daughter was simply drinking her milk from her mother's breast. But the fact remains that I was jealous and angry at my own baby. I feel so sick in admitting the extent of my total spiritual depravity. Jealous at my own baby!

Why? That Jasmine was drinking "too much" from the breast was my own disturbed interpretation of what I was feeling about the breastfeeding, which I would watch with *intense jealousy*. At that point in time I was, I suppose, like most people not introspective enough to wonder about the causes of their emotions. But some years later, when my eyes were opened, I questioned (maybe even compulsively) almost every emotion and behavior in my past. This particularly strong feeling of jealousy, which I came to question most intently, contributed to the demise of my relationship with Geena many years later.

Remember the story about my feeling jealous when the baby *hamsters* suckled their mother? How sick of me to get jealous at baby hamsters! I felt the same then as I did in 1976 when my daughter Jasmine suckled Geena. The emotive responses to the two scenes were identical! What was going on in the deep chambers of my soul? What primordial or infantile instinct or memory did the suckling scene connect to? What sick or pathological pattern was called forth by this? I know it is not normal for fathers to feel this type of intense jealousy at their baby suckling.

I was a very sick infant masquerading as an intelligent grown man. What shame came upon my heart years later when I entered therapy. What a disgusting human being I had become—competing with my infant daughter for my wife's breast. Someone should have killed me, for I really was not human, I was a monster from hell, a totally sick and depraved maggot, a vampire set upon the earth to torment those unfortunates who happened to cross paths with me.

When I entered therapy in 1985 I was shocked to learn of the multitude of symptoms which had invaded by psyche throughout my life, this jealousy having been one. Apparently somewhere deep inside my soul (psyche) there was a part of me that regarded Geena as a mother (here we go again with this sickness), so much so that I felt an infantile possessiveness towards her breast, even against my own baby daughter. This interpretation can also help explain why I felt profoundly lonely and abandoned when Geena would get mad at me, so much so that I felt that I had to use illicit sex to drown out this overwhelming despair. This strong feeling of jealousy was obviously not under my control for there was nothing that I could do to stop its manifestation within me as soon as my eyes saw Jasmine on Geena's breast. My reaction was as automatic as the combustion of gasoline when a match is lit next to it, and neither I nor the gasoline had a choice about igniting under those conditions. The one thing that I could have done, in retrospect, was to leave the situation immediately or beforehand so that the scene would not distress me; but, at that time I did not have the knowledge or the wisdom about what was happening to me nor the ethical foundation to behave appropriately in spite of my personal feelings about the situation. Because of my own issues, I unjustly caused distress and discomfort to my wife Geena and my infant daughter Jasmine. As I look back at how my infantile heart attached itself to Geena, I can see that in spite of the pathology, it was a vast improvement over how I had related to my first wife Katherine, for with her I exhibited a constellation of behaviors typical of a two-year-old. Furthermore, even though I still would have problems with sexual and appropriate boundaries with my children, they would be less severe than with my first-born, Sarah.

In spite of my feelings of jealousy, I very much loved and enjoyed our baby. I'd help care for her in every way. I would feed her the bottle (!), I would change her diaper, carry her all over town in my arms, bathe her, play with her, cuddle her, take pictures of her. No matter how cranky she got I found I had the patience to carry her around or deal with her in whatever way was necessary for her care. I was loving (almost) every minute of Jasmine's babyhood.

Sometimes she would get on everyone's nerves because she suffered from colic, as the pediatrician said. But when she was not in pain she redeemed herself by cooing and playing with all of us. As soon as she began to crawl she did something unusual: backwards crawling! That earned her the nickname of "Cruise-o-matic" which we all affectionately called her. Because she liked pickles we then switched to "The Pickle Lady." And her first solid food was Mexican refried beans. She loved them. We loved her. In this respect we were all happy.

So Geena and I persisted with our relationship in spite our terrible fights, my jealousy of the breast, and my rampant infidelity. Soon we bought a modest house on which Geena and I worked hard to redecorate and improve. Jasmine was up and running, and even at age one was showing a solid, hardy body (the refried beans, no doubt!) that earned her the additional nickname of "The Mack Truck." And soon Geena was pregnant again. This time she and I decided to legalize what we had been doing for more than a year and tie the knot. In February of 1978, Geena, seven months pregnant, and I got married in a private ceremony performed at our own home by a female Methodist minister. Jasmine and Sarah, and Geena's sister Julia were witnesses. I can truly say that I felt very happy marrying Geena.

In May of 1978, early hours of the morning: blond, blue-eyed Gabriela was born very quietly at the East Kansas State University Medical Center. She too was a joy to my heart, and I carried her in my arms wherever we went, showering her with more kisses than the Mexican pinto beans Jasmine loved to eat. I was thoroughly delighted with my three daughters.

Meanwhile, I was becoming supremely bored and unhappy at the college for the curriculum was too elementary and the salary was pitiful. Through hard work at publishing I had already been promoted to Associate Professor and awarded tenure, yet my feelings and my professional goals started to change—I started feeling that academia did not mean much to me for I had an inner restlessness growing daily inside me. Wife, three kids, and the same miserable university salary. I was growing professionally but not financially. I knew I wanted money—lots of money, maybe even millions of dollars. Yes, I knew I was destined to be a millionaire, that being a professor at a university was kidstuff, that it was meaningless, that it was a useless profession. Big cars, large home, European vacations, money to burn: That is what I was wishing for all along. Money, money, money. That was my new focus in life. Money, money, money. Forget history and teaching. Money, money, money. My sights were set way beyond the horizon on humongous amounts of power, prestige, and money. "I want it all no matter what it takes to get it."

The years-long desire that I had had for enormous amounts of money was reaching a fever-pitch and obsessive-compulsive intensity in 1978. My narcissistic ego-balloon was inflating at a rapidly without my knowing that it was even there. And all the while I truthfully thought that I was "highly motivated," "ambitious," "a hard worker," "going places," "a doer not content with the status quo," "a person with enormous potential," a "go getter," "one who produces results," a "high achiever," and someone "not born to have only mediocre material things in life." I had become obsessed with money and possessions; they were to be acquired at any cost and by using people to advance my goals. My inner selfishness was expanding seemingly on a weekly basis. I did not know it then but the "achievement motivation" which undoubtedly helped me to survive through grammar school and later propelled me through graduate school, was of the "jungle survival" kind: that is, it was good to me for it helped me to cope with the hell of my childhood, but unfortunately it became anachronistic in my adulthood, a continuation of a strategy of psychological survival "by any means necessary." I was a supreme Narcissist. Nothing could stop me.

Was this real? Was I taking a realistic view of the future and our goals? Or was I becoming more emotionally unstable?

This drive to "achieve" some "higher level" of performance proved to be fateful in my life, for it prompted me to take very risky steps which later turned out to be disastrous. If I had only known.

But there was also another factor which silently but relentlessly kept influencing how I related to Geena and how I planned for the future: My jealousy of Geena for having a family of origin while I essentially had none. My children were now growing up with *one* grandmother, Geena's mother. I deeply and spiritually resented that I did not have a mother to be a grandmother to my children. Why did Geena's mother have to be *the* grandmother of my children? Why did Geena have brothers and a sister who could be uncles and an aunt to my children while my own brothers and sisters were faraway in Texas and essentially unavailable emotionally to my children? I had no family I could proudly show to my children and make part of their lives! It was the same pathetic jealousy which had stressed my relationship to Katherine; it was now raising its ugly head again in my life. Unfortunately for our marriage, I unjustifiably directed some of this existential and spiritual anger at Geena. She was innocent; her crime was that she had a family of origin while I did not. Her crime was that she breastfed our children. Maybe she means to aggravate me, I thought. Yes, she deliberately wants to put me down. She wants to humiliate me. Yes, that's it—she wants to destroy me! But nobody does that to the Macho Chicano. Nobody!

In the years since I had left high school (1964) I had made many attempts to reestablish relationships with all my brothers and sisters, including all my aunts (Julieta, Sonia, Marisa) and my Uncle Felipe, but the results were always the same: There was no family love there, only the vague notion that we had all come from the same "family" (or the same litter of hyenas). But I stubbornly persisted in "reigniting" brotherly love among us all, not realizing until many years later that there never was any real affection among us. In this area too, my intense overwhelming desire to "have a family of origin" blinded me to the truth before my eyes: We had never bonded as a family, so there never were spiritual and emotional forces that tied us together. My long trips to visit my "relatives" were based more on a profound "need to belong" than on feelings of family ties. I discovered this too late, and along the way I made critical life decisions based on this delusion about the family I thought

I had. I ended up suffering greatly for it. Geena and the babies suffered too. It proved to be a destructive force.

These two new demonic forces inside me—my narcissistic need to climb to greater heights, and my desire to move to San Antonio to be near my (pretend) relatives—combined to prompt me in 1978 to consider leaving academia and go into the business world to make "millions." I was convinced that with the "right plan" I could succeed at anything, even in the business world, which was totally foreign to me. In early 1978, I discussed with Geena my thoughts about moving the family to San Antonio and going into business; she gave her support as long as we seriously considered moving to her native Oklahoma at some point in the future.

It was not easy deciding on a "career" in business, for I had not taken a single business course while in college and was totally ignorant of all business principles. Yet (delusionally) I "knew" that I would find a solution to this problem, something that was confirmed to me when I was having a conversation with a "friend" of mine who was a real estate agent. Over coffee he gave me the complete description of what it would take to earn a living selling homes and businesses, making big commissions. I knew I had found the answer.

From Kansas City I started contacting real estate firms in San Antonio, determined to make my crazy dream come true. Most were not hiring new trainees for their firms, but I did find one willing to put me through some aptitude tests to determine if I had the "right personality" for the job. Within a month they had accepted me and asked me when I could start.

In November 1978 we sold our house, packed up our cheap furniture, and I, with dreams of millions (or billions) of dollars ahead, left Kansas City en route to San Antonio. It was all for the wrong reasons. I was just spiraling down into a world of madness. It was the beginning of the end for Geena and me.

Chapter Eleven
The Downward Spiral

$\mathbf{P}$erhaps I went into the business world in San Antonio because I already had delusions of omnipotence and grandiosity about achievement and future wealth, yet the gestalt of the high-powered real estate office where I was stationed, and the fairy-tale-like optimism of the training sessions, added significantly to my delusional notion that if I set my mind to it I could achieve any goal and any level of wealth on the face of the Earth. I feel now that, quite paradoxically, it may have been necessary to be delusional in order to generate internally the vast amount of energy and motivation that this high-stress job required, and to avoid becoming disenchanted or even despairing by the enormous amount of rejection that was part and parcel of our daily sales presentations. Potential workers who were contemplating coming into the business but who may not have been delusional probably saw the true torture and rejection and uncertainty that went along with any sales presentation, and opted to seek a career elsewhere. That left only the egomaniacs like myself who endured the torturous "aptitude tests" which were routinely administered: Maybe only the truly greedy, the narcissistic super-achievers, the obsessive-compulsives, the bipolars on a manic high, the hyperactive workaholics, and the grandiosely delusional could stomach that torture and the grand over-optimism of the indoctrinating training programs.

Yes, I was enjoying a great degree of success because I was taught to be ruthless in my sales presentations, to "take no prisoners," to never take "no" for an answer, to address every objection as an impediment to my financial success, and to extract some benefit out of every sales call and home presentation. Even my family could be used as an incentive, for some trainers suggested that we place a photograph of our children on our desks and think about them when we felt bouts of depression or disillusionment about the torrent of rejections of that day, for the problem of rejection was a real one that affected each of us in different ways, especially us newer agents who had not yet developed a wide base of "repeat" customers.

Motivation to achieve. Desire to succeed in sales. Ability to stay focused on my goals. Unflinching belief in my ability to make the sale. Concern for the potential home or commercial business buyer. Professional desire to learn more to serve the customer better. Professional ability to present a home well so that customer may benefit from it. Professional ability to regard even unproductive cold calls as productive since the next call may produce the sale. This is what the surface picture showed, and I believed most of it at the time. In reality the truth was quite disturbing as I realized many years later.

There was little or no respect for the customers but they were treated well insofar as they brought commission money into the firm; those commercial customers who bought more often were sent Christmas cards and bottles of wine or other small gifts on special occasions. Customers had value as long as they permitted us agents to define their view of the investment property world; that is, they were treated as children who were told what to do with their money and were regarded as hostile if they challenged our sales presentations. Customers were not respected as human beings but were rather seen as pawns to be used for the purposes of the property brokerage firm. Yet we lived with the delusion that "the customer comes first." Not so. The customer came last after the needs of the firm and the agent had been met. In fact, this sales philosophy fit me well because it was very similar to the techniques of seduction I had been using for many years on women: Flatter them and tell them whatever they want to hear to get them in bed, in very small steps.

Professional desire to succeed in sales, to stay focused, to learn more about properties to better serve our customers? Hardly professional. All knowledge that we gathered about homes and properties and about the customer was used *against* the customer to whittle down his resistance to the sales pitch. Product information sheets routinely accentuated the *attributes* of the property that could push the *buying* hot buttons of the customer, and deemphasized the risks of the investment which could jeopardize the sale. The "professional" part was how we expertly seduced the customer into buying what we wanted him or her to buy.

With my clearer perspective in the present time I can say that in a very real sense we were seducing our customers in a manner not so different from how *Don Juan* seduced young women to fulfill his own selfish desires. Like the sexual seducer, we wanted the victim to permit us to do something to him or her. When the victim said "No!" on our initial approach we refused to stop. We were already determined that we were going to get what we wanted, so that a clear "No!" was not taken to mean "No!" Instead we came up with sweeter words to assuage the concerns of our victim, and repeated this approach over and over until the victim, or customer, gave in. Of course, there was no respect in the beginning and even less after we triumphed over this reluctant customer who made us work hard for our reward—the commission. We all did it, including our colleagues at other firms.

So the real picture was more like: Delusions. Grandiosity. Greed. Manic pursuit of the sale. Hostility towards uncooperative customers. Disrespect. Blind to our ethical follies, or, worse, unconcerned about them. Everything seemed to fit well with my pathology at the time.

Less than a year after I began my new career, I was making five times what I was making as an Associate Professor at East Kansas State University. There was no tenure in this business, only professional longevity guaranteed by my continuous production of commissions on a daily basis. No sale, no commission. No commission, no pay. There also was no way to just "coast" or "fake it", for it was crystal clear if I was doing my job or not: At the end of the month my manager would tell me that I had done well for the month, that I was a great asset to the corporation. Or, just as easily, his warm and appreciative demeanor could turn to dagger-like icicles shooting from his constricted pupils as he would ask me if I was feeling well, for he wanted to know why my sales had been so poor on that particular week or month. All of us knew that his personal liking of us was based solely on how our commission efforts lined his pockets and those of the firm. He, like all other managers I came to know, was a chameleon when it came to personal relationships. It must have been a requirement that only men with no capacity for empathy for coworkers would be considered for the position of manager. He was a snake, and I could see it in his eyes. Of course, we all were.

Soon after I had started the job I knew that anxiety would be a way of life in this business, only I did not know that it would compound my own miserable personality problems. Of course I was full of grandiose ideas, but those were my own, generated by my internal problems of self-esteem which I did not even know I had (for I was destined to make millions). When this plan of mine became externalized by the requirements of the job it created almost intolerable levels of anxiety and discomfort within my soul, for now it was the manager who was telling me that my usually good levels of commission production were no longer good enough and that I should really be producing 10 or 20 percent more. Only by the desperate determination to make more calls and more property presentations, and to be more aggressive over the phone, would I increase my production by the percentage he wanted; but my success and pride at my accomplishment would be short-lived, for almost immediately he would revise his expectations for me to produce even more. The more I produced, the more he expected of me. I was desperately chasing a rainbow on the other side of the planet. With this kind of set-up I was constantly chasing ever elusive commission production goals, I was never good enough, I could never, ever be able to say I had reached any meaningful goal. The intense pressure was unraveling my sinister personality.

As a consequence, I was no longer enjoying the high levels of production which made me one of the fastest rising stars in the office. I was not a "great producer" but a maniac broker making hundreds of phone calls a day to unappreciative "suspects" who for the most part did not want to be bothered with sales pitches about investment properties. Sure I was bringing in vast amounts of money for the firm, and my income reflected that, but I was not enjoying my accomplishments because my focus had become the absolutely unattainable "infinite income." Somewhere deep in my soul, my mental and emotional program had become that I would not rest and I would not stop to enjoy the fruits of my labor until there were no other income levels left to conquer! By default, and perhaps quite subconsciously, I was saying to myself that only "infinite income" would make me realize that I had indeed arrived at the Nirvana of my dreams: total and absolute wealth beyond the limits of all imagination. In retrospect I know it sounds sick and absurd, but at that time it was all very real to me. I actually believed I could attain infinite income, and I was desperate in my relentless perseverance of that goal. I can see now that I was going mad.

One day I was talking over the phone for the third time to a cold-call prospect I was trying to convince to buy a 25-unit apartment complex in West San Antonio. I already knew he had money, so it was just a matter of making him see that it would be to his advantage.

"But, Mr. Wells, look at it from the point of view of monthly cash flow. With these 25 units you'll easily generate about $15,000 income per month—that's $180,000 annually. Now, you did tell me last time you wanted to retire from your job with the electrical company, right?"

"Yeah, I still do, " responded Mr. Wells.

"Wouldn't it feel great to just relax at the New Braunfels Springs with your wife and collect $15,000 per month without lifting a finger?" I asked him provocatively. "And I really mean that you wouldn't have to do anything because we can also take care of property management for you."

My prospect quickly fired back: "That sounds good but I am concerned. What if property values start going down—I will lose big money here. I can't afford to lose money at my age. We just want to retire. Maybe we should just put that money in a certificate of deposit."

We were trained to always have a good comeback for any kind of objection the prospect might have concerning the sale. The manager always told us that there are no valid excuses for not buying.

"Yes, I suppose you could do that. But it would generate only about $50,000 in interest for you and your wife—that's $130,000 short of what you would be getting with the apartment building. And in just two years you would be more than one-quarter million dollars short. Do you think you could find something great to do with that kind of money?"

"Quarter-million, eh?" said Mr. Wells. I knew I was gonna get him. The word "million" turned out to be his hot button.

I continued. "Look, let's do this, Mr. Wells. Tomorrow afternoon I have a time slot open to show you the property. You don't have to buy it, you don't have any obligation. Just look at it. See how that property in just two years can start you on the way to be a millionaire. Would you prefer 4:00 or 4:30 tomorrow?"

Just like seducing a woman I was able to take little steps along the way to my goal—steps small enough that prospects often were not aware of what was happening.

It was my inability to question the absurdity of what I was trying to do that left me vulnerable and blind to the impossible demands of my managers, and which further damaged my tortured soul, making me more hostile, less accommodating, and a living hell as a husband.

Poor Geena, she was trying to live the dream with me, only I did not know that in reality there were some sick agendas behind it—it was a nightmare which neither of us recognized as such. Most of the time we felt good about each other, except when we had our monstrous arguments which I can best characterize as titanic power struggles. For whatever reason we each wanted to have things our way and unfortunately it appeared that we did not have sufficient love, respect, or integrity to serve as our spiritual bond while we worked on honest disagreements. I know for a fact that I did not respect Geena, and from her behavior I can infer that she did not respect me either. My womanizing continued unabated and unencumbered by guilt or remorse, for that had gone out the window a long time ago. Filthy and cutting words spewed from our mouths, further eroding our tenuous foundation and encasing our hearts in concrete tombs as a protection against further attack. I called her names, and she would threaten to take the children away from me. Within two years of arriving in San Antonio to chase our sick dream, we were blasting hateful verbal volleys at each other with total abandon and doing irreversible damage to our relationship. Who knows for sure where a particular battle got started, but once we locked horns there was no love, no respect, no ethics, no common bond of parenthood. We both were guided by raw animal instinct to win the battle, even if it was being fought with bayonets of fire on the sinking ship of our marriage. Maybe we saw it and maybe we didn't, but we did not seem to care that the winner would eventually stand triumphant on that burning and sinking ship that represented our delicate marriage, afloat only barely, and guided by torn sails being blown by pathological winds from the memories of pains past. I lament now that things had gotten so bad and I did not have the fortitude to do my part in correcting them. Perhaps it was the unverbalized rage that I held against Geena.

Unquestionably I inflicted horrendous damage on our marriage by my unbridled and remorseless escapades with women, something that I felt I needed like a drug. And as always it was just pure sex, for in my heart I still felt "Please Don't Ask Me To Kiss You." I could go to bed with them, yet I did not hold their hands or kiss their lips for real. Even though I did not tell Geena what I was doing I am sure that she sensed something because I never was able to tell her that I was 100 percent faithful to her. In this respect she was totally justified in feeling anger or even hatred towards me for my actions. Maybe because of this anger she threatened me dozens of times that she was going to take the children away from me (two by this time), a threat that hit me at the deepest core of my being. In spite of my being a loose narcissist with little or no ethics, I still felt very much attached to my children, the loss of which would have brought spontaneous and enormous devastation to my life. So when Geena threatened the very first time to take them away from me, I felt an extremely ugly revulsion in my heart, a debilitating dread in my heart against a demon plotting to take my children away. Of all the possible weaknesses in my soul, Geena had shrewdly zeroed in on my most fundamental one, for it centered on the extreme wretchedness of my own childhood and how years later I had bonded to my children, only to face a new Satan, a new Devil, a new betraying force which was about to open the flood gates of traumatic childhood abandonment by taking my own children away from me. Hadn't I suffered enough losses in life? Now my children? Hell had come to Earth even if it was never far from me. From that day on I felt unequivocally in my heart that I had married my worst nightmare, that The Devil had risen from his sepulchral bed, had borrowed some features from my mother's cadaver, and had come back to hunt me again, to take my children away, and to really kill me like he had planned all along. It wasn't as if I could quickly shut the door or pull the covers over my head, for all this evil was already inside my house, and I felt totally powerless against it, just as I had been as a child when relationships could never be counted on and when the forces of the universe threatened to take away what little there was to have. When I was face to face with Geena during a vicious argument and she calmly threatened me, I felt somewhere in my heart that I was face to face with the reincarnation of the supremely evil Devil and that I, even as an adult, could not defend myself. Geena's threats horrifyingly replicated the infernal agonies which I had suffered face to face as a child as the heinous Devil routinely abused our mother to the edge of death while we watched in helpless horror, not knowing if, in the aftermath, we would have a mother or a cadaver. It was this chronic heart-wrenching uncertainty about my mother being there tomorrow that had given me a perpetual anxiety about losing significant relationships, and my children were the most important relationships in my life. There was absolutely nothing that I could do to diminish the torment of the threats. I was feeling hopeless and in a deathly panic. It didn't matter that I was an adult now, for I was still a very horrified child in the middle of the night, expecting to be pulverized at any moment. My life was desperate.

To be fair about the matter, I may add that maybe Geena felt that this was her best weapon against the way I would disrespect her, the way I would treat her. Each of us felt totally justified in whatever we did or said to win our caustic arguments, even if we had to burn our house down to win.

We tried to be better with each other, enjoying good moments many times, but, often, I would have to force myself to feel positive toward Geena even days after a fight. In 1980, she had said to me that she was pregnant for the third time, news that made me feel even more insecure, for my vulnerability to her threats would then be even greater. Nonetheless, in February of 1981, our only boy, Andrew, was born. He was to be our last child.

I knew how to be a father to three girls (or I thought I did), but I had no idea how to behave toward a boy. Do I have to kiss him? Do I hug him in the same manner? Besides, I'll have to teach him how to be a "man." I wasn't sure that I knew how to do these things. In spite of my fumbling, Andrew started to develop into a nice little boy, maybe, too, because Geena made every effort to give him love and attention. She was an excellent mother. Sarah, Jasmine, and Gabriela had a good time with their baby brother. We all were happy with

Andrew, and I was happy with all my children and took them everywhere for outings, especially carnivals.

But something awful was coming to a head, as the fights between Geena and me intensified. I would work longer hours, then I would come home and make several more dozen calls from the house. We felt that we had to see another marriage counselor to determine if we could put an end to our caustic disagreements, but the several that we visited offered no help or ideas that we accepted or could work for us. Still, we kept on trying, seemingly banging our heads on the wall, maybe not being able to maturely see that our marriage was already dead.

Geena made the appointment after we agreed upon it, and we arrived with our complaints already stored in our separate bazookas ready to bring each other down in front of the counselor. Christine was in her 30s, and had a beautiful and very femininely decorated office.

"Well, I want to thank both of you for agreeing to this meeting. Just to let you know that I will not be in favor of one of you and against the other. We want this to work so I need your trust. Is that pretty clear?" asked Christine. We both nodded.

"I need to hear from each of you what the nature of the problem is, only from your perspective and not the other person's. Who wants to go first?" Geena and I looked at each other and understood it was OK if she went first.

"There are so many things wrong—I really don't know where to begin. We fight all the time, but Victor says it's just because I want to win no matter what. But he's very selfish, always going out with his women. His voice is very loud, he looks at me with hate in his eyes, he wants to intimidate me. I'm a career woman but he has never respected that. I'm just tired of it all."

After Geena finished, Christine waited the better part of a minute to see if Geena wanted to add anything, and then looked at me to let me know it was my turn.

"With the women it is true. But I need to do that and I don't know why. Geena contradicts me on everything I say even if deep down she knows she's wrong. We can't agree on anything and when we argue she threatens to take my children away from me. That is something I cannot stand. She just bosses me around. I don't like that shit."

Christine then asked both of us the question at the very center: "Why are you two still together? Do you love each other?" She looked at me waiting for an answer.

My soul was telling me that I could not possibly love the Demon who was threatening to take my children, but I also knew I had to be very careful how

I answered because it could very well be that Christine herself was another Demon in disguise waiting to collaborate with Geena to take my children away. But without honesty we cannot resolve anything. And if this session fails, Geena's hand will be strengthened. Am I assessing this correctly or am I being paranoid? No, I can't take any chances with this question or with Christine.

I answered diplomatically. "Most of the time we feel good about each other but then when we fight we don't feel like we love each other."

Then Geena exploded. "You bastard! You don't even love me, you forced me to move to San Antonio when I didn't want to, you spend money without any regard for our finances, you are always fucking those women, and you want to teach my kids to be shitty Mexicans like you!"

We were now engaged in battle in front of Christine. "Your kids? Go fuck yourself, you stupid bitch. You're the one who's always trying to control me, and threatening to take my kids if I don't do what you want! Well, fuck you!"

"No, fuck you, you chicken-shit Mexican bastard!"

The counselor ordered us to stop the verbal vollies. I can't recall how this miserable session ended—I just know we did not go a second time. We drove home without saying a single word.

The way I see it, in life if you have a secure and loving childhood, your soul will grow to be complete, beautiful, and ready to give love to another. But as an adult the soul is ready to cleanly split down the middle as we leave our parents who represent the receding half of the soul, the force that formed it. The part we are left with is strong and well formed, but spiritually it yearns to find another similar half to create the paradox of two individual halves to make the whole—the relationship. When Geena and I went to see Christine the Counselor, in essence we were asking her to help put our souls back together from the pieces we brought her—our individual halves were not even complete to begin with. There were missing pieces, and pieces which should not have been there. But not even God could have made an integral soul from the broken parts of our painful childhoods.

It was looking rather hopeless as we drifted in our own sea of disrespect and mutual spiritual attacks. I continued to demonstrate very little respect for Geena, and she increased her barrage of threats to take the children. Little did I know that my absolutely worst and catastrophic nightmare was just around the corner, waiting to tear my insides apart in a convulsive breakdown which I could never have imagined even if I had stared at the walking corpse of The Devil coming at me with a screwdriver in his hand, ready to finally plunge into in my heart, just like he had always wanted! The evil seeds were ready to sprout. Only a few final ingredients were needed to unleash their awesome, unforgiving, and ferocious power against the delicate balance holding my mind together, for the high anxiety at work and the chronic siege of the threat of losing my children were dual tormentors stabbing my throat on two fronts. Time was running out.

One day at work I received a mysterious phone call from an "agent" who refused to identify himself but who did divulge that he was working for a "very prestigious" investment property firm in the same city, a firm, he said, that was interested in talking to me about the possibility of my working for them. I felt maximally paranoid that there might be something illegal about the whole matter, so I simply said that I was not interested, and I hung up. But, before I did he mentioned that "the firm" could offer some "cash incentive" for me to transfer my clients and my efforts over to them. So I inquired with other agents, discreetly, and soon learned that—yes!—these offers were common in the industry. Other agents told me that when a broker is doing exceptionally well the word gets around and soon other firms want to entice him to switch jobs. A-ha! So now I was really interested in talking to the mystery man. *I hope he calls back!,* I thought.

Of course, he did. And he knew the business, so they would not take "No!" for an answer. This time I was prepared. The caller still refused to identify himself, asking me in a hushed tone if I was free to talk over the phone. No, there are other people in the office! "Well, could we meet at my hotel room where I can give you more details?" said the caller with a nervous voice. I had to think quickly. Was this a plot by Geena to entrap me? Was this some kind of FBI sting trying to force me to do something illegal? Could it be corporate espionage? Russian KGB agents? Undercover CIA counterespionage operatives trying to catch some foreign mole within our ranks? My greed and my paranoia ran wild and vied for supremacy and action. It took a great leap of courage and wanton suspension of my apprehension to agree to meet with this weird stranger at the other end of the line, for I even suspected that his true motive was to lure me to the hotel to kill me. But not even my life was that valuable, so I had to go there so as not to miss an opportunity to get on the boat to financial Valhalla where the Garden of the Gods sprouts billions of dollars just waiting to be harvested. Yes, I must go there! But what if? My usual paranoia made me even sicker.

The dark man had given me the address of the hotel, with instructions to ask for "Mr. Jaspers." Was that his real name? I wondered. At the front desk the clerk directed me to room 317, and I was soon on the elevator to meet either death or a golden opportunity. I could handle either, because I was "destined to make millions or billions." As the elevator stopped on the third floor, I took a deep breath so as to be ready for fight or flight should a threat appear suddenly before I got to the door. But no, there was no one on the long and dark hallway where I suspected that financial fairies mixed with the demons of quick death, for they could be one and the same for all I knew. In front of me I soon saw Room 317; I was on the threshold of something big.

One knock on the door was all it took, for a well-dressed man with a weasely face opened it as if his hand had been on the doorknob awaiting my knock. He introduced himself again, this time with a face that went with the voice over the phone. He proposed to me a deal whereby I would leave my current real estate job and immediately start with the firm he was representing. But, why would I want to leave a position where I was already making lots of money and where every month I would be making even more? He had an answer for me: His firm might consider an upfront cash bonus payable to me on day one at my new job. I agreed to meet with the executives of the new firm at a later date. The man with the mysterious face would arrange all that for me.

On the way down the elevator I actually felt proud of myself for having scored a positive on an endeavor that I was very apprehensive about, something that reinforced my longstanding belief which had helped me escape the agony of life in the Mexican ghetto: take a risk, even if all intuition points to the contrary. This had worked for me so many times, and I had a lot to show for it. Unfortunately, a short time later this dear belief of mine would cause me to make a decision which would have disastrous results for me and my family.

A few days after this secret hotel meeting an executive from the competing real company called me, identifying himself and his firm as the principals which had solicited the services of the agent whom I had met at the hotel. I agreed to meet him and his colleague at a restaurant far from the San Antonio area where there would be less of a chance of any one of us being recognized by other diners. At a very elegant restaurant all three of us met, and soon we were having lunch and discussing the vicissitudes of the investment property markets, a natural topic for us but which I suspect was brought up not because of a vocational interest but rather because the two executives wanted to gauge my level of understanding of these matters and how they impacted on how I marketed certain properties. Even though it had been a relatively short time since I had begun studying the facets of the real estate business, I knew that I had to give a grand performance, not too technical, for they would feel that I would scare away customers with jargon, and not too simplistic, for that surely would not impress sophisticated investors who generally expected their brokers to be geniuses about the international economic forces that affected their multimillion-dollar portfolios. My real attention was on *how I presented information* as well as on the content, so I followed their lead and elaborated only slightly on the topics they brought up for discussion. I must have passed the test for they then wanted to know if I would consider going to work for them immediately. Of course, in the investment property business there is no such thing as giving notice to your employer, for he would immediately confiscate all your account books. One quits the minute one gives notice, I was told, and practically runs to his new employer to call all one's current property customers to persuade them to switch investment property firms. In the meantime the former employer also calls on the same customers to tell them that the agent has left the firm but that the account will now be handled by someone who can give them even better service. It is a race to see which firm can contact and persuade as many customers as possible in the shortest length of time. I felt that it would be a very hectic and anxiety-producing event for me.

So at that lunch the executives offered me a modest bonus if I'd join their firm, and I said I would think about it. Over the next several weeks they raised their offer a bit and I finally accepted. The date of the actual move to their firm was set, leaving me plenty of time to get nervous and to tell Geena what I was planning on doing. Since we were getting plenty of money she did not protest. On the day of the big switch I was maximally prepared by having made notes about all of my clients. Then I took a deep breath and left my private office en route to my manager's. The dreaded moment was here. She was surprised that I was quitting when I was doing very well at the firm, especially since recently I had gotten a new office, a new computer, a client expense account, and a personal sales assistant. But then again, she was not surprised because she knew that good agents always got offers elsewhere. Was I going to give all that up? Yes, my mind was made up, and I needed to hurry on down to my new office with the other firm so that I could immediately call all my customers with the news of my move. Even as I was walking down the hall towards the exit I saw my manager hurrying towards my office, undoubtedly to get control of all my account books so that the remaining agents could call all my clients immediately to offer their own version of why I was leaving and then to entice them to form a new relationship with a new agent in the same office. Because none of my customers knew ahead of time of this move (I dared not take the risk of informing my clients ahead of time for fear of the news leaking out prematurely, for then surely I would have been fired, effectively cutting my bargaining position in half in future negotiations with a new firm.), I then had to literally run to my new office to begin the frantic job of calling my hundreds of clients before my former colleagues did. All my old "friends" at my former real estate agency, those whom I socialized with, joked with, and lunched with, were now my enemies, for friendship would have meant that they would not touch my clients. Since they could make lots of money by calling my clients, they, in effect, chose to steal my clients and forego the friendship with me. Bottom line: All these friendships were for the moment, and another Brutus would take another stab if there was money in it. It truly was a dog-eat-dog-eat-master world.

After hundreds of telephone calls I was able to reach most of my clients, persuading most to switch firms so that I could remain as their real estate property investment manager. Then came the tedious job of transferring vast amounts of investment assets which my former firm held as agent for my customers. After about two months of laboring through all the details of hundreds of transfers, I could finally settle down to the job of raking in the commissions, which was the only reason why my new employer hired me anyway.

At home we started using the money to buy things that we had been wanting for some time, like a lawn mower, an electronic sewing machine for Geena, and a new car for me. One day I surprised Geena by driving her to a nice neighborhood in town and telling her that we were going to buy the nice house with the little brook in the backyard. We were definitely awash with cash, allowing us to take vacations almost weekly, something that the kids soon dubbed "two-door motels" because we would get adjoining rooms, and preferably the bridal suite with as large a living room as possible. This was the life.

Not surprisingly, this enormous financial success served to buttress my belief that I was invincible, that my next switch to another firm would be for a bonus of *several million dollars in cash*, that all I needed to do to realize my (narcissistic) dream of having infinite income was to continue to amass a larger base of clients who would then be persuaded to buy, thus bringing in more commissions for my firm and strengthening my image and subsequent bargaining position in the future. Day in and day out, I would have even wilder dreams of bigger accounts, larger transactions, and even more stratospheric take-home commissions. No doubt about it, the future was *glorious*, just there waiting for me to reach out and take it. I was on the way there; I was on the train to heaven on Earth. Who wants just a BMW? How can we possibly be content with our spacious five-bedroom home in a clean, quiet neighborhood where the kids can bicycle to their hearts' delight? And "two-door motel" vacations only once a week? How cheap! No! We need more. There is more to be had. There *are* bigger homes, aren't there? How about ten bedrooms and some huge acreage? My BMW? After a few months I got bored with it so I gave it to Geena, who was all too happy to drive it down the interstate on cruise. I got another brand-new luxury car. And for vacation how about *buying* the motel instead of just renting it? I know I was meant for more; why settle for only mediocre status? That huge account is just around the corner. The millions will start rolling in pretty soon. Need to brush up on European cities. Need to take the kids on a voyage around the world. Two-hundred cities, minimum. Vast riches soon enough.

Yes, I was invincible. I had the magic touch in sales. I could convince anyone to buy anything at any time. And since the rejection that was intrinsic to the sales job did not bother me, I could simply go on and on selling, not feeling anything underneath. Infinite power, infinite wealth. I even had my business cards with me during my "off" days (which weren't too many) so that I could hand them out to people I met at restaurants, at the mall, even at turnpike ticket booths. No opportunity would be lost, for every person on the planet Earth was a potential client and thus a potential source of commission money and wealth for me. It was a sickeningly grandiose fantasy that permeated all my waking moments.

But with all the cash came responsibility, which I did not have. At every opportunity I spent money without the slightest regard for the future—and without any adherence to a budget. It was an intoxicating experience to have thousands of dollars per week, plus the upfront bonus from my firm. Never in my life had I had so much money. For me, the Mexican kid who came from the hunger-stricken neighborhoods of El Paso, Texas, this amount of money was beyond what I had imagined possible just a few years earlier. All throughout my childhood we had struggled with just a few dollars a month, eating bricks, Catholic communion wafers for lunch, and filthy scavenger pigeons for supper, so there never was a need to budget our dollars, for we spent them on food, water, and, if any were left over, on the electric bill. Having a budget was alien to our family as well as to the hundreds of other destitute families in our area. As is the case with any family living on the edge with even the basic necessities missing from their lives, money becomes an obsession or fixation, something connected to a highly volatile impulse which immediately comes to the surface as soon as one has money. Rational expenditure of funds is unheard of, for, in a person who comes from poverty, it's the emotional side that's in "control" when it comes to money rather than the more logical, rational side. The emotional, histrionic, impulsive, irrational side: That was me. I had no idea at all about how to manage my own money, and here I was "managing" the millions of other peoples' investment property monies. How ironic. How pitiful.

Actually, there was a part of me, the "rational" part, which did know how to manage funds, but it was typically overruled by my irrational, impulsive side which always wanted to buy whatever my whim desired, papering the problem over by rationalizations about how I "truly needed" that something, or, worse, denying to myself that there even was a need for a budget. In this fashion we were spending thousands of dollars per month on frivolous products and services when we should have been saving our money in a more rational manner. I was so blind but happy to spend the dollars which I had so desperately wished for as a child. A little bit late, but they had finally arrived; the wishful child in me had some dreams to catch up on.

Of course, at that time I did not understand these psychodynamics within me—I just felt an enormous impulse and desire to spend money any way I wanted to. Not surprisingly, Geena disagreed with me on many of my financial decisions, leading to more combat between us. Just one more thing to argue about.

Quite ironically, as I was reaching ever higher levels of commission production and income I was also feeling more paranoid, sometimes even simultaneously with my grandiose feeling about myself. That is, I felt that I could achieve any goal, yet I also had an uneasy feeling that it was *not I* who was producing these wonderful commissions for which I was loudly praised by my manager. Deep inside me was a voice (or a realization) that I did not deserve this kind of success. It was as if I had an internal saboteur always telling me that I was not good enough for this, that my new success would soon crumble. In fact, on two or three occasions I told Geena that she should not get too comfortable with our opulent lifestyle because "the whole thing can come crashing down at any time." Understandably, she was perplexed. I was truly concerned about my doubts which seemed to be at work to undermine my grandiosity. Grandiosity, paranoia, doubts, immense greed, irresponsibility, narcissism, power struggles, pathologically high need for sex with Geena and other women—my God, I was getting worse, I was going insane. The convulsive climax was near.

Somewhere along my way to financial success I also became progressively less tolerant of Geena as she became more entrenched in her positions on practically everything in our lives. As I grew disenchanted with my new firm because their departments did not perform as they said they would, Geena began to hound me about us moving to Oklahoma to be closer to her parents. It never occurred to me at that time, but she too found our marital situation unbearable and wanted the comfort of being closer to her parents. In my unabated paranoia I simply thought she was trying to make life hard for me. That was indeed unfortunate.

While I complained to corporate headquarters about the terrible service that several accounting departments were giving my customers, I was coming to realize that in this firm I could not make the millions or billions of dollars that I was absolutely destined to make. My honeymoon at the new firm was short-lived. I knew I had made the wrong move, but it was too late to do anything about it. All the real estate companies in San Antonio knew of my decision to leave my first employer for the second one, so I knew that if I did not make this current position work I would have a hard time finding a new employer.

One day Geena was more ugly and cold than she had ever been in our life together. She might as well have been a walking cadaver. Her expression sent chills down my spine and struck terror in my heart for I knew somewhere inside me that there had been a fundamental change in her attitude towards me and our marriage—and it was not for the better. But everything about the rapidly sinking dream depended on us getting along and acting cooperatively, even if only on the surface, for I knew that we were like two massive continents inexorably and abrasively moving past each other, driven by titanic forces which neither of us understood or recognized. Her face made me sick. Her face was the look of doom. I knew that deep inside me was a scream of terror, a torrent of panic, a feeling that my disturbed personality would soon unravel. It was as if I could no longer keep the door closed against the army of demons that my insecure and stressed life had awakened. Their evil and guttural growls made my knees weak and my stomach nauseous. They were knocking louder and louder at my door! *Yes, they have come to disembowel me!*

Chapter Twelve

The Final Collapse

Under Siege From All Fronts: The Volcanic End

Worsening conditions at work made me ever more irritable, leading perhaps to even more frequent and more bitter fights with Geena. She continued to threaten me as always. This made me resent her to the point of hatred. If we had had a warm and honest relationship we would have presented a united front towards all our problems, but our energies were fiercely divided, and oftentimes we did things that undercut each other when we should have been supportive. My pitbull boss had begun to illegally withhold my commissions because he felt that our department should be doing a lot better, an act that put immediate financial strain on me because of the considerable mortgage which I had to pay on our very large home.

All the while Geena kept criticizing me about my inability to solve these financial problems, something which made me feel that indeed I had no value left in the relationship. The crowning statement from her came a few months later when, after more financial setbacks, she told me, "You deeply disappoint me."

Those words haunted me for years because I interpreted them to mean that she had stayed with me that long because of the continuing stream of material rewards that she was receiving as a result. Of course, I was no prize as a husband, but it did hurt to hear those words coming from her mouth. At the very least it drove another wedge between us, preventing me from speaking to her openly about the panic that was engulfing me. I was all alone in facing the mounting problems. And I guess that Geena must have felt alone too, married to a paranoid man with the cold stare.

Then came the catastrophe. In late summer of 1984 the real estate firm fired me when I pressured them into paying me the commissions which they had illegally withheld from me. Soon we put our house on the market, we lost Geena's BMW coupe, my luxury car, our real estate investments in Florida, our stock investment portfolio, my pension plan, and whatever cash we had left. Never in my life as an adult had I felt as powerless as I did when all the financial dominoes around me started to topple each other, and there was no one whom I felt I could turn to. I trusted no one to empathize with my situation, and indeed none of my relatives came forth to offer even moral support. At that point my inner tension was proportional to the discrepancy between my dream of having millions, or perhaps infinite wealth, and my realization that my dream lay in total ruin and devastation. To make matters even more personally painful, this cataclysm had unfolded dead center near my relatives, all of whom I had impressed with years of accomplishments and even higher expectations for the future. Finally, I could not legitimately continue to point out to Geena that my "judgment" was always correct when I wanted to do something that she disapproved of. It was a colossal failure on all fronts for me.

Not surprisingly we filed for bankruptcy—my second in my impulsive life—to attempt to save at least our house. But it was not to be, for whatever equity we had was soon consumed by the arrears in payments, which were considerable. From millions (billions in my dreams) to bankruptcy. It was hard to believe this was happening. Maybe my mental health was getting even worse. Well, there was the continuing problem with the cat.

We had this tan cat with a very dark, almost black face which we kept inside the house and which I did not particularly like. At about the same time when all these marital and financial problems were exploding, something very peculiar started to happen, although at that time I did not understand what it was. As if I did not have enough problems, the cat started to make fun of me. Yes, for real—laughing at me, and talking behind my back. When I looked straight into its eyes I felt that those eyes were staring at me defiantly, almost as if she too wanted to mock me in my time of woe. I know it sounds weird, but it's true. And I could sense without any doubt that she was just laughing inside, laughing at me! Never before in my life had I seen that in an animal, so I was frightened and angry at the beast for daring to look at me in that manner.

There, she did it again. Did you see it? Oh, my God, what's happening?

"Stupid!" I heard the cat say. Yes, for real. And then she said, "Loser!"

She's looking straight at me and laughing because of my problems. How did she learn to humiliate me? Keep your eyes on her because... Look! Now she's sticking her tongue out at me. Why? Why is she tormenting me?

When I turned my head away from her I heard her laugh at me again!

Fuck off, you chicken-shit Mexican bastard!

Why is she doing this?...

Even though I suspected that it was just my way of interpreting things, my feelings told me that indeed this cat was "trying" to be defiant and was also laughing at me. Was I just imagining this, or was I now fully mad? As a consequence of that feeling, I would kick her when I had a chance, something which I knew I should not be doing. But she kept laughing at me, for real! Imagine that—even the cat was laughing at me. It is quite sobering for me to now look back at this psychotic episode in my life and realize the degree of moral turpitude and pain which had engulfed my life so completely at that time.

Poor cat, she was not the one who was psychotic; she just happened to live in the house of pain. But maybe not! She definitely was sneering at me. I just knew it. I highly suspected that it was Geena who put her up to it.

Our arguments got uglier by the day, our power struggles more strident. Geena's threats were coming more frequently, more viciously. My fear, my distress, my panic intensified. Our children were witnessing our obnoxious battles, and in spite of our loving them we were still using them in our power struggles, for whatever Geena ordered me to do with them I would do practically the opposite, as when I permitted them to sit with me and watch violent action movies on TV. Against my better judgment I did that to have them next to me, for there was no one else to feel close to. Then I failed again in exercising proper judgment, resulting in an incident in the bathtub.

As had been my ignorant custom on occasion, I would take showers or baths with the kids, and aside from the events which I already detailed in the case with Sarah, there were no incidents of any kind with Andrew, Gabriela, or Jasmine as they were growing up. But sometime in 1985 in San Antonio I was taking a bath fully naked in the jacuzzi with all three kids while Geena came in and out of the master bathroom several times. After about 30 minutes two of my kids got out to shower while one of the girls remained behind. Within about a minute she started soaping my penis, something that I should have stopped immediately since I felt that she should not be permitted to do that. But somehow I did not have the fortitude or courage to do it, for at the same time my penis started to become partially erect, which scared me but which again I did not stop. At that time Geena came into the master bathroom, saw what was happening, and said that we should both get out of the jacuzzi. I felt embarrassed about what had happened although I did not even think about the possible emotional damage to my daughter. I did not give this any more thought until some weeks later when another nuclear-bomb's worth of emotional upheaval would stop our moribund household from continuing in its present form.

I also began to lose my temper more easily with my children and started to hit them with my leather belt on their legs, leaving welt marks. I always apologized to them afterwards, but I would end up doing it again and again when they did something that irritated me. Oftentimes I would secretly lament my actions, but I dared not confide in Geena so that we could talk about it, for I feared that she would throw it in my face at the next argument. Instead we just became polarized on this issue, just as we had on the hundreds of others which had brought us to this totally ruinous situation in what was to be the crowning glory of all my (narcissistic) achievements in the great city of San Antonio.

Geena Sees the Therapist, Alone

As I have said before, Geena and I had consulted several counselors but none of them were able to provide us with any substantive help we could benefit from given the sorry state of our trust and willingness to accommodate each other. In early 1985 Geena told me that she was going to go see a counselor by herself, and I responded that I did not care either way. She had been reading some counseling books and had gotten some ideas about how to improve herself if not the marriage. About two weeks later she told me that her therapist wanted to meet with both of us at the next meeting. Immediately I felt very suspicious if not outright paranoid, thinking that Geena had already succeeded in advancing her viewpoint with the therapist and that I was being invited not so much to help improve the marriage but for the therapist to see for herself what a wretched individual I was. In spite of the insufferable calamities which were already heavy upon my heart and sense of self (or what little I had), I accepted the invitation on the outside chance that we could work something out. That's not what happened.

On the day of the meeting, Geena and I behaved rather coldly towards each other—as usual by now—but managed to get there, in North San Antonio, with no incident. Glenda Watson, who appeared to be in her thirties, was pleasant enough. She asked us to sit down on the floral design sofa in her nicely decorated office. I must have repressed the initial stages of our conversation for I do not remember just who said what, yet I do recall the ugly manner in which I blew up at Glenda towards the end, rabidly raising my voice:

"I know why you called me in here. Both of you bitches want to join forces against me! I know the God-damned plan you have to sink me. You want me to kiss your dirty feet as the price for not calling the social workers because of what happened in the bathtub, right? Don't look surprised—you're both bitches and you know it. Both of you should just fuck yourselves, you bitches!"

She calmly diffused the situation, but I was still angry at her as we walked out. It had been an ugly meeting, which was also obvious from the manner in which she and Geena exchanged glances as we left (or was I being paranoid?). I did not know it but the stage was now set for the last leg of our paper empire to break, sending us all in a maximum state of crisis.

May 1985. My oldest daughter Sarah, still back in New Jersey with her mother Katherine, was graduating from high school and she wanted me to attend the ceremonies. The mutual suspicions between Geena and me were at an explosive level, enough to keep my stomach churning almost on a 24-hour basis. Geena began to sleep upstairs and our level of communications was the worst that it had been in all our ten years of hellish marriage. My instincts told me that something terrible was in the works, that a catastrophic event would finish whatever we had left of the empire, of our marriage, as sick as it already was. Sarah's invitation put me in a very difficult position since I did not trust Geena to maintain the status quo if I went for a few days to New Jersey for Sarah's graduation. Yet I also did not want to miss this very important event in my daughter's life. So I kissed Andrew, Gabriela, and Jasmine, and with a horrible feeling of doom in my stomach I boarded the plane to Jersey, as if I was going somewhere and I was not sure that I would be alive much longer. That final minute before I had left our home-for-sale in San Antonio was to be the last we all ever spent as a family.

Sarah's 1985 high school graduation was a joyous event. My ex-wife Katherine, looking prettier than ever, was there with her new husband and two kids. She had always been courteous to me after our divorce in 1969. Although I was enjoying every moment of it and reminiscing about my own graduation from high school in 1964, I nevertheless could not help but wonder just how my other three children were doing in San Antonio. During the next two days I made several phone calls to our house in San Antonio but the phone would ring unanswered. I knew something was wrong, and my level of paranoia increased several fold and my nausea was constant. I even attempted to move up the date of my departure to San Antonio, but there were no available flights. My stomach was getting sick from the tension. I did not sleep for three days in Jersey.

"Where Are My Children?"

Tuesday, June 5, 1985. I shall never forget that date. The plane ride from Newark International Airport to San Antonio had been uneventful except for my near panic state imagining the worst. From the terminal I ran to my car, which I had left in long-term parking, and raced down to our house. As I pulled into the driveway, I felt that the moment of truth was just a few seconds away. Were my children going to be there so that I could kiss them, or was Satan waiting to carry me down to hell as he had been threatening for the last ten years? I knew I had to open the door and meet the fate which had already been decided for me one way or another. With extreme dread and trembling hands, I was like a child making himself open his eyes in the dark to see if the monsters are still there. I inserted my key into the door and flung it open. *Horror! Satan had been there!*

I had just opened the door into my worse possible nightmare! Death was preferable! Torture, dismemberment, decapitation, and death were preferable! I needed to die! The Demons of Crisis and despair were upon me, inflicting a level of pain that up until now existed only in the abandoned child who still lived in the deep recesses of my subconscious. Whatever defenses I had had, they were destroyed instantly by the momentous realization that my children were gone! Gone! No longer a fear but a catastrophic reality.

The door opened into the kitchen, which was bare—Geena had taken the furniture and my children. But maybe it was not so. Like a madman I quickly ran to other rooms only to painfully reconfirm my initial realization. Empty. Old boxes here and there, but the furniture was all gone. I ran to the children's bedrooms. Empty. Where are their little clothes? Gone! My pain was like no other that I had felt before, including when my mother died. Waves and waves of uncontrollable despair and extreme panic overcame me as I searched the empty house for my children, hoping that I had somehow neglected to check a closet or corner of a room. But no. It was empty. They were gone. The despair boiled over into total panic as if my children had been kidnapped by a terrorist and I would never see them alive again. Where are my children? *Where are my children?* For the first time in my life, I was in total and paralyzing panic, total despair, and in a profound psychological crisis which made every other pain in my life seem so insignificant. My physical agitation was such that I was hyperventilating, so I dropped to the floor and I wept and sobbed and wailed and vomited as I never had in my life. My children were gone. My putrid life was over.

Deep in my heart I knew that Geena had taken our children to Oklahoma City as she had threatened to do many times. I had passed out on the floor and came to after a few hours, mustering enough energy to get up again and make several more rounds of the house, just to make sure that I had not missed anything. Empty. Pictures, furniture, kitchenware, books. My children's beds. Gone. On the kitchen counter I found a short unsigned note by Geena stating something about going away and taking the kids. My reaction was: Fuck you. You can go away but leave my kids here. I finally got the idea to call one of my local cousins, and she confirmed that Geena had taken the kids to Oklahoma City. On the 20th round of the empty house I found a booklet by the Texas Department of Social Services addressed to me informing me that a complaint had been filed concerning my abuse of my children, and that I should contact the indicated social worker for more information. Immediately I called but they said they could not tell me anything, that I would have to go to their downtown offices get more information. That added to my panic, for now I had a dreaded social service agency on the case. If there ever was any time to die, this was it. My despair and sense of loss were incalculable. It felt hopeless. Not even my narcissistic delusions could save me. Will I ever see my children again? Can I talk to my children now? Where are my babies? I miss them. I know Geena hates me, so she will never let me see them again. What will happen when four-year-old Andrew says, "Daaaaaaaddyyyyyy," in the morning and I am not there to rush to his bed to pick him up and kiss him? And who is going to take Gabriela and Jasmine to the playgrounds and carnivals if I am not there? It was time to die. Life should not be like this.

I must have collapsed on the floor again because when I woke up it was already night-time, at around ten. I should have stayed unconscious since I began to cry uncontrollably as soon as I woke up. Too much pain. Too many losses. My children were the only human beings on the entire earth whom I truly loved and for whom I gladly toiled. There was no one else to trust. I could serve them without fear of betrayal. I enjoyed loving them. There was no one else to trust. Too much pain. I was hoping that I would not wake up again as I started passing out again. The Devil had my children.

The next morning I woke up on the floor, drained, with my stomach full of acid and an awful knot in my throat. Only after about an hour did I muster enough energy to lift my wretched body off the floor only to realize that I had to deal with this catastrophic situation all over again. The panic and horror of the previous day had given way to general tremors throughout my body, as if I had the extreme chills of malaria. Several times I dialed a number on the phone, but my trembling hands made it difficult to get the number right. Still I felt that Geena's hatred would make it practically impossible for me to ever see my children again, for I now knew that she was fully capable of carrying out her threat to take them and to never let me see them again. Without my children life was hopeless. Everything else could be replaced. Who cares about BMWs or millions of dollars? Who cares about having a big house? What good is a home if the children are gone? Did they miss me? What were they told about the clandestine move? Everything under the sun was replaceable except my children. There was not much point in going on without them.

Wednesday, June 6, 1985. My inner despair was deepening by the hour. Within my soul I was feeling my children were dead. My "relatives" were not much help, as I had expected. No one to trust. Even opening my eyes was painful for in front of me I saw the raw devastation of our lives and our family. All my children were gone. All the cars were gone. All the furniture was gone. All my night stories were gone forever. Through the years I had invented hundreds of bedtime stories for them—all featuring a magical coffee shop where one could order anything in the world... No more *Coffee Shop* stories for my children.

I had to get a grip. My car now was a ten-year-old Chevy. Since losing my job I had sold most of our valuable collectibles. No more investments. The house was already many months behind in mortgage payments and a few weeks away from foreclosure. And my proudest glory—my children—were also now gone. My journal entry for that day: "...nothing matters now."

In spite of the heavy burden of despair which had now come to totally envelope me I mustered enough energy to go see the social worker at the Social Services Department in South Central San Antonio. If they said I had done something wrong with my children I needed to know. Yes, the "complaint" by some unknown person stated that I hit my children with my belt, that I let my daughter play with my penis in the bathtub, and that I was showing my children lots of XXX-rated films. I told the lady truthfully that, yes, I did hit my children with my belt; that, yes, I did once permit my daughter to play with and soap my penis in the bathtub; that, no, I did not show my children XXX-rated films or any kind of sex films. Sure, I was a pervert, but I had not watched any sex films for many years. As completely as possible I confessed, and I realized suddenly that what I did to the children was wrong. The social worker said that "the case" would be transferred to Oklahoma City since that is where the children had been taken. I then replied that I would try to deal with the problem as per the recommendations of the Social Services Department in Oklahoma, and then I left with more angst and pain than before. Besides Geena, now the entire State of Texas and the State of Oklahoma would band together to prevent me from ever seeing my children again. It was hopeless. I did not see much point in going on with my life. I was a disgraceful failure.

For some hours on that Wednesday (Day 2) I stayed away from the house, not having the courage or the coping power to look at the savage emptiness that was left behind, the rotted-out shell of the grandest of my dreams. It was time to think about how this tragedy came to unfold. But I also noted I was feeling numb instead of panicky.

"If I am so great and such a genius in everything, how is it that I am in this mess? Why are these people telling me that I did something wrong with my children? Is it possible that throughout the years Geena may have been right when she and I disagreed on critical child-rearing practices?" I had a nagging feeling deep in my soul that perhaps I could be wrong about my beliefs about life on this earth. My intellectual style had always carried me forth so well. "Is it now failing?" I asked myself.

Thursday, June 7, 1985. On this day, I got out of the House of Despair as soon as I could, forcing myself out of my bed on the floor. Aimlessly I drove around San Antonio, desperately seeking ways to distract myself from the suicidal tidal wave which was engulfing me maybe irreversibly. Every couple that I saw with children sent new shock waves through my soul almost as reflexively as the moth goes to the light. I turned my face but the arrow had already gone through my heart, time and time again.

I went for dinner at my cousin Lilly's home (my Aunt Julieta's only child), and afterwards she sat me down and started again on the subject of forgiveness and Jesus Christ, but for the first time in my life I did not react with disdain and anger at the mere idea of God and his omnipotence. "Let Jesus be your guide, Victor, because we all fail and we all need direction in life. Accept his principles and let him help you with this terrible problem. There is no other way," said Lilly lovingly as she always had before. "Is it possible that I need a guiding light in my life—that I have not been able to make it work properly because I have been too selfish and self-centered?" I asked myself, critically introspective as I had never before been. After pondering the issue not so much intellectually but with a heart sinking with the weight of depressive despair, I told Lilly that I did need help in cleaning up my life so that I could someday be able to see my children again. "Then close your eyes and repeat after me," commanded Lilly as we held hands and I pledged to follow Christ's principles as the Way in my life. That same day, after nearly 25 years of hostile denial of the supremacy of God, I purchased my first Bible ever (for $9), and began to find out more about proper moral principles. I found out I had had practically none.

Friday, June 8, 1985. Yet, the next day I was still walking in deep despair, feeling that I needed something more earth-bound to offer me support because I had a feeling that I could not go on much longer, that within a day or two I would cease to function or exist. The very thought of "ceasing to function" was scary to me, for I had always thought of myself as a survivor who could tackle any task, any challenge, and any monster at any time. How could it be that I was starting to shut down from the intolerable pain of the loss of my children?

I was finally able to contact Geena in Oklahoma—it was an ugly experience I will never forget, for she was hateful and she had my children. Deep in my heart I felt the most vile repulsion in having to negotiate with Satan, or, worse, with the reincarnation of The Devil, the Chief Tormentor in my life, for that is how it felt to me. She did not even let me talk to my children. I knew that my emotional crisis was deepening. I was not omnipotent as I had believed for many years. The end was near; suicidal thoughts were getting harder to ignore. I called the only counselor I knew in the San Antonio area: Glenda Watson, Geena's previous therapist whom I'd screamed at and viciously insulted. I was hoping she would not tell me to go to hell in my time of need. It would not be professional, but I couldn't blame her either.

She was surprised that I called her, but quickly responded positively when I told her that I needed her help. Although she did not come out and say it, she already knew of the crisis that I was in, so I conjectured that Geena had been in contact with her from Oklahoma. Never in my adult life had I bowed before anyone to ask for individual help, but now was the time to do it for I felt that I was absolutely at the end of my rope, that the next day or two could be fatal.

"Should I check into a psychiatric hospital?" I asked her, halfway mumbling, and she replied that it might not be a bad idea given the extreme level of my despair and suicidal thoughts. I asked her to check with whatever insurance coverage we had left and to call any hospital. I just waited while I prayed to God to please keep me away from the path of no return, for the thoughts of running my old car in a closed garage were coming at me by the minute. I knew that this split between Geena and me involved vast hostility, if not outright hatred, and that because of this she would never let me see my children again. Ten years of bitterly contentious matrimony had laid the groundwork for a vengeful refusal to let me see my children, I thought, so I went even deeper into the suicidal despair of hopelessness. No pain that I had ever felt in my entire sick life could come close to matching the hell of this profound loss that I felt deep in my heart. This was not life.

Glenda Watson called me back and told me that she had already made all arrangements for me to sign myself in at Hamilton Psychiatric Hospital in North San Antonio. With barely enough energy I packed a few things and entered a new chapter in my life—that of a mental patient, which I never would have thought was possible. The end of the San Antonio dream had come at last.

Chapter Thirteen
The Edge of Sanity

Driving north on the Highway 35, I had a few moments to reflect on the wisdom of going to a psychiatric hospital, yet I felt that there was no other way to handle my extreme pain and feeling that I could not go on. For years I had been fiercely independent, taking great pride in how I had survived many calamities in my life, and with no need for the support of a wife for anything. The current crisis made me realize that all my cockiness and grandiosity of the past was possible because I always felt my children were in good hands when I left them with Geena—I could give myself great freedom to advance without worrying about them. That was no longer the case. Besides, my desperation was so acute that I had to bring other people into my inner spiritual turmoil in order for me to survive. Yes, I had to go into the hospital. It would also afford me the opportunity to look at my life to see what needed to be changed. Besides, I felt that all my innate coping power—which our biology affords us for an entire lifetime—had been spent.

Hamilton Psychiatric Hospital was located on beautifully green acreage, surrounded by lots of trees, nicely trimmed hedges, and a few narrow pebble roads—like an estate, really. I pulled into the parking lot wondering just when it would be that I would be driving away from this hospital, if at all, for I had no idea what kinds of problems they would discover in me or just how the issue of my not being able to see my kids would resolve itself. Maybe they should just keep me here forever if I can't see my kids; I wouldn't be able to go on anyway. So at exactly 5:13 P.M. (I'll never forget it; I made a mental note of the time) I entered through the sliding front doors and went to the admissions desk where they sat me down and asked me innumerable questions about insurance and a few about my background, and then I was led towards what they told me was the Adult-General Unit. In spite of my numbed consciousness I became apprehensive when I saw them taking me through several sets of doors which the nurse locked behind us.

"Do you think I am going to escape?" I asked her nervously.

"No, not you, but there are some patients who wander and we want to make sure that they don't walk out," was her very diplomatic response, as we came upon the nursing station in the center of the Adult-General Unit. And there I was, in my new home in a psychiatric ward. From father to condemned pervert in this psychiatric ward. It was agonizing to contemplate the precipitous losses which I had suffered in the last few days. My hands and arms were trembling almost uncontrollably.

But the nurses took charge right away and did not give me a chance to obsess about my pain, for they started to look through my bag for "sharps" and removed my shaving razor plus a few glass bottles of after-shave lotion and other toiletries, including wire hangers. They similarly checked my pockets and asked me to hand over my key ring, which I promptly did. It was beginning to feel like the pat-down the police give all those criminals on TV. As this spectacle was unfolding the other patients on the unit were beginning to mill around, so I got a good look at the other people with whom I was going to share my life for God knew how long.

Some introduced themselves with shaky voices, others looked at me with scared and suspicious eyes from dark corners of the hallway, wondering, I was sure, just how I was going to fit in with their established distant relationships. They all looked sad.

Suzanne, the blond nurse, took what was left of my bag and said, "Come, let me show you to your room," as she briskly walked ahead of me down the long, narrow, and shiny corridor, on both sides of which were patient rooms, many with doors decorated by colorful art which I later discovered had been created in art therapy sessions. Almost at the very end of the corridor we entered a room on the left and Suzanne introduced me to a lanky young man of about 20 who was lying on the bed closest to the window. I was sure he had his own private demons to deal with.

"Victor, this will be your roommate. His name is Sam. Sam, this is Victor."

Suzanne showed me the limited number of items in my Spartan room, decorated more to the likes of some hermit monk who intentionally may have wanted as little as possible of the material things in life. I quickly noticed that the three built-in lamps in the room appeared to be of a heavy duty metal with matching indestructible lens cover, presumably to discourage tampering for suicidal purposes. Inside the closet there were no traditional hangers and no hanger rod for the same reason. The mirrors over the dressers and in the bathroom were of shiny metal, not of glass, which could be broken to produce razor-sharp shards to stab someone or to cut one's own aorta to end it all in the quiet terror of the night when demons usually come from inside one's mind to torment the soul. Even the commode was smartly constructed for it had no obvious parts which could be dismantled.

Once the nurse left I put my belongings in the dresser drawers and tried to strike up a conversation with my roommate Sam. Up and down his arms I noticed that he had scratches or scars, yet I could not imagine what could have done that damage. Well, he volunteered to tell me even if I was not going to ask him.

"My father doesn't want me," said Sam with a strange grin on his face, what I learned later to label as "inappropriate smiling." "He told me many times to get out of the house, so I had to run away when I was 12. That is why I had to hurt myself on my arms to forget about it," he said, this time with a sad look that betrayed the fundamental anguish that I sensed was just beneath the plastic smile.

"So why are you here?" I asked him.

Pointing to his forearms he said that he had tried to kill himself by cutting his arms. It looked to me, though, that judging by the number of scars, this was not the first time he had tried that. I am so glad, I thought, that I came here before I got to Sam's stage. I was already learning something. Poor Sam, he wanted to talk a lot longer than I cared to listen; my mind was still on the fact that I had not seen my kids for about a week, and I was missing them terribly. Even though they were not with me I knew that Geena would take good care of them. In fact, for years I envied her because I secretly knew deep in my heart that she was a far superior parent than I was. Through no fault of her own, it created an undercurrent of hostility in me because it made me feel inferior in how I was able to love my children.

As per regulations I had to eat my supper in the lounge area and not in the patient dining hall; their brilliant justification for this was that they needed to observe me to see that I was "OK." "OK?" Of course I was NOT OK! I was miserable and felt like just crying all night because of the pressure on my chest, a tension that approximated the subjective sense of the "knot" in my throat. But I complied because I wanted their help in fixing my life as a wretch disguised as a successful academician and prolific salesman. The part that had been missing all along was a genuine sense of decency.

Nothing much happened after supper. A nurse took my blood pressure, pulse, and temperature. Normal. Then I went to my room to contemplate more of the day's events. Fortunately I already had a diary which was several years old and which I had brought into the hospital. This afforded me the opportunity to record in great detail my thoughts and the activities of each day. My brand new Bible (N.I.V.) was on my desk so I began to read The New Testament to get an idea of what Lilly and Jesus meant by the process of cleansing and "sanctification." Quite serendipitously I opened my Bible to *Romans 7:14*, where the Apostle Paul wrote a very timely message to all Christians in Rome: "We know that the law is spiritual; but I am unspiritual, sold as a slave to sin. I do not understand what I do. For what I want to do I do not do, but what I hate I do."

That made sense to me, for I interpreted Paul's words as indicating that he and all people everywhere have to struggle with "sinful" desires which eventually get us all in trouble. Maybe that had been my major problem in life—satisfying whatever urge or desire I felt without regard for morality or consequences. After many years of having rejected it outright, I was beginning to make some sense out of the Bible. I needed direction in life. But more importantly I needed to have Andrew, Gabriela, and Jasmine with me. *Where are my babies? Why did they take my babies from me? I will gladly give up anything in life just to be with my children again.* When I finally went to sleep that first night on the psychiatric ward, my pillow was spongy wet with tears for my children, and there was also another stream of tears about to break forth which a huge dam of denial had blocked since the early stages of my childhood. The dam was about to break.

During the night I found out that Sam slept fitfully, tossing, grunting, whining, and getting up several times. Since I did not know him I felt obliged to keep an eye on him, for he might have felt like taking out his anger on me. To my surprise the nurses came into our bedrooms in the morning urging us all to "rise and shine." Why were they so happy? Did they have any personal problems? Within minutes I got into the shower and felt an uncontrollable urge to cry—no, wail—to no end. If it had lasted only a few seconds it might have been OK, but this kept on and on. It was a primordial cry from the depths of my soul, saddled with sadness, depression, and loss. But I felt personally embarrassed because I was crying like a child, almost like a baby. Yet I remembered what the nurses had told me, so I knew that I should express whatever feelings I had. This infantile crying spell in the shower lasted for about 15 long minutes, and left me drained and puffy-eyed. There really would be no dignity in opening up our hearts to admit our pain and our sins. That in itself was a terrifying thought—I was exhausted and it was only early morning.

After breakfast the staff told me that I had to attend "therapy groups" to help me deal with my problems, so over the next two days I attended Men's Group, Art Therapy, Bereavement Group, Biofeedback, Parenting Group, Sexual Deviance Group, Healthy Sexuality, Men & Women Role Play, and Rational-Emotive Therapy Group. These first 48-hours on the unit opened up my eyes to a new world of psychology which I had never known in spite of my extensive reading. More importantly, I learned about decency and morality in human relationships, concepts foreign to me prior to this. I was learning how to identify feelings. And the one which I was most interested in was the agonizing panic-pain of not being able to see my kids. "Can you help me with this?"

In one of those groups I got acquainted with Diana, a woman of about 28 who was in the unit due to trauma from a rape. Maybe "acquainted" is too hopeful of a word, for she was very defensive about associating with men on the unit, quite understandably so given that she was a rape victim. Then we all went to Group Discussion.

Thomas: "Victor, tell us how you feel about how husbands and wives should resolve differences."

Victor: "Well, I think that...."

Immediately Diana interrupted...

Diana: "You think? That was not the question. Thomas asked you how you felt. Express how you *feel* not how you *think*."

For a few seconds I had to pause to ponder what Diana had just said to me. She was right! Why do I always say "I think" when I am attempting to describe something that more accurately should be classified as a feeling. For the next two days I studied the idea and felt some kind of revelation within me. This simple process of identifying and labeling feelings correctly was something that I did not know how to do too well, even though for "normal" people this was probably second nature. Even in pain I was learning a lot, yes, learning a lot from others in pain.

Also in the group was Bob, the young truck driver who was psychiatrically hospitalized subsequent to the trauma he had experienced after his 18-wheeler rig had tipped sideways onto a small car, completely flattening it and killing its three occupants. Bob was still in a daze, talking almost dispassionately about the tragedy, yet saying in the same sentence that he was giving up trucking. He, too, had been battered by the forces of the universe—greater than us all. But I was learning from him the art of sharing intimate feelings with other human beings; the art of being vulnerable in making a connection to another person. He was a "macho truck driver," but the nurses and the staff encouraged him to "open up" and express his feelings in "this safe environment."

I took a quick liking to Joe "Granpa," an old man of about 60 whose wife had recently left him and who alternated between weepiness and fits of anger towards his wife. In group therapy all of us would confront him on the painful realities of his life, realities which he was trying to avoid at all costs.

"All these years I treated her like a queen. I mean, I did everything that she asked of me. Why did she leave like this? She was so ungrateful," he lamented in front of all of us, laying his life open for all to see. That was something new to me. People do have problems. These are feelings.

Diana, the most astute social observer on our unit who had already reprimanded me for saying "think" instead of "feel," immediately shot back at him, saying, "Joe, do you really think that a woman who is being treated like a queen is just going to pack up and leave her husband out of whim? There's something wrong here, don't you think?"

"But I tell you, I did everything for that woman. Sure I was not a model husband, but I did love her. She was so ungrateful," reiterated Joe as if reading some kind of hidden script, obviously not listening to Diana's confrontational observation. My mind was working on what I was hearing in group therapy. Our misfortunes are not simply the result of the whims of Gods or Demons, but have grounding in our past, in our behaviors, in our attitudes. To some degree we create the fruits of our lives. Well, maybe I was to blame for the mess in my marriage and for my kids having been taken away. "I have got to be honest about this, even if Joe is not about his treatment of his own wife," I thought.

"Joe, you are not listening and you are avoiding the question or the issue. I am sorry that your wife left you, but if you don't face up to what role you may have played in her leaving you then you'll never correct the problem. If you want her back you are going to have to confront whatever shortcomings you may have had as a husband," Diana said, this time with a more forceful and less sympathetic voice. Apparently she regarded herself as the informal unit psychologist, dispensing (quite accurate and helpful) advice to her peers, even if they didn't request it. The group leader and the nurses just nodded their heads in approval.

But old Granpa was in his feeling-sorry-for-himself mode, and started his diatribe again, only to be interrupted this time by Mitchell, the husky lineman for San Antonio Power & Light who recently had lost a child in a car accident:

"Listen, Joe. We know how tough it is to lose someone. I know; I just lost my young daughter in a car accident. But you have the opportunity to get your wife back if you would only talk to her honestly and listen to what she has to say. We cannot guarantee it, but I am sure that she will tell you what went wrong. In fact, I feel that you probably already know what went wrong but are having a hard time accepting it."

Other group members jumped in to buttress the support line that Diana had started, but Joe was not going to budge on this one. He firmly believed he was blameless. It made me think of how I used to be just a few days before when I accepted responsibility for nothing when things went wrong. Joe's impenetrable defense against blame was so crystal clear to all of us, yet I conjectured that Joe himself was totally blind to it. So is the nature of defense mechanisms. Unintentionally, the group's efforts had benefitted me more than they did Joe. Did others look at me in the past as we are now looking at Joe? With incredulity at my stupidity? Very sobering.

And so it went for the next few days as I went from group to group, trying to contribute to help others, yet always getting more from each group. It was revelation after revelation, as if my eyes were opening for the first time in my life, seeing things that "normal" people had been seeing for years. My mind had been dull and blind and impervious to the truth that is essential for proper relationships between human beings. All those years in the universities and in my two marriages I had been living in the shadows, plodding along by massive delusions and blinded by pervasive defense mechanisms which helped me cope but robbed me of authenticity. I had been a fake, a fraud, I wore disguises so people would not see the intense insecurity in my soul. The light was finally coming in! But I had to make a gargantuan effort to get excited about these excursions into the light, for my real mood was one of acute anxiety, loneliness, and desperation.

Still unanswered was the most profoundly disturbing question: Will I ever get to see my kids again? Without any "defenses" I had to think realistically about this question which emotionally made the situation one of life and death for me. I had spoken several times over the phone with Geena after I had checked into Hamilton Psychiatric, only to feel even closer to madness after each call. Her mood and tone were caustic, and she would even tell me to just stay in San Antonio as Social Services in Oklahoma was going to prevent me from ever seeing my children again due to the abuse. Those words and the prospect of not seeing my children ever again were intensely painful, so painful that I thought and dreamt constantly of suicide. It was like a triple death in the family. My hand tremors got worse, and only my pillow knew of the continuous tears which came uncontrollably from my heart at night. My eyes were swollen every day.

Soon enough I had a private talk with my psychiatrist, Dr. Brownwood, who came in to see me for about ten minutes every week. What can one accomplish in ten minutes? He asked me basic questions like how I liked the unit and if I was feeling better (yes and no). I asked the staff to have my real therapist come in to see me.

I was so happy to see Glenda Watson on the unit; somehow I felt that she really did empathize with my situation. I also felt that her being a female therapist was a big factor, since I felt very needy for a sympathetic woman's ear. For the first few minutes after we met in the corridor we had to go hunting for an empty therapy room, a practice that became standard for us. Finally we were settled in a small room with just a table and two chairs.

Very painfully I told Glenda how I felt about losing my children, and even about my losing Geena. But I also knew that this hospitalization was not just about losing my kids but about how I had behaved as a person throughout the years, how I had behaved as a father and as a husband. She responded by telling me that my pain had roots in my early childhood experiences, and that we should start with that.

It was shameful. It was disgusting. It was sickening. Those things that had happened to me and those things that I had done. If I told Glenda about my childhood—especially if I told her of the disgusting things I had done—she would *know* that I was a *worthless* individual. She might not even want to be my therapist anymore, and she will tell the hospital staff never to let me out of this unit! One saving grace here was the courage I saw in the other patients' willingness to discuss their most profound, shameful, and painful secrets with staff and in front of others. There is no other way. Glenda must know that I came from hell as a worthless cockroach infant.

For the first time in my life, I began to relate to another human being the darkest and most shameful secrets of my childhood and my vile life as an adult, as a predatory vampire of the night, masturbating into towels while sucking blood from women everywhere. Even in ten years of marriage I had not dared tell Geena any of this, principally because I could never trust her—I knew (or *felt*) that she would vengefully use it against me if she ever got a chance. Story after story, the feces of my life and the maggots of my spirit all came out into the light where they could not hide from the discerning eye and ear of a person who knew about ethics and proper moral standards—Glenda Watson. Cunnilingus at age four, my using a safety pin to inflict pain on myself at age three, the bamboo incident, sex with the janitor at age six, seeing The Devil stomp on my mother, threatening to slash my own wrists at age six, seeing my baby brother Benito's head slam repeatedly onto the concrete floor, eating bricks for breakfast, communion wafers for lunch, and filthy pigeons for supper, butchering the three puppies, neighborhood boys and men having sex with me, the midnight raid by Social Services in El Paso, how I was sexually abused hundreds of times at the foster home, my masturbating dozens of boys for money, the endless nights of hunger, my terrible sexual contact with two of my daughters, my mother showing me her huge breasts, my mother's death, sex with ranch animals, my marriage to Katherine, my sickening penchant for pornography while I was living in New York City, and my endless and meaningless string of affairs with women, several of whom became pregnant. It took several sessions; each time I felt that Glenda was going to get up and leave because she *knew* I was a hopeless pervert with no worth on this Earth. But she did not leave; instead she said she understood how those things happen. It was enough to make me cry almost uncontrollably, as if the demons and maggots within me were being forced to confront the light, *the real light* that can destroy them. It was a cleansing process that I had never experienced in my life: the sharing of the vilest, darkest, most disgusting crimes against nature that any human being is capable of committing. That was me, full of decaying filth inside my soul, full of sewage and pus from old wounds that never healed, bursting with the maggots of pornography which had found a convenient dead spirit to feed on, to metamorphose at night into a stalking vampire which lured women into bed for their sexual organs, only to see the bloodsucker vanish deep into the rot of my soul after having feasted, leaving the rest of my spiritual carcass exposed for further putrefaction. That was me. For the first time ever I was feeling that I was not so great. I was not destined to the greatest heights of Texas. No, I was simply a rotting corpse. I should have been butchered and then buried when I was a child of three, except that my mother was too blind to see that my spirit had died. Or maybe she was just a cadaver herself. Maybe my mother had no spirit.

With each story that came out of my soul I realized more fully that I had been living all of my life in a perverted and delusional world, the world of "psychological defenses" set up to protect against agonizing pain and gut-wrenching anxiety and terror, like the one we felt when Satan stomped on my pregnant mother while she was on the floor and we were by the corner, watching helplessly as El Diablo, The Demon, The Vile One, The Devil, did his terrifying deed. As is the case with these childhood defenses, my soul was able to curtail some of the terror of our daily life to allow me to continue to function biologically, but the price was the setting up a system of defenses to cover my real broken self, thus effectively robbing me of an opportunity to grow up with a "normal" personality. In talking to Glenda I was listening to myself spew the venom of my life, and I knew that I was not normal. The endless childhood traumas and the subsequent massive defenses had taken a grievous toll against my "inner self."

Years later I discovered that it was psychiatrist James Masterson, who in his excellent book *The Search For The Real Self* (1988), said it best:

"*The Search For The Real Self* is also about those with an impaired real self who are unable to accomplish the task of finding a fit with their environment, and are compelled to resort to self-destructive behavior patterns—evidence of a false self—that protect them from feeling 'bad' at the cost of a meaningful and fulfilling life. The false self, unable to experiment, induces a lack of self-esteem as the person has to settle for rigid, destructive behavior that avoids life's challenges, but leads to feelings of failure, lost hopes and unfulfilled dreams, and despair."

Not only was my material empire in ruins, but as I listened to the discussions in therapy groups, as I spoke privately with the other patients, as I spilled the blood of my soul, as I listened to the careful advice of Glenda Watson, I realized that inside me was an even greater ruin, for my inner self was a vast wasteland.

Why am I in this "Sexual Deviance Group"? I'm no deviant! But as I listened to the pain coming from the other patients and the supporting words from the army of therapists on hand, I *knew* that indeed I was not normal! You mean it is not OK to take baths or showers with your growing children? You mean it is not OK to even playfully touch their private parts? That it is wrong to show children pornographic photographs? Isn't that art? Doesn't that enlighten them about the beauty of the human body? Masturbation wrong? It's a healthy outlet! That *my* masturbation was an addiction? How can a sexual act be an addiction? Sounds silly to me. How many times? About 1,200 times a year, or about 42,000 ejaculations in the last 35 years. That puts it in perspective, and it sounds real ugly to me now. Healthy adults don't do that? I thought everybody jerked off at least several times a week. How could I have been so wrong? I had been on the edge of true ethical and moral madness. It was a sickness of my soul.

It was from unit therapists Richard Ramirez, Tom Lyvers and Esther Schube that I learned much about healthier ways of responding to other human beings. As I was coming to realize that my life was fully contaminated by perverted sexual feelings, Esther Schube was busy helping me to develop more normal responses in her group, "Healthy Sex and Parenting." For what seemed like centuries I believed with all my heart that sex was for ejaculation of sperms into the female and nothing more, and that her job was simply to lie there passively with open legs while the Macho Chicano delivered the sperms inside her. "Intimacy" for me had always meant being able to suck a woman's breasts while playing with her clitoris, or, more preferably, getting a blowjob where the woman begs for the opportunity to swallow one's sperms. "No!" was Schube's response. As strange as it may sound I was dumbfounded by her different interpretation of the concept of "intimacy."

In fact, she was able to draw upon my experiences in New York, where the streams of sperms ran for blocks and emptied into foul-smelling sewers at every corner.

"Victor, didn't you say that in New York you used to feel terrible after you had sex with a strange woman and that you wished secretly to quickly disappear from her bed after you reached orgasm?" she asked me. "Intimacy has nothing to do with sex; it has to do with trust, sharing, loving, and being deeply honest with each other," she added.

Esther Schube was speaking in a foreign language to me. Trust? How stupid I would have to be to trust, I thought, since any rational person knows that we cannot trust anyone! WE CANNOT TRUST ANYONE! That was the voice from the inner sanctum of my soul. But Schube seems like a nice person. She seems loving. She says it with conviction. While my eyes and my ears were busy assessing the threatening idea of trusting someone else, my inner soul was demanding that I keep my time-tested strategy of knowing that the world is dangerous and that you cannot trust anyone! Esther was confronting me on this fundamental issue in life.

So in "Men's Group" I asked a fellow Chicano, therapist Richard Ramirez, for his view. He said that he was happily married, and that he "trusted" his wife. "But don't you worry that she might use your trust against you? That she might betray you? That she might one day take your children and bring out the secrets you entrusted her with?" I asked him incredulously. Richard was very self-assured when he answered that he was not worried that she would ever do that; or, alternatively, that he was able to tolerate the negligible risk. I secretly admired Richard for having a trusting relationship with his wife. In my two marriages I had been unable to do that. I just knew at the center of my soul that women could never be trusted!

For the next several days I pondered the enormous and revolutionary idea of "intimacy," struggling within myself to comprehend this strange human phenomenon. In spite of all my intellectual education I still was having a difficult time understanding, from an emotional perspective, just what the concept meant and why people would ever want it in the first place! So my perplexity reached into Tom Lyvers' group, "Sexual Deviance," although he was to offer a challenge of his own.

In Tom's group I soon learned that my Macho Chicano desire to copulate with as many women as possible was also a sexual addiction; he even introduced me to the "12 Step Program" to help me to deal with the "addiction." But I thought that addictions were things like alcoholism and smoking tobacco, or even an uncontrollable craving for food. But sex with women an addiction? That did not sound true to me; they were trying to stretch the limits of psychiatry here. I was not an "addict." I was merely exercising my Macho Chicano instinct to bed as many women as possible, to keep score, to remember and delight myself in my hard-fought conquests. I was not an addict. It was my "free choice" to have or not have sex with women, and I had chosen to have sex with them. Other men had other sports and hobbies; I had the past-time of having sex with women. There is no addiction here, I felt. But I listened to what Tom Lyvers had to say.

The central theoretical model that we used here was the thesis expounded by Patrick Carnes in his very influential and popular book, *Out of the Shadows: Understanding Sexual Addiction*. For starters I was told about the basic belief systems of all addicts, especially sex addicts:

(1) There is a sense of abandonment.
(2) Addict believes that "I am basically a bad, unworthy person."
(3) Addict believes that "No one would love me as I am."
(4) Addict believes that "My needs are never going to be met if I depend on others."
(5) "Sex is my most important need."

Carnes went on to state that the sex addict exhibits ritualized behavior, periods of escalation and de-escalation, delusional thought patterns, massive denial of painful reality, futile attempts to stop the behaviors, is abusive, and most importantly, has a secret life. That was me! All that was me! My memory quickly went back to the hundreds of times in New York when I knew ahead of time that if I took this woman to bed tonight, I would feel sickeningly repulsed after the orgasm—perhaps, I know now, because of the pitiful lack of true intimacy in the relationship. Yet, this *force* inside me would compel me to go ahead with the seduction in spite of the dire warnings from my wounded soul. It was almost as if I had been just a passive player listening to my inner vampire's voice say, "You must do it. You must get her in bed tonight. You must have intercourse with her no matter what, even if you don't like her and even if you have to lie to her in order for her to open her legs. Do it!" When my vampire took over, my true soul could not offer a credible counterforce. Yes, it was beginning to look as if I truly had been a sexual addict *all* my life, beginning at around age four! And, yes, it also made me feel that I was a maggot in the cesspool. What a sickening realization.

I didn't fare any better with my honest reports to my many group therapists about my years of masturbation, a practice which I must have begun at about age eleven. Yes, it was compulsive, for I did it even when I did not feel sexually aroused. Thousands of times when I was in bed alone, especially in my agonizing years in New York City, I would fight with my limp penis so that it would get up and provide me with a much needed orgasm. It was almost as if I had to convince my dick to perform for me.

Thinking back I remember that when I lay in bed, I was defenseless against the inner pain and depression, something which I had to fight against, and my only weapon was my penis and the orgasms which it provided to me. Usually in the aftermath of the pleasant feeling of the orgasm I would fall asleep, having accomplished my task of drowning out the anxiety and the pain, first with an orgasm, and then with a quick exit into my dreams.

And I also was an exhibitionist, for subconsciously I enjoyed walking naked in front of my children. Oh, my God, why? And a voyeur of pornographic magazines, looking at the human body and the sex act in the vilest of manners, respecting nothing about the integrity of human beings. It was all now clear to me: Sex had been my drug. And I had been in the mucus-filled gutter as a down-and-out addict.

Glenda Watson didn't think that all these years I had simply been exercising "free will" in making my decision to go to bed with women, but rather that the force of the addiction had propelled me to engage in these behaviors. My delusion had been that I, in a free act of will, had opted for the perversity. Thinking back on that, I can add another dimension to it, basically, that the "addiction" was not some "foreign" force that "made me" do these despicable things, but rather that the "addiction" was simply another facet of my personality, albeit a sick part of it. Whatever I did, whatever I thought, whatever I felt (however good or wicked these may have been), they all came from different chambers of my soul and my personality, not one being more or less a product of the total "me." It was all me, in badness and whatever goodness there may have been.

But maybe this is just coming from the "scientific" side of me which I cultivated during my education, the side which still had some connection to the "truth." In that hospital and in my experiences in the counseling afterwards,

I saw how many people opted to ascribe their socially undesirable traits or behaviors to foreign agents within them, agents such as "the disease," "the addiction," and even "the mood." If we do not want these behaviors, the best we can do is to state that "there is a part of me that rejects my desires and my behavior in question, although these desires and behaviors come from a real part of me deep within my soul." Labeling our undesirable behavior as an addiction might just be a mental slight of hand to disown our problematic urges and character traits.

As I learned more about real psychology in the Adult-General Unit, I began to feel a compounding of my depression, for the therapy groups were exposing the vast character pathology of my life, a development which essentially led me to realize that I had been a selfish, exploitative, narcissistic, and sexually perverted intellectual. True, I was very smart, but I also had significant emotional problems which had begun probably a few months after birth. Intelligence and emotional health, I found out, were two entirely independent facets of the mental life of a person. The hopelessness of my anxiety and depression produced agonizing emotional pain which I had never before felt in my life. Unlike more normal individuals with a healthy sense of self who had some family for moral support, I was almost all alone in this crisis, and, had it not been for the budding hope which I was getting from the Bible, I would have sunk in irremediable despair and would have simply taken my life. Losing my children and my psychological defenses almost simultaneously was a double blow against which I had no defense, until a few days after my admission when I discovered that Hamilton Psychiatric had a Christian psychiatric unit! I was ecstatic!

One day I was in the crowded patient cafeteria when a woman of about 25 asked if I would share my table with her. Of course. Terry had long black hair, quite a few adolescent pimples, and a warm personality which I was guessing had something to do with the "glow of Christ" in her life. Within about a minute I learned that she was a patient at the hospital, yet I also knew that she did not reside at our Adult-General Unit.

"I'm staying at the Christian psychiatric unit where they let Christ heal your soul. I'm very happy there; I think it's the best unit here. Do you want to come with me for a visit?" she offered with a girlish enthusiasm.

"Terry, you mean that instead of using regular therapy you ask Christ for forgiveness and you let Him cleanse the sins of your life?" I asked, barely containing my joy at finding this fountain of hope right *within* our hospital.

"Sure! We have Christian nurses, Christian counselors, Christian therapists, and our own Christian psychiatrist, Dr. Morgan. They are all very much with the Lord—they can help you to make peace with yourself no matter what your problem is. I can arrange for you to come visit me on the unit if you want."

It was wonderful—this idea of a Christian unit in the hospital. The pain from the secular therapy had gotten too great, and I needed more support from Christ on a daily basis. The therapy in the secular unit was like surgery without anesthesia—painful but necessary. Support in the Christian unit would be like having the much needed pain medicine during and after surgery. I already was praying for about two hours a day, yet I felt that I needed to devote more time to Bible study and therapeutic prayer to God. That same day I asked Ruta, the evening head nurse, to get me permission to spend some time at the Christian Unit. Even though I secretly yearned for Ruta's motherly care, I knew in my heart that I had to follow Christ's path as the only possible path towards my children. That was my only hope.

Promptly the next morning I met with Dr. Morgan, the affable, thin, and unassuming Christian psychiatrist for the Christian Unit. Even though it had been only about two weeks since I had become a Christian I was already having some conflict between what my heart wanted—to be a devoted Christian—and what my intellect was telling me about inconsistencies between Christian and secular approaches to psychiatric counseling.

"Dr. Morgan, will we be talking about our individual problems in the Christian groups, or will we be studying the Bible?" I asked him nervously since I had no idea what a Christian psychiatrist believed was the source of problems in people's lives. Were there schools where they taught medicine and psychiatry from the Biblical perspective? I didn't know what to expect.

"We talk about each person's problems and we ask God to intercede for healing. We also pray and ask God to cleanse our souls of everything that may be bothering us, including loss of children and wife," responded Dr. Morgan in a gentle and reassuring tone.

After about a half-hour of conversation he said that he would allow me to attend group sessions at his Christian Unit. "You can start today if you wish." Yes! Within a few minutes I had Tom Lyvers, my treatment coordinator, adjust my schedule to include some therapy sessions at Christian.

That morning I was let out of the locked doors of our unit into the common hallways of the hospital, where I soon made my way down a long, sunny corridor and stood in front of the similarly locked main doors of the Christian Unit. The nurse at the nursing station inside buzzed the electronic lock and let me into the quiet chambers of God's unit. As I walked down this unit's hallways I had a pleasant feeling in my heart, a feeling that told me that everything in the end would be OK. That I would eventually see my children. That God was on my side. That God would see to it that my children were taken care of while I was dealing with these terrible problems. Yes, this was a wise move for me. I felt like an infant who needed more of the spiritual nourishing from The Source—from God.

In the nicely carpeted therapy lounge were lots of easy chairs already occupied by Christians in turmoil, mostly women with the unmistakable look of depression on their faces, each with a copy of The Bible on her lap. This session was being led by Dr. Morgan, who quickly started the meeting with a prayer, and then promptly went to Jesus' Sermon on the Mount (Matthew 5:3):

> "Blessed are the poor in spirit, for theirs is the kingdom of heaven.
> Blessed are those who mourn, for they will be comforted.
> Blessed are the meek, for they will inherit the earth.
> Blessed are those who hunger and thirst for righteousness, for they will be filled.
> Blessed are the merciful, for they will be shown mercy.
> Blessed are the pure in heart, for they will see God.
> Blessed are the peacemakers, for they will be called Sons of God.
> Blessed are those who are persecuted because of righteousness, for theirs is the kingdom of heaven."

Dr. Morgan's view was that God's message was very clear in the Beatitudes, and that all faithful Christians could take comfort in knowing that God had already proclaimed in the Book of Matthew that our suffering was never in vain, that it had some meaning which currently we may not understand but which in the future would be very clear to us. It was almost as if God Himself had uttered those words for I felt instant comfort in knowing that this acute suffering which I was going through was not simply the result of capricious "forces of the universe" but somehow was related to God's plan. Maybe God wanted to punish me for the vile life which I had led. Maybe I had had sex with too many women. Maybe it was the thousands of times which I had masturbated (no more of that!). Maybe because I had been a perverted father. I was a mere mortal, so I could not figure out what God's plan was, yet I felt a comfort in knowing that by leading a more righteous life I was indeed getting closer to God through the process of sanctification. We all had our unique situations and our way of interpreting what God wanted to do with us. I knew that my pain was containable. There was hope for the future.

But Rebecca did not think so, for she was very angry at God for having ignored her for so long. She was about 65 years old and quite querulous and rambunctious, complaining about everything in the lounge from seats to lighting to the company she kept. It was difficult for me to understand what she was angry about, or indeed to see that she was a Christian in the first place. From her tone of voice I could tell that she was merely listening to Dr. Morgan's sermon and that her heart was not *feeling* it. Well, I got a lot out of it.

After that first session at the Christian Unit I had the opportunity to chat more at length with Terry—she was happy to see me there.

"So how do you like it? Is it the way that I described it to you?" she asked me with a wide grin while holding on to her Bible (she was serious about studying).

"Oh, I love it! This is heaven on earth. I had no idea when I came to this hospital that I would have a chance to study more of the Lord's message. I am very grateful to you, Terry, for having told me about this. Praise the Lord!" I said very enthusiastically to her.

"Well, now that you know you like it, why don't you ask to be officially transferred to our unit? We have some beds empty right now. How about it?"

"I still need to meet with the other therapists. Who knows, I may just do that," I replied, noncommittally.

The next Christian therapy session was led by Jack Tinin, the Treatment Program Coordinator for the Christian Unit. He was more laid back than Dr. Morgan, preferring to sit on a generous chair with his legs crossed, Bible on his lap, while he asked us questions about our personal situations. I desperately needed to *know and feel* that at the very least God was still on my side, since I suspected that because of my wickedness no other human being on the planet would want me. And I also needed to know that God would soon return my children to me. Jack always managed to find the right scripture which would reinforce my faith that God would prevail against the forces of evil that were attempting to take away my children permanently. My anxiety and depression would subside significantly after each session.

Usually I would stay behind to talk to other fellow Christians about their problems and about the Bible (of course). Katie looked like she was about 45; she had been a Christian most of her life (compared with my two-weeks' tenure). Family problems. Husband ran away. She had that look of a "permanent depression" on her face, as if she had lost all hope of ever feeling good again. Three times in the last several years she had tried to kill herself. Some time later I learned that her diagnosis was "dysthymia," or neurotic depression. In spite of her having Jesus Christ to support her and to give her hope she still had a hopeless outlook on the future. In fact, it was painful for me to learn about her case because I realized that I too felt hopeless in spite of my wanting to feel hopeful with God on my side. Still, it was better to have some small scoop of hope, or I would have simply closed my eyes to die.

So for the next two weeks I divided my time almost equally between God's Unit and the secular Adult-General Unit, getting support and insight from both. From the very first day I figured that the Christian counseling method could not stand alone, for it concentrated on faith and hope, tools for allowing one to live a little longer when the situation appeared essentially hopeless. What it did not do was to tackle the agonizingly serious reason why the person was in the hospital in the first place. That was the job of the Adult-General Unit; it offered just the facts, and some support. Together these two units worked miracles for me, given the heavy burden I placed on both. Praise the Lord! And Praise the Adult-General Unit staff!

One day I was having my regular session with Glenda Watson and I was talking about my mother. Glenda conjectured that I had very powerful feelings about my mother, given the history which I had been relating to her over the last several weeks, and she suggested that I write my mother a letter.

"But, Glenda, my mother died in 1958 when I was 12. She's been in the ground for 27 years. What do you mean 'Write her a letter'?" I asked incredulously.

"Yes, I want you to write your mother a letter telling her how you feel about all those things that went on when you were a child. It does not matter that your mother is dead. We know that. But your heart will pretend that she is listening and you can communicate your feelings to her," replied Glenda in a warm, soothing tone.

That night after I had gone to all the groups and the day's "wrap-up" meeting, I walked to my room, knowing full well that I had a job to do. I needed to talk to my dead mother.

For years and years I had had only minimal feelings about my mother. Intellectually I knew that I had had a mother—maybe it was on another planet, or even in a different century—but I had put the whole matter to rest when the Barrientos family took me into their foster home shortly after my mother's death. So tonight I had to open the chapter of my life that had been plaguing me in an unrecognized way for the last 27 years. Making sure that I was all alone in my room and that I would not be disturbed, I looked back at the terrifying agony of my childhood and my memories of my dead mother. With rivers and rivers of tears cascading onto my yellow notepad I managed to pen these few lines to the spirit of my mother:

July 2, 1985

Dear Mami,

You've been gone for so long. In fact I never did get a chance to say "Goodbye" to you. I know that now you are in another world, so I hope that God relays my words to you.

We were so out of control but I still wanted your warmth—I miss that. After you died I never had it again. It felt better with just you in our home, when The Devil was not there, even if we didn't have any food—that didn't matter. I also want to talk to you about other things.

I feel that you should not have had so many relationships with men. There are so many stories about you—I don't know which, if any, are true. As a consequence I feel confused. What happened to me at that house on Lincoln Avenue? Who was that babysitter? Did you suspect sexual abuse? Did you abuse me sexually? Is El Diablo (Merengueno Zalmar, The Devil) the father of Benito? Did you want that baby? Did you love that baby? Were you negligent in caring for Benito? Did you want him dead?

I, too, did many things that were wrong. I engaged in homosexual sex with many boys;.I felt so ashamed of playing sex games with my sisters when we were still at home and you were in the hospital that I wished for a moment that you died so that you wouldn't have to know about it. I am sorry, Mami.

I know that you, too, suffered a lot. Your marriage to The Devil was miserable right from the start. I think that your only happiness was the children. I am sorry we didn't turn out great. And I am sorry that you never found true happiness.

I cried a lot at your funeral, but it was all inside because I was embarrassed. You were in that horrible box and I knew that I would never see you again. I felt so lonely because there was no one else I could trust. And you know The Devil—he was such a fiend that I could not even count on having at least a father after you were gone. You were the only parent I knew, so when you died there was nothing left.

Mami, I really am sorry we didn't have more time together. I am sorry for the bad things I've done. I'll be better and then you can be proud of me like you wanted to be. I am sorry if I have sullied your name. I do want you to rest in peace—you deserve it.

I'll work with God in your name. You just rest. Bye, Mami.

Victor

As my soul reluctantly released these words to my mother, I got a new knot in my throat on top of the other one I had been carrying for weeks after the loss of my children and wife. It was a good thing that I could close the door to my room, for I would not have wanted anyone to see me cry like a child that night for hours. I was feeling a profound sadness about the enormous calamity that we had all suffered as children—that indeed fate had robbed us of our childhood, that we had to defend ourselves as well as we could from a very early age. Remembering the wise words of my hospital therapists like Glenda Watson, Richard Ramirez, and Esther Schube, I could not help but compare the vile wretchedness of our own childhood with the examples of "healthy childhoods" they gave us.

"There are some things children should never see, and some emotions they should never feel," the counselors would say.

The more I opened my eyes to the concept of a "healthy childhood," the more clearly I saw the sickness of our childhood and the perversity of my conduct as a father to my four children. Waves and waves of harsh reality were finally pounding on my soul, demanding acknowledgement that was many years overdue. I had simply been living in a world of psychological repression, sub-consciously covering up the terror, anguish, and RAGE so that I could continue to function in other areas of my life. Somewhere along the way I had added sexual addiction and perversion to my life of sickness, thinking stupidly that I was very "liberated" sexually—that I had no "hang-ups." Perversity from the Devil! Further along, my grandiose delusions of infinite wealth had served to further buttress a grievously damaged inner core, keeping it alive by artificial means. The damage had already been done by the thousand snake bites from the pit from which we all arose. My soul was at last almost completely stark naked, all its vilest secrets and most painful wounds exposed, stripped of its pathological masks which had destroyed my two marriages and had led me to believe that my irresponsible and perverse behavior as a father had been the sign of "liberation." Up to that point I had sincerely believed that I was a great person, destined for infinite wealth. But it had all been lies, lies, lies. Sinister lies that come from within the secret chambers of the mind and which are directed towards the authentic soul to keep it at bay. This malignant source had lain deeply coiled within me, almost totally invisible to my consciousness and attention. That shadowy quality is what made it sinister—it really was like having a vicious vampire inside me. Slowly I was exposing this monster.

The more I learned from Glenda Watson and others, the more I wanted to know about my ailments. So I read voraciously from the hospital and unit library. I learned that I had been wearing a mask all these years—a mask to hide my wounded inner self. The revelation to me was incredible yet terrifying. I was desperately trying to come to terms with this phenomenon I'd never read in graduate school. All these years I had been essentially a mask—a perverted one at that—attempting to interact with other people and failing because I was not genuine. In fact, the mask of grandiose narcissistic delusions had fooled *me* too, for I genuinely had faith in my glorious future, believing that nothing and no one could stop this fate from becoming a grand reality. It had been this sickness that had prevented me from expressing genuine love for my two wives, Katherine and Geena, if indeed I had even been capable of loving them at all.

The terrifying part about this interpretation was that these lies about myself had been created internally without my knowledge or full awareness. Initially that sounded almost impossible to me, but the more I talked to my therapists and the more I read, the more convinced I became that indeed I had just burst the previously impenetrable bubble of narcissistic delusional thinking. It was scary to think that there was some structure within my psyche that had taken it upon itself to create an elaborate web of lies, unbeknownst to me, so that I could keep at bay the torrent of unrecognized panic and depression within my soul. In psychoanalytic theory, what had been happening to me, as far as the narcissistic delusions were concerned, was that my ego, that executive and "managing" part of my psyche, had exercised its "defensive" function by first repressing the considerable number of memories of terrifying feelings from my childhood, and then actively constructing an elaborate honeycomb of denial and delusions around my abilities to succeed and my great destiny, All this time my "Id," that fundamental reservoir of needs, desires, anxieties, fears, and other emotions, had to be partially covered or "repressed" to allow functioning in everyday life.

After I had tearfully reviewed my Letter to My Mother in front of Glenda, I was asked by her to continue the process with a letter to my stepfather, The Vile One, The Sinister Scum from the Sewer, The Devil. It had been only while hospitalized that I had begun to recognize that I had anger—no, RAGE!—towards the filthy worm, for prior to that I would easily have said that I remembered what he had done to us but that it did not matter anymore. Not so! That night I prepared myself just like I had the night I wrote to my dead mother, but this time around I first had to pray to God to ask him for advance forgiveness for the dirty task which I was about to undertake, for I knew fully well that God and the Bible did not approve of foul language and certainly not of using expletives in describing another person. Initially I had been torn between my desire to adhere to the spirit of propriety as clearly embraced in the Bible and my wish to expunge my soul of the rage which I was beginning to feel against The Evil Tapeworm—The Devil. Maybe delusionally or maybe wisely, I felt that God would want me to rid my body of anger, wickedness, and rage, and that he would allow me the opportunity to vent toxic spiritual fumes from my heart, for I had an honest and worthy motive for doing it. Besides, I thought, I really would not be hurting anyone by my venting.

After I turned on the lights in my room to a warm, yellow glow, I sat down to write on the same notepad that I had used the previous night, and my pen began to spew hissing venom from its tip as I wrote to The Corpse, reminding him of all the irredeemable injustices he had done to me, my brothers and sisters, and my mother. Line after line I called the monster every odious and denigrating name that I could think of, cursing his face, the day that he had been born, and the fact that he was there at the *Plaza de las Rosas,* "looking for someone to be ugly with." As I was attempting to recall memory pictures of my experiences as a child when The Monster was around, I could feel strong revulsion and a desire to kill, to destroy, to cut to pieces this wretched and ugly bastard who impersonated a father. How dare he even say that he was a father! No! He was a hyena at best, a rabid one that tore all of us to pieces. As I wrote, my hands trembled with rage, for I could not write fast enough to express the torrential outpouring of bloody pictures which were coming back to me dozens at a time and the homicidal rage which was making my whole body quiver. I was feeling an uncontainable desire to kill, kill, kill!

"This motherfucker needs to die—he does not deserve to live!" I felt and thought as I was vividly recalling and reliving the horrendous time that The Devil stomped on my pregnant mother, with all of us young kids there are witnesses, forever freezing the image of the ugly trauma in our hearts. As I sat there in my modest but clean and warmly lit hospital room, I was feeling a rage and a liberation, for this time around I could pretend in my mind's eye that I was not a passive witness to the horror, but that I was now able to intercede on my mother's behalf and destroy the advancing demon with my bare hands, impacting my steel fists into his hideous face before finally cutting off his head.

"No, motherfucker! You will not hurt my mother. Fuck you. This time around you will die!"

Even as I was expunging my horror and my rage, I was scared at this homicidal fantasy which was vivid but also necessary for my soul. It was my deep trust in Glenda Watson, Tom Lyvers, Esther Schube, and Richard Ramirez which helped me to continue with my catharsis from the bowels of my soul, a venting which simultaneously brought an inner feeling of cleanliness, for the demons of horror, rage, and shame were slowly being dealt with and felt to their vilest levels.

After two hours of vivid recall and fantasy I felt drained. It was time to take out my now-tattered Bible and pray to God to ask for dispensation for the violent and rageful thoughts which I had had. I knew He would understand.

For many days I read and reread that filthy letter to The Devil. I talked about it with Glenda Watson, and I reviewed it in a therapy group. It had opened up the door of repression which had kept this rage behind the scenes, a rage operating as an "unseen hand."

In fact, I was learning that most of my behavior throughout my life had been guided by the unseen hand of powerful and pathological subconscious forces which operated in secret, exercising preemptive control over "my" decisions to engage or not engage in certain behaviors. As I see it now, it had been a mere illusion that "I" was making decisions about my life on a purely rational basis; that is, it was a delusion, for I clearly did not have real freedom in feeling a certain way or another in, say, interpersonal relationships. In my relationship with Katherine the unseen hand of my desperately needing a mother had effectively but surreptitiously guided my entire repertoire of feelings and reactions to her, while my unfortunate emotional status as a young child within my adult body provided me with the strong feelings of entitlement so typical of a two-year-old, leading inevitably to the temper tantrums which destroyed our initially passionate and romantic relationship. Even today I lament the loss of this relationship because of the wonderful memories which I have of the romantic bliss and passionate feelings which I had for Katherine in the beginning. It was my great loss and misfortune that, having found such a loving and beautiful woman, my inner soul did not have the emotional maturity and the moral rectitude to nourish the relationship in a responsible manner.

Then, too, the "hidden hand" had been making its sinister maneuvers in my soul in the manner in which I had related to my children. Throughout the years I never questioned *why* I had the desire to show pornographic pictures to my children, why I secretly enjoyed parading nude in front of them after I took a shower, why I felt that it was a "harmless" game to "playfully" pinch some of my kids' crotch area, and why I spoke of things sexual in front of them. As previously explained, I had thought all along that I was simply "totally liberated," that I did not have the usual sexual "hang-ups" that other people had. In reality it was the pervasive sexual contamination of my inner soul which prompted me with its hidden hand to relate to others, especially all women and all my children, in a sexual way. It is only by the grace of a "higher power," perhaps that of Providence, that I did not have sexual intercourse with any of my children. It is sick enough to have to say to myself, "Thank you for not having had sex with your own children."

My therapists said that the sexual and shameful contamination which our wounded inner child feels will cause our adult mental functions to operate in pathological fashion directly related to the exact nature of the wound in our childhood. In my case fear, anxiety, abandonment, and sex were the main engines which drove my life as a child, and which continued to dominate it as my mind matured intellectually but not emotionally. As a result I ended up as an adult stuck emotionally at the child level, where the damage had occurred.

It made sense to me, what my therapists were saying: That there are some things that children should never see, and some emotions which they should never feel. For me it was too late, for as a child I had already seen the unseeable and felt the unfeelable. I was hoping, lying there all alone in my hospital bed one night, that my evil and sick nature had not contaminated my children, and that my reprehensible behavior towards them and in front of them had not damaged them beyond repair.

As I did every night at Hamilton Psychiatric, I cried myself to sleep, for I missed my children and had no idea what they were doing in Oklahoma. Life without them was unthinkable. The knot in my throat was a painful and constant companion. Sleep was like a temporary and welcome death for me.

Every morning the nurses' wake-up call at my door brought me back to the world of pain, the world of anxiety, of uncertainty, of hand tremors, of shame. What new deficiency in my personality would I uncover today? What new revelation would point out to me the innumerable transgressions of my sorry life? I was getting used to the idea that what my proud "intelligence" had told me throughout the years was not intelligent but rather perverted. If I cannot trust my inner "sense" to guide me in life, whom or what can I trust? When will I see my children? Will I ever?

This realization that my cocky sense of "values" throughout the years had been all wrong made me feel rather insecure about the future since I knew I could not depend on "intuition" for guidance. Painfully, I learned in many of my therapy groups that certain situations create reactions in all of us, and that we must reflect upon what these situations remind us of.

So I was crying less; the torrential rivers of tears had slowly dwindled to small streams. The panic subsided. Only in retrospect did I realize later that my face was also showing a constricted range of emotions. At the time that it was happening, I took that as a sign that I was ready to leave the hospital, that the major work had been done. So I asked Glenda Watson and the other hospital staff to please release me from the hospital. After a few consultations with Glenda, the psychiatrist, and my treatment coordinator, Tom Lyvers, I was discharged uneventfully from Hamilton Psychiatric Hospital on Tuesday, July 10, 1985. But there was more pain ahead.

I got an eerie feeling as I walked out of Hamilton Psychiatric towards my old Chevy station wagon. In a period of about six weeks, I had done more for my mental sanity than I had done in the ten years that I had spent at universities searching for the ultimate truth of the universe. Driving south that cool night I felt glad that I was on my way to Aunt Julieta's house in South San Antonio, for I dreaded with terror the idea of going for the night to my now-empty house which was pitifully up for sale. My imagination fueled the gastric acids in my stomach as I imagined that the ghosts of my children would come up to the kitchen door, like they always did in happier days, not to greet me this time, but to strike terror in my heart because their ghostly forms would blend with the terror of an empty house, a sign of the fundamental abandonment despair of my life. In my heart I knew that in the night I would be overcome by my own demons from within my soul, that I might not survive, that I would be found in *rigor mortis* the following morning, done in by self-inflicted terror. Yes, going to my dear Aunt Julieta's house was a wise thing to do.

She was so happy to see me knock on her door, my Aunt Julieta. "Come in, Victor, come in. I am happy to see you again. How do you feel?" was her welcome. "I have prepared a few little things for you. Do you want coffee? I also have popcorn. Tortillas, beans, rice, you name it!" It was nice to be with my mother's sister. All her life she had worked like a horse doing research at a real estate title company. She was now a widow, lived alone, and in the old days she had been fun to be with. After I ate a few little things, not much, for I could not stomach anything, Aunt Julieta showed me to the bedroom which she had prepared for me. "It is not much, but the bed is clean, and you can stay as long as you like. Is everything OK with you?" she asked, detecting that I was not my usual talkative, cocky self. "Let God help you with this big problem, Victor. Why don't you ask God to help you get your children back? Sometimes God has to test you to see if you are a real Christian—to see if you can pass the test."

"Test me? Why does He have to test me? I am being sincere in my desire to be a better person, to be a better father to my children. But, on the other hand, I have been very evil and God may have to test my sincerity. Why is life so painful?" I thought.

That night I just lay in bed after we turned off all the lights, and I found out that I needed a small night light to scare away the demons of the night who apparently had assumed strategic positions just outside my bedroom door, inside the closet, and, most terrifyingly, under my bed. I dared not let a wayward hand or foot protrude outside of the edges of the bed for I knew that the starving gargoyles would immediately grab it, if not to eat it then simply to torment me. It was an inner prison of terror which I could not share with my Aunt Julieta because I feared that she would think that I was being silly, or, worse, that she would conclude that they should not have let me out of the hospital in the first place. Of course, my intelligence knew that there were no demons anywhere, but my heart was deaf and blind to my rationality as it cowered from my own inner terrors, the products of long-ago traumas, when perhaps there had been demons or terrors in the middle of the night, just large enough and threatening enough to have left their evil imprint in my infantile soul forever. One of these demons was The Devil. And I can only guess that there had been more, perhaps even as an infant in my grandparents' house in Mexico, for I suspect that my grandfather had sexually abused all his children—that is, my mother, all my aunts and my one uncle. It was not a foreign demon but rather a tragic corruption of the soul based on the influence of degenerate forces during critical stages of childhood development. Just as a crooked tree is nonetheless a tree, my inner turmoil was all me, for there were no current forces which I could blame for the torment I felt. The corruption of my soul was all mine; my inner safety had been grievously compromised years ago by tormentors whose shadows still haunted me in the obscurity of the night.

And so it was that the little night light with its feeble attempt to push back the forces of darkness was the only ally I had that night, and every night after that, against the encroaching tentacles of the spirits from the other side of my subconscious.

Midnight, then two then four in the morning. I could not sleep. I could no longer cry. The rivers of tears had run their course, yet within me I felt some sadness but I could not feel the full impact as I had been able to in the hospital. On many nights I got up from my bed and sat on the couch in the living room, looking straight ahead into space, almost catatonic, for hours, *thinking* about the loss of my children but unable to *feel* it. My Aunt Julieta got up many times to ask me if I wanted anything, like *leche caliente* (warm milk), but I simply said no. I just wanted to sit there expressionless for a few hours. Suicide was the next phase.

Something was definitely happening that was different from what I had felt at Hamilton Psychiatric. Soon I was no longer eating and had very little interest in going out of the house. I was sinking fast into a deep depression. My outpatient psychiatrist prescribed an antidepressant for me—desipramine. Day after day I could see my condition deteriorating as my hand tremors spread to my arms; it felt as if I was shivering in the 105-degree weather in Texas. It was a good thing that I had Glenda Watson to lean on.

Before I left the hospital I had asked Glenda if she could continue to offer me therapy on an outpatient basis and she responded affirmatively. One day that summer I visited Glenda at her usual office away from the hospital.

Like most office buildings in San Antonio this one was immaculate, smartly adorned with abundant plants in the lobby. Glenda's office was warm, cozy, and decorated with a feminine touch of lavender and pink around the soft easy chair and sofa. I was happy to see her, although I was not able to *express* my delight at seeing her or at the warmth of her therapy room.

"Glenda, thank you for agreeing to see me on short notice. I appreciate it," I said as my mouth crackled from the symptomatic dryness caused by the antidepressant.

"I can see your mouth is dry, Victor. Do you want some water?" she said as she left the room and came back with that welcome cup.

Looking at the floor so as to avoid shameful eye contact I softly mumbled, "Glenda, I think that I am very near the end of the line. I have no more coping power left. I can't go on. I am thinking of killing myself." In spite of all the pain that I had gone through I had never before felt that the end was near; I had never told Glenda or anyone else that I wanted to end my life. The hope-lessness of the last few days was real; this was a new low for me.

"Do you feel that you need to go back to Hamilton Psychiatric Hospital?" she asked me softly. Back into the hospital? What could they do for me, any-way? My situation is hopeless. What can they do about it? I thought for a few seconds. Then I shook my head.

Throughout the many sessions which I had had with Glenda at the hospital, I had always expressed some emotion, sometimes nervousness, sometimes fear or anxiety, and sometimes anger at the things that had hap-pened to me. But this time around I had nothing to express; my face was blank, my eyes half shut as if to symbolically close out that painful world. The shutdown from the depression was evident all over my lifeless face and my monotone voice.

At one point in the session I told Glenda that perhaps I should go to Oklahoma to attempt to see my children in spite of what Geena had said about the Oklahoma Social Services not allowing me to because of the abuse. But then they will try to prosecute me for what I had done. Maybe prison. But these are my children! How can I *not see them ever again!* But I had no money to get there.

Towards the end of this session I assured Glenda that I would not attempt to kill myself, and we scheduled another visit. As I drove away I felt some profound sadness inside me again, a sadness that was being held back by some block that was beyond my control. My feelings were disappearing. I was glad that I had Glenda on my side. Bless her heart.

Meanwhile my Aunt Julieta did everything she could to lift my spirits. She joked with me about her ever-present popcorn that she ate for breakfast, lunch, and supper, and I managed to let out a few giggles. She took me to garage sales where she always got the lowest rock-bottom price possible, outwitting even the most clever salesman. She took me to many of San Antonio's Mexican restaurants, but I could not force myself to enjoy the wonderful food that had been so dear to my heart.

My cousin Lilly and her husband included me in their family and church activities, but, again, I could function only perfunctorily at them. For the most part I just read the Bible on that desperately lonely couch in my Aunt Julieta's home; I read for hours during the day and almost all of the night. My body was starting to shut down too.

One night I called Geena in Oklahoma, and she informed me that she had already filed for divorce—that I should be receiving the papers soon. It was another painful arrow that pierced my soul. When will the relentless assaults end? I then told her that I might want to go to Oklahoma to be near my children, irrespective of what Social Services was saying. "Don't bother," she said. "You might as well just stay down there."

There were some people who were advising me to "rebuild" my life there in San Antonio and not to think too much about the past or about my children. I had family here in San Antonio. I had my irrepressible Aunt Julieta, Cousin Lilly and her husband. There was the Mexican culture which was dear to my heart. "Besides, there are a lot of beautiful Mexican women around here who would love to marry you and have children with you," they'd say to me. But I could not just discard my children. I missed my babies! I couldn't imagine my life without them.

It did not matter to me that if I went to Oklahoma I might end up in prison because of the child abuse. One concern was a practical one: Did I have the emotional strength to make a long trip, still suicidal, to be closer to my children?

On my next visit to Glenda I asked her for her opinion on whether I could make the trip from San Antonio to Oklahoma City. She hedged, explaining that it was up to me to determine if I wanted to relocate because of my children. But when I told her again that my children were the most important thing in my life she got off the fence and stated firmly, "Well, then, yes, you should go there and see what you can do."

This was a decision based on what my heart was telling me, not so much on what was right. It did not matter if I had all my relatives around me in San Antonio if I did not have my children. It did not matter if I had a beautiful Mexican wife if I did not have my children. It did not matter if I was surrounded by the finest Mexican food in the United States if I did not have my children. It did not matter if I avoided Social Services but I did not have my children. *In fact, nothing mattered much if I did not have my children.* It was a gnawing void deep within my soul.

In spite of still being in an almost catatonic depression, I set out to plan my relocation to Oklahoma. I had absolutely no money. All the equity in our house had been sucked away by months of non-payment of the mortgage, while I still had no job. In an unprecedented act of desperation I went to several churches in the San Antonio area, explaining my predicament while begging for a loan which I would repay with interest. They all asserted that they could not help for a variety of reasons. Depressed and desperate, I resorted to selling what few articles remained in our now abandoned house.

Finally, I had a little bit of money to finance my car trip to Oklahoma and sustain me for about one month while I found a job. I was going out on a limb, a long one, but I saw no other way.

Scared, depressed, and unsure about what I was doing, I made the final preparations in early August of 1985 to drive my old Chevy from San Antonio to Oklahoma City, Oklahoma, with minimal cash to support myself during the trip and while I looked for a job. With my trembling hands I packed only the bare essentials, feeling that I was planning to go into the unknown in Oklahoma, with no familial or other supports there. What if I got more depressed and became critically suicidal to the point of actually going through with it? But I wanted my children. It was a risk that I had to take. I asked God to give me the strength to survive the long journey.

On Saturday, August 4, 1985, I got up early and left fateful San Antonio on my way to Oklahoma City. I was hoping to work on getting my children back, but I really did not know just what to expect.

Chapter Fourteen

Learning to Love for the First Time

Mile after mile up Texas' highways I listened to religious music, getting much needed inspiration to continue on a trip that made me feel both hopeful and very scared. In two days I arrived in Oklahoma City. Along the way I had called Geena, and she had told me that I must first make contact with the social worker before I see the kids. How many more obstacles did I have to overcome? Nonetheless, I was glad to be there. Geena did say that I should not touch her! She said she felt funny and scared. *Well, I'll be cooperative all the way; I will ask for God's help in putting my family back together again.*

Late that first night I had to search for an available room in one of the numerous motels in the area, finding one at the end of Route 482. I knew that I was perhaps just a few miles from where Jasmine, Gabriela, and Andrew were that night, yet I did not know if there was a bottomless canyon between us, making it next to impossible to be with them. After reading my Bible I took my antidepressant and anti-anxiety pills with water and crackers and laid wide awake in bed until the cracks in the ceiling became familiar tributaries and rivers, finally falling asleep with the feeling of a heavy stone on my chest.

By about 5 A.M. I was already up, unable to continue my fitful sleep. There were three harsh realities which I had to deal with: (1) When do I see my children? (2) Where can I find a really cheap apartment? (3) How long will it take to find a job? The very first thing I did was call the social worker from Oklahoma Social Services; she promptly told me that the child abuse case had been transferred from San Antonio to Oklahoma City, and that she was not placing any restrictions on my seeing my children! Had Geena lied to me? I was ecstatic. Now I could see my children! Praise the Lord! Thank you, Jesus!

After a quick phone call Geena agreed to bring the kids in two days to meet with me at a restaurant on Memorial Drive on the outskirts of the city. I was overjoyed to know that within 48 hours I would see my babies again! Praise the Lord again and again!

Thursday, 09 August 1985. 9:18 A.M. "I am moments away from seeing Geena and the kids!" I thought. It had been about two months since I last seen them and my nervousness was intense as I drove my car to the appointed place. "How have they changed? Do they still love me? Will they recognize me? Have they grown a lot?" A few seconds later I spotted the restaurant and drove into the parking lot with my anxiety at a peak from the anticipation. No, they were not there. Had Geena decided to play tricks on me? I just waited. A few moments later I saw her car pull into the parking lot, with the familiar faces of Jasmine, Gabriela, and Andrew anxiously looking my way. "Thank you, Lord! They are here!"

As Geena parked, the doors of her car flew open, and my three kids jumped out and ran at full speed towards me screaming, "Daddy, Daddy, Daddy!" With tears already running down my cheeks I ran towards them and managed to kneel a split second before all three ran into my open arms. "At last! At last I have my babies in my arms again!" I hugged them. I held them close against my chest. Their little arms were wrapped around me tightly. Their faces were now covered with tears and as we exchanged frantic kisses our tears of joy mixed and mixed again. Cries of joy were intermixed with crying and laughing as I looked into their eyes and saw the familiar sparkle that I had seen in them since they were babies. Over and over again we all took a breather from the very tight hug that we were giving each other, momentarily looking at each other's faces as if to ascertain anew that this was real, that indeed we were together again. In all it must have been about ten minutes that we spent on that very small spot on the restaurant parking lot, glued to each other to compensate for that terrible separation that we had all suffered through.

And Geena must have been standing nearby. I cannot remember. Whatever indecision I felt about how I was going to greet her (or hug and kiss her) evaporated like a drop of water on a hot skillet as she approached us and said with a stern voice, "OK, that is enough of that. Let's go inside the restaurant." Those were her words after we had not seen each other for about two months.

So inside we went as I held three little hands in my two, hands which I had held countless times before in crossing streets and while walking endless miles with my kids. We continued looking at each other, almost not believing that indeed we were together, if only for a few moments. I hugged them again and again as we ate I can't remember what. We said over and over, "I missed you!". The pain of the separation slowly melted away into the background with each kiss, each squeezing hug, each intense look that we gave each other. Then it was time to go. Geena said so.

Many times more I kissed my kids as they got back into Geena's car, their little faces looking my way as the car pulled away and I stood alone in the middle of the hostile parking lot, blowing them kisses which they gleefully returned, much to my delight. In a few seconds the car disappeared from sight, and the churning in my stomach came back with unmitigated vengeance.

Within a day or two I found a small studio apartment in the little town of Yukon, just west of Oklahoma City, a basement apartment which consisted of one 12 by 12 room plus a bathroom. The contrast of this tiny dwelling to the mansion which I had had in Northwest San Antonio was striking and painful, a vivid confirmation of the drop in my station in life. But, no matter, I thought, for I was now in the same area as my children and was determined to set up an arrangement so that Geena and I could share time with them more or less equally.

But it was not going to be that way. Within a day the social worker from the Social Services department dropped a bombshell on my lap: The department was changing its mind and was not going to allow me to see my children for an unspecified period of time.

I was devastated. "How could this be? These are my children. Minutes, hours, and days already seemed like an eternity without them. The urgency within my heart was just a parent's who has lost sight of his small kids in a busy park—*seconds* and minutes are agonizingly long and strike terror in the soul since the separation is forced upon the vulnerable heart of the parent. I have covered my sins in therapy and have made an earnest effort to improve! How did they feel? I am their father; I cared for them and I loved them! Is there no end to the pain in my life?"

Depression and Anxiety—my constant companions. News about this restriction sent me into a deeper crisis as I contemplated the possibilities about the future: "When will I see my children again? A week is too long. They are growing. I know they miss me and I miss them. A month? A year? Is Social Services thinking about an eternal restriction? I can't live like this. There is no hope for the future. It's as if they all died at the same time. It's hopeless."

At night in my dimly lit basement room, surrounded by threatening shadows and the usual torment of the creeping silence, I agonized in my private crisis, my personal hell in a city of polite strangers too busy to share a word with me. My mind could not function so that I could distract myself with a hobby or other past-time that normal people usually enjoy when they are at home. Instead I was being eaten alive by pain in my stomach, feeling that no matter what I did I could not defeat the hostile forces dominating my life, a life that I was struggling to improve.

For hours at night I thought. It is so hard to love someone. It is so hard to have children to love, for part of my soul is outside of me, in them, and thus I am extremely vulnerable to attack from the wretched forces of the world. If I did not have any children I would be less vulnerable, and would then laugh at prospective attackers who tried to make my life miserable, for I could definitely defend myself against any and all threats with the full force of a strong and defiant soul. But he who takes my children has struck a fatal blow to the center of my being, effectively cutting my soul to shreds and precluding my being able to fight back or even to visualize a tolerable future. There is no other way—I have children, so I must tolerate whatever pain comes my way to learn to love them properly.

With crisis-level anxiety and trembling hands I managed to call Social Services back, and I made an appointment to see the social worker so that I could understand the basis of their decision. When I arrived at the local office the social worker took me to a sparsely furnished conference room and explained to me that the complaint in San Antonio had indicated that I had hit my children with my belt, that I talked to them about sexual matters, and that I had permitted my daughter to play with my penis in the bathtub. "Yes, all that is true, but I realize now that it was wrong" I answered. I added that I had been seeing a therapist about the matter and that I had already improved on my parenting attitudes and skills. She asked me to sign a document attesting that I agreed that indeed the allegations on the complaint were true. I readily agreed. She also indicated to me that the district attorney in the area would be forwarding my statement to the DA in San Antonio to see if he wanted to file charges against me. "Yes, why not? Everything else is going wrong," I thought. Besides, I had made a commitment to myself and to God in San Antonio that I would clean up my life and make every attempt to be more honorable—for my children and for me. Again the possibility of jail became a reality, but I was determined to be more ethical if I truly wanted to set the right example as a good parent to my children. There was no other way.

Much to my dismay, the social worker was not able to give me any indication as to the length of time they wanted me to stay away from my children, stating instead that the department needed more time to evaluate the situation.

In line with my new-found ethics, I promised the social worker that I would cooperate with them in any manner they wanted. With my heart heavier than before, I left the office, en route to find a church which could help me in the last days of my life.

It was a battle that I felt that I was going to lose, and I had no allies in Oklahoma City or anywhere near there. My cousin Lilly had advised me to attempt to contact churches as soon as I got to Oklahoma City—that they could give me spiritual support in my hour of need. I tried. Maybe a dozen churches. I prayed to Jesus Christ to help me with the gargantuan task of pleasing the behemoth Social Services, to adequately do what they wanted me to do so that I could again see my children. But even as I prayed I felt terribly alone, alone while surrounded by several hundred devoted Christians, all committed to the principle of brotherhood and sisterhood among the followers of Jesus Christ. Oftentimes as services ended I would remain in the main chapel or sanctuary, desperately hoping to make human contact with other Christians with whom I could share some of my sorrow and panic about my children. Yet, it never quite worked out that way, for we all made trite conversation, and afterwards everyone left with people whom they were obviously very familiar with. Even in church I was falling apart. Crisis. Desperation. Anxiety and Depression. No job yet.

Friday August 31st, 1985, 3:47 P.M. "This has been my **worst** day here in Oklahoma. All day long I've been feeling high anxiety attacks, nervousness, tremors all over my body, and I've been thinking again of suicide. Everything seems so hopeless. Can't talk to my children. Social Services and the social worker are real monsters—can't seem to please them on anything!

"Suicide—suicide—suicide—end it all—end it all. Suicide—suicide—suicide—suicide—suicide—suicide. End it all—end it all—end it all—end it all. Too much pain—too much pain—too much pain—too much pain. I miss my kids—I miss my kids—I miss my kids—I miss my kids. Help! Help! Help! Help! Help! Help! Help!" I passed out after making this journal entry, I think.

I called Social Services again. We met at her office at headquarters and she told me the "service plan" was that I was supposed to get treatment for my sexual aberrations by a therapist who could certify that I would never again be a threat to my children. My cautious optimism was soon squelched as I started remembering some of the psychology which I had just learned at Hamilton Psychiatric Hospital, namely that it probably was impossible for any therapist or person to certify that another would *never* engage in such behavior. Very nervously I asked the social worker about this, but she stuck to her demand as she handed me the name of a therapist in the area who specialized in the treatment of sexual deviance. While I was on my way out, she gave me the only good news that I had gotten in a long time: that the district attorney in San Antonio had decided that his office would not attempt to prosecute me for my offenses against my children. So with phone number and address in hand I left, determined to do whatever I could, as always.

As I had nervously expected, the therapist flatly told me that he could not certify that one of his clients would never again engage in aberrant behavior, and that he was surprised that Social Services was requiring such a determination. But, he did give me the name of another therapist who had done a lot of work with hardened sex offenders. Hardened sex offenders? They still considered me a sex monster? His name was Steve Miller.

Leaving his office, I was full of shame knowing that I was referred to a therapist who specialized in career sexual offenders. "I am no sex offender," I thought, as I reflected on my current abstinent behavior and compared it with the perversity of my life before I had gone into Hamilton Psychiatric Hospital. "I was a pervert delighting in voyeurism, masturbation, empty and impersonal sex, fraud, exhibitionism, pornography, interpersonal manipulation, and poor sexual boundaries with my children. But I am now more aware of my failures and character flaws, and am making the effort to improve myself," I said to myself. Still, I had to go see him. I feared that he was just going to inform me about my death sentence.

I met Steve Miller for the first time at his office in the little town of Midwest City just east of Oklahoma City. He was about 50 years old, had a firm, muscular build, and a reassuring and easy-going smile about him. Very briefly, I told him about all my problems in San Antonio, the current crisis of not being able to see my children, and the demand by Social Services that a therapist be able to certify that I would never again harm my children. I cringed as I told him about the requirement, expecting him to shoo me away as an impossible client just as the referring therapist had basically done. But no, he said that he would work with me to provide me with treatment so that I could someday again see my children. Praise the Lord. I was overjoyed! There now was HOPE. He had accepted the challenge.

Soon he asked me to fill out countless questionnaires, or "protocols," related to paraphiliac tendencies, formerly known as sexual perversions. I truthfully admitted on these long True-False questionnaires that in the past I had had these impulses and desires, and truthfully stated that at the present time the impulses were greatly diminished. The fact was that I had not attempted to seduce a woman in several months, had not masturbated at all in that period of time, and had not sought pornographic materials for more than a year. It was my honest belief that if I was to be a good parent to my children, I had to confront these issues as I had at Hamilton Psychiatric Hospital and with Glenda Watson. I was committed to the path of ethical and responsible behavior. Soon enough I signed all the necessary papers so that Glenda could send him a copy of my therapy and hospital file to bring him up to date.

But it was going to be hard, very hard, for in the second session Steve suggested that in addition to the therapy I should start attending group therapy as provided by the Oklahoma Society for the Prevention of Cruelty to Children (OSPCC). It was for hard-core sex offenders and child molesters, he told me. "Hard-core?" *Am I that bad?*

Steve Miller had instilled in me a hope that I had not felt in a very long time, so of course I was willing to do anything that he asked of me because I trusted him—I felt he was not simply trying to make my life difficult. But I was not prepared for the shock that was coming.

With much apprehension I arrived at the evening meeting for group therapy at a location near downtown Oklahoma City. The two-story brick building was nondescript; I had been wondering if it would have a sign outside reading: "Irredeemable Sex Perverts, Degenerates, and Maniacs Enter Here Please," with a large red arrow pointing toward the door. It was a remodeled old factory building. No, no signage. As previously instructed I went up a few steps and entered the building, closed the massive door behind me, and then I entered a surreal world in Meeting Room 132. There were two therapists—one male, one female, both apparently in their 40s.

"You must be Victor," said Braxton as he shook my hand. "I am one therapist here and the other is Thelma, over there. Please, sit down and join us." She was sitting at the opposite end of the large meeting room which measured approximately 40' by 40.' There were about 20 men aged 18 to 80—all of whom in one manner or another had sexually abused young children. There in front of me, sitting in a circle, were the fiends of the world—the scum of the earth. Sitting in the same room with these repulsive men was ugly and repugnant to me , since I felt I didn't belong there, that *they* were the offenders and that I was not in the same category. I looked at them with disdain, I looked at their unshaven faces and the hair coming out of their ears, I looked at their primitive understanding of human psychology, I looked at their rotting teeth, at their pot bellies, at their sneaky and paranoid demeanors, at their filthy hair and cigarette-stained fingers. "This is not happening to me; why am I in this group with these dregs of the earth, these weird men who have sex with children? They all look like irreparable perverts to me. And why are they smiling and laughing if they are child molesters?" I thought to myself. Sitting in a circle with these monsters I almost went numb—I was in culture shock. "There must be some mistake; Steve Miller really did not mean to send me here."

Soon I learned that all except me had been convicted of sexually abusing children, that they had been adjudicated as being sex offenders, and that the courts had required them to attend these group therapy sessions. After a few minutes for roll call and a few words about payment schedules, we began talking about the conditions which led to our having abused children.

We all came from different walks in life; we all had different histories; we all had suffered as children in our own individual ways; we all had crossed the boundary of decency and had had sexual contact with a child; we were all now here to talk about how to prevent any more future transgressions. I gathered quickly that some of the men in the group still had not gotten even to the first stage in the sexual recovery process, that of fully and unequivocally acknowledging their transgressions. Joe was very much still in the denial stage inasmuch as he continued to maintain that his girlfriend's ten-year-old daughter was the one who enticed him.

Joe: "I hear what you guys are saying but I am having a hard time with it. I did not seek her out; she was the one who would come to me and she wanted me to wrestle on the floor with her. She would get on top of me and put her fanny square on my crotch; hell, she would even rub her breasts on my chest. Even though she was only ten she knew more than some women that I know who are 30. I am not made of stone; I got sexually turned on. Damn."

Braxton: "But you were the adult and you were supposed to have exercised restraint and proper judgment. If you noted that you were getting sexually excited, could you have told her firmly that it was not a good idea to wrestle with you?"

I listened to the interchange intently because I could see a parallel of some sort with what I had done in San Antonio while in the bathtub with my own daughter. Even though I had processed this transgression many times with Glenda Watson, with numerous therapists at Hamilton Psychiatric Hospital, and a few times with Steve Miller, I still felt some confusion about the social and psychological dynamics which lead one to engage in such moral violations against children. As in Joe's case, I had done something against my daughter without any prior planning, and once I got into the tub with all my kids the sequence of events proceeded until she was soaping my penis and it started getting hard. How disgusting it all now felt!

My thought process was broken as the discussion continued.

Joe: "Well, what the hell was I supposed to do? It was not me who went after her. She knew that she was teasing me. It's not me only; she teases lots of the boys in the neighborhood. Remember that I did not rape her; she willingly participated. In fact, I could almost bet that she was not even a virgin."

Then Arturo, the 55-year-old mechanic convicted of raping his niece, spoke up.

Arturo: "Joe, I like you, man, like I think that you are missing the point, man. It don't matter what she did or said to you. Like you are the adult—the big guy here. Like you are not supposed to do them things. Maybe if she have been like 18 or something like that might have been OK. But she was not 18; she was like 10 years old. You cannot have sex with a kid. I think that's why we're all here. Do you get that point, man, do you?"

Joe: "I hear you, man, but I tell you that I didn't do nothing wrong. It was not rape. As far as I'm concerned, she knew what she wanted and she did not say no."

Most of us clearly saw the infraction, yet Joe evidently did not feel any moral restraint against sex with children. Or, alternatively, I suspected that he might simply have been in a stage of denial so that he would not feel the guilt of his actions. As I compared his case to mine, I saw similarities and also differences, but, of greatest importance, was my insight about how I had not had proper restraint and proper boundaries in regards to sexual behavior, for I should have known that placing myself in a situation such as being naked with my kids in the bathtub could conceivably result in even more breaches of the boundaries of propriety. So I thought that maybe *subconsciously* I may have wanted to place myself in such a situation. That is, given that I had had other sexual infractions with my children (e.g., showing them pornographic magazines, walking around naked, etc.), I suspected that somewhere, deep inside me, I may have had some sexual impulse that defined, in part, my relationship to my children.

The more the perverts spoke, the more I thought. The more I thought, the more I reflected on my past and on my motives. And the more I reflected on my past perversities, the more I saw similarities between myself and these unclean fiends in the room with me. No, they were not simply depraved men—they were men consumed by sexual impulses or crippled by a lack of empathy through no fault of their own. They were men who long ago had been innocent little boys, and something had made them take a wrong turn. Now it was up to each one of us to turn from our wicked paths.

Men like Joe were in the minority, for most of us were readily admitting that we had done something wrong and were willing to listen to others to gain whatever wisdom we could so that we would not re-offend in the future. With each weekly meeting my initial disgust and repugnance at being in the presence of these "degenerates" were slowly melting into an empathic understanding of them and of the personal and family dynamics that had led these men to commit these crimes in the first place. In subsequent group sessions, I no longer saw their pot bellies, their emaciated bodies, or their poorly maintained teeth, but I did see the paths of destruction which each of them had been on for most of their lives, consumed by alcohol, self-doubts, personal tragedies and traumas, and a gross lack of proper parental modeling when they were children themselves.

Yes, I was like them, they were like me. I was in the right place. The initial shock which I had felt when I came into their presence for the first time had been due to my unacknowledged realization that they were the flesh-and-blood personification of my own perversity, that gross lack of ethics which I was now trying to put behind me as my ugly past life, that of vampire of the night. These men were just variations of the theme of my life—they really were my brothers in spiritual sickness.

On a subsequent night, Mike, a grandfatherly man of about 75, said, in interrupted phrases, that he had begun having sex with his granddaughter when she was about seven years old, that he had been feeling very lonely since his wife had died. He acknowledged that he should not have done that, but, yet, I found it unbelievable that he would have started abusing a child that late in life—that this was the very first time that he had crossed the line. On many of our evening group therapy sessions he would cry, perhaps in part because he was scheduled to go to prison for his deed, and at his age, I am sure that there was a chance that he might not even get out alive. It was a tragedy for the child and for the perpetrator.

Our group sessions were always gut-wrenching as we wallowed in the spiritual mud that essentially had been our lives for some of us and still was for others. They had been where I had come from, minus some particulars: frenzied masturbation, child pornography, snuff films, voyeurism, fire setting, breaking and entering, exhibitionism, theft, rape, alcohol, cocaine and heroin addiction, gross dishonesty, sado-masochism, animal torture and killing, physical assault, and for some, manslaughter. We were a wretched group of men with souls that had come from hell and had arrived on this earth to suck blood from the innocent and spew spiritual devastation wherever we went. It was not an easy task that the therapists had, for it was their duty to professionally empathize with us perpetrators who had engaged in so many heinous deeds. We were the dregs, the maggots, the rot, the decayed putrefaction of society—some of us knew it and some didn't.

Between the weekly sessions with the men, I would meet with Steve Miller for individual therapy, and he would assign readings for me so that I could learn more about the various sexual disorders that had consumed my life in the past. On my own I also read whatever I could about psychoanalysis and child development, when I was not too depressed.

One thing that struck me as very interesting was the moral structure which I noted in myself and in the other men in the group. For years I had thought of myself as having been a highly moral person based solely on the fact that I didn't do certain things I considered immoral—like using drugs, stealing cars, getting drunk, robbing banks, and killing people. That made me moral, I thought. Most men in the group still thought of themselves as basically good individuals except for "a few areas" of their lives in which they had not acted properly (such as the sexual abuse). Yet on closer inspection I noticed that our having abstained from such immoral acts was not in fact an act of conventional morality but rather simply a case of practicality. That is, we had had no desire to engage in these behaviors to begin with. So it cannot be said that our *sense of morality* prevented us from having behaved in this immoral fashion. If a person abstains from engaging in some immoral behavior, we cannot then say with certainty that this was due to his moral values since he may have acted thus out of purely practical considerations. Just because you *behave* morally doesn't always mean you're a moral person.

As I reflected on this in group therapy I could not help but think of the delusion which I had had for many years. I had believed that I was indeed a person who had a sense of moral direction who helped others whenever possible. Yes, my behavior was truly charitable towards others even when I was still living in the dark, consumed by perversions and addictions. But if I was such a moral person, as my behavior might *have implied*, why then did I behave so immorally towards my children, towards my two wives, and towards the many women I deceived and then summarily seduced with total disregard of their feelings and welfare? As I sat there in the circle of spiritual corruption I was feeling that of course I had not been a moral person, that my belief about my being charitable had been no more than a narcissistic delusion to reinforce the grandiose notions that I had had of myself. If in fact I did have any morals, these had been compromised many years ago by the ravenous appetite of my pathological sexual desires and by my feelings of terror surrounding issues of abandonment from my pathetic childhood.

That may explain why I now feel like a worthless individual with no moral conscience and unworthy of life itself. But in my view, my feeling worthless is now preferable to my former life of grandiosity, sin, and perversity. I was spiritually dead. No better than a cockroach.

Other men in the perpetrator group had similar moral confusions, although I came to believe that they were not entirely aware of their internal contradictions. It was incredible to listen to Josh as he related to us all how much he loved the daughter he had had sex with.

"Yeah, it happened to me. I guess I must have had, you know, sex with my daughter about a dozen times, maybe more. But I want you to know that, that, that I love my daughter. Very much. That she means everything to me. OK?"

"Josh," interrupted Thelma, the therapist, "let's do a reality check here. Can you perhaps explain to us what it means to love your child and still be able to permit yourself to have sex with her?"

He was stumped by the question and looked at the ceiling for an answer as he rubbed his chin nervously. "Man, that was when I was all fucked up. I was on drugs, you know, drugs. Pot, cocaine, the Big H—you name it. I didn't know what I was doing. Life was just a blur; you know what I mean?" Josh looked mostly at the floor as if consciously avoiding the 20 pairs of intense eyes that were on him as he explained his transgressions. He continued: "I don't know. I loved her, you know, when she was born and I loved her when I was doing it and I love her now. I just love her, and that's the truth. It's hard to explain."

Actually, he couldn't explain why some fathers who love their children have a desire for sex with them, and why they are not able to stop from crossing the line. It is one thing to have thoughts about it and quite another to give in to them. As I listened to the therapists' tough questions, I started feeling, that perhaps it was not love after all but some other perverted need to possess these children as objects, perhaps as trophies of our manhood. Why then were these children placed so low on their fathers' priority lists, coming after selfish desires for drugs, alcohol, and sexual liaisons?

There were few behaviors talked about there which I could identify as being "loving." Besides the verbal assertion of "I love my child" there was not much else. It was beginning to look like either we all had misidentified our emotions, or we had all been subconsciously delusional about our supposed love for our children. We were learning a lot from the therapists, but learning a lot more from each other's experiences in hell.

It was painful for me to have those thoughts, those many nights that we spent doing spiritual autopsies on our dead or dying past lives, those lives which we had lived in the dark—like the cockroaches. I doubted myself too, wondering if indeed I really loved my children. If I loved them, why did I parade naked in front of them? That was not right. If I loved them, why did I contaminate their little souls by showing them pornographic pictures? That was wretched. If I loved them, why did I take baths with them since babyhood and not stop at some appropriate age later on? That might have prevented the bathtub incident. So I mustered the courage to ask myself: "Do I really and honestly love my children?" It was paralyzing just to consider that appropriate question in the first place.

I had already learned from the hundreds of hours of therapy at Hamilton Psychiatric Hospital that I had to continue to face realities even if they were painful, especially when I detected an internal reluctance to look into the issue. And so I could not hide from this nagging suspicion about the nature of my love for my children.

At my next session with Steve Miller I thought I would bring up what we had talked about in group.

"I've been thinking about this idea of love. When I listen to the men in my group I get the feeling that everybody thinks about it differently," I said to him. "I've always thought love was love."

"What do you think it is?" Steve asked me noncommittally.

I had to pause since I thought he was going to give me his opinion to help me with my obvious confusion.

The thought that came to my mind right away was my Uncle Felipe's assertion many years earlier that my mother had truly loved us, and my vehement—no, almost violent—protest that she did not. Steve knew I was seriously thinking about it.

"So like you've said before, you believe that your mother really didn't love you. What makes you say that?" asked Steve in his usual non-challenging tone. Yes, his tone was not challenging, but his questions nonetheless did force me to put things in perspective.

"Well, she married this worm who became our stepfather, and I've told you about what a terrible person he was. He made our lives miserable. But besides, my mother didn't really care about us. We kids were on the streets all the time—she didn't care. I was repeatedly raped by the janitor and she never noticed. We had no food. She asked me to lick her vagina and all that."

"You are on the right track when you recognize your mother's failures," replied Steve with an approving half-smile. It meant the world to me when I could talk about my disgusting history, about my real feelings, and not have the other person condemn me to hell. All my life I had shielded my true feelings for fear of rejection—I had developed my false sense just to survive.

And then he said something which struck me like a bolt of electricity.

"You know, Victor, it seems to me that all your life you have been very needy for real love and that may have been what was happening between you and your children. You have been feeling that you were giving them love, but maybe it was that they were giving you the affection you so desperately have been needing. Does that make sense to you?"

Steve had turned my long-held belief upside down. I had been using my own children to give me comfort and reassurance all these years. I felt good about it and returned the affection. I looked at the floor, feeling like one of my last great saving graces, my love for my children, had just been evaporated with a few simple words—I did not even put up a fight. I had to accept the obvious reality.

This could also help explain why so many of us in the men's group kept insisting that we loved our children and could not account for our unloving behavior towards them. We could only insist that "…in spite of everything I did I still love my children." It was clear to me that when you love someone your *behavior* has to be loving.

Yet it was patently clear to me that we sex abusers and assorted perverts maintained in believable fashion that we very much loved those whom we had abused sexually, physically, and morally. The resulting painful and inescapable conclusion was that all of us had been essentially delusional about how much we "loved" those whom we had abused. The assertions of love were credible because we *believed in our souls* that we had genuine love for these children, yet the true underlying process was a mere illusion of loving.

Many hundreds of hours at night, while I lay in my dark dungeon all alone in the city of faceless strangers, I pondered over a theory of love to help me to understand my own true feelings, if I could only decipher them, and my behavior towards my children. I said to myself, "There has to be *something wrong* with any definition of *love* which includes patently non-loving behaviors, such as acute episodes of abuse or neglect, along with caring behaviors which are beneficial to the long-term well being of the person who is the object of our affection. Or could it be that some people are simply not able to love on a full-time basis and periodically decay into abusive and exploitative parents? But if that is so, are we justified in still calling their positive affections and behaviors *love?*"

"Did my own mother love me? If she did, why did she act so unlovingly? If she did, why did she fondle my penis? If she did, why did she entice me to put my tongue inside her vagina? If she did, why did she show me her breasts when I was raging with adolescent hormones? If she did, why did she hold me as an infant with disdain on her face?" Every night I pondered over these uncomfortable questions.

From the various therapists I had consulted I received what were basically "cop-out" answers to the question of whether my mother had loved me or not. "Well, she loved you in her own way," was the usual noncommittal answer I got, but "in her own way" was the poisonous part of the explanation, for it contaminated the concept of love which all of us parents should understand as clearly as possible. Given all the perverse explanations of love I had heard from patients at Hamilton Psychiatric Hospital and now at the group therapy sessions with us sex offenders, I knew in my heart that I had better face reality (if there is such a thing) and confront the issue of love from a psychological, moral, and spiritual perspective.

But I had to be careful in developing my own ideas on the fundamental nature of love, for in the past I had gone astray by depending only on my own interpretations of the world to the exclusion of everybody else's. Without realizing it I had become encircled by delusions based on my own pathological desires and inner forces, and this had played a major part in creating my sick behavior towards my children, my two wives, women, and people in general. So, as Steve Miller put it, I had to do a *reality check* with him on a regular basis to see to it that my thinking was on a more even keel and less reflective of trauma and pathology.

By talking with Steve and by listening to the life stories of the other men in the sexual offenders group, in time I reached the conclusion that indeed my mother had not loved any of us, that in fact she had been incapable of loving her children in a mature, responsible, and healthy manner. My mother may have believed with all her heart that she truly loved us all, but if my theory of love is correct, she was simply delusional about it, for if she had stopped to reflect on *how* she loved us she would have readily seen that her *actual behavior* towards us all was tragically deficient in almost all areas of maternal care and concern, and morally abusive in others. She loved us, yet she never disciplined us. She loved us, yet she demonstrated grave indifference when I as a six-year-old boy would walk alone for miles and hours on end all over the city of El Paso, subconsciously drowning out my childhood sorrows. She loved us, yet she stood vainly adorning her face and hair in the mirror as my baby brother Benito crawled his way off the bed on many occasions, finally being swallowed by the cold death of the unforgiving concrete floor in our welfare apartment at the Jacinto Projects. She loved us, yet she stood around the house talking to us but not doing any housework to clean what we ignorantly called "home." She loved us, yet dozens of times she sent me out to school in the biting cold in shorts and smelling like urine when it would have been within her means to get me clean winter pants. She loved us, yet she never kissed us. She loved us, yet she made me her child accomplice when she would meet secretly to fuck with her lover at the Hotel Central in El Paso. She loved us, yet she always referred to all her daughters as "virgins." She loved us, yet she walked around naked or with an open blouse. She loved us, yet because of her other shortcomings she placed us in a horrifyingly abusive situation at the hands of The Devil, a life decision which she apparently did not know how to reverse. And she loved us, yet because of her probable undiagnosed mental illness she never knew she *could not* love us. It was a tragic life for her. And for us.

In another session with Steve I brought up something which I had been thinking about for many years.

Steve asked me, "Victor, is there something in particular you want to talk about today?"

"Yes." Then I hesitated for a long moment. "There is this photograph of my mother. I first saw it when I was about six or seven years old. It's pretty large, about this size." I motioned to him what would be about an 8x10. Steve knew this was no ordinary photo.

"It's black-and-white, a portrait of my mother dressed really beautifully in a sleeveless dark dress. She must have been around 25 at the time. Wearing a necklace and earrings. Full make-up, her hair bright, shiny, elegantly done. She looks very pretty. But it bothers me intensely."

Steve looked perplexed. "What's wrong with the photo of your mother? I don't get it."

"It's the look on her face. She has that haughty look. She is not smiling and she is raising her right eyebrow, just the same way she always did when men on the street would whistle at her. It's a proud look, disdainful—an unmistakably conceited look. The identical face she would make when men would give her salacious looks when we walked together on the street. Now as an adult I can figure that her look told me that she was relishing the attention or the whistling, but she just looked straight ahead with a raised eyebrow."

"Well, OK, Victor, I guess your mother was proud of her looks, her face," said Steve, unmoved by what obviously was bothersome to me.

"You know what is real shitty about that photo, Steve? The bitch has me in her arms! I was a two-month old baby and she was giving her haughty and proud look for the photographer! As an adult, I came to realize that something was wrong because normally parents tip their heads towards the child they are holding when a photo is about to be taken. But not my bitch mother.

Her head was straight, vertical, and there was an unusually large distance between her face and mine. She was modeling for the photographer, and I was just some sort of prop or baggage or bag of shit in her arms. Damn the bitch and her conceited look!"

Steve always had good comebacks for my complaints about my childhood, always acknowledging them but then putting some sort of positive spin to make me feel better. This time he was quiet a few seconds too long. I detected that.

He mustered his take on it. "Maybe she was not really conscious of what she was doing. But besides that, how does it make you feel?"

I was ready with the answer even before he asked the question. "I hate that stupid baby in the picture. He looks totally stupid and fucked up. I feel I could spit on the little sombitch. He's smiling, the stupid fool, not knowing that his bitch mother is paying more attention to the photographer than to him. Just throw him in the garbage and quit pretending that his mother is really holding him as a baby and not as a dumb piece of shit. And fuck the bitch too. Fuck the baby and fuck the bitch-whore." Yes, there was a lot of bitterness in my words. Another sore spot with pus.

"You certainly have a definite opinion of that photo, Victor. What else are you feeling?" asked Steve to prompt me to continue.

"I was thinking, Steve, that an adult can be wise, or, perhaps just regular and normal, or he can be a fool. But I have never, ever heard anyone say that a baby is a fool, but in this picture I am a big, fucking fool. That's how I feel. I feel like a fool even though I was only about two months old. Can you imagine an infant being a fool? Inconceivable! But in that photo I am one. I am a fucking fool for being a mere prop in that photo! Had I been able to, I would have just walked out of that fraudulent photo session after looking at my mother's haughty face. What a fucking fool I was to have stayed there!"

Steve just looked at me, and then I just looked at the floor. More calmly I then added, "When I look at that photo I really feel at that moment like punching that fucking baby in the face for being a fool." But my ire grew instantly. "Get out of that photo, you stupid mother-fucker!"

"You keep saying, 'That baby,' when you refer to yourself in the picture. It's almost as if you want to dissociate yourself from who you were at that moment in time."

"Yeah, I guess so, Steve. It's easier for me to say that the bitch is holding that baby instead of the bitch is holding me. But really, it's a pervasive feeling of being an infant asshole when I look at that picture. I feel stupid and I feel angry at the bitch. I really think the bitch should have drowned me in the river instead of taking me to the photographer's studio. In the river I would just be an innocent dead baby, but at the photographer's studio I was a fucking imbecile baby in my bitch mother's arms! Those are my feelings, my reactions to the photo."

"Do you think that your mother was aware that something was wrong when she was holding you to take that picture?" asked Steve who seemed to be running out of pertinent questions on this issue.

"No, I doubt it. She looks immensely proud in that photo, but not proud of me. Proud of herself, or her beauty, of her eyes, of her dress. Her facial expression seems to be saying, 'Photographer, eat your heart out, you are looking at the goddess of beauty!' So why the fuck do I have to be in the picture with this conceited bitch?"

"But, Victor, where do you get this idea that when two people are about to be photographed that they get closer to each other for the camera?"

"Steve, I've seen so many photos of families and have noticed that family members lean slightly toward each other for the pose. I believe that in their hearts they feel that '*we* are about to be photographed.' If they share an emotional closeness they feel like a *we*, and if they don't feel close they feel like separate individuals about to be photographed together. I doubt very much that a loving mother holding her infant would subconsciously feel that 'Oh, my, the camera is ready to take *my* picture.' If she's a loving mother *she will have to feel* that, 'Oh, my, the camera is ready to take *our* picture.' She would move the baby closer to her bosom and place her face closer to the baby. She would feel that mother and baby are one unit. I feel very strongly about this, Steve."

"Well, what you feel certainly makes sense, Victor. I'm glad you brought it up because we have to talk about everything that has caused you anguish and trouble in the past."

Steve and I went back and forth about this photograph issue for a couple more sessions and then we went back to the topic of love and how some people have a pathological definition of it and other emotions.

As to the concept of love, I was all screwed up. There was no other conclusion for me to reach since I was making an effort to *develop* a healthier concept of love which would help me be a better parent to my children. Even if it hurt I had to strive to break through the sickness of pathological delusions surrounding my evil interpretations of love so that I would not make the same mistakes with my children in the future. I knew in my heart that I would not want to end up interpreting love in the same fashion that my mother had almost four decades earlier. So that brought me back to the question of self-analysis: Did I love my children? It was only fair to apply to my own behavior the same standards which I had viciously applied to my mother's. Instinctively I knew the answer.

There was a logical part of me that thought that if I judged myself according to my new healthier standards of what it meant to love, I would fall painfully short of the mark. In the several months I had already spent in therapy with Steve Miller I had come to learn about "appropriate" and "inappropriate" behaviors for parents. I had begun to learn about this at Hamilton Psychiatric Hospital but it came into focus with Steve's direction. These standards which I had diligently pondered because of my desire to be a better parent, and because I valued Steve's ethical advice, were fast becoming my own, and led me to conclude that indeed, as my mother and stepfather had failed us as parents, so too had I failed my children as a father. Clearly, I had not been a loving father. I "loved" my children but had behaved in ways which were unquestionably non-loving and abusive towards them. As Steve had conjectured in his tentative explanation of my sickness, maybe I had used my children to satisfy my own infantile and selfish need for affection, much to their detriment because of my spiritual blindness. I had used them like a vampire of the night, protecting them because they represented my only link to humanity and because without them I would feel the full fury of my subconscious abandonment terror. Maybe subconsciously my heart regarded them as "objects," like morsels of food to be protected only because they represented affection and security, and perhaps even survival. That was sick love. I had not loved my children properly. Perhaps I had not loved them at all. It was all my delusion based on my selfish need to survive an otherwise cold world of treachery, insecurity, and abandonment. And they had innocently been my life raft in a sea of anxiety, loneliness, and depression. This was a conclusion which added to my inner terror and further eroded my feelings of self-worth. I was not worth the air I breathed; perhaps I should end it all. Too much pain. Suicide. Suicide. How could I have been such a parasite upon my children's spiritual health? For many months now I thought I was just a sick cockroach, but now I wasn't even at that level. Yes, my mother should have drowned me—I just came to this world to suck blood from my innocent children. Now, how can I criticize my own mother when I had been more wretched than her and perhaps should have known better, given my level of education? Truth was painful indeed; that is why my soul created my delusions—to help reduce and mask the inevitable feelings of anxiety, worthlessness, rage, and total abandonment.

So, engulfed in this maelstrom of ugly feelings, I continued with my sex offender group meetings every week while I saw Steve for individual therapy just as often. I looked forward so much to meeting with Steve because he always seemed to have faith in me, that I could continue to improve. In fact, I was feeling incredibly worthless but he still expressed a willingness to work with me towards my goal of becoming a better father for my children and a better person in general. When Social Services was condemning me for what I had done, Steve was praising me for the painful work that I had already done to uncover the evil psychological processes within my soul which had been the center of my wicked life.

With near panic apprehension I would periodically ask him: "Steve, do you still think that it is realistic for me to hope that in the future I will be able to see my children?"

"Victor, your children are your children. From all the notes I have read about this case I can see that you have done many good things for your children," Steve would answer, with a warm smile and a spiritual calm which was hard for me to understand, given the panic anxiety which I chronically felt within my insides.

"Yes, but Social Services hates me. Geena hates me. They all say that I am an incurable sex abuser of my children. Maybe even my children will not remember me; I haven't seen them in a long time. How long will it be for me to see them?" I would ask with a burning pressure at the center of my chest.

"Your children will always be your children. You are their daddy. They won't forget you. We need to continue with this therapy and then maybe in the next few weeks you can begin to write up a draft of an apology letter to your children. How does that sound?" said Steve optimistically as usual.

It was hope when I felt there was none. For ten years I had taken care of my children with Geena (18 years, counting Sarah, with Katherine), and in spite of my shortcomings as a father, I still felt that I loved them, or, at least, that I needed them. The subjective feeling was that I wanted to do what I always did with them: to hug them, kiss them, have dinner with them, take them to playgrounds and carnivals, help them with their school work, tell them *Coffee Shop* bedtime stories, and just be their father, minus my past perversions. Every day was agonizingly long as I dealt with the fate which had in effect kidnapped my children and which was uncompromising in its demands for their return. As hard as I was working on my own issues it was still painfully slow, so it added to my anxiety and my relentless suicidal depression. The time without my children was intolerable.

Perhaps this fatalistic depression showed very obviously on my face and in my demeanor, for I was having a very difficult time finding a job in Oklahoma City. When I was at Hamilton Psychiatric Hospital I made a decision not to go back into real estate investments since I felt that the temptations for "infinite wealth" would be too great, and I feared that my greed or grandiosity might come to the surface to contaminate my behavior again. After several months I finally found a job as a salesman for a retail electronics store, something that interested me because of the electronics involved.

The salary was at the minimum wage, barely enough to pay for my rent and the few utility bills which I had. And I worked selling all types of electronic equipment and gadgets to customers. The thing that was unusual about me this time around was that I treated all customers honestly, providing them with the real information they needed to make an informed choice about what they were buying—quite a contrast to the days when I was a shameless Machiavellian, telling customers whatever needed to be said so that I could make the sale. And when my mind tempted me while I was in the stock room about the many items which could easily fit into my pocket, a flashback into my former kleptomania, I made the conscious effort not to take even a pencil which was not rightfully mine. It felt good to have an arena to show myself that I could walk a clean and ethical path. I was like an alcoholic who had to make a conscious effort to avoid the bottle.

Yet there were many painful moments, like when fathers would show up with their children to buy them a little radio or some other gadget. As I waited on them a painful knot would develop deep within my throat, and my chest would feel as if it could not expand to take air in—a suffocating condition. How lucky they were, I thought, to have each other and to be able to go out to do simple things like buy a radio. Quite often tears would cascade down my cheeks, so I would have to turn my face away from the customer and pretend to inspect some nearby product. Without my children the job was meaningless, and my life was painful. Only Steve was able to help me see the role that this job was playing in my overall recovery from hell.

Time after time as I confessed to Steve how I had acted in the past, how I had cheated and lied, how I had taken so many women to bed, how I had mercilessly decapitated the three innocent puppies, how I had been full of the maggots of pornography in the worst years of my life in New York, he would be supportive and tell me that, yes, all those things were terrible, but now we have to improve and move on into the future. It surprised me every time that he gave me his therapeutic support, for I always had this terrible feeling in the pit of my stomach that at some point he would simply tire of all the sinful and shameful acts in my life and justifiably conclude that I was irredeemable, that I was too corrupt at the core, too depraved, to ever see my children again. Against this toxic angst from my soul I forced myself to trust

Steve Miller because I knew that I had to continue to clean up my life for the sake of morality and for my children. I was walking a very fine line between the extreme anxiety of paranoid trust and outright madness because of my inner belief that indeed I was rotten at the core for all the terrible things that I had done in the past. For all I knew maybe Steve was as blind as me—how could he feel I was worth saving? My head was swirling with questions and paranoid thoughts. I was becoming more aware of the intricacies of appropriate social relations between decent people.

One day when Steve and I were discussing one of the readings he had assigned to me, I asked him if he felt that I had completely "conquered" my previous propensities for pornography, meaningless sex with women, and masturbation, for I had not exhibited any of these behaviors for several months, something which I had never done in my life. He replied that sometimes these sexual addictions go "underground" or become "dormant" when there are other major issues preoccupying the person, and that oftentimes when life is more normal the impulses may come back with full force. Almost in the same breath he added that perhaps it was time to shift gears—to stop going to the sexual perpetrators group and to start going to the self-help meetings for sexual addicts, much in the same manner as recovering alcoholics go to Alcoholics Anonymous. The name of the group was "Sex and Love Addicts Anonymous" (SLAA) and it met weekly a few miles east of Oklahoma City in the small town of Shawnee.

One very dark night the following week I made the 30-minute trip from Oklahoma City to meet with the group, contemplating my new label of "sex addict" as I drove alone in my car, my shame my only companion. As I drove east I had plenty of time to think of how much my life had been out of control, of how I had been asked to attend therapy with other sexual perpetrators and now therapy with love and sex addicts. Was there anything redeemable in my character? Was I now or had I been a sex addict like someone who is addicted to alcohol or some other sinful drug? In spite of my self-esteem being at its lowest point in my whole wretched life, I was feeling even lower, knowing that my own therapist had recommended that I attend self-help sessions with love and sex addicts! Soon I reached my destination and parked my vehicle in the lot next to the meeting hall. With much apprehension I walked the short distance to the building. A new low in my wretched life. Sex and love addicts!

It was dark outside the meeting hall, so I was not able to see the faces of the other strangers who meekly entered through the double doors of the small building which housed our meeting room; I was hoping that there would be no one whom I would recognize, for I would have to flee immediately because of the shame of exposure and recognition. Soon I would be surrounded by sex addicts! Sex perverts! Sex fiends! Sex degenerates! Sex monsters! Sex deviates! The depraved dregs of society! All in one room! Do we even belong to the human race?

Once inside the meeting room with heavy curtains I saw about fifteen men and women ranging in ages from about 18 to 60, all chatting amicably with each other. They did not have weird raincoats, nor were they masturbating openly in their chairs, violently beating their penises or furiously manipulating their clitorises as I had ridiculously imagined they would be. No, they were friendly, and they welcomed me into the group as we all stood around, chatting about life's vicissitudes, waiting for the meeting to begin.

We all sat on easy chairs arranged in a large circle in this meeting room illuminated only by an incandescent bulb at the center of the ceiling, providing a warm but not bright glow in the entire room. As in AA meetings there was no therapist here, for all of us were sex addicts who depended only on each other for therapy and support. All were quiet as the informal leader, a thin young man of about 22, spoke first, reminding everyone that all conversations in this room were confidential and that no one should talk to nonmembers about the discussions. He then continued.

"This is the East Oklahoma City weekly meeting of Sex and Love Addicts Anonymous. Hi, my name is Rick. I am a sex and love addict."

The group responded: "Hi, Rick."

On cue the person next to him then spoke:

"Hi, I am Carol. I'm a sex and love addict."

Everyone introduced himself or herself with the same line, to publicly acknowledge our addict status to the other members. It was then my turn.

"Hi, my name is Victor. I am a sex and love addict." Never in my life had I declared that to other human beings in a group. That hurt.

In front of other human beings I had just stated that I was a sex and love addict, the first step in my continuing recovery from the tentacles of the severe urges and desires which had effectively ruined my life and impaired the life of my children and my two wives along with the countless number of women whom I had used to satisfy the sexual vampire within me. "But I'm not like them," I thought, "because I have already dealt with all my issues and am no longer an addict." It did not take long for me to realize that each person in this group was at his or her unique stage of the recovery process, obviously painful, as exemplified by Tom, the teacher who had ruined his career and his life because of homosexual pedophiliac desires.

"My name is Tom. I guess this must be my 60th or 65th meeting; I can't remember. I lost track. I've been doing better; we're going back to court on Tuesday; my lawyer says that the judge may go easy on me since I've been coming here and have been seeing my therapist. I don't know; maybe he'll give me six months' probation. I hope so. Anyway, my urges to go to the park to catch a glimpse of some….some little boys playing around is greatly diminished, but I still have it. I stay away from the Sears clothes catalogs too; I used to collect them to see all the young boys in their underwear, and, and, I would masturbate while looking at them. But I have not done that for about one year. I've been sober for about one year. I still think about it, though. My "addict" is still there. If it wasn't for my wife I would not be here. I'd be dead. She's been a great help to me."

As Tom was speaking to all of us in a low, shaky voice I could not help but wonder just how much this man had done in his life of pedophiliac sin, consumed by his internal demons that relentlessly demanded satisfaction with the bodies of young boys. He continued.

"I guess I need to say it again. The last time I did this was about 18 months ago. It was one of my students—he was about 13 years old." Tom hesitated, wringing his hands in nervous reaction to the obviously difficult task of divulging something shameful in his life. "Initially I thought I was just attracted to him because he was intelligent; but he was also handsome and I liked his body—its shape. I'm not sure how it got started but I met him one day at the barn. Behind the school. And we had sex. Then it became pretty regular. It got so that I looked forward to meeting him there several times a week. But the whole thing fell apart….when his mother showed up at my house….and told me that her son had told her everything. That was the most horrible day of my life, although my therapist thinks that it was the most fortunate day of my life….because it essentially brought my addictive sexual urge into the light. Before that not even my wife knew about it."

"Anyway, my addict is on low right now. I still struggle. I'm still sober. I'll pass the ball to someone else now."

I learned quickly that people "passed the ball along" to someone else when they felt they wanted a breather from their confessions or summaries of how they were doing with their "addict." All the time while Tom was speaking not one person said anything. The unwritten rule was that there would be no interruptions when one was talking, and no feedback (positive or negative) in the presence of the entire group. What that meant, of course, was that all sorts of sexual behaviors would be talked about, and that none of us would pass judgment as to the propriety or morality of that sexual practice. How could we? We were all in the same boat. We were all sex fiends trying desperately to disengage the depraved sexual vampire clutching our damaged souls.

In a way I liked the philosophy of the group because I felt right away that I could talk about the dastardly things I had done, and I would know that no one would be telling me how sinful I had been. And the same time I would feel common bonding with other human beings who had suffered in their lives because of the immorality of their sexual desires. Yes, this was the group for me. They all had inner maggots and vampires to deal with. Steve had been right in sending me here.

There was about a minute of silence after Tom stopped his confessional abruptly. It was OK to just say nothing and to let the silence move a soul into action. Jim, a hairy guy of about 29, spoke next.

"Hi, I'm Jim. I'm a sex and love addict. Mostly sex. That's my addict. I can't seem to stay sober for more than about two weeks. Last weekend I acted out again. As early as Wednesday I knew that I would have a bad weekend—or, rather, a good weekend, and then a bad feeling. I thought that maybe I should go to an SLAA meeting, but the closest one on Thursday was about 40 miles farther north, closer to Stillwater, so I didn't go. On Thursday I began to think all day long about the hookers on Union Street. I called my buddy and we talked for about an hour, maybe more. But by the end of the day I was already thinking about how I was going to dress up for the night and jump in the sack with a prostitute. Now, I know better. My bottom line is when I start cruising near Union Street—that's my point of no return. I have to have her once I cruise along the street and see one of them wave to me. That's my bottom line. I know that I cannot stop myself if I have gotten that far in my cycle. As I said, this weekend I did it again. I felt rotten afterwards. But all I can say is that I'll try to stay away from Union Street. That's all."

It was incredible to hear Jim talk about his addiction to sex with prostitutes. I felt sorry for him (as well as disgust), for I knew that he was exposing himself to a variety of very lethal venereal infections, and probably was already infected without knowing it. Besides, I thought, who would want to have sex with and put his penis into a vagina that was already crawling with sperms from about five different donors and infectious germs from about a hundred others? How disgusting! And do you have to kiss her? Kiss the same mouth that sucks dick every night? Do her Johns squirt all their sperms into her mouth every night? And then you have to kiss that mouth, knowing that she will transfer some of that semen to your lips? How sick! All this was absolutely disgusting to me! In the past I had had sex with prostitutes maybe three times, but,I had never felt a burning desire to search them out specifically.

But then, I thought that each of us had a nauseating story to tell, and that my own addictions and perversions might appear justifiably sickening to other persons. Nonetheless, I did feel repulsed by Jim's story. Maybe in a way that was good because it indicated that my inner soul had some decency left. Yet I still wondered, what in the world made Jim have this obsession/compulsion/addiction about prostitutes?

In the back of my mind I always worried that the addiction octopus inside me was "entrenched" much like a cancer with parasitic dendrites burrowing into all of the surrounding areas of my soul, and that I would never get rid of it. Some therapists which I had read about had asserted that "once an addict, always an addict" the same way an alcoholic would always be an alcoholic. But did that mean I would always want to have meaningless sex with many women? That I would masturbate forever or until my penis shriveled and then fell off? That I would enjoy looking at the sinful pornographic magazines until I died? I was scared. My focus came back to Jim's continuing confession.

"After many years of doing it with hookers I know my cycle pretty well. Or, I think I do. It starts when I am at work, like it did this past Wednesday, as I said. I start obsessing about being in bed with her and how wonderful the orgasm is going to be. That I will be in extreme happiness. Of course, it never works out that way. But for some reason I have not been able to learn from it. That's my addict. For years I have had this problem. Anyway, I obsess about it but I know that I should try to stop the obsessing, you know, while I am still far from my bottom line—where I will not be able to stop. Maybe I had a rough week—that is why I was obsessing. That's all I could think about. The thoughts kept coming at me, you know; I could not control them, even if I tried to think about something else. I could not fight it. I could not work."

Jim continued. "So when I got home, hell, I quickly started doing some work around the apartment, but I felt lonely. It never feels right in my apartment. It is too lonely. I finally went to visit a friend of mine and we went out for pizza. But…. Friday…. it was worse. My addict was asking to go to Union Street. To see the ladies. When I got home Friday afternoon I showered, even though I knew that whenever I do that it means my addict is in full control and that I will go out into the street to see a hooker. But I guess I was also delusional, because I kept telling myself that I was going to shower…because it made me feel better. The addict is the one who wanted the shower as foreplay to sex with a hooker that evening. It's funny how that delusion works every time. I know it's false but at the moment I don't believe I'm doing what I'm doing just to get to the hookers."

"I got in my car all dressed up and still believing I wasn't going to act out Friday night—I would just drive along the empty city streets with no particular direction in mind. In the back of my mind there was a little voice that kept telling me that driving around always lands me on Union Street. And the hookers."

Jim did not elaborate when he mentioned this little warning voice in the back of his mind, but his train of thought somehow clicked with my experiences with women and I just imagined what struggles must be going on inside his head and soul on Friday nights.

"Jim, be careful. Don't think that driving around is just driving around."

"It would be glorious to feast on her breasts and get deep inside her!"

"I guess I can just drive around the city, you know, just relax and enjoy the lights."

"Pure ecstasy, is yours for the taking! It's Friday night!"

"Jim, are you going to do it again? Be careful!"

"You know how heavenly it is when you come inside her! You know how you are in Nirvana when you suck on those large, inviting nipples!"

"I'm not really driving to Union Street but I gotta pick up some groceries near there."

"Jim, are you sure you're not lying to yourself? Driving near Union Street?"

"I am being honest—I really do need some groceries and the store is close to Union Street. That's not my fault!"

"Pure joy, the highest high, what could be better? You've been to paradise before and you loved it! Let her fondle your dick and your balls—you'll be euphoric! Nothing else on planet Earth matters when she has your dick in her mouth—you love it! Right? Right? You love it, damn it!!"

"Jim, get those thoughts out of your mind or you'll get in trouble again. Get them out of your mind, get them out of your mind."

"I am OK, I am OK, I'm alright, I'm not going to fall into it this time. I just have to get to the grocery store, but, hey, there's too much traffic on this street, so I'll take a short-cut through Union Street, real quickly, I won't stop, I need to get to the grocery store."

"Jim, I sense something is going wrong. Are you failing? Don't do it. Get the groceries somewhere else."

"She's waiting for you! Her big tits are in her bra just begging for your attention! She's not too far from here! You know how you love to remove her panties! You love it, you yearn for it, you desire it, it's your moment of pure rapture when you open her legs! You love it, you need it! Your body is trembling, right? Right?! This means you want her, you want her, you want her, you want her now! Now! Now! Now! Go fuck her! Go fuck her, you damned bastard, go fuck her now!!!"

"Oh, oh, oh, there she is, there she is. I want her, I want her tits, I want her now. Oh my God!"

"Jim? Jim? Ji...."

I had gotten lost within my mind as my imagination exploded and created these images and surreal conversations about what may have been going on in Jim's head. It helped too that Jim had been silent and the group had been waiting for another member to speak. But it was Jim who finally spoke and that broke my very deep train of thought.

"Well, I don't have much else to say. My name is Jim, and I'm a sex and love addict."

The group waited for the next person to volunteer a story. But my heart wanted to finish the story that my imagination had concocted of the titanic struggle of the vampire addiction to prostitutes that was ruining Jim's life. With trepidation I recognized only too well it resembled my struggles with my addiction to meaningless sex with women. That night, sitting silently with that group, I felt that I quietly, to myself, just wanted to add to that imagined story what I would feel after I had gotten my orgasm with those women in New York and Kansas City. My soul wanted to bring to my full awareness the ugliness it was forced to endure.

"This feels so good, oh, God, so good, oh God......aahh... Oh-oh. She's looking at me, she's hugging me. Was she doing this before? She's kissing me! I don't want this! She wants my hand, no, she wants my hand! Why am I naked? I gotta cover myself! This is terrible, it's embarrassing! Oh, Lord, I don't want to be in this bed, God, help me!"

Those flashbacks of mine made me remember well the agony in my soul when my vampire just went into hiding after my orgasm, and I was left naked in bed with an essentially strange woman whom I did not want to kiss, hug, or even touch. It was a deplorable situation for me and also for the innocent woman who thought she had had an intimate moment with me. In actuality she had gone to bed with my vampire, who now was nowhere to be found to kiss and cuddle. A few moments later I would cry and feel nauseous because I had raped her soul and mine.

The 14 other faces in the circle expressed neither contempt nor approval of Jim's behavior, as most just stared at the floor as if in a stupor brought about by the meaning of what Jim had just said. It was clear that we all wanted to do what was right in our lives, but that all of us were driven by immoral forces hard to control—forces that took over our behavior, supposedly against our will. This periodic loss of contact with reality was about as close to psychosis as one could get without being labeled as an outright psychotic or schizophrenic.

But I also thought of it as self-rape or self-seduction. My soul would fight against the urge, but the vampire would just keep whispering to me about how wonderful it would feel, how ecstatic and magical the moment would be. It's almost as if I was being seduced, but not by her! After the sex act I would just lay in ruins, sick and nauseated about what I had done to her body, to my body. Something or some force there in the dark had forced me to have sex with the innocent woman, to seduce her even though I did not even like her. But when I regained my senses I saw that there were only two of us in her bedroom…

As I sat there in the circle of admitted addicts, I felt that indeed we all were very much alike in that we had a "sensible" self which could see reality as well as any normal person, but that we also had an internal beast—the sexual addiction—which demanded nourishment for its ravenous appetite and was able to take over the thoughts and actions of the person for its own purposes. It was like Jekyll and Hyde, or a higher-functioning form of schizophrenia, or dual personalities—a "milder" form of Multiple Personality Disorder—or some malignant dissociative process, or a severe form of obsessive-compulsive disorder. My thoughts made me shudder at the gravity of the mental impairment which I had had, and which I prayed to God I no longer had. "Please, Lord, make it be that I am no longer an addict. This is a terrible disease of the soul. Help me, Jesus!" As with the previous group of sexual perpetrators I had just left, here at SLAA I soon felt that I belonged. We had to band together to fight our internal demons.

On subsequent SLAA meetings, I thought more of the powerlessness which many of us felt or had felt when we were in the grip of the addictive monster. I started remembering clearly how many times while I lived in New York City I had agonized about my desire to go out and seduce a woman into bed, but struggling against this enormous urge because I felt and I knew in my heart that it was bad for me, for my soul, and for the woman. I recalled how many times I had felt the unrelenting urge to fill a woman with my sperm to impregnate her, for some reason still unknown to my full consciousness, while at the same time thinking that if I succeeded in my goal I might create grave problems for myself, the woman, and the resulting child. This is exactly what had happened with the Chinese woman whom I had impregnated, only to regret it deeply afterwards. Night after night the urge was incessant and uncompromising, calling me to go outside, to prowl the streets, the parks, or the bars, to make small talk to a receptive woman, and to bring her home to my bed for impregnation. It was almost as if I had been a predatory spider bringing conquered prey back to my wicked lair, the bed of abandonment, despair, and rivers of sperms. I believed quite delusionally that she wanted my raw dick inside her with no condom or other contraceptive. She needed my sperms to get pregnant. My reason and my weak ethics struggled painfully against this inner tormentor, valiantly attempting to keep my behavior within some moral limits. Yet always at a certain point in the painful struggle the superior forces of darkness overran my battle-weary soul, and with the perverted sexual urge firmly in control my thinking would then turn delusionally psychotic: I would dismiss risks as being negligible or non-existent, while I would come to believe that in the end everything would work out fine. "She looks alright to me," I thought. "She doesn't look like she has any communicable diseases. Besides, I know that she just wants to have a baby, and after she has it she will go away. I know that this time I won't feel bad afterwards because she has a nice body. This is heaven on earth!" Like a malignant spirit I would then proceed to go outside and begin the hunt. I was sick all the way to my inner core—truly abominable.

It had been the same everywhere within my mind: The titanic forces of the addiction waging a full scale war against the combined forces of reason and ethics for total and complete domination of my soul. Reason and self esteem always ended up with deep wounds and impaired functioning every time the battle was fought. In this respect I thought that perhaps there should be another category of mental illness to unify the various addictive disorders that we were all suffering from: *episodic delusional psychosis.* Those of us who had felt the intense inner pain of the battle within our souls were in fact better off than those people who were not yet part of SLAA because they had not even *recognized* that their entire soul had been taken over by the blood-sucking tentacles of the addiction. These persons were deeply in *denial,* so I conjectured that it was possible to classify them as being in the stage of *chronic delusional psychosis,* an umbrella term for numerous forms of delusions which by definition run counter to reality and reason. If the person then somehow managed to break through the denial—often the result of some painful event subsequent to the acting-out behavior—then he or she would enter the stage that most of us in the group were in: episodic delusional psychosis. That is, our delusions and our abandonment of proper ethics would reappear episodically as required by the insatiable appetite of the addiction. Metaphorically, it was the usual Jekyll-and-Hyde syndrome.

In time I came to know many people who were regulars at the SLAA meetings in Oklahoma City, and for the most part I felt a camaraderie with them. How ironic it was for me when I met Ellen, a young woman of about 25 who had had hundreds of lovers in her short years, for in my former life I would have thought it lucky to have found a group where women with insatiable sexual desires met for conversation. But all of us were now beyond the sex game, and would never consider a sexual liaison with anyone within our close-knit group. It was like we were all brothers and sisters. One night Ellen spoke softly.

"Hi, my name is Ellen. I'm a sex and love addict. I've been coming to these meetings off and on for about three years, and it's been about ten years since I knew I had a problem with sex and love. I've been staying away from men, from relationships, for some time. Relationships are always bad for me, but I don't know why. Maybe I'm just looking for love but can't seem to find it in the guys I end up with. I always think that a new relationship will solve all my problems, but don't we all? Actually, it's more like I think that sex with a new man will be what I've been looking for, but, I don't know, it does not seem to work that way. Maybe it's not the sex I'm after. I just want someone to hold me and tell me he loves me. It's bars, the park, at work, at church, anywhere. I meet someone and I quickly want to get him to bed, because I have this urge to do it. It's hard to explain. I've done it with 200 or 300 men. It's like guys lose interest as soon as they orgasm. Maybe I do too. Then I just want him to leave, to get out of my apartment and to leave me alone. This weekend I did OK. I called some girlfriends of mine so we went out for pizza dinner and it kept my mind off the sex thing. I usually cry myself to sleep.

"Sometimes I think that my father has a lot to do with my addiction—at least that's what my therapist thinks—but I can't be sure. He's a psychiatrist, very respectable, but he did not ever give us any attention. Neither did my mother, so I really shouldn't pick on him. I'll keep trying. My name is Ellen. I'm a sex and love addict. That's all for right now."

As Ellen spoke she looked at the floor, as many of us did when we forced ourselves to let go of a shameful secret which contaminated our souls from within. From her inflection and tone I could tell that she wasn't sure whether she was telling us her story or asking us how she was doing with bridging her soul to ours. We gave her our support by not condemning her.

On those nights when the group did not meet we could call each other by phone to discuss the particulars of our own struggle, or to ask for moral support as we felt the pangs of withdrawal from that wonderful drug—sex and love—that we craved. Even though I had not had sex with any woman for months, and had not masturbated for the same length of time, I still felt the urge to engage in heated sexual union with a woman, or at the very least to masturbate to release the tension. I asked Steve Miller if there was "legitimate masturbation" which would not be construed as "acting out addictive behavior," but he could not answer that beyond telling me that when masturbation becomes very frequent and takes the place of normal sexual relations with a woman, then it could be construed as part of an addictive cycle. But then I thought privately: "Then at what point is the sexual relation with a woman part of an addictive cycle and when would it be 'normal'?"

Throughout my drying out period, as I increased the length of my sobriety I still would look at women on the street and in the stores, but I made no attempt to seduce anyone and even turned down one or two offers which my addict instinctively knew would lead into the bedroom. I clearly was committed to making an earnest effort to stay away from meaningless and disgusting sex with women and also keeping my promise to myself to refrain from masturbation. My other problem, the addiction to pornography, had been subsiding throughout the last few years, and by the time I met Steve Miller I did not consider it a significant part of my sexual addiction.

It was important for me to mention to Steve that I had told my SLAA group that only with my two wives did I ever feel that I wanted to cuddle after sex, for I remembered fondly how I would play with Katherine's hair, and many years later, how I would "spoon" Geena as we both were ready to fall asleep. Their bodies were spiritually warm, and I felt a loving attachment to their hands, their lips, their hair, and their faces. It was regrettable, I told the group, that I had been too sick to have had the emotional capacity to nourish the relationships properly, and that because of my actions and perversities, both marriages had collapsed. Two good and decent women, two disastrous relationships. Because of me.

In juxtaposition to my warm feelings towards my two wives were my feelings of disgust and vomit after I had sex with women who were strangers. Or maybe I thought that *I* was having sex with them but it was in reality *the addict* who was feasting on their bodies, while the "real" me was coping with the naked body and genitals belonging to a woman whom I was not spiritually intimate with. During one of the many nights when I told various parts of my story and my struggle to the group, I started thinking that in retrospect it may have been *a good sign* that I felt disgusted and felt like vomiting during my perverse sexual escapades, for it signaled that at least a part of my soul was rebelling against the immoral behavior which my addiction was forcing me into. Had I felt totally comfortable during these acts, I then would have had reason to suspect that my entire being was corrupt, and that there would not have been even a small candle of decency to struggle against the forces of evil from within me. It was therefore good, I said, that all of us were in the midst of our own internal struggles, because this indicated that there were parts of our personalities which were still genuine and which could ally themselves with good people. I should have known what the vomit was all about when I was in New York, but at that time I did not have the wisdom nor the introspective capacity to interpret what was going on inside my soul. Hamilton Psychiatric Hospital, Glenda Watson, Steve Miller, and the two sex therapy groups which I had joined had pointed me in the right moral direction and had forced me to look deep inside myself for the answers to my emotional and behavioral problems.

In the meantime all this talk about "deviant urges," "unnatural desires," "my addict," and "irrepressible impulses" had an unintended effect on me, besides the valuable therapeutic one, when I started reading more about sexual deviance and came upon some texts on serial killers, something about which I have already expounded. In the book *Inside The Criminal Mind* (1984), author and criminal psychologist Stanton E. Samenow asserted that common criminals are able to "compartmentalize" their ideals, morals, and behaviors to a degree that allows them to keep on engaging in immoral behaviors while maintaining a belief that indeed they are "good" citizens. In addition he asserted that these criminals routinely saw people merely as pawns to be used for the satisfaction of their goals. It did not take too much effort on my part to see my behaviors described in Samenow's profiles and to ask myself why I had not also turned out to be a vicious criminal. It was unnerving to see what kind of company I was in.

Steve also recommended *Psychopathy: Theory and Research* (1970) by Robert Hare, an excellent book that delineated the disturbed world of the highly functioning psychopath who is able to lie, cheat, use, abuse, and manipulate others through his charm, but is unable to feel empathy or to establish ethical, long-term relationships with others. I just knew that he was referring to me, or rather, to the way that I had been as a vicious narcissist in the many years prior to the painful collapse of my grandiose dream in San Antonio in 1985. Several years after I had started with the SLAA meetings, Dr. Hare, considered by many to be the world's authority on psychopathic behavior, published another influential book, *Without Conscience: The Disturbing World of the Psychopaths Among Us* (1993), that further illuminated the profile of the psychopath: "Psychopaths are social predators who charm, manipulate, and ruthlessly plow their way through life, leaving a broad trail of broken hearts, shattered expectations, and empty wallets. Completely lacking in conscience and in feelings for others, they selfishly take what they want and do as they please, violating social norms and expectations without the slightest sense of guilt or regret." Even years after the initial shock of realizing fully that my behavior during my adult life had been sociopathic and immoral, I still was encountering further research material that reinforced this idea and added to my inner feelings of worthlessness. I indeed had come from hell.

In fact, all this self-analysis may have turned into a compulsion for me, as I read voraciously about clinical practices and psychiatric assessments. Not that I was too objective about the social desirability of my traits, for Steve Miller felt that I was mostly thinking unflattering things about myself in my quest to read more psychological studies about personality. I figured that he was right, not because I had a compulsive bias against myself, but because I believed that *it was indeed true* that I was a worthless individual undeserving of anything good in life. I had done too many bad things to be considered redeemable at this stage of my life.

After several months and maybe 20 meetings at SLAA, Steve Miller told me that I was ready to "graduate" to the next phase of recovery: I would switch from the regular confessional/progress meetings of SLAA to the "Step" meetings of SLAA held on different nights and in the small town of Chickasha, southwest of Oklahoma City. At these meetings we did not actually concentrate on our background stories, but reviewed in front of everyone how we were doing in practicing the 12-Step Method in our sobriety. I made an earnest effort to implement each and every one of the 12 steps, stating dutifully and honestly to the other group members that for many months I had been "sober" and had not "acted out" on my addictions. That is, I had been behaving ethically in my sexual behavior and in general with all other people.

In spite of still feeling that I was essentially worthless, I could nonetheless see that my life had greatly improved in the area of ethical behavior towards other people, especially in the area of sex. I was no longer prowling for women, and I even began to feel more conservative and reserved in regards to the issue of pornography. Whereas in the past I had salivated salaciously over glossy color photographs of naked women with their legs fully spread, now I felt that the human body was to be respected and that neither women nor men should display their bodies in any manner that violated general decency or that suggested raw sexuality without spiritual bonding. Steve Miller, along with the small army of other therapists who had counseled me, had taught me some of the basic rules of decency, good parenting, and appropriate sexual responses to other human beings. I had never heard such words from my mother or stepfather. Indeed I was embarrassed to admit that I had not known about proper sexual boundaries concerning my own children. How stupid of me.

While I struggled with my recovery from hell I still ached profoundly about not having my children with me. Major parts of my therapy with Steve were simply the support he so eloquently and warmly gave me as I moaned and cried for my children in his office. In fact, it seemed to me that at this stage of my recovery I was still in a chronic state of *crisis* due to major changes which had taken place and were still taking place in my life. Having to cope with not being able to even see my children would have been difficult by itself; yet I also had to adjust to my new life free of my old comfortably sinful ways, including my pain-numbing practices of sexual seduction and masturbation. At every meeting I devoted part of my allotted time to cathartic lamentation about my children while my group peers listened attentively and offered moral support. For me each day began as a crisis since I had no idea what to expect from Social Services. Would they prohibit me from ever seeing my children? What role was Geena playing in either facilitating or hampering me in seeing my kids? Would I have enough energy to make it through the day? I felt lonely, but I knew now that I cannot seek a woman for empty sex to drown out my lifelong sorrow. As psychiatrist M. Scott Peck had said in *The Road Less Travelled* (1978): there is necessary pain that we must feel under certain circumstances in order to maintain proper mental health. Maybe I had avoided the terrible pain of my life for too long. I had been wearing a sinful mask, that of an almost conscienceless narcissist and sexual pervert, to avoid feeling the pain of terror and rage from my childhood. *Maybe this pain of losing my children was necessary to rupture my otherwise impenetrable shell of delusional narcissism which had kept me afloat in my inner sea of bitter despair.* But even if this pain is legitimate, can it go too far? Could it exceed my coping ability? Could it send me over the suicidal edge? I had to continue to seek help from God, the only possible source of comfort against these unforgivingly hostile forces. *I need my children, Lord.*

Traditional psychotherapy with Steve Miller was certainly helping me to deal with my long-term issues of sexual addiction and my other maladaptive impulsivities, but Steve alone could not possibly function as therapist and 24-hour spiritual supporter. Oftentimes we talked about my efforts to get better acquainted with the Christian Church, which Steve encouraged me in. Because of the pain I had experienced in the almost twelve months I had been in therapy, I came to conclude that spiritual counseling in the form of Christian devotion was what I needed in addition to the very necessary secular therapy. Seeing Steve at our appointed weekly meetings was a significant boost for me, but I needed someone else in my life—someone or something I could count on, say, at two in the morning if my anxiety became too great.

In time I did find a church which helped me considerably as a support for my weakened and battle-bruised soul as I opened door after sinister door with my therapist and groups, combating the many demons which had been tormenting me since the day I was born into a despicable family.

Piece by piece I told the pastor stories of my life and to my surprise he did not reject me—he did not even say what a terrible person I had been in the past. Instead he told me that all my sins would be wiped clean if I truly repented and asked God to cleanse my soul "with the blood of the lamb, Jesus." I was so grateful that the pastor did not reject me during my greatest hour of need, when I felt that my tasks were difficult if not impossible and I felt so worthless because of the wicked personal history which I was continuing to acknowledge and face up to. To make it worse, living up to Christian standards of righteousness was very difficult; the worst part of this was the simultaneous comparison of my previous life of perversion with the Christian standards: they were miles apart. Indeed I felt I had come from hell—how could I be a Christian?

I fully confessed to the pastor when I gave him a copy of a very detailed letter of sins which I had written to a woman whom I had been dating and who had broken off the relationship with me. Even though I did not manage to win her back, I did feel a sigh of relief knowing that I had been totally honest with her and with the pastor, in letting both read this letter. When I visited him in his study after he had had a chance to read it, I was quite apprehensive, expecting the worst. But he told me, "My friend, it seems that you have been to hell and back. But with the power of Jesus all is fine. Just ask him to remove all these things from your soul and you are forgiven of everything. Your heart will be clean. As the Lord said: "Though your sins are like scarlet, they shall be as white as snow" (Isaiah 1:18). I was overjoyed. Thank you, Jesus.

I saw him many times after that, on each visit relating to him what I was doing in my secular therapy. For my chronic anxiety he even helped me by giving me a couple of sessions of relaxation therapy. Then he told me that he wanted me to study his sermon techniques because he might ask me in the future to deliver a sermon in his church.

"But I'm such a sinner," I thought in my new self-denigrating manner. "How can I stand up in front of all these people and preach about salvation, ethics, and the concept of sanctification when I am probably one of the worse sinners on the planet?" It is not that I was afraid of speaking in front of people, for I had years of experience delivering university and community lectures on history to thousands of students.

"We're all sinners," said the Pastor, "and we all fall short of the grace of God. You can do it. Let's practice next time."

It felt like a high honor to be asked by the pastor, but even though he mentioned it to me several times I did not have my heart into it, and it never came to be. But it did solidify a conviction that I had about general therapy, an idea that I had started to develop when I was at Hamilton Psychiatric Hospital in San Antonio. And this was that secular and spiritual therapy do not work as well just by themselves, but complement each other magnificently when applied jointly.

As I started to feel better with the separate help of the secular and the spiritual counseling, I began to feel that I wanted to get into the field of counseling and therapy, and wanted to stay away from the deceptive and manipulative world of real estate investments. Through the years when I had been teaching I had also counseled students at universities and at community centers, although not people with serious psychiatric disorders. The therapy at Hamilton Psychiatric Hospital, from Steve Miller, and from the Pastor convinced me that secular therapy plus spiritual support worked far better together than each separately or singularly. In fact, I was so enthusiastic about that revelation that I began to apply for jobs in the field of counseling and psychiatric interventions. It proved to be a momentous decision in my life.

In spite of having a graduate university degree, I had very little formal education in the area of clinical psychology, but a lot in other types of psychology. My keen interest in history involved knowing why governments, and cultures, and individuals did what they did to leave their mark in history. Most of what I had learned at Renwick U and at International University dealt with general psychological topics such as obedience, group relations, the famous Skinner boxes used in learning experiments, personality and Freudian theories, plus other esoteric subjects which seemed rather intellectual at the time, but which now seemed of direct application to my situation. Besides, throughout the years I had been developing my own opinions and theories about many aspects of human behavior, notions which I had to reformulate when many of my delusions were burst in those painful days at Hamilton Psychiatric Hospital.

I didn't get the first two jobs I interviewed for, possibly because they required applicants to have enough experience in the clinical area of psychology. But the third and lengthy interview brought an immediate offer for a fulltime position as a crisis clinician at the local crisis center. The stipulation was that I had to go through a brief training program. I was elated.

Oklahoma Municipal Crisis Center (OMCC) was a state-funded agency responsible for providing telephone and face-to-face support for people facing either acute or chronic psychiatric crises in their lives. A popular term once used for services of this sort was "suicide hotline," although OMCC provided much more than support and advice for those contemplating taking their own lives.

Housed in a two-story building with the Oklahoma Department of Mental Health (ODMH), OMCC provided 24-hour psychiatric support services for persons distressed because of divorces, deaths in the family, rape or other assaults, suicidal or homicidal thoughts (ideation), or other events or changes in their lives which pushed them into a state of crisis. It also provided continuing support and psychiatric management services for long-term, chronically mentally ill patients who required regular support by telephone or in person.

Given my new-found and intense interest in clinical psychology, I considered myself fortunate to have gotten a position at an agency so rich in psychiatric knowledge and techniques. Little did I know that I would soon be thrust deeply into the world of the most serious, most dangerous, and most devastating mental illnesses known to the field of psychiatry.

On day one I was introduced to all the day-shift clinicians in the crisis room, a collection of desks, telephones, voluminous files, and busy workers handling distress calls over the wires. Being brand-new, I felt overwhelmed by the avalanche of crisis calls, hospital emergency room referrals, therapists' names thrown around, references to psychotropic prescription drugs, calls being traced, and psychiatrists being consulted by the small army of front-line crisis clinicians in the "workroom." "How can we keep track of the hundreds if not thousands of names and agencies that are being discussed?" I asked naively. "Well, after you get the hang of it you will have no trouble remembering who is who," was the reassuring response from one of my colleagues-to-be. Many months later I would finally merit that vote of confidence.

That first week at OMCC was difficult because I had to study and quickly learn procedures and policies concerning our protocol of responses to a multitude of crisis situations. My in-house training began right away under the direction of my immediate supervisor, 48-year-old Berthe Newton, a very compassionate yet level-headed clinician who seemed to have an uncanny ability to assess new clients, even with a minimum of information about symptoms. Whereas we phone clinicians in general had to have significant levels of symptom-related information and social history in order to make an assessment, Berthe would arrive at essentially the same diagnosis but considerably sooner than any of us. Indeed, she was a vast storehouse of clinical insight and information. And her level of self-confidence was something I very much admired. I should be like her.

While the clinical training was progressing at a fast pace, I was also getting a much more valuable education from Berthe in the area of prudence in dealing with clients. On more than one occasion Berthe had to talk to me privately about my naive lapses of judgment which showed I needed direction. Once I had taken a female mental patient from our crisis room back to her apartment in my car, with no incident of any sort. "But given her mental condition, Victor, what if she had accused you of something?" was Berthe's disturbing question. She was right. There had been no one else to take the patient home and I had volunteered with honest intentions. But, as a matter of prudent and professional policy, I would have to be careful about possible risky situations like this in the future. I indeed had been dangerously naive.

On another occasion when I had gone to the home of a family of a patient, I asked the mother of the patient if she would give me permission to take a look at the patient's room and have a look in one of his drawers to get a better idea of his personal habits, which might help us to make a diagnosis at the hospital where we had just sent him. She agreed and with her present I opened one drawer but saw nothing out of the ordinary. Well, back at the crisis room Berthe got really mad at me for this "off the wall" idea of looking inside the drawer. Even though I explained to Berthe what my intention was she insisted that we should not look at patients' personal effects or drawers. I took that ethical principle to heart since I respected Berthe for her knowledge and for the compassion she showed towards our patients. In my heart I realized that she was also right on this issue. Again, I had been stupidly naive.

These two early reprimands by Berthe instilled in me a heightened awareness of respect for procedure and respect for our patients, plus a realization that good intentions alone were not enough,. They should be combined with a keen knowledge of ethical principles in the treatment of our patients. Even though it had been unpleasant for me to have Berthe call me out like this, I wholeheartedly accepted her criticisms and was eager to learn more.

Every day I was learning more and more of the clinical material to help me make accurate diagnoses of the people who would call our crisis line for help. Most of my time I spent listening to other, more experienced crisis clinicians and answering calls myself. The many telephones in the workroom were always ringing, so consequently there were usually several clinicians on the phone asking questions about vital information and attempting to de-escalate persons in distress. Conversations most often contained key words such as fire, kill, sad, rope, gun, razor blade, safety, promise, divorce, etc. When we determined that we could not diffuse a volatile situation over the phone, we would then call the police and meet them at the residence of the person in distress. On many occasions we would also call an ambulance when it was deemed necessary to transport the person to the emergency room for a more detailed psychiatric assessment.

In the beginning I handled the less intense phone cases which required an assessment and a recommendation for subsequent therapeutic services. One of my very first cases involved an extremely distressed mother who called to ask for help in controlling her 15-year old son who was not obeying her and who was getting into trouble with the neighbors—throwing trash in their backyard and calling them names. Quickly I was able to determine that there was no emergency since no one was being threatened and the son himself was not making any threats to hurt himself or others. After I asked the mother many questions over the phone, I recommended that she enlist the services of the court system through a program that is called "CHINS" (Child in Need of Services), whereby the legal system would assign a social worker to the son and with the full force of the power of the law require him to make use of therapeutic services to address the problematic behaviors subsumable under the diagnostic category of *conduct disorder.*

After my supervisors saw that I was making correct and reliable diagnoses, they sent me out to the field with another clinician on more difficult cases. One of these was a neighbor's complaint about a mother who was screaming and acting strangely in front of her apartment building. This was the case of Kate and her robotic children.

With several years of psychiatric assessment experience, my colleague Tammy was a valuable resource to have along with me on what would turn out to be an especially sad case. When we arrived at the address indicated by the neighbor, we did not find anyone screaming in front, so we knocked on the door.

"What do you want?" came a hostile and distressed voice from the top of the stairs.

"We are looking for Mrs. Kate. Are you Mrs. Kate?" Tammy asked, even though we could not see the woman beyond the door.

"Yeah, I'm Kate. Go away. I don't want no visitors. Get away!" was the angry response.

Tammy and I persisted since by now we knew that the woman's voice indicated that she was in distress. After we identified ourselves she gave us permission to enter through the front door and walk up to her second-floor apartment. We could hear a baby crying.

We walked rather apprehensively up the stairs, for we did not know what to expect at the summit. The voice gave us permission to enter through the second door, and then we found ourselves in the middle of the dining room. A disheveled woman of about 35 sat nervously on a long sofa in the adjacent living room, with a very small baby precariously positioned on her shaking lap, its head almost hanging off the edge of the woman's legs. As soon as we started walking towards the clearly visible living room the woman became more agitated and started screaming complaints at us, waving her hands dramatically above her head. Without any hesitation we stopped in our tracks, noticing that she was no longer holding the baby. A few times it looked as if she was about to get up from the sofa without first getting a firm grip on the baby, and we feared that it'd roll right off her lap onto the hardwood floor.

During a very tense ten minutes Tammy and I spoke gently to Kate, trying to reassure her that we were here to help her, that we would leave if she asked us to. As we spoke we gently suggested to her that she might want to hold the baby more securely in her arms. She finally did and then stood up. After a little more coaxing she was able to put the baby in the crib, and we then all sat down at the kitchen table to determine the exact nature of this crisis.

Kate was still very agitated, very nervous. Even though she was an attractive woman she obviously was not taking care of herself, as her clothes were all rumpled, and her hair looked unkempt. We did notice, however, that her apartment was clean and that everything seemed to be in order.

Her shifty eyes, paranoid demeanor, and hyper-vigilant gestures suggested to us right away that Kate was under extreme stress and that she might be suffering from some chronic mental disorder. After we determined the whereabouts of her other children we then proceeded to de-escalate her in an attempt to decrease the volatility of the situation, and about 30 minutes later we asked her a few questions about herself. The conversation then shifted to an assessment of other psychiatric symptoms.

We had already determined that Kate lived alone with her children, yet she told us that there were "intruders" in her apartment.

"Yes, I am afraid because there are people who just come into my house. I know the door is locked, but sometimes when I am sitting down I see someone walk down the hallway to my kitchen, but when I go to check there is no one there. I don't know where they are coming from. Sometimes they even call my name."

It was clear to us that Kate was suffering from a psychotic disorder, although we could not yet identify exactly what it could be. Was she a schizophrenic? Was she suffering from post-traumatic stress disorder with psychotic flashbacks? Or was it possibly something like brief reactive psychosis? What was clear to us was that this woman's contact with reality was impaired and she was having a difficult time coping with her parental duties.

We determined that she was fully oriented as to place, time, date, and knowing her own name. Yet, there was something distant in the manner in which she looked at us, strengthening our suspicion that she had a serious psychotic disorder, perhaps with symptomatic feelings of not being connected to her own body.

"Yes, sometimes I do feel strange. Like my body is not my own. Like someone else gets inside my body and makes it do things that I don't want to do," said Kate, with peculiar expressions and continuing to shift glances between Tammy and me nervously.

This symptom, classified as "depersonalization," again buttressed our conviction that perhaps Kate was exhibiting the symptoms of paranoid schizophrenia. She added that strange people on the street stared at her for no reason, and that she could hear others always talking about her just about everywhere that she went. More frightening though, was what she told us next.

"No, I do not sleep well. Usually I sleep for only a few minutes at a time. Almost every night I wake up in the middle of my sleep and I sense that a strange man is lying next to me in my bed. I am terrified to turn to look at him, but I just know that he is there next to me. He wants to have sex with me," she said, explaining her horrific midnight terrors and crying in the process.

We had already called Social Services to come to the apartment to help in placing the children with relatives, and we called for an ambulance to take Kate to the emergency room (ER) at the Medical Center for further assessment, for we both felt that her mental state was so deteriorated that her impaired judgment would make her a threat to herself and others. An emergency room psychiatrist concurred with our assessment of paranoid schizophrenia and signed the legal papers to have Kate committed to a psychiatric hospital for a ten-day period for further assessment and observation.

This had been a very emotional crisis assessment for both Tammy and me, so we talked about it at length in the workroom. Fortunately all our colleagues knew about the emotional difficulty of having to deal with very sad cases such as Kate's, so they provided us with the support that we needed.

Several months later I received a call from the triage nurse at the emergency room of the Medical Center informing me that Kate had been sent to the emergency room again after neighbors reported smoke coming from her apartment. Kate had been released from the psychiatric hospital several weeks prior, and apparently had started a campfire in the middle of her living room. Police had subsequently brought her to the ER for assessment due to the bizarre nature of the fire. Berthe then asked me to go to the emergency room to make the required psychiatric assessment to determine the extent of mental impairment and the necessity for another psychiatric hospitalization.

By now I had made perhaps dozens of assessments in the fast-paced environment of the Medical Center emergency room. As usual I walked past the emergency entrance guards and right to Charge Nurse Neti who of course already knew about the case. Neti briefed me on the facts about the fire as reported to her by the police, and then pointed to the room where Kate had been placed for assessment.

That night I saw the usual number of medical emergency cases at the ER: gunshot and stabbing victims; auto accident victims; old folks who had fallen and broken a hip; small children wailing like sirens with the intolerable pain from falls, broken bones, or the symptoms of the flu; and the regular batch of hypochondriacs who always felt rejected and disappointed when they were told to go home. A small army of nurses, assistants, and doctors walked busily from cubicle to cubicle, trying to remember what patient name went with what symptom, and spewing out long lists of medications to be used on the battlefield that was the emergency room. After stepping past numerous patients along the way, I finally reached the cubicle in the ER where Kate had been placed.

She was lying on a stretcher-bed, secured by a four-point restraint on her wrists and her ankles so that she could not hurt herself or others. As the charge nurse had told me, Kate had been totally uncooperative about coming to the ER, and had to be restrained when she became assaultive towards the staff. That in itself told me that she could not control her impulses.

Kate recognized me immediately, saying, "You are the one who came to my house the other day." I wasn't sure whether I should reply enthusiastically or not, because I suspected that her spontaneous statement might be hostile. After I reestablished new rapport with her I asked her a few questions about the fire.

As Neti had warned me, Kate did not think there was anything wrong with setting a "bonfire" in the middle of her living room. "I was careful about it. Why are these people giving me trouble?" was her symptomatically indignant response. As in the past, she was paranoid, shifty, and suspected that everyone was going to do her harm. That she was strapped onto the bed did not seem to bother her too much. Periodically she would exert significant force against the wide leather straps as if to test their tensile strength, looking at them with incredulity yet not complaining at all about them being there.

It was actually painful for me to see this woman whom I knew was trying to be a mother to her children yet was not able to do it properly because of the internal demons of her schizophrenia which had impaired her perception of reality so significantly. Her psychosis was pervasive: She stated that she could communicate with others in any country by just thinking about them, that her head was really a machine, that she had two bodies, that in reality she had given birth to twins but that nurses stole her other baby in the delivery room, that other people kept changing her legal records at the courthouse, that she had made a copy of her own body, that someone kept injecting her in the middle of the night, that the bruises on her leg were caused by the strange man who quietly climbed into her bed every night, that all her food was poisoned, and that she felt like cutting herself with a knife.

She continued. "Do you know that someone in my house keeps moving objects around? Someone is trying to confuse me. They take objects like lamps, books, dishes, and they put them in places that I don't like. Someone in my house keeps moving objects around! Damn!"

I tried to give Kate the benefit of the doubt when her answers to my questions were not clear, trying to spare her another hospitalization, yet I was feeling that she probably would have to be committed again because of her impaired judgment. Momentarily I shifted the discussion to her children.

"As I understand it, Kate, Social Services took you to their offices so that you could visit with your children last week. How did that go?" I asked her cautiously. I had to swallow hard to utter the phrase "social services" without any rancor, for I felt they were my mortal enemies! In spite of my negative feelings I had promised myself to always do the right thing for the kids and the patients.

Her affect changed dramatically as a wave of sinister expressions covered her face. With an ugly look of disdain on her lips she told me, "Oh, no! That's what they want me to think! Sure, they said they wanted me to go to their office to see my children. I went there." Her eyes shifted from left to right as if to ascertain that no one was listening as she told her secret. "But when I got there they brought in these three kids which they said were mine. Liars! They were robots! Robots given plastic masks so that they would look like my children! Liars! They didn't fool me. I told the robots to get away from me. Get away from me!"

Tears rolled down my cheeks as I looked at Kate and tried to imagine how her kids must have felt when their own mother repudiated them after a long absence. For years Kate had struggled to be a good mother, but her illness was now making that almost impossible. She was so far from reality. Her children, too, were the victims of this terrible disorder which was robbing Kate of her sense of judgment. I knew at that point that we would have to hospitalize Kate again to prevent a tragedy due to her severely impaired judgment: She was not able to assess safety and risk properly, and her delusional belief that she had two bodies, combined with her expressed desire to stab herself, made it extremely likely that she would harm herself due to the impairment from the schizophrenia.

According to protocol I called Berthe Newton back at the crisis center from the phone at the hospital emergency room to confer with her about the symptoms Kate was exhibiting. Berthe needed to feel comfortable that the symptoms that any patient was exhibiting were significant enough to require hospitalization. That is, she needed to make sure that the patient presented a risk to herself or to others because of the impairment of the illness. After I described Kate's condition to her, she concurred with my opinion that Kate would have to be hospitalized because of significant exacerbation of her para-noid schizophrenic disorder. Consequently I filled out all the paper work for a psychiatric committal and the psychiatrist signed it. But before we could hospitalize Kate we had to clear this with the institution to which she would be sent: Wellington State Hospital.

After Berthe's approval I quickly called Dr. Noonfield at Wellington State Hospital to advise her of the proposed transfer of Kate to her unit. Dr. Noonfield gave her approval and the transfer became official.

While I still had Berthe on the phone I told her that I was feeling sad about Kate's condition and especially about her rejecting her own children as robots. Berthe gave me a few moments of empathic support and we moved on to the next crisis.

Everything I was learning in my work at the crisis center was helping me to understand myself better. I saw the concept of delusions, so central to the study of addictive cycles and addictive behavior, come alive in my study of my patients. With some patients the delusions were prominent and easily discernible by almost any observer. But in others they were very subtle, and only careful and meticulous interviewing would ferret them out, especially with patients who were very "guarded." In either type of case it appeared that delusions were a fundamental part of the psychodynamic structure of the person. I thought of my own previous delusions whenever I did an assessment of a patient in crisis.

For some time before I even started work at the crisis center, I had begun to live more ethically, and my work with all types of patients permitted me to exercise this new morality with real people. I can truly say that Berthe Newton's lectures about ethics were painful yet necessary for me to continue to improve my professional skills in psychiatric assessment and intervention. In fact, it was making me feel better about myself because I was placing an ethical rule above my personal wishes, something which still was relatively new to me.

Every week I would tell Steve Miller what I had done at work and how I had treated my patients. He, too, was pleased with my efforts and continued progress. The crisis job was not just educating me about normal and abnormal human behavior, but was also providing me countless opportunities to do the right thing in my relations with other people.

But by far the most important area that Steve helped me in was parenting, for he directed me in clarifying the many attitudes and habits which I had had as an ignorant and pathological parent from the moment that my first child, Sarah, was born. My poor Sarah, she had the misfortune of being born to a father who had never seen a role model of a good parent, a father who on the contrary knew only strife, hunger, sexual abuse, misery, neglect, physical abuse, violence, and terror as the daily ingredients of family life. Yet I do not offer this as an excuse for my failures as a father, for I believe now that every child has the right to expect love and security from his or her parents, while these parents have the moral obligation to provide a loving home to their children, even if the parents themselves never knew the comfort of a kiss, a hug, or of reassuring words when the night was too dark. That is easy to say but difficult to do. I know. Any moral ideal requires pain and effort, especially if it is not native to the personality structure of the parent—as in my case. But to invoke explanations for a failure in parenting, however logically legitimate, would violate the innocent expectation of the child, a child who in turn would grow up without the moral imperative to show love to his own children. Explanations of parenting failures benefit the parent and sacrifice the child's right to express indignity and moral grievance against the parent when something has gone wrong. It is only through this process of moral grievance and indignity that a child can maintain an integrity of moral rectitude in parenting when the time comes for him to be a parent himself. If we legitimize our excusing to the point that it becomes part of the culture, then we will have sacrificed our ideal and moral duty to be loving parents no matter what, for the heart of the child understands no excuses for the absence of love and security.

In my daily work at the crisis center I also saw that bad parents produced generally bad children who grew up without the slightest idea of what loving parenting was all about. These children, in turn, grew up to become parents who engaged in the same pathological behaviors which they had seen modeled in their homes when they were growing up. In the saddest of these cases parents were convinced that they were being good parents when in fact their type of "love" was abusive, dependent, conditional, or narcissistic. Their vast delusional systems would not allow them to see the path of destruction that they forged for their children—a path which was all too easy for us clinicians to see.

So with the benefit of real life examples I compared my own new parenting philosophies with those that weren't working for our patients. I was constantly revising the ideas I had learned at Hamilton Psychiatric Hospital, at the sex therapy groups, at the SLAA meetings, at the crisis center, and from Glenda Watson and Steve Miller. Steve would talk to me about privacy for all family members, about respect, about sexual boundaries, about appropriate and inappropriate topics of conversation with children, about limit setting, about proper discipline, and about role modeling. These ideas had been like revelation to me when I first learned about them at Hamilton Psychiatric Hospital, and now with Steve I was learning how to apply them.

At a session with Steve around June 1986 I brought up the topic of why my mother had failed us so catastrophically. This question had always been in my mind through the years, but it came to center stage when I first entered Hamilton Psychiatric.

"I am sure there are many reasons, Victor. But I suspect that your mother did the best she could under the circumstances," Steve said, not being specific enough for what I was fishing for. I had given the question and the answer hundreds of hours of my time, so I was ready to tell Steve what I felt, given my broader view of things at this point.

"Yes, Steve, I am sure my mother was a complex human being with her own history being the driving force behind her soul and her behavior as a mother and as a person. But to me the biggest clue to this tragic mystery is that painful photograph of her and me, the one we talked about."

"Yes, I remember that very important photo, " said Steve, nodding his head.

"Well, looking at everything I know about her and of my brothers and sisters and me, I can only conclude that my mother's overriding psychological trait was obsessive, almost pathological, vanity. Above everything else she needed to look pretty, so much so that her relationships to her children were easily just a secondary priority. I cannot tell for sure but I suspect she might not have liked the idea of my nursing at her breast when I was a newborn—something that filled me with neuroses later on. In fact, she did not nurse any of us. I suspect she wanted to maintain shapely breasts. She would often preen herself pretty in the mirror. Most tragically this was what was happening when our brother Benito fell several times off the bed onto the concrete floor.

"And remember her regrettable decision to ignore the doctors' various warnings about her breast cancer and their repeated recommendations that she get a radical mastectomy? It was her top priority to maintain her breasts and her beauty, even though one of them was almost totally wasted by the cancer. She did not think of how this would impact all of us kids."

Steve then added, "It sounds like vanity may have been one of your mother's problems, although from everything you've told me throughout the year I suspect that your mother was also depressed and tormented by fear and anxiety, don't you think, Victor?"

"Yeah, most definitely. I am sure she must have had a hellish childhood herself."

"So if she was pathologically vain, how does that make you feel?" Steve probed.

"You know, Steve, I the adult can understand why my mother failed. And the child in me has forgiven her. I had to cross that bridge before I could realistically hope to be a decent parent to my own kids."

Several weeks later Steve called me at the crisis center and told me that he wanted to see me in his office later that evening, that he had good news for me. He did not have to ask me twice.

That evening he told me that he had informed Social Services that he felt I was ready to begin seeing my children, although with supervision at first. He told me that he did not feel that I was a threat to them or to anybody else. *Praise the Lord!* I almost jumped up and down with joy. *Is it true? Will I see my children soon?* I was ecstatic as never before in my life. I cried in his office, but this time out of joy!

Two weeks later Steve, Social Services, and my kids' therapists set up the meeting at the therapists' offices. I was asked to arrive at a specific hour, no earlier, no later, so that my kids could arrive early and leave after I did. I arrived at the exact appointed hour.

I was very nervous—trembling—but I walked into the building and went to the room that had been indicated to me. As I opened the door, Jasmine, Gabriela, and Andrew ran towards me, just like they had at the restaurant a year ago, and again I kneeled just in time to take them into my open arms. We hugged and hugged and cried and cried with joy. "Daddy, Daddy, Daddy!" was all they could say. I loved to hug them and hold them in my arms. My babies, my babies! The separation had been painfully long—an eternity for a parent and his children. I was so happy to have them in my arms again. Truly a miracle!

Maybe ten minutes later I noticed that there were three therapists in the room with us, including Steve. I had feared and expected that the other therapists would give me hate stares, but on the contrary they were quite friendly and accommodating. It surprised me to see they too had tears running down their cheeks. Because they did not interfere at all with my interaction with my kids, I was able to make maximum use of the one hour which I had been allotted. We talked, we joked, we asked each other questions, we tried to catch up on lost time. It felt wonderful just to see them next to me—their beautiful little faces, their bright and happy eyes. This is what life is all about, I thought.

And then it was time to leave.

From the way things went, I knew that all three therapists were satisfied that my interactions with my children were wholly appropriate, indicating to them, I hoped, that we should continue with the visitations in the near future. Indeed, Steve told me several days later that we should develop a schedule of increased contact time with decreased supervision. I was so happy that I could see the end of the worst unimaginable nightmare that had turned our lives upside down, but which ironically had also saved my relationship with my children. Our lives were on the mend.

Over the next several months I saw my kids on many occasions, each time with less and less supervision. One day Geena called me and said that Social Services had informed her that it would be OK for me to take the kids on a three-hour outing without any supervision. I was ecstatic! This was it! This was the beginning of the end of Social Services' involvement!

In no time I rushed over to Geena's house and picked up my kids. They, too, were very happy that only us four would be going out together. We had a wonderful time at a local pizza restaurant, savoring our time together about as much as we did the excellent pan pizza. It was an incredible and momentous time in our lives.

Then in late November 1986, after I had been seeing my children for several months with no supervision and with no incidents of any kind, Social Services informed Geena and me that they were closing the case. The nightmare was finally over. We were all still alive.

Very soon after that, the divorce became final, with Geena and me having joint legal and joint physical custody of our three kids. Subsequently we developed a schedule that allowed Jasmine, Gabriela, and Andrew to spend about half the time with each parent—which I was all too happy to do. My apartment soon became a haven for my kids, and we all started learning how to be a family with the new ethical order: going to roller rinks, telling *Coffee Shop* stories at bedtime, doing the laundry, going to parent-teacher conferences, me serving as chaperone for my kids' field trips, taking them to the doctor, staying at home with them when they were sick, taking them to their soccer or baseball practices, teaching them manners and morals, setting an example for them, cleaning the apartment, taking them on long trips, hanging their artwork all over the apartment, and a million other activities! This was about as close to "normal" as I could get, and a vast (*vast!*) improvement over what I had been more than a year prior. I was happy to parent them, this time appropriately and maturely. I was happy to hug them, I was happy to love them and care for them. Even my relationship to my first-born, Sarah, improved dramatically, even though now she was no kid but a young woman of 20.

And Geena? I spoke to Steve about that a few days later but he seemed to agree with me that both Geena and I had done and said so many vicious things to each other that the relationship would be difficult to repair. Maybe Geena and I never did function well together—perhaps we were just irremediably incompatible, but we had been too blind with lust to have noticed it when we first met. Still, that does not erase the many wonderful memories of the good times we had even under the dreadful conditions of our marriage.

So I am left with the insoluble issue of how I feel, or should feel, about my mother. The small army of psychotherapists, counselors, pastors, clinicians, psychiatrists, and group leaders and members who brought me back from the clutches of insanity all gave me their experienced views of what it means to be a parent—but especially what it means to be a mother who came from a childhood home as sick as the one she would eventually be a mother in. And what does it mean to be the son of an abused mother? My poor mother never had a chance to talk to someone like Steve Miller, someone who could have listened to her heavy heart and given her unconditional support and respect for her as a person, just as he selflessly did for me. But it was not to be—tragically, her sadness and sorrow accompanied her all the way to her early grave. The whispered details of my mother's childhood experiences shall forever remain a mystery, but had I known them as a post-recovery adult I would have readily understood why she acted the way she did and why she just didn't have it in her to mother us properly and lovingly—she gave us what few kernels of love she had. Today I understand maybe why my mother spent so much time looking in the mirror; she was painting herself to hide the hopeless and lifeless face underneath. And now that I have traveled on the dark path of terror and madness I realize too that my mother must have walked on that same pernicious path many years before I did, and that the fog of sorrow and loneliness prevented her from sparing all of us the same insufferable fate. My mother—she had little to give because her own parents had sucked the blood out of her heart for their own pathological necessities when she was but a young, innocent girl.

So finally I can put my mother's mournful spirit to rest. Finally I can begin to honor her for her suffering and for setting an example of how to endure an empty, savage life. And finally I can now say from my heart that, yes, she is my precious children's grandmother—the grandmother they will never know.

————

www.ingramcontent.com/pod-product-compliance
Lightning Source LLC
Chambersburg PA
CBHW020323180626

46812CB00001B/25